# LADY
# UNRIVALED

# Books by Roseanna White

LADIES OF
THE MANOR

# A

# LADY
# UNRIVALED

## ROSEANNA M. WHITE

BETHANYHOUSE
a division of Baker Publishing Group
Minneapolis, Minnesota

© 2016 by Roseanna M. White

Published by Bethany House Publishers
11400 Hampshire Avenue South
Bloomington, Minnesota 55438
www.bethanyhouse.com

Bethany House Publishers is a division of
Baker Publishing Group, Grand Rapids, Michigan

Printed in the United States of America

Library of Congress Control Number: 2016938542

ISBN 978-0-7642-1352-6

Unless otherwise noted Scripture quotations are from the King James Version of the Bible.

Epigraph Scripture quotation is from the New King James Version®. Copyright © 1982 by Thomas Nelson, Inc. Used by permission. All rights reserved.

This is a work of historical reconstruction; the appearances of certain historical figures are therefore inevitable. All other characters, however, are products of the author's imagination, and any resemblance to actual persons, living or dead, is coincidental.

Cover design by Jennifer Parker

Cover photography by Mike Habermann Photography, LLC

Author represented by The Steve Laube Agency

16  17  18  19  20  21  22      7  6  5  4  3  2  1

To David, the real-life Cayton to my Ella.
You are strong where I am weak,
bold where I am quiet,
realistic where I'm a dreamer,
and yet you dream alongside me every day.
I'm so glad we get to travel this crazy life side by side.

# CHARACTER LIST

## Ella's Family

**Lady Ella Myerston** Sister of the Duke of Nottingham. Called Lady Ella.

**Charlotte, the (Dowager) Duchess of Nottingham** Ella's mother. Called Duchess or Duchess of Nottingham by peers, Your Grace by the public, Charlotte by friends.

**Duke and Duchess of Nottingham** Ella's older brother and his wife, Brice and Rowena from *The Reluctant Duchess*. Called Your Grace by commoners, Duke and Duchess of Nottingham by peers, Brice and Rowena by close friends and family.

## Cayton's Family

**James Azerly** The Earl of Cayton. Called Cayton or Lord Cayton almost exclusively.

**Susan, the (Dowager) Countess of Cayton** Cayton's mother. Called Susan or Lady Cayton.

**Lady Adelaide Azerly** Cayton's infant daughter, called Addie.

**The Countess of Cayton** Cayton's deceased wife, Addie's mother. Formerly Miss Adelaide Rosten.

**Duke and Duchess of Stafford** Brook and Justin from *The Lost Heiress*. Justin is Cayton's first cousin. They have one son, William, the Marquess of Abingdon, who is also called Bing.

## Other Characters

**Kira Belova**    A ballerina in the Ballet Russe (Paris) until a recent knee injury; mistress of Andrei Varennikov. Hired as Lady Pratt's lady's maid, using name Sophie Lareau.

**Andrei Varennikov**    Wealthy Russian mogul living in Paris.

**Catherine, Lady Pratt**    Widowed viscountess. Called Lady Pratt by most, Catherine or Kitty by friends. Son, Viscount (Byron) Pratt, died as infant.

**Lord Rushworth**    Catherine's brother, given name of Crispin. Called Lord Rushworth, Rushworth, or Rush.

**The Earl of Whitby**    Brook's father, called Lord Whitby, Whitby, or Whit.

**Dorsey**    Lord Rushworth's valet.

**Evans**    Cayton's valet; Tabby's brother.

**Tabby**    Addie's nursemaid; Evans's sister.

**Mrs. Higgins**    Housekeeper at Anlic Manor.

**Felicity**    Mrs. Higgins's niece, maid at Anlic, best friend and childhood companion of Adelaide, the Countess of Cayton.

**Lady Melissa Harrington**    Brook's cousin; former romantic interest of Cayton.

Now hope does not disappoint,
because the love of God has been poured out
in our hearts by the Holy Spirit who was given to us.

—Romans 5:5 NKJV

## One

Lady Ella Myerston knew more than everyone thought she did—and more than they thought she should. She pressed her back to the warm stones, sliding silently behind an evergreen hedge to avoid a servant. Breath held, she waited for him to pass before daring to take another step.

Silence. Silence was absolutely essential if she intended to go unnoticed. One foot carefully down, and then another. Barely breathing. Reaching out inch by inch until her hand closed around the warm metal latch of the door. *Victory!*

She pulled open the heavy wooden slab and stole inside. "Drat." Not the room she'd expected—this door brought her nowhere *near* the library that had been her aim.

Well, she was accustomed to such things. Creeping forward along the hall on silent feet, she reviewed her plan of attack. Get into the library. Find the book she needed. Escape back to her chamber before her friends and hosts, the Duke and Duchess of Stafford, were any the wiser. They didn't need to know that she knew about the diamonds—much less that she intended to intervene before the things could bring more harm to her brother and his expectant wife. If the duke and duchess realized her intent, they'd probably ship her straight back to Midwynd Hall.

Not acceptable. The rest of them had already paid a steep enough price. They needed a reprieve, and if Ella couldn't give it to them openly, she would resort to the underhanded.

A hushed giggle reached her ears, propelling her into the shadowed space behind a suit of armor that looked properly medieval. Not the best hiding place, but the two housemaids who scurried along the corridor didn't notice her. Their heads were bent together, their giggles pulling a grin onto Ella's lips too. Probably whispering about some handsome footman or groom. Were she at Midwynd, where she knew all the maids and footmen, she might have joined them.

Were she not about covert business.

Once their footsteps had faded, she disentangled herself from the knight's shadow and resumed her creeping, making it to the library unhindered. A bit anticlimactic, but she would chalk it up as a job well done and get on with it.

The Stafford library was vast and thorough. Intimidatingly so. She'd known it was big, of course. She'd just forgotten *how* big.

Well, there was nothing for it but to dive in and pray no one interrupted her—or noticed her absence from her borrowed bedchamber upstairs. Nothing for it, that is, except for the catalog cabinet nestled in the corner, praise be to the Lord. Ella scurried over to it and flipped through the neatly typed cards in the D drawer.

*Diamonds. Diamonds.* Surely they had books on diamonds. Surely if anyone in this world had books on diamonds, it would be . . . "Aha!" Ella did a little jig . . . and clamped a hand over her mouth when her outburst echoed back to her.

Some spy.

But no one came bursting through the carved doors, so she took the direction from the card, shut the drawer, and headed to the appropriate section of shelves. One twelve-foot climb up a ladder later and she had it in her hands. The book she hoped would fill in a few of the blanks that remained after her previous attempts. It would certainly tell her about the rarity and worth of red diamonds. It would tell her where they originated. It would tell her all the scientific, factual data she could ever want.

What it wouldn't tell her, she knew, was about the Fire Eyes specifically, and how they had ended up first with Brook and then with Ella's brother, Brice. It wouldn't tell her why Brice and Rowena had fought over them so bitterly in the first months of their marriage. It wouldn't tell her about the curse her sister-in-law had feared would rip apart their world.

And their world had been ripped.

Maybe it was the curse, or maybe it was just the people who so greedily searched for the gems her brother had stashed somewhere or another. Ella didn't much care which was at fault. She just wanted to keep the diamonds from doing any more damage to the people she loved best in the world.

"Ella? I thought you were resting before our ride."

Ella shrieked, spun, barely thinking to clutch the book and its incriminating title to her chest.

Some spy indeed.

Brook, Duchess of Stafford, stood just inside the door. Blond hair coiffed, riding habit impeccable, amusement in her gaze. "*Désolée*. I didn't mean to startle you."

At least Ella had the wherewithal to laugh at herself. It would have looked beyond strange to her friend if she hadn't. "I *was* going to rest. But a book makes for the better resting, you know."

Brook flashed a grin right back. "That it does. What have

you selected? Did you find the latest Sherlock Holmes novel I told you about?"

"Oh." Ella waved a hand and slid the book around to her back, praying it looked merely dismissive. She headed for the doorway, ready to edge her way around the duchess standing sentinel in it. "No, not yet. You've so many books in here, I thought I'd be adventurous."

"You always find a way to be." Brook's brows lifted. "Though I can't think what might be in these esteemed shelves that would require hiding it behind your back. What have you? Some cautionary tale your mother had forbidden you to read?"

"No, nothing like that." Ella's laugh wasn't forced, exactly—though it may have been a bit more nervous than she wanted it to be.

"Then what?" Brook reached out, fingers wiggling in an unspoken demand. As if Ella were the duchess's small son, to just hand over whatever forbidden object she had discovered. Not that little Lord Abingdon ever did either, come to think of it.

Ella lifted her chin. "You can have it when I'm through, but you'll not be stealing my reading material from me again, thank you very much. Don't think I've forgotten how my copy of *The Lost World* mysteriously disappeared at Midwynd while you were visiting."

Brook laughed—and lunged for her. "Desperate times. *Your* library is not so well stocked. Come, Ella. Show me!"

"Never!" Knowing Brook would just think it a game—praying so—Ella squealed a laugh of her own and made a break for it, meaning to sidestep her nosy hostess and make for the door.

She should have known Brook would be too quick. She spent her days chasing an errant toddler, after all, despite having a team of servants to do it for her. And despite one last shriek of protest on Ella's part, the duchess pried the book from her hands.

Ella sighed and turned to face her friend, knowing well what was coming.

Brook was never one to disappoint. The good humor on her face changed in a flash to temper. "*Diamonds.*" She lifted narrowed eyes to Ella. "Do tell me you're just plotting what kind of engagement ring you'd like when you finally decide on a suitor."

As if any of those stuffy men in London—who saw her only as a connection to her brother, the Duke of Nottingham—would ever get so far with her as to present a ring. But Ella smiled. "You're always so astute."

Brook blustered out a growl and raised the book in the air as if in testimony to Ella's insanity. "You know. You know about the Fire Eyes, and your brother is going to kill me for getting you involved in all this, and I'm going to kill *him* for taking them to begin with after I *begged* him to leave the trouble to me and Justin, and . . ."

From there, the rant moved into Monegasque. Had it been French, Ella would have had at least a hope of following, but not Monegasque. She listened for a moment . . . and then tried to snatch at the book Brook wielded like a sword. That just propelled her friend back into English. "You don't understand, Ella! This is not some . . . some adventure story. It is *real*, and it is deadly, and I won't have you involved!"

Ella stiffened, her chin coming up. "I know perfectly well how real it is, and how deadly. You almost died over those gems. My *brother* almost died over them, and his wife."

Brook visibly drew her emotions back in and took a deep breath. "It was not the diamonds that nearly killed Brice and Rowena."

"No." Ella's nostrils flared as that ache, still fresh, consumed her. "It was *my* oldest friend who did it. My oldest friend, with whom I'd spent every day last autumn—and I didn't see it. I didn't see what Stella had become."

What else hadn't she seen—*didn't* she see?

"Ella." Brook slid closer and rested her long, tapered fingers on Ella's wrist. "You can't blame yourself for that. No one saw it."

No excuse—but there was nothing she could do about the past. Nothing except determine to make the future something different. To pay attention. To do whatever she must to protect her family. "It may have been Stella Abbott who pulled that trigger six months ago—but it was the Rushworths who used her because they wanted the diamonds. The Rushworths who used Rowena. The Rushworths who sent that monstrous Highland laird after her."

"And the Rushworths who have retreated altogether now." The fingers squeezed on her wrist. "They are not even in the country. You needn't worry."

Worry was a waste of time, true. But consideration . . . Consideration wasn't to be neglected. "They will be back—you know it as well as I. And when they come . . ."

Ella shook her head and pulled away. "Brice took the diamonds from you because you were just married, starting a family. Now *he* is the one who will be a father within a few weeks. I'll not let him pay the price the Fire Eyes seem to demand. I won't let him or Rowena or their child suffer, not when there just *may* be something I can do to stop it all."

Brook turned back toward the shelf and the ladder Ella had just climbed a few minutes prior. No need for *her* to check her catalog to know where it belonged. "There is nothing you can do. There is nothing anyone can do—not now."

"But there is! We can *learn*, Brook. You, of all people, should know that. We can learn more about the Fire Eyes, about this curse, about why the Rushworths want them and—"

"Is that why you invited yourself to Ralin?" Temper sparked again as Brook shoved the book back into place with a *thud*. "Not to visit me, not to give your brother and his wife some time alone before the baby comes—but to snoop around my library?"

Ella tried on a cheeky grin. "Well, if there's any library in the world that could help me, it's yours. You know it's true."

There—a breath of laughter as Brook gained the ground again. "Let it drop, Ella. I beg of you. Let's just enjoy your time here and forget all about the Fire Eyes. Find your adventure somewhere else, go and get lost in the wood. Imagine a few good stories about the faeries in the hills. Just not the Fire Eyes. *S'il te plait*."

Everyone in her world thought they had to protect her—that she had to be coddled, that she hadn't the stuff it required to stand up and fight for what she loved. No one ever listened to her when she tried to speak hope into life—they just assumed her naïve.

Well, she wasn't. Perhaps her judgment had proven faulty in the past, but not anymore. And she would prove it. With or without their help.

"Now." Brook drew near and wove her arm around Ella's. "If you're not going to rest, how about that ride?"

Her hostess certainly wasn't going to leave her alone in the library just now, so why not? Ella produced a mischievous smile and let Brook turn her toward the door. "Can I ride Oscuro?"

Her friend glared, but with a hint of amusement back in the corners of her mouth. "It isn't *my* decision, *mon amie*. It is he who will not allow it. But you can take his sister. Tempesta is nearly as quick."

"Ha!" The stallion was indeed finicky about who he would let near. So far as she knew only Brook, Stafford, Brook's father, and one jockey had ever managed to keep their seat in his saddle. She would, frankly, prefer Tempesta, but appearances must be upheld—so she put a bounce in her step as she headed for the library's door. She would come back tonight, when everyone else was asleep.

"There is a reason *she* isn't the one you take to the races, Brook, and don't think for a moment I'm fooled by your blaming it all on the horse. I am a natural, you know. Utterly irresistible to any living creature. Animals and children all flock to me." She charged through the doorway, Brook's chuckle already following her. "And the gentlemen! We cannot overlook how they all fall—"

"Whoa!" The warning, deep and urgent, came too late.

Ella squealed like a ninny as she plowed directly into a solid, nicely clad chest and nearly tumbled backward from the impact—likely would have fallen had strong hands not caught her about the waist. She looked up, expecting to find Brook's husband, Stafford, or perhaps Brook's father, Lord Whitby, who was also visiting. Embarrassing, but they would have laughed it off—and teased her about the claim she'd been in the midst of making regarding how all the gentlemen fell at her feet.

But she looked up into deep green eyes, not blue or brown. A face somewhat familiar, given its resemblance to Stafford's, but capped with warm brown hair instead of blond or silver-streaked raven.

Lord Cayton, it must be. Stafford's cousin. And his scowl was exactly like the duke's.

Funny though . . . Stafford had never made her stomach knot up like it did just now, nor made heat surge when he happened to touch her. Not like it did when Lord Cayton's hands slid from her back to the sides of her waist, testing her balance before releasing her.

Would she be too much a ninny if she swooned a bit, just to force him to hold on a few seconds longer?

Probably. So she forced herself to straighten her spine and say, "Pardon me." At least she tried to say it, though her voice sounded odd—all fluttering and uncertain—to her own ears.

Lord Cayton just stared at her, the scowl deepening, and let her go.

"Hello, Cayton." Brook—probably in the doorway, given the nearness of her voice—sounded only slightly amused. "Looking for Justin, or are you here only to bowl over my friend?"

"Your friend." His voice was exactly what a man's voice should be. Rich and deep, but not *too* deep. A lovely, honeyed baritone—if tinged with a rather baffling accusation. "I thought I knew all your friends. I don't believe I've met this one."

Ella may have been irritated at being spoken of as if she weren't present, had his gaze not remained latched so unwaveringly upon her face. She could only hope the thundering of her heart wasn't audible. Or visible. Were this one of the romantic tales she so loved, birds would start singing in chorus, Brook would vanish, and Lord Cayton would declare his instant, undying love.

After, of course, he stopped frowning at her.

Brook edged into Ella's periphery. She, too, was frowning. "Of course you have. Haven't you? This is Nottingham's sister. Lady Ella Myerston."

"Lady Ella." This was usually where the fawning began, where eyes lit with longing—not for her, but for her associations and dowry.

Not Cayton. His eyes flashed some message she couldn't decipher as he took a giant step back. He sketched a quick, abbreviated bow and focused his gaze on the space over her shoulder. "A pleasure to make your acquaintance, my lady. Forgive me for bowling you over."

"I think we all know it was my fault. But I shall graciously forgive you, if you're so determined to accept the blame." Her smile felt a little off, a little shaky. He certainly wasn't behaving like most men. But then, why should he? Lord Cayton was no stranger to dukes—he was grandson to the late Duke of Stafford, after all. She searched her mind for what else she knew about him.

Those knots in her stomach turned heavy. He was the one who had been courting Brook's cousin, Lady Melissa, only to toss her over for a rich, sickly heiress two years ago. His wife had died the very weekend Brice and Rowena wed, if she recalled aright, after giving birth prematurely to a daughter.

Not her type of gentleman. Not at *all* her type of gentleman, if he cared more for shoring up his bank accounts than for true love.

And, for that matter, if his true love were another woman.

Which was just as well. It would be difficult enough to achieve her purpose here with Brook set against it—she hardly needed the distraction of possible romance. Her galloping heart would just have to calm itself and her logic get a rein on her imagination. Handsome as he may be, Lord Cayton was obviously not the man she'd been awaiting for her fairy-tale romance.

Though when his gaze landed on her again, his frown smoothing out, that logic nearly fled. "Gracious of you indeed, my lady." He edged backward another step, turning his face toward Brook. "I thought Stafford would be in the library this time of day."

"A report just arrived from his holdings in Africa—he's looking it over in his study in the tower."

18

"Ah. Then I shall . . ." Taking another step backward, he cleared his throat. And darted another vaguely accusatory look Ella's way. Which was so baffling she couldn't help but find it fascinating. What could he possibly have against her when they'd never even met? "Good day, Duchess. My lady."

"Cayton, wait." Brook took a step after him and with a hand on his arm halted his flight—he had already spun and looked ready to dash down the hallway at full speed. "You're coming on Friday, aren't you?"

Friday—the Staffords were hosting their annual Cotswolds Ball. Ella had known about it before she invited herself for a visit. To hear Brook tell it, every family of note in the entire region came, some from three counties away.

Cayton sighed. "Brook . . ."

"You need to get out once in a while, James."

Ella frowned at the use of his given name. True, Brook used them more than most, but Ella had never heard her do so in reference to this cousin of Stafford's whom she didn't much care for. She obviously had some motive as clandestine as Ella's.

Now the duchess tried on a persuasive smile. "Bring Addie with you, and plan on staying the night. She and Abingdon can play. You know how they love seeing each other."

"But—"

"You haven't missed the Cotswolds Ball in a decade—the neighborhood needs to see you. They all miss Adelaide. They need to speak to you of her. Of Addie."

His shoulders went a bit more rigid with each word she spoke. "Do you never tire of bullying me?"

To Ella's eye, Brook's grin looked a bit forced. "*Jamais*. And your only recourse is to give in. I'll not relent."

Mumbling something about the likelihood of being hunted

19

down in one's own home, Cayton jerked his head in a nod and strode away.

Ella sidled next to Brook, watching him until he turned a corner. She couldn't quite hold back the hum of appreciation. "I think the only time I've seen him was a glimpse across the lawn at the house party your father hosted, before I was out." She had badgered her parents for a solid week to convince them to let her attend with Brice, only to have the party cut short the day they arrived by the death of Cayton and Stafford's grandfather. "I didn't realize what a handsome man he is."

Brook tilted her head to the side, but her face remained stony. "He does bear a certain resemblance to my husband, I admit." With a blustery sigh, she looped her arm through Ella's and led her toward the stairs at the opposite end of the hall. "You are the sister of a duke, Ella, and pretty as a picture. You can have any gentleman you want. Don't set your sights on that one. For my sake, I beg you. I don't think I can watch him break the heart of another of my dearest friends without taking drastic measures, and I would hate to leave poor little Addie an orphan."

And Brice accused *Ella* of being dramatic. "Lady Melissa, wasn't it?"

"*Oui.* He courted her for nearly a year, enticed her to lie to her mother and meet him in Eden Dale when she was visiting us at Whitby Park, made all manner of promises, declared his love, and then . . ." She snapped her fingers, and the muscle in her jaw pulsed from where she clenched her teeth. "Just like that, he marries another. Without even the decency to tell Melissa before it was announced in the papers. Without the decency to face her since, for that matter, though he claims to be a new man. Well." She lifted her chin, the set of her mouth going smug. "That's about to change."

Alarm beat a rapid pulse in Ella's chest. She pulled Brook to

20

a halt at the base of the stairs that led to the guest room where her riding habit waited. "What are you planning?"

When Brook grinned in that particular way, trouble always followed. "Did I not mention that my cousin is due to join us tomorrow? I keep forgetting to bring it up, it seems. . . ."

"Brook." Admonition—and perhaps a dose of horror—saturated Ella's tone. She leaned close so any passing servants wouldn't hear her words. "Have you no compassion whatsoever? You're going to sic your cousin on him without so much as warning him to brace himself? Are you mad? She's *terrifying.*"

Brook—who, granted, could make Melissa look tame in comparison—merely laughed. "That's exactly what your brother said when she forced him to take her to Hyde Park the day she discovered Cayton was engaged."

Though Cayton was likely halfway up the tower stairs by now, Ella looked over her shoulder. "He probably has good reason for not wanting to face her—these days, I mean. Not that I intend to make excuses for how he treated her."

"Ella, I know you always want to see the best in everyone, but trust me—it's high time those two clear the air. They will either end up engaged before the night is out or part amicably. Either way, an improvement over the current situation."

Engaged by the end of the week—was that what Brook's cousin would be hoping for? Recalling those deep green eyes, the way his hair fell so perfectly over his forehead, Ella had to think it was. She knew for a fact that Lady Melissa Harrington had been collecting proposals for the last two seasons, turning them all down—and this must be why. Because she still loved Cayton, and now that his wife had passed away . . .

*Oh, drat it all.* For just a moment there she had thought . . .

Brook and Justin had found their love story while dealing with the Fire Eyes nonsense. Brice and Rowena too. For one instant, with his hands on her waist, she had imagined the same for herself. Love and adventure, hand in hand.

But no. Life didn't work that way, and fleeting impressions certainly couldn't be trusted. That ache pulsing, Ella shook it all away. Even long-standing impressions couldn't be trusted. If she hadn't been able to gauge the nature of her oldest friend correctly, she certainly wouldn't assume she saw anything but good looks in a man she'd known all of a blink.

She'd do better to focus on diamonds.

# Two

James Azerly, Earl of Cayton, paused his charge up the tower steps when he reached the landing with the window. He always stopped there, had since he was a boy old enough to stretch on his tiptoes to see out the panes of glass. From here, one could look for miles across the rolling Cotswolds. The Stafford pastures, now filled with horses grazing, running, leaping. And beyond it, the nearest village with its thatched-roofed stone cottages.

It looked like a fairy world, had *always* looked like a fairy world, and he didn't imagine it would change anytime in the near future. Gloucestershire had always been where he most felt at home, despite the fact that his own house was in Yorkshire. This view, right here, was the first thing he had sketched that he had taken any pride in. He still had that little drawing stashed somewhere, didn't he?

But no, he didn't want to think about his drawings. Not just now. Not when doing so made him want to spit out a few curses. He settled for muttering, "What a blighted fool you are, James Cayton," and forced himself to turn from the window and keep going.

The door to his cousin's study stood open at the top of the stairs. Cayton didn't bother knocking, just strode in and sank into a chair with an indolent slouch that would have earned him a cuff from Mother, had she been here and not off on the Continent having a grand time without him.

It had been his decision to stay behind, but at the moment he rather regretted it.

He slouched a little more and tilted his head back so he could look at the plasterwork on the ceiling. "Your wife is a bully. I don't know how you tolerate her, unless it's because *she* can tolerate *you*."

At the familiar jest, Stafford snorted a laugh. "She only bullies those she loves—or who very much deserve it." A paper rustled. "Take a look at this, will you, Cay? See if it adds up properly."

He obligingly sat up and took the piece of paper his cousin held out, noting the columns of figures upon it. Cayton had never spent any more time with numbers than he had to for his lessons—but when Stafford had helped him sort through his books awhile back, they had discovered he was rather good at mathematics.

Proving that he *could* have done better with his estates than he had. He could have, had he bothered focusing upon them before he was forced to do so. But he had chosen failure, like with so many other things in his life.

He glanced down the columns, tallying in his head as he went. "He's off by two pence."

"Well then, I'll obviously have to sack him." Their grandfather might have—Stafford, however, reserved his wrath for those more deserving of it.

As Cayton had been a time or two. He handed the paper back and scrubbed a hand over his face. "Why is she so determined to get me to this blasted ball on Friday? And don't give me that line about never missing one. I hosted it for you while you were traveling two years ago, don't forget. I know all about the long history of the Duke of Stafford's famed public ball. That doesn't mean anyone expects to see me here this year, so why is your wife insisting that I must attend?"

"You think I understand the mysteries of Brook's mind?"

Cayton just stared at him. Blinked. Though his cousin didn't do him the courtesy of looking up to see his spot-on glower. "According to you, dear cousin, yes. You do."

"I would never dare claim something so impossible." He scribbled a note onto another paper before him and then looked up. "Just humor her, Cayton. And be glad she's worrying for you rather than just grumbling about you as she did for so long."

He'd had no intention of attending the ball before, and certainly not after he'd collided with Lady Ella downstairs. She was sure to be there, and he had no desire to be if she were. Not that he had anything against the lady, of course. It was just . . .

It was just that her hair was a shade of red so much deeper than he had recalled.

That the line of her shoulder made his fingers itch for his sketching pencil.

That her eyes danced with a light he thought for sure he had imagined.

He pinched the bridge of his nose and tried to clear her image from his mind. When had he even seen her before? For the life of him, he could remember only her face, not the backdrop behind it. Which was dashedly disconcerting.

He pushed himself to his feet and strode to the window that gave the best view of the Forest of Dean. Such an endless sea of greens and browns. He could fill a whole palette with varying shades and still not have enough of them to do it justice. "You failed to mention that Brook was expecting guests."

A crash from the desk brought Cayton spinning around—though he didn't know whether to laugh or frown when he saw Stafford had knocked over a cup full of pens. His cousin wasn't usually the type for clumsiness.

Nor for wide eyes, like he had now. "She *told* you?"

Suspicion dug in a few claws. They weren't trying to make a match, were they? He couldn't think so. Brook didn't like him nearly enough to try to set him up with one of her dearest friends. But why this reaction? "I met her downstairs just now."

Stafford's face moved back to neutral. "Oh, Lady Ella."

Another claw dug in. "Of course Lady Ella. Who did you *think* I meant?"

"No one." Stafford busied himself righting the pens.

As if Cayton didn't know him better than that. He moved to the desk, leaned on it. "Stafford. Who else is coming?"

His cousin sighed. "She may have invited Regan and Thate to spend some time with us soon."

"Oh." Cayton straightened, well able to imagine why they wouldn't want to tell him that. He and Thate had never particularly gotten along—especially after Thate married Melissa's sister and Cayton had gotten engaged to Adelaide. "When?"

He would make his escape to Yorkshire before they arrived. With Regan and Thate would come too many thoughts of Melissa—of old dreams, old regrets. Too many hours spent wondering how she ever could have loved the man he had once been, when Cayton hated that man so much now. Too many hours when even lifting his brush to canvas would accomplish nothing, because every time he did he would remember that he'd never been truly honest about who he was. And how had he meant to make a life with a woman when he was afraid to show her his true self?

He'd always been a blighted fool.

26

"They won't be coming for some time. After the Season." Pens all back in place, Stafford looked up at him with that soft but unyielding expression that meant he was about to deliver a speech about something he deemed to be for Cayton's own good. "You needn't run off just because Brook's family is coming. You know that, surely. Water under the bridge and all that."

Water that would be happy to carry him away and drown him. "Call me a coward if you must, cousin. But I can't face them. Not yet." Not when even thinking about that family brought the waves of guilt crashing down—made him wish for a different past, one less shadowed with bad decisions and regret.

Stafford rose. "They are her cousins. You are mine. At some point peace must be made. Cay, this is ridiculous."

"Easy for you to say." He turned for the door. "I'd better get home before Addie wakes up."

"Cayton, you're not that man anymore. Let them see that."

The words brought him to a halt a step from the exit, but they couldn't quite overcome those crashing waves. His fingers curled into his palm. "You don't understand, Stafford. You never hurt anyone like I've done."

"Haven't I?"

Cayton pivoted to face him again. "It hardly counts when you end up married to the woman you hurt."

"She might disagree."

Arguing with Stafford was always so unsatisfying. Yet somehow, he could never resist. "You and Brook merely had a misunderstanding. I quite deliberately broke Melissa's heart. Quite deliberately chose my own gain above anyone else's interests. Quite deliberately chose silence when speaking of my concerns about Pratt's intentions could have saved your wife a lot of pain and tribulation."

There, the wince that said he'd hit a nerve. Though for the

life of him, he wasn't sure why he'd wanted to. Why could he never let it rest? Why could he not simply accept the forgiveness Stafford and Brook had offered him when he'd confessed to them six months ago that he'd heard a bit of Pratt's plans to kidnap Brook but had said nothing?

Perhaps because he simply couldn't believe they meant it. Not when the duchess still looked at him as if she'd as soon kick him as say hello. And not when his cousin regarded him with such pain.

"There is no point in dwelling on this, Cayton. You made mistakes. You admitted them, you repented of them, you have embraced the redemption from them that the Lord offers. It's time to forgive yourself."

A task he had yet to figure out how to do. "That's why I came, actually." Though he edged toward the door, ready to dash back down the stairs if his cousin thought his suggestion foolish. "I thought perhaps . . . I appreciated our talk the other day—when we were discussing that chapter in Ephesians. I thought, perhaps, we could . . . make a habit of it?"

Stafford straightened, all shadow leaving his eyes, brightening them. "I was going to offer—I didn't know if you'd be interested. We could meet here in the mornings. You can bring Addie. She and Bing can play in the nursery."

A bit of the tension in Cayton's shoulders eased as he nodded. "I'd like that. Starting tomorrow?"

His cousin smiled. "Tomorrow it is. This is a good step, Cay."

He certainly hoped so—he was due for a good step. With a nod and a wave, he turned and headed back down the stairs, a prayer thumping along with every footfall.

A prayer that, this time, was answered positively when he made it all the way outside without running into the duchess and her guest again. Not that it stopped his mind from conjuring up Lady Ella's face.

Just an appreciation of beauty and good humor—that was all. Of the way the light caught her hair and set it ablaze. The line of her shoulder.

It had nothing at all to do with the way his throat had closed off when he'd looked down at her and realized . . . well, that she was real.

Troubadour snorted a greeting as he neared, and he swung up into the saddle after giving his horse an obligatory pat. "Let's go home, boy."

It still felt odd to trot away from the familiar stones of Ralin Castle to the nearby house he had shared so briefly with Adelaide. In all his memory, the duke's castle had been more home to him than his own in Yorkshire. After his father died when he was small, he and his mother had spent most of the year at Ralin, with Grandfather. He had terrorized the ducks down at the pond as a boy. Learned how to jump a horse in that paddock to the west. Had stolen his first kiss from the stable master's daughter—and gotten his first slap for his fourteen-year-old bravery.

He pointed Troubadour down the drive and didn't look back at the beloved towers, the stone walls. Not until he was eight had he realized that, though he was the older of them, his cousin would inherit the duchy, not he. That Ralin Castle would never be his, because he'd been born to the duke's daughter instead of one of his sons.

If he were being honest—which he was trying to be these days—he would admit that it had caused him no little jealousy as he grew up. That was, perhaps, why he and Stafford had never much gotten along as young men.

But losing Grandfather had forced them to put all that aside. And seeing the mess the estates had been in, how much work his cousin had put into setting it to rights . . . it was good Stafford was the one in charge of it all and not Cayton. He'd managed his own, much smaller, estate poorly enough.

It took only a few minutes to canter the mile to the picturesque manor house set against the wood just before the village. As a boy, he had never spared more than a passing glance at Anlic Manor. Though the honeyed-stone house had been standing every bit as long as Ralin Castle, the Rosten family had only purchased it a generation ago, with the profits they made in the mills.

He owned those now, too, as well as the fifteen-acre estate that Adelaide had loved so well. And which he knew Addie would love every bit as much. Like her mother, she would grow up dipping her toes in the little stone fish pool, escaping her nurse to frolic in the grass that grew tall and waving by the small lake. It wasn't as large as Azerly Hall, their home in Yorkshire, but it was better situated. Warmer. And somehow when he was here, he remembered Adelaide as she would want him to—he saw her smiling, happy. At Azerly she had never been so well.

"Back already, milord?"

He smiled at the groom who emerged from the small stable to take his horse. "Must be back before the lady awakens, you know, Gregory."

The groom, with his grey hair and ample wrinkles, had been at Anlic some forty years. He grinned. "The nursery window's open, but we haven't heard a peep from the little lady. You've time yet, I'd think."

He wouldn't complain about that either. The day was always more pleasant when Addie enjoyed a nice nap. "I'm sure I shall find a way to fill it." After dismounting, he handed the reins to the man.

Gregory nodded. "Mrs. Higgins would like a word with you, I believe."

"Ah." His housekeeper here spoke with him more often than the one at Azerly did, but he had a good idea of what she would want to talk with him about today. "How is Felicity?"

The groom just shook his head, worry deepening the lines that smiles had wrought. "Poorly, so far as I can tell. Don't know how much longer she'll be able to work, milord."

He and Mrs. Higgins had already lightened her niece's duties several times, but if Felicity was still overtaxed . . . "We'll see she's cared for, Gregory. Even when she cannot work any longer."

"She won't take charity—you know she won't. She'll work for her keep or she'll leave."

But she couldn't leave—that was what the man's eyes said when his lips stopped. She had no other family left, no home to go to. And if the babe she carried sapped her strength here, it would sap it all the more in another position.

He nodded and headed for the house. "We'll find something that she can manage."

Mrs. Higgins must have heard that last bit, for the aging housekeeper met him at the door with a frazzled sigh. "I don't know what else to give her, my lord. She is already on the lightest tasks. And I swore to you when you agreed to keep her on that I would show no favoritism, despite she's my niece, but—"

"Hush, Mrs. Higgins." He smiled and motioned that she should lead the way into the rear entrance. "And I assured *you* that favoritism is not ill-placed in this situation. Felicity was Adelaide's longest, truest friend."

They had been companions as children, the housekeeper's niece brought in specifically for that purpose, given Adelaide's infirmity. She had never made friends among society. Felicity had become her lady's maid once they were old enough—really, demoting her to a mere housemaid after Adelaide's passing was an insult, but she'd insisted on working for her keep. "My wife made me promise to see to her care, and I intend to do just that. She will always have a home here. Always." Even if some scamp had married her just long enough to get her in a family way and then run off. It was hardly her fault.

Mrs. Higgins pressed a hand to her forehead. "I suppose I can put her to polishing the silver again."

He smiled and patted her shoulder—something his housekeeper in Yorkshire would never have invited nor tolerated, but they moved at a different pace here. And the Rostens had never insisted on the formality that his parents had.

"There now, Mrs. Higgins, I knew you would think of something. And when the silver has been polished, I have long been thinking that we should continue the late Mr. Rosten's work cataloguing the books in his library. Perhaps she could do that . . . with young Ronald to fetch and replace the books for her while she sits at the table?"

The woman's eyes lit. "Oh, she would enjoy that. Thank you, my lord."

"Certainly." Satisfied that such a huge task would keep young Felicity busy long after the babe came, he nodded his farewell and slipped up the back stairs. A peek into the nursery showed him that Addie still slept peacefully while her nurse sat by her crib with knitting in hand, so he continued on his way, up to the garret with its generous windows and slanted, dark-beamed ceilings.

He had known the moment Adelaide showed him this room that he must fill it with color and paper and canvas. Its size was perfect, its lighting ideal. Here he had put his wide, simple desk where he sketched. His easel remained always by the window, where morning light could spill just so onto the canvas. The smell of oils lingered always, along with the potent bite of turpentine.

*Heaven must smell like this.*

He jammed his riding gloves into his pocket but decided that changing into fresh clothes could wait. Another task called, and too loudly to be ignored. He headed straight for the cabinet he had positioned under the slanted eaves and opened the topmost drawer, drawing out the sketch pad he had begun after Adelaide's death last year, when everything had seemed so bleak and hopeless. When the world had felt as though it were collapsing overtop him.

Stafford had told him to pray. To ask God to reveal himself.

So he had prayed. He had prayed that God would do just that, and that He would show him some slip of light to cling to. That He would prove there was hope left in the world.

He had drawn countless things. Flower gardens in spring, sunshine bursting through clouds. Happy children, doting old women with well-earned lines in their faces. Then he had cast about for laughter. For smiles.

He flipped past those first drawings to one in the middle and stared down at the face of Lady Ella Myerston. He hadn't known who he was drawing—he had thought her just an ideal, like so many other figures he had sketched from nothing more than imagination. But there she was. That graceful line of her shoulder. The eyes that sparkled with hope, with a light he had given up on.

He had done a handful of sketches, as was his usual way— seeing her from different angles, different expressions on her face . . . but all of them variations on a smile, a grin. Always happy. Laughing.

Just as she had been when she came plowing out the library door and straight into his arms.

He put that book aside and reached back into the drawer, for the stack of thicker stock he had used with his pastels. In the one of these he'd done, he had tried to capture her coloring.

But his imagination had failed him, it seemed. Her hair was much richer a shade than he had given it credit for being. He had erred on the side of orange, but that wasn't right at all.

Drawing out the box of pastels, he reached for the scarlet and got down to business. He worked steadily, correcting his earlier work until his imaginary Laughing Lady became a truer representation of Lady Ella.

Funny though . . . The more accurate he made the representation, the more vibrant her smiles and laughter seemed.

He had just pulled out a fresh canvas and put the first stroke of a sketch upon it when a halfhearted cry from the floor below brought him to a halt. Grabbing a rag to wipe off any remaining color from his fingers, he abandoned the canvas and headed downstairs. Even the idea for a new painting couldn't compare to being the one to reach into his daughter's crib and pick her up as she awoke.

Tabby still sat with her yarn and needles, though she looked ready to set it aside. "I thought you would be down, milord. Shall I go and ring for her luncheon while you have her?" At Azerly Hall, she would have under-nurses to do such menial tasks for her—here at Anlic, they kept only a skeleton staff.

"Yes, go ahead." For a moment, he just stood there and looked down at the little girl who blinked up at him, stretched her chubby little arms, and grinned. She tied his heart into knots with that grin. He returned it and stretched his arms into the crib. "Are you ready to get up, my sweet girl?"

She answered with the one word she'd managed thus far. "Da! Dadada."

Answer enough for him. He scooped her up, cradled her against him, breathed in the scent of talcum powder and lavender as she snuggled in and closed her eyes again. The sleepiness wouldn't linger long, he knew, but he would enjoy it while it

ROSEANNA M. WHITE

lasted. In another moment she would want down to crawl about the room and pull herself up on anything she could.

For now, he took the chair Tabby had vacated, held his daughter close, and shut his eyes. When he had prayed for proof of hope, God had opened his eyes to this too. To these quiet moments that meant the world.

If only the rest of the world would forget about him and let him enjoy it. But the letter in his pocket proved they wouldn't.

He should have shown it to Stafford while he was there, but . . . tomorrow would be soon enough for that.

# Three

Kira Belova tucked her hand into the crook of Andrei's elbow, made sure her prettiest smile was in place, and prayed her knee didn't give out. "*Oui*, Andrei. You know I would love to."

Her patron smiled and patted her hand. "I knew you would, *mon amour*. Come. I have hired a car to drive us. You like the automobiles, *n'est pas?*"

She hated them—the terrible vibration of the engine, the way they bounced over every cobblestone in Paris—but *he* liked them, so she had claimed bliss when he'd taken her for a drive last week. "Of course I do, *moy durugoy*." The Russian tripped off her tongue, as it so seldom had the opportunity to do in recent days.

She missed Sergei, barking orders at her in a mix of French and Russian. She missed the other ballerinas, muttering and cursing as they stretched their bodies to the limits. She missed the feel of a cold barre under her fingertips, the stretch and strain of muscles. The applause as she transformed arms and

36

legs and back into poetry and music before a crowd of adoring theatergoers enthralled by all things Russian.

Her knee ached, reminding her to keep her smile bright. "Where are we going today?"

Andrei's gaze was on the sleek metal contraption he had hired—this one a gleaming green, where the last had been black. He was still trying to decide what model to buy, he had said, and so was testing out a few.

She would never dare say that they all made her wish for her babushka's stubborn old farm mule. If ever she said such a thing, Andrei would shake her off him like dust, and then where would she be?

She had begged and pleaded with her family for years to send her to St. Petersburg to study ballet at the Imperial School. She had pulled every possible string and called in more favors than she was owed to get an audience with Sergei Diaghilev after his Ballet Russe had debuted to such critical acclaim. She had given up everything—everything—to move to Paris and dance. She wouldn't go back. She wouldn't. Her knee would heal, Sergei would take her back into the corps, and though she might not immediately return to the prima ballerina role, she could earn it back. She could. She would. She *must*.

"La Musée National des arts asiatiques Guimet." Andrei helped her into the car and closed the door behind her. This car had a roof, and he paused for a moment in that way she hated, just looking at her, framed by the metal.

Just another statue for his entryway. Another painting for his wall. That was all she felt like when he looked at her like that—a piece of art in his collection, bought and paid for because she was the prettiest dancer in the ballet. The same reason he carted her around Paris in the finest silks money could buy—just showing all his friends and competitors that he could have the best.

He leaned in, pressed a kiss to her lips, and then moved around the idling car, humming.

She took the moment's respite to draw in a deep breath and push it out, pushing all bitter thoughts out with it. To rub at her knee while he wouldn't notice. She must purge herself of these terrible thoughts. She had worked hard to get his attention—he, the wealthiest Russian in all of Europe, the man every ballerina and actress and singer had vied to win. She had flirted and smiled and played coy, she had darted toward and away again for a solid year. And oh, the victory when he had finally made her the offer all the others had hated her for.

A house of her own, filled with servants. She could open the windows there and smell the fresh baguettes baking. She could ring a bell and have her *café au lait* delivered to her boudoir. She had commissioned a wardrobe to put any princess to shame, had her dark hair regularly styled by a professional *coiffeuse*. He took her to the nicest restaurants, draped her neck with jewels, introduced her to dignitaries and royalty and other wealthy merchants—and all she had to do was keep him happy.

She tried not to think of what Babushka would say. The sorrow that would fill her eyes at knowing Kira had freely chosen what she had striven all her life to escape.

Sliding into the driver's seat, Andrei flashed her a smile full of even white teeth. He was a handsome man, if fifteen years her senior. Kind, most of the time. Generous, when it suited him. And though he had left his previous mistress in so poor a state that no one else dared speak to her, Kira wouldn't let that happen to her. She would make sure that, if they parted ways, it would be amicably. So that she could simply crook a finger at one of those princes or dukes and keep the lifestyle she loved. Not find herself in a gutter, penniless and scarred—the price of betraying Andrei Varennikov.

No, Kira wasn't stupid enough to betray him. "I don't believe I've been to this museum. From its name, I assume it specializes in Asian pieces?"

There was nothing Andrei liked more than talking of art, of antiquities, of all the fine things he surrounded himself with. "*Oui*. They have recently acquired a display from Tibet."

*Tibet*. Kira scoured the map in her mind, trying to place the name. Before Andrei, her knowledge of geography had been poor indeed, but she quickly determined that if she wanted his attention, she must be able to speak intelligently. Finally, she smiled and snuggled close to his side. "I have read that the monasteries in the mountains are breathtaking."

"Mm. They have nothing on our Optina, but they are beautiful. I saw the display last week with Jacques Bacot, who collected it all, and it was quite intriguing. But we are not going through the main display today, *ma belle*."

"*Non?*"

"No. Monsieur Guimet is trying to sell me some of the pieces in his storage room."

She made an impressed noise, knowing how he loved seeing what the public couldn't. Just last month, right before her injury, he had dragged her through the basement of the Louvre for an endless four hours.

Hopefully the Guimet's storage rooms were considerably smaller, because there was no way her knee would hold out so long. She would be forced to ask for a respite, which would remind Andrei of her condition, which would in turn prompt him to ask how much longer she would be away from the ballet . . . and that was not something she wanted to discuss. He liked her because she was on display, because being her patron sparked envy in his friends.

But the public's memory was so short. Another month or

two, and no one would remember Kira Belova. How she could leap farther than the other girls, how she could hold a pose without her muscles shaking like theirs did, how she could make the audience weep with her perfectly controlled movements. The posters with her face upon them would come down and be tossed out with the rest of the garbage.

The streets of Paris moved by her window—all the boutiques and cafés and delicatessens that had become so familiar. She watched the café owners set up the tables and chairs outside their buildings, just so, while their dogs lazed about underneath them, no doubt eager for the patrons who would toss them a crumb now and then with a deep Gallic laugh. Shopkeepers swept their entryways with ancient twig brooms, pausing to shout now and then to acquaintances who would rush over to exchange kisses upon their cheeks. She had thought it strange, at first, how this bustling city managed to capture bits of village life.

Andrei prattled on about this *comte* and that duke, the Russian prince he had dined with last night, the trip he was planning to Monte Carlo in a few weeks. She made all the appropriate responses, exclaiming over how she had enjoyed Monaco when the ballet was there for a season three years ago, when she'd just been getting her career off the ground—but her focus was on the young mothers with their wicker baskets full of fresh produce, on the old men sitting at tables, sipping their coffee and enjoying a cigarette along with their newspaper. Everywhere, people old and young bustled about with baguettes tucked under their arms.

Finally, they turned onto Place d'Iéna and parked in front of the museum. Above the buildings she could see the Eiffel Tower stretching skyward, gleaming silver in the morning light. Kira waited for Andrei to help her out, smiled up at him from beneath her lashes, leaned just enough upon him as she got out to make him think himself necessary, but not so much that he was reminded of her ever-aching knee. It would likely be swollen again after this outing, but with any luck she would have time to ring for some ice before whatever event he had planned for the evening.

He led her through the double doors, ornate with carvings, and through the busiest room in the gallery, pausing here or there when the other patrons glanced their way. Kira knew her role well. How to tilt her head to showcase the diamonds gleaming in her ears, the musical laugh she should loose—quietly—whenever he whispered something in her ear.

Life with Andrei was as much a ballet as when she danced upon the stage. Just as choreographed, just as polished.

Sometimes, in the dark of night, she wished for a lively tambourine and a room full of rhythmic clapping to dance to.

"This way, *ma chérie*." He led her through an arched doorway with a hand upon her back. Sunlight angled in through a narrow window into a small closet of a room with a desk and shelves covered with books and papers. Organized, no doubt—the French were *always* organized—but with a system only the owner of the piles and books could understand. An older gentleman looked up from his chair behind the cluttered desk, smiling.

"Monsieur Varennikov, *bonjour*! You are right on time. And Mademoiselle Belova." The man—Guimet himself?—held out a hand for hers and, when she'd placed her fingers into his palm, leaned over to kiss her knuckles. No doubt now that they had been introduced, their farewell would be marked with kisses upon her cheeks. When he straightened and met her gaze, it was with sparkling eyes. "I saw you in *L'Après-midi d'un faune*. You were . . . enchanting."

"*Merci, monsieur.* You are too kind." She tried not to think of what her father would have thought of that particular ballet. It had caused a sensation, to be sure. And had earned her many, many adoring fans eager to take on Andrei's role.

She reclaimed her hand and tucked it against Andrei's arm with her other. Silks and jewels weren't all he gave her—he also lent her his protection from would-be suitors. Not that this elderly gentleman before her was a threat.

The man shook himself and motioned back toward the hallway. "Come, come. I will show you downstairs and tell you about anything you wish. I think several of these pieces would be an excellent addition to your collection, *monsieur*."

Stairs? Kira kept her smile in place, but she also readied her stage mask. The one that allowed her to dance on toes that were bloodied and occasionally broken—it could surely cover the relatively easy pain of her knee. It had nothing on what her feet had suffered.

Why, then, had it been so debilitating? She could have danced through the pain. She could have, if only it hadn't become so *weak*.

Between Andrei and the railing, though, she made it down the stairs and into the dank, cool basement without any mishaps. The two men chatted for a few minutes, lamps were lit, explanations of several pieces given. Then Andrei asked if he could wander around on his own, and the older man left them with a flurry of niceties—and no doubt franc signs dancing before his eyes.

Andrei waited until he had gone, leaned over to press a quick kiss to Kira's lips, and then tugged her toward the section where relics from India were apparently stored. "This way, *ma chérie*. It is a statue I want you to see."

Her brows knit. "But did he not say they were primarily

religious artifacts? Andrei, since when do you have any interest in such things? Do you really mean to buy any of this?"

"Perhaps to appease him. But that is not what I wish to show you. Here." He stopped her before a shelf, shuffled a few boxes around, and finally pulled forward a rough stone figure, recognizable even in the light of a single lamp. "What do you think?"

She blinked at the animal, trying to determine what about it had caught his interest. The material was crude. The craftsmanship was crude. The very stance of the small-scale beast was crude. Since she had no insight, she widened the eyes she turned on him and went for endearing. "I can tell you it is a tiger, *mon amour*. Beyond that, I am afraid I need you to explain it to me."

Rather than grow exasperated with her, he chuckled. "You are exactly right, Kira. It is a tiger, crafted thousands of years ago, its origins unknown but thought to be somewhere in Bengal. But it is rare, because though the tiger god has a name—Dakshin Ray—they rarely carve statues of him, given that the beast itself roams the jungles. He is a god more feared than loved. He is a god who destroys villages and feasts upon them."

A shudder stole up her spine. Perhaps she *did* see what he saw in it, then. "You have other statues of tigers—what strikes you about this one?"

"What it lacks, *ma chérie*. What it lacks." He turned the carving so that she looked into the beast's face rather than its side. "What do you *not* see?"

Usually such questions made fear take hold of her stomach, or impatience well up. This time, the answer was obvious—staring quite literally back at her with empty sockets. "It has no eyes, but holes for them. Not like most statues. More like . . . like it had separate eyes that have come out. Stones, perhaps."

"Not just stones, Kira. Jewels." He stepped behind her, his

hands resting on her hips, and lowered his head to her level, putting his mouth at her ear. "Diamonds."

"Diamonds? In such a simple piece?"

"Simple, yes. Crude, to be sure. But it has a certain primal power, *n'est pas?*"

It did, at that, and was decidedly unnerving as it stared at her with its missing eyes. *"Da."*

"Now imagine it with red eyes staring you down."

"Red?" She turned her face a few inches so she could see his profile. "How?"

"Red diamonds." His thumb stroked over her hip bone, though it seemed more absent than suggestive, given how his attention remained riveted on the statue. "The rarest gemstone in the world, and there are two of them, a matching pair."

Another shiver overtook her—this time more because of the man who stared at it so intently than the statue. "What happened to them?"

"They were stolen—no one knows when. They have popped up from time to time in India, only to disappear again after men have murdered over them. Often enough to keep the legend alive, but no one has heard anything about them for twenty years."

Her throat went tight. If no one had heard anything, then he wouldn't be bringing up the story. "Except . . . you?"

He breathed a laugh and moved to her side again. "You know me well, *ma chérie.* I have made it no secret to all the major jewel traders that I am interested in any rare gems they come across. Two years ago, an Englishman made contact. He said he had two red diamonds, twin stones. He called them the Fire Eyes."

"Fire Eyes." Perhaps it was the damp, the chill that made her shiver for a third time.

"I have done my research. That is what the natives called the jewels that belonged in this statue." He tapped the tiger on the head and then pushed it back into place. "Not that the man claiming to have them knew anything about the statue. And not that it matters—I won't have such a crude tiger in my house."

But the jewels . . . the jewels he would want. "Did you buy them?"

"I offered to." He repositioned a box in front of Dakshin Ray and straightened his shoulders. He was broad, powerfully built, and though nearing forty, still strong as an ox. Evidence, she had heard it whispered, of his common, country origins.

Origins he was forever trying to outpace.

Kira shuffled backward a step. "Did he not accept your offer?"

"He did. And accepted a deposit on the gems—but failed to deliver them."

A corner of Kira's mouth pulled up. "More the fool him. And where is he buried?"

But Andrei didn't smile. "In Yorkshire, England, but not of my doing. He was killed before he could get me the jewels. But I will have them, Kira. And once I do, Prince Vitaly will no longer be able to deny my worth. He will let me marry his daughter. *Nyet*, he will *beg* me to marry his daughter, when I promise to put the Fire Eyes around her neck."

There were many moments when she didn't enjoy being Andrei's mistress, but these—when he had that fevered glint in his eye as he spoke of the princess he wanted to marry—these she hated. "I am certain you have sent men in after them—"

"They have found nothing, and I do not wish to harass the man's widow outright. I am not a monster, Kira."

"Of course not." Her smile didn't waver. Even if all those whispers about scarred women and dead men did steal into her mind. "What, then?"

He stilled, pivoted. Stared at *her* much as he just had the statue—as a means to an end. "She is in Paris right now. With her brother. They do not know who I am, of course, certainly not that I am here—all dealings have been through one of my agents. But I have kept a close watch on them. And they are *here*, Kira. *Here*."

Instinct told her to back up another step. But he was watching, so instead she slid forward until she could rest her hands on his chest and tilt her head up to look at him. "Will you approach them? Ask them about the jewels?"

"*Nyet.*" Though his mannerisms were calm, the Russian word told her his passions were high. Dangerously high, given that he continued in them instead of switching back to French. "They already contacted my agent. Asking, yet again, for more time. I need to know what is going on, *milaya*. I need someone inside their house when they go back to England."

"A spy." She trailed a finger down the lapel of his jacket. "If anyone can find such a person, it is you."

"I have already found her." He reached into his inner pocket and withdrew a . . . ladies magazine? She recognized the article it was open to, having read it just yesterday. But he flipped it over to the advertisements and handed it to her.

He had circled one. "This is the widow you speak of? Who is looking for a lady's maid?"

"*Da.*" He said no more.

She read the notice once, twice, but it was just like every other such request. The only thing of note was that interviews were being held today. "So you have sent someone to secure the position?"

"Not yet. But Sophie Lareau has an appointment in two hours. Just enough time for you to go back to your flat and change into something more suitable for such an interview . . . Sophie."

"*Quoi?*" After slapping the magazine back to his chest, she stepped away. "*Non*! I will not! I will not be a *servant* to some English lady. I will not be a *spy* for—"

He caught her by the wrist and held her still. "Have you anything better to do just now, *mon amour*?" No threats flashing in his eyes, no heavy hand. He didn't need them. He had men to do such work for him.

But she shook. Not from fear but from fury. All she'd given up to avoid the life of a servant, all she'd worked for, and he wanted her to demean herself, to bow and kowtow and clean up the slops of another. "I'll be back on the stage in a few weeks. I have a *career*, Andrei, and I cannot drop it all to go chasing after diamonds that you intend to give to your spoiled little princess so she'll finally agree to be your wife!"

Now his eyes flashed, and he dragged her against him. Still not hard. His grip wasn't painful, but it was somehow all the more insistent for its gentleness. "I have spoken to your physicians, Kira. You will never dance again."

"*Nyet*! What do they know? It has only been a few weeks. They are wrong. They are all wrong! I will strengthen it. I will defy the odds. I will—"

"You will do exactly as I say, and you will continue to live the life you love so well—just off the stage." He released her, set her away from him, and ducked his head a bit to meet her eyes straight on. "Do you hear me? Do this for me, *milaya*, and I will put the house into your name. I will set up an account for you, just for you. You will never want again."

She could only stare at him and wish away the tears that burned. How could he say that she would never dance again? How could *anyone* say such a thing to her? It was her life, her whole life, everything she had ever yearned for. "It cannot be as bad as they say. I will prove them wrong. I will."

His smile looked almost paternal as he tweaked her chin.

"Perhaps you shall—you have the Russian spirit, after all. But if not, you will not suffer, *ma chérie*. You will live well, answer to no one but yourself. You can have your babushka come and stay with you if you want." He leaned forward, feathered a kiss over her temple.

She turned her face away. Was this how he broke things off? Gently, generously? Asking a favor of her? "She would hate Paris. She would hate anything but home."

"You could afford to visit her there, then." He kissed her cheek, settled his hand at her waist. "I can trust no one as I trust you, Kira. But you—how could they see you and not hire you on the spot? Who could better navigate that strange world than a girl who has proven herself capable of flourishing no matter where she ends up? You are my best hope, Kira Belova. My only hope."

She kept her face averted. "You speak of washing your hands of me in one breath and of your admiration for me in the next?"

"You think I *want* to part ways with you, just because your career is over?" His breath tickled her ear. "*Milaya*, you underestimate my affection for you. But you have made it clear you will not be involved with a married man, *n'est pas*? And Princess Alyona will soon be my wife. Our *affaire de coeur* is bound to end soon, by *your* decision, not mine."

She felt as rigid as that stone tiger—and just as fragile. That was her future, ready to topple and shatter. All her dreams, all she had slaved for, had sacrificed for, had compromised for . . . gone. Like smoke, blown away with the first stiff breeze.

No one would remember Kira Belova in another year. And she certainly had no way of making a living without the ballet . . . other than *this*. Doing a man's bidding in exchange for a roof and clothes. Fine ones for now—she still had face and figure and that remnant of fame.

But her skin would wrinkle, her belly would sag, dark curls would go grey. Then what?

A house of her own, money of her own . . . It was an offer she couldn't pass up. Which Andrei, of course, knew. With a sigh, she rested her forehead on his shoulder. "A *servant*?" Babushka remembered too well being a serf, bound to the whim of a master. All of Kira's life Babushka had whispered that the greatest gift of their family wasn't their artistic flair, wasn't the strong health that kept so many of them alive. . . . It was their freedom to use health and talent as *they* willed.

"Only for a month or two, *ma belle*. Then it is back to Paris, back to your house. You put the diamonds in my hand, and I put the world in yours."

She closed her eyes and imagined, for a moment, that she could hear the carefree laughter of her brothers, the booming voice of her father, the gentle admonition of Babushka, saying always the same thing. "Do what you should, *rebenok*."

But there was no *should* in life, not in hers. There was only *must*. "So be it."

# Four

The day was mild enough that Ella left her wrap inside, content with the warmth her morning dress's sleeves provided. She tilted her head up to receive the spring sunshine, blithely ignoring all the memories of her mother chiding her about freckles. Some things were worth the sacrifice of a little vanity, and these first warm days certainly merited a dusting of freckles across her nose.

Birds chirped, a gardener hummed, and Ella followed the sounds of deep belly laughs to the flower garden at the rear of the castle, where she spotted little Lord Abingdon, tiny heir to the Duke of Stafford, running a bit unsteadily from his mother. Something sparkled in the fist he waved in the air.

Diamonds, likely. And after her midnight study session, Ella was fairly certain she could have examined them and identified their grade. Not that she dared mention her newfound knowledge to anyone at Ralin Castle.

Abingdon waved the gems as if they were no more than glass beads. The boy had blond hair, like both his parents, and his mother's mischief always in his eyes. Ella absolutely adored him—and greatly pitied his nurse, who always had a frazzled look about her, even though Brook spent far more time with her son than most ladies did. Now Ella rushed into his path with a laugh of her own, arms open to intercept him.

But he knew her too well, and knew that she'd pry whatever he had stolen from his fingers. With another happy baby giggle, he squealed and changed directions, toddling and weaving his way toward a blanket someone had spread out, strewn with toys. His knees folded at one point, and he crawled for a step before pushing his way back to his feet and starting again.

Ella chuckled as Brook came to her side. "What has he stolen this time?"

"My bracelet. How he managed to get the clasp undone, I'll never know. Smart little monster." Grinning with pure maternal pride, Brook flipped away a curl that had fallen into her face . . . and then touched a hand to her stomach. "Perhaps the Lord will take pity on us and send us a calm, sweet little angel like Addie next time."

"Next time?" With a happy squeal, Ella drew her friend in for a joyful embrace. "Congratulations, Brook! Is *that* why your husband had such a proud gleam in his eye at supper last night?"

Brook gave her a squeeze and drew away with contentment in her eyes. "He accused me of planning it this way so I'd have an excuse to stay at home for the Season."

"The happiest excuse one could ever devise." Lord Whitby's words preceded his arrival from beyond the hedge by a second or two. "Though I have already begun trying to lure them to Yorkshire for the summer, if they eschew London." He stepped directly to his daughter's side, pressed a kiss to her head, and crouched down, holding his arms wide. "Come here, Bing. Come to Grandpapa."

The miniature marquess had his grandfather wrapped firmly around his little finger, and well he no doubt knew it. The boy

51

emitted another happy noise and changed course again, barreling toward Whitby and tumbling into his arms. The earl stood, his brows in a frown but a smile hovering about his lips as he tugged the bracelet from the toddler's fingers. "Found your grandmama's jewelry again, I see." He angled a sharp look at Brook.

She held her hands up, face all innocence. "I didn't *give* it to him, Papa. He took it straight from my wrist while I was playing with Addie. I was just telling Ella how I hope this next baby is a girl, and calmer."

Whitby snorted a laugh and tickled his grandson's tummy. "Don't let her fool you, Bing. You have inherited your mischief directly from your mother, and it serves her right if you manage to outdo her in it."

Ella's mind had snagged on that *playing with Addie*. If Lord Cayton's daughter was here, that meant *he* was here. Which meant she may see him again, and she wasn't sure what she thought about that. Brook had spent much of the evening seething about his treatment of her cousin, Melissa, of her hopes that it would all finally be put to rest.

By the time Ella had sneaked back down to the library, she was fully convinced that he was a man to be avoided.

Never mind that he was so very handsome, and that her pulse had sped so deliciously at his touch. A bit of romance wasn't worth heartache, which he seemed to bring with him.

She turned away from Brook and Whitby, listening now for other baby sounds and the soft coo of a nurse. It was hardly the daughter's fault that her father was a rake, and Ella could never get enough of children. A few steps along the white gravel of the path, around a hedge, and she spotted child and caretaker, headed their way with a smile.

Addie, about three months younger than her energetic cousin, crawled through the grass, but not upon her knees—she rather seemed determined to spare her gown any stains and was on feet and hands, her little bottom straight up in the air. So charming a picture did she make that Ella couldn't help but laugh.

The nurse looked up and curtsied upon spotting her. "Good morning, milady."

"Good morning." Not wanting to startle the little one, Ella eased closer. "What a little darling. She is about nine months old, if I remember correctly?"

The nurse nodded. "Lady Adelaide Azerly, though we all call her Addie." She said it with pride and affection and then dipped her head as if afraid it was misplaced. "I'm Tabby, milady. Been her nurse since the day she was born."

"Lady Ella Myerston." Gaze still focused on the girl, who had paused and now looked over at her, Ella crouched down much as Whitby had just done. "Hello, sweetling. Aren't you the prettiest thing? I don't believe I've ever seen such beautiful large eyes."

They were a brilliant blue, making a striking contrast against her cap of feathery dark hair. And when those perfect pink lips parted in a grin, Ella was quite willing to declare herself in love. Another happy laugh tickled her throat when Addie shifted course and crawled toward her. "Are you coming to make your own introductions? What a polite little girl."

Addie came directly to her, going so far as to pull herself upright using Ella's knees.

Tabby lurched forward. "Oh, milady! Her hands are grubby, she'll soil your lovely dress. Let me take her—"

"Nonsense. It doesn't matter." To prove it, Ella sat down in the grass so the little one could crawl into her lap. Lewis would have had a fit—but then, her maid wasn't there. Ella had sent her on a holiday to visit her family, not wanting anyone from

Midwynd with her while she sought out information on the Fire Eyes. And here was another added benefit—no familiar maid to sigh and scold and badger her for every stray stain and misplaced shoe. And brush. And book. And necklace. And . . .

Addie obligingly settled in Ella's lap, fisted her hand around some grass, gave a tug, and held up her treasure with those wide, guileless eyes.

Yes, Ella was most assuredly in love. And a baby, still so innocent, she was in no danger of misjudging. She took the proffered gift with a smile. "Why thank you, Addie. I shall cherish it always."

Tabby settled across from her with a bit of a frown. "She's usually wary of strangers. You must have a way with children."

"Children and animals, as it were. Right, Ella?" Brook's voice came from behind her, but Ella didn't turn her head away from her little guest to see her friend. Brook would probably read in a flash that she'd been in the library again last night when she should have been sleeping and would take the liberty of locking the doors tonight lest she repeat the infraction.

"You cannot deny the evidence." She stroked a hand over Addie's silky hair. And if ever she found the right gentleman—after she'd managed to ensure Brice and Rowena and their babe were safe from the Rushworths and the Fire Eyes business—she wanted nothing more than to settle down and obtain a passel of children. And puppies. Perhaps a kitten or two. Blessed, precious chaos.

Addie loosed a high, happy sound and grabbed another handful of grass. This time, she tossed it in the air and clapped when it rained down.

Tabby scolded. Brook laughed and said, "Beautiful adornment. Though no doubt full of bugs." Her fingers skittered over Ella's shoulder, up onto her head.

Laughing, Ella batted her friend away. "You are as bad as the children, Brook. It's no wonder your son is so wild."

"They bring out the best in me. Just wait until they're grown enough to handle cricket bats and tennis rackets. I shall teach them all manner of ways of terrorizing their fathers." This last part she said more loudly.

Ella turned her head enough to see Stafford approaching on the path, grinning. And Lord Cayton beside him.

*Drat.* There it was, that same flutter in her chest that made her breath catch and butterflies perform acrobatic stunts in her stomach. It was simple attraction, she knew that. But she had noticed handsome men plenty of times before. Why did it tug so strongly this time, when he was quite clearly wrong for her?

Addie clapped grass-scented hands to Ella's cheeks and declared quite seriously, "Dadadada."

Ella grinned. "There he comes indeed. You are as brilliant as you are beautiful and charming, my lady."

She expected the child to lift her arms toward him, or to Brook or the nurse, but she seemed quite content to kneel precariously on Ella's legs and stare at her. And the why soon became apparent, when with another happy squeal she abandoned her cheeks and reached with both hands for Ella's hair. One tug and pins went flying.

Really, Ella had no choice but to laugh again, though to hear the other women scold, one would have thought the little one had committed some grave error. Ella held her steady and made no move to free her hair from the insistent little fingers.

Tabby rushed to one side of her . . . and Cayton appeared on the other.

"Apologies, milady!" The nurse sounded more than a little chagrined. Which was probably why her shaking fingers managed only to create more of a snarl.

Ella chuckled. She would *not* be bothered by Lord Cayton—neither by his nearness nor his list of heartless infractions. "It is no great matter, Tabby. No need to fret. She just wanted to guarantee my undivided attention is all. Well, you have it, my little sweetling."

Addie grinned her appreciation.

Cayton went to work on the little fingers nearest him. "I daresay she is simply intrigued by the shade, my lady. I don't know that she's ever seen red hair before."

Behind her, Brook snorted a laugh. "Oh, now you've done it. Back away, Tabby, before you take some of the shrapnel. Cayton, I shall sing a requiem at your funeral."

The nurse, confusion on her face, stood up. Cayton's fingers froze. "Pardon?"

Ella reached up to take over where Tabby had left off, freeing that one side relatively quickly. Handy, since that meant she could turn her head to glare at Cayton. Whose face was close enough to hers that she nearly forgot to be angry and focused instead on memorizing the way his brows fit so perfectly over his eyes. Nearly.

Instead, she added the gravest of all infractions to his list of them. "She is referring to the fact that I get a bit defensive, my lord, when someone mistakes my hair for red—when, really, anyone can see it's *auburn*."

Most gentlemen had the good sense to stutter out an apology when they had committed that particular crime. This one just lifted those perfect, strong brows and met her gaze. "No. Auburn is equal parts brown *and* red. Yours, Lady Ella, is quite simply *red*."

Ella glared. Even if his fingers in her hair made her scalp tingle. "My apologies, my lord—I didn't realize you were color-blind."

He had the gall to grin. "No, no. *My* apologies, my lady. I didn't realize you were delusional."

"It is not delusion, just simple fact." She reached up, knowing she had better put some distance between them so she could school her ridiculous reaction to him. But if she tried to free her hair on that side, her fingers would brush his. And she could hardly stand with any grace from this position.

*Drat*—she was stuck. And, if she were being honest, enjoying it just a bit. She set her hand on Addie's back again.

His fingers moved, quickly loosing his daughter's hold. In the next moment he was rising, chuckling, and helping her to her feet along with him. "Obviously a sore spot with you, though I cannot fathom why, Lady Ella."

He had obviously never had crowds gawk at him and whisper words like *vulgar* as often as they whispered *lovely*. It was one thing to end up the center of attention due to one's wit and charm—quite another to have it foisted upon one because of the beacon of one's hair.

He held out his hands for his daughter. "Come, Addie. Time to go home."

Tabby dipped a quick curtsy. "Shall I go and gather our things from the nursery, milord?"

"Please do, yes." Cayton's face had fallen into a frown again, though. Probably because Addie still made no move to go to his arms. "Come to Dada, Addie."

The little one smiled at him but kept an arm looped round Ella's neck—then lunged, but not toward her father. She reached out a hand toward the bushes growing at the edge of the garden just beginning to bud, her shift pulling Ella a step toward the path.

Ella was happy enough to oblige. "It seems Addie and I are taking a little promenade before you leave with her, my lord."

Cayton, however, kept pace beside her. "If you let her, she'll steer you all about the estate like that."

"And a better way to explore it I cannot imagine." Settling the girl more comfortably on her hip, Ella let her lean whichever way she wanted to go. Perhaps a conversation with the little one's father was all it would take to make Ella push aside attraction and forget any silly notions about him.

She glanced over her shoulder to see if Brook was scowling a warning at her, but her friend was talking with her husband and father, not seeming too concerned about Ella wandering off with Cayton.

He obviously wasn't *that* much a reprobate, then.

She smiled up at him, a bit of softness creeping in when she saw the way he watched his daughter. "You seem to be quite involved with her. Most men I know would simply leave a babe to the nurse's care in your situation."

Given the storm clouds that gathered in the green of his eyes, it must be as much a sore spot with him as her hair was with her. "She's *my* child, not the nurse's."

Yes, definitely a sore spot. But Ella's smile didn't waver. "I didn't mean it as an admonition, my lord, but as a compliment. Surely you aren't so unfamiliar with them that you can't tell the difference."

He sighed, the clouds parting. "My apologies. My wife's last words were that she knew I would be a good father, that I would love our daughter. Stafford insists I'm so determined to honor her vision of me that I'm going to extremes to prove her right."

"I'm sure your cousin speaks from concern for you. But how could you *not* dote on her? Look at those eyes." When Addie turned them on her, Ella laughed. "Yes, sweetling, I'm talking about you. But all good things, I promise you."

Addie grinned, showing off gums with two teeth just beginning to poke through, and leaned to the left. Ella happily abandoned the path and cut through the lawn.

Cayton was frowning again. "She doesn't usually take to people so quickly."

"She must be an excellent judge of character." Unlike Ella.

"Ah, right. I believe you were in the middle of saying something about children and animals loving you when you were coming out the library yesterday—though I interrupted you before you could finish your claim about gentlemen. How is it we are to respond?"

She wouldn't flush, she *wouldn't*. So she chuckled instead. "I believe I was about to claim that they all fell at my feet in adoration, but I may have been exaggerating slightly for Brook's benefit. To be honest . . ." She leaned his way just an inch or two. Looked up into his evergreen eyes. "I haven't quite the way with animals I claimed either. Oscuro tried to nip at me yesterday when I dared compliment the sheen of his coat."

Amusement gleamed in his eyes. "That horse is a menace, my lady. A magnificent menace, I grant you, but you needn't take it as an indictment against your charms."

Addie reached for a butterfly fluttering overhead, apparently done with steering. So Ella angled them away from the garden. "You needn't worry for me, my lord," she said on a laugh. "Neither my confidence nor my lies about it can be shaken so easily."

"You do that a lot."

His tone was far too serious, contemplative. Her brows drew together—she had only been jesting. "Lie, you mean?"

"No." His lips twitched up but settled back into a serious line again. "Laugh. Smile."

"Oh." Her shoulders relaxed, though she realized only then that she'd tensed them. "I do, at that. And why not?"

"One might ask instead *why*." He motioned toward the sky—

blue overhead, but clouds gathered on the horizon. "Life is as much cloudy days as bright ones. More, oftentimes."

"Well, we *are* in England." When Addie rested her head upon Ella's shoulder, she reached to smooth down a wisp of that impossibly soft hair. "And yet most people never realize how many of those clouds can be broken through with a bit of sunshine. Why shuffle about in the dark on a cloudy day when one can brighten it oneself?"

He fastened his gaze on the horizon. "You think a smile can actually change things?"

"It absolutely can, when aimed at a person who needs one." And the certainty slithered inside her that this man at her side most definitely needed one. He wore weariness in the line of his shoulders, a bit of dejection in the angle of his head. She hadn't noticed it at first behind his utter handsomeness and the stories of his mistakes, but there it was. "And what changes things even more is hope. Faith. When we believe, my lord, amazing things happen. Ours is a God who delights in providing for His children, who charges us to be whole, complete, to find joy in all our circumstances through Him."

The breath he drew in looked as if it barely sustained him, much less fortified him. "I am learning to believe that . . . but it is difficult when one sees only what one has lost. No matter how we believe, people still die."

"They do." There were still times she found herself wanting to run and tell her father something. Still times Mama's eyes would flood with tears at the mere mention of him, or of something he had loved. It had been only a year and a half since his heart had failed him at their home in Scotland, and sometimes the pain hit with as much fierceness as it had that day when she realized he was gone. "And it will always hurt to lose those we love. But if we live in fear of losing them, or of dying ourselves, or if we focus only on the hole their passing leaves behind . . . then do we not cheapen life? If we value it so highly that we mourn its passing for years, then ought we not live it to the fullest?"

"Hmm." It was a thoughtful hum, his gaze remaining locked on the distance. But the line of his shoulders lifted a bit. "You do have a point."

Ella feathered her fingers over Addie's back. "Of course I have. I am as wise as I am witty, you know."

Another hum, this one brighter. He glanced her way with a smile in his eyes. And made it rather difficult to dislike him merely on principle. "I don't know if we can call it wisdom, Lady Ella, until you admit that the fiercest hope cannot change *some* things. You can believe it all you want, but your hair is not, and will never be, auburn."

Or maybe *not* so difficult. Her laugh bounced back at her, making her feet come to a halt. They were behind an outbuilding, but she wasn't sure which one. Or how exactly she had led them to so unlikely a place.

Cayton's gaze took note of their surroundings, too, and his amusement gleamed all the brighter. "Do you always take your promenade to the gardener's shed?"

She bit her lip, though it did nothing to hold back her smile. "I don't believe in traveling the beaten path. One never knows what one might discover when one strays from it."

"Mm, well." He bent down, plucked two dandelions from the higher grass that grew against the wall of the shed, and handed one to Addie, who fisted it with a thankful squeal. The other he held out to Ella. "This seems to be all that's around to be discovered today."

Just a weed, most would say, common and soon to go to seed. So why did it look more beautiful than any of the hothouse flowers she had been sent in London? Ella took it with a smile, telling herself that being a wee bit charmed was no great thing in the grand scheme of keeping one's distance from a man. "A bit of sunshine. You learn quickly, Lord Cayton."

"These days, I hope." Appearing as though the brush of their fingers hadn't sent tingles up his arm as it had hers, he reached for his daughter.

Addie went without complaint this time, a yawn hinting at the approach of nap time. Ella's arms felt dreadfully empty with her gone, but her heart beat so full it nearly hurt as she watched the girl snuggle contentedly against her father's chest. It was terribly cliché to be attracted to a man just because he was a good father . . . and handsome . . . and clever . . . and charming. And Ella hated to be a cliché. She must get ahold of herself.

His daughter settled, Cayton looked up again at Ella. He didn't smile, not with his lips. But his eyes shone green and bright. "I suppose I shall see you tomorrow, Lady Ella. At the ball. Perhaps . . . you will save me a dance?"

She ought to refuse. Politely of course. Somehow. "Perhaps I shall—if you promise to stop calling my hair *red*."

He laughed, full and deep, and it sent a thrumming all through her. "I will not lie, my lady. But you'll dance with me anyway."

"Will I?" She twirled the bright flower between her fingers.

"Well." He backed away, still smiling, his daughter still happy in his arms. "I *hope* so. Is that enough to make it become reality?"

She shouldn't like him. It couldn't possibly bode well. "We shall see, Lord Cayton."

He chuckled as he turned, as he made his way back to the garden. Ella watched him go, leaning onto the wall of the gardener's shed with a sigh. She shouldn't like him, and couldn't trust the fact that she wanted to—not given her poor history with judging a person's character.

And, besides, Lady Melissa would arrive tomorrow, and they'd be engaged before the night was out.

All well and good. And to show herself she wouldn't care a bit, Ella would do her best to turn a few heads of her own. She'd wear the new ivory evening gown that she had just commissioned for the Season, the one with the overlay sprigged with flowers of red and yellow. The pendant that drew attention to the intricate bodice of the dress. Her hair up, with her mother-of-pearl combs. And she'd top it all off with the earrings she kept "forgetting" to return to her sister-in-law, the ones dripping Nottingham rubies from a cluster of gold and diamonds.

Pushing off from the shed, Ella brushed grass and dirt from her dress. She'd brush him aside just as easily. No investment, no disappointment.

Still, her fingers clutched the dandelion stem as she headed back for the house.

## Five

Cayton cast yet another glance to the envelope sitting on the top of his chest of drawers. Though it was closed, the letter folded neatly inside, the words kept scrolling before his eyes. *Paris has not done my sister the good I hoped, so we will be back in England soon. I may need your help, Cayton. I will say no more now, but I look forward to seeing you in Yorkshire.*

He knew the script. Knew the tone. Knew too well that Rushworth thought he could appeal to him for help because he had never once stood up for what was right in the past. Had been—regardless of what Stafford said—all but complicit in crimes by doing nothing to stop them.

And he hated himself for it.

A light tap on his bedroom door and it opened enough to admit Evans, Cayton's evening jacket in hand. His valet took one look at the direction Cayton faced and sighed. "Shall I tack it to the wall for you, my lord, so you might glower at it every time you look up?"

"You are, as always, infinitely amusing." He frowned at the choice of jacket Evans laid out on the bed. "Why did you have *that* one pressed?" He hadn't worn it since Adelaide's funeral—

it being his best and that event being the last he'd attended that demanded such.

Evans's blink was all innocence. And didn't fool Cayton for a moment. "It was my understanding there's a young lady you might wish to impress tonight, my lord."

Cayton picked up the snow-white shirt already set out for him and jammed his arms through the sleeves. "You've been talking with Tabby." Who had been babbling incessantly about the saintly Lady Ella for the past twenty-four hours.

A small snort was all the laugh Evans permitted himself. "She *is* my sister, my lord."

After making quick work of the buttons, Cayton held out his wrists for Evans to insert the cuff links. "Blasted bother to employ so many people who are related to one another. I don't know when I'll learn my lesson."

Evans put in the diamond-studded links with a few expert motions. "Shall I go and tell Mrs. Higgins to toss her niece to the drive, then?"

"I'll toss *you* to the drive, if you don't learn to mind your tongue." It was about as likely as Troubadour reciting a sonnet, which Evans well knew.

His valet reached for the tie that had been waiting beside the shirt. "Did you show His Grace the letter?"

"Mm."

"And?"

Cayton had heard stories of people whose servants minded their own business—or at least pretended to. Fantastic, glistening tales of valets who went about their work stoically, silently. Such was not, it seemed, his lot. "He thought it must have something to do with the diamonds, though he had no better guess than we did as to why Rush would need *my* assistance."

Evans's brows knit as he knotted the tie. "Was he concerned?"

"Only for me, not about the situation. I received yet another lecture on letting go of the guilt, since I'd accepted forgiveness for the actions."

"Perhaps you would stop receiving said lecture, my lord, were you to follow the advice." Evans made a quick adjustment to the tie and then spun for the jacket, held it up.

Cayton sighed. "Really?"

Evans didn't so much as twitch. "You would prefer the one with the ink stain that wouldn't come out? Or perhaps the one with the fraying cuff that I have been begging you for a year to have replaced? Which of those shall I fetch for you?"

*Blast it.* He turned his back to Evans so he could slip his arms into the sleeves and the man could smooth the fabric over the shoulders.

Evans did so chuckling. "She must be as pretty as Tabs said."

"I have no interest in Lady Ella Myerston." Why, then, *why* had he asked for a dance? *Stupid. Foolish. Dangerous.* "But if I show up looking like a vagabond, Stafford will probably drag me upstairs and force me into one of *his* jackets." He'd done it once before, when Cayton had forgotten that he was coming for a dinner party and had happened by more by accident than design just in time to be snapped at.

"Tabs said Addie took right to her. Didn't mind having grass thrown all over her or her hair pulled out of its style. Can't say as I've met too many ladies like that."

Cayton looked to the mirror across from them, lifting his brows at his valet's reflection. "Rubbing elbows with the ladies when I'm not looking?"

"Always keeping an ear out for which other houses would suit me, you know. So that when you kick me to the drive, I know where to go." He tugged Cayton's sleeves down over his cuffs.

"With the recommendation I'll give, you'll only be accepted as a scullery maid."

A laugh slipped out before Evans pressed his lips against it. "Yes, milord," he squeaked in a high-pitched imitation of the young girl usually hired in that beginner's position. "Sorry, milord."

Cayton's gaze shifted to that blamed letter again. "I don't like it. I've a bad feeling."

"As my mum would say, don't go borrowing tomorrow's troubles, my lord, when today's are troubling enough. Hands."

Cayton turned, held out his hands, but let his gaze go unfocused. "If I hadn't acted as I'd done with Pratt—if I'd just *said* something . . ."

"You were distracted with your new fiancée—you've a bit of cadmium on your right index finger."

"It's no excuse, and Adelaide would have been the first to say so. I let my friend kidnap Brook, when a simple word from me could have stopped it all."

"You made a mistake, you shrugged off what you shouldn't have. You've admitted it to Their Graces, and they've forgiven you. Let it go—you've a bit of ochre on your left ring finger too."

Cayton, sighing, lifted his hands before his eyes until he spotted the small specks of paint he'd missed. A few scratches chipped off the sneaky remnants of his afternoon's activities. "It isn't so easy."

"The worthwhile things never are. Like subduing your habit of rubbing at your neck when you've paint on your fingers—you've a great smear of blue right under your collar."

He strode to the mirror and leaned in close. How had he missed *that* when he was bathing? He picked at the flakes.

Evans moved to the satchel sitting on Cayton's bed, put a

comb and a change of shoes into it. "I found it very interesting when Tabs mentioned Lady Ella was a redhead."

Cayton paused, scowled, turned. "You were snooping in my garret again."

And hadn't the grace to look abashed about it as he fastened the bag closed. "Curious what book those sketches were in, if you only just met her. I could have sworn that was the one you filled up four months ago."

Cayton leveled a finger at the man's nose. "Stay out of my garret or I really *will* sack you."

Evans grinned. "You know, my mum would adore a portrait of Tabs and me for Christmas."

*Of all the . . .* "I'm not a portrait painter, and I certainly don't make a habit of taking commissions from my staff." And before his mind could go to good ways to position the siblings down by the pond in the morning light, he stomped from the room. He was, as usual, running late—he'd already sent Addie to Ralin with Tabby, so that the children could play tonight and in the morning. And to give himself an excuse to slip away from the ball and check on her. He'd granted Evans the evening off.

Soon he was settled behind the wheel of his Renault. Someone—likely Gregory—had already cranked it for him, so he had merely to switch on the magneto and set off down the drive.

Evening light was doing amazing things to the clouds drifting across the sky, making him wonder what colors he would mix to achieve just that shade of rose-gold. And how it might set Lady Ella's hair ablaze if he happened to stroll through the garden with her before the sun went down.

*No.* He shook his head to clear it of such thoughts.

It had only been two years ago—while Stafford, so newly the duke, had been traveling in India or Africa or wherever in blazes he'd been at that point—that Cayton had played the host at the Cotswolds Ball at Ralin Castle. It had been Cayton who had greeted each nobleman, gentleman, and merchant who had crowded the ballroom. Cayton who had bowed to Miss Adelaide Rosten and remembered that she was, aside from Stafford himself, the wealthiest individual in Gloucestershire . . . and that she looked at him with the exact same shade of adoration as she had when they were children.

He had realized only a couple months before, when his steward had passed away, that his estates were in a precarious position. The answer—after gambling had failed him—had seemed obvious. He'd kept Adelaide at his side all that night. And a week later, he had proposed to her.

Last year had been her first and only Cotswolds Ball as a countess. Lady Cayton. A title she'd held such a short time.

His fingers tightened on the wheel. He had tried. Perhaps his reasons for wedding her had been self-serving, but he had tried to be a good husband. He had tried to make her happy. Tried to deserve the affection she gave him so readily. Tried, even, to love her in return.

If only they'd had more time, maybe he would have succeeded. He'd managed to get over Lady Melissa—surely falling in love with his wife would have been the next step. .

It would have been easier to forego the ball this year. That had been his plan when Mother had expressed concern about traveling with Aunt Caro and thereby missing it. She would have stayed just to support him through it, had he asked. But he would have felt like a child, admitting he didn't want to face a ballroom full of neighbors without his mother nearby. No, he'd just sworn off going. Planned to avoid the probing, condoling gazes of the friends and neighbors Adelaide had grown up with. A pox upon Brook for making him abandon his perfectly sound plan.

The moment he turned up Ralin's drive, he hissed out a breath at the number of carriages already there, along with a slew of automobiles. Most would be staying at inns and hotels, or traveling back to their own homes after the ball, but Cayton knew a few of the more prominent families would likely be staying overnight.

Why in blazes had *he* agreed to do so when he had such a short drive to his own bed? He ought to tell Tabby to take Addie home after her visit with her cousin, that he would be back by midnight. But the moment he parked and switched off the magneto, a rotund gentleman descended upon him, all wide smiles and energy.

"Lord Cayton! Bully to see you. I feared you wouldn't make it this year, but Mrs. Ipswich assured me your cousin would see you came, and here you are."

Cayton's hand was being pumped up and down even before he managed to shut his door behind him. "Mr. Ipswich, good evening. And how is your wife?"

"Hmm?" His focus had gone to the car, but the jolly gent grinned his way again. "Oh, fine, fine. Thought I'd better intercept you and warn you that all the mothers are lying in wait, ready to introduce you to the young ladies inside. No one has forgotten that you made a countess of one of them, and they're all eager to be next."

A small groan slipped out before he could stop it. "I thank you for the warning, sir. I shall just—"

"Face it like a man—that's what." Ipswich slapped a meaty hand to Cayton's back, propelling him forward, away from his car. "Everyone appreciates that you're still grieving for Lady Cayton, my lord, but your girl needs a mother, and you yet need an heir. Adelaide would have been the first to tell you to move on."

No. Adelaide would have been the first to tell him never to marry for the wrong reasons again. Never even to consider it unless he could find a wife who fulfilled a daunting list of criteria. If there were a next Lady Cayton, she must be someone he loved, whom Addie loved, marriage to whom would not damage his daughter's position in any way—which ruled out many of the girls no doubt in there dreaming of being made a countess, at whom society would scoff. Someone who could speak to his soul as well as his heart and mind. Which ruled out Melissa. Someone who would accept all he was, failures and successes both. Which ruled out . . . pretty much every other young lady in England.

Cayton merely grunted his response to Ipswich.

Others spotted him too, hampering all those thoughts still running through his head of slipping back to the car. And while tempted to glower about it, Lady Ella's words from yesterday floated through his mind, reminding him that he cheapened life by not living it fully.

Reminding him that somewhere inside, she no doubt beamed sunshine into the evening.

A footman opened the door for them and the other couples meandering that direction, and the butler greeted them with a bow. Ipswich had apparently already been announced along with his wife, and Mr. Norton hardly required a card from Cayton, though he collected one from the others to follow him in. He trailed the old butler toward the ballroom door, though people spilled from every room on the ground floor.

The Cotswolds Ball was aptly named—it seemed the whole region turned out to enjoy the duke's hospitality. Every blasted gentleman and shopkeeper, and all their unmarried daughters besides. It was enough to put a man into an apoplexy.

They paused in the doorway, Cayton a step behind Mr. Norton.

His gaze drifted of its own will over the sea of gaily clad people. He spotted Brook in one corner, glistening and gleaming and playing the hostess to perfection. Last year, her first time doing so, she had left the region in a blissful dither over their new duchess. He had heard whispers for months afterward about how the young duke had chosen a veritable princess for himself, and proud they all were to call her their own.

They had obviously none of them felt the lash of Brook's tongue.

"Are you ready, my lord?" Norton asked under his breath.

The concern in the butler's tone relaxed Cayton's shoulders. Some people, at least, understood how difficult this was. His gaze tracked to the corner of the room opposite Brook, where a flame of red hair drew him like a moth. "I suppose so."

The pleasant little flip of his stomach faltered and turned to a lump of lead when he spotted another head of hair beside Lady Ella's, one far closer to the auburn she claimed to be.

Norton cleared his throat and boomed out, "The Right Honorable James Earl of Cayton."

A pox upon them. All of them. Ignoring the murmurs and the faces that turned his way, he managed half a pivot before a familiar, treacherous hand landed square on his back and propelled him into the room. "Don't even think about it."

Hardly caring what the region thought, he scowled at Stafford. "You lying, manipulative—"

"Friend. And cousin. Who only wants the best for you." Stafford somehow managed to look perfectly at ease as he forced him another step inside the door, out of the way of the next couple to be announced. "You haven't spoken to her for two years, Cayton. This has to stop."

"Your meddling in my life? Yes, I'd definitely agree that it has to stop."

Stafford speared him with a quick glare before directing his ducal smile back over the crowd. "You're not any longer the man you were two years ago. It's time to prove it. Go, talk to her and get it over with."

He'd rather slip out the door, charge up the stairs and to the nursery where Tabby and Addie would be, gather his daughter into his arms, and go home.

Melissa and Ella had both spotted him. He didn't care to put a name to the myriad of emotions that flitted through both sets of eyes. If he looked closely enough, he would surely discern disapproval in them both, even from this distance.

But if he slipped away, they'd both call him a coward and worse.

He stood up a bit straighter and promised himself he'd punish his traitor of a cousin on the tennis court tomorrow. "I can't believe you lied to me."

"You mean as you did to me two years ago, when you said you'd spoken to her before your engagement announcement appeared in the papers? You have no idea the fight Brook and I had that day, all sparked by you forcing me blind into a dratted uncomfortable situation. Turnabout, my friend. Turnabout."

What happened to not being that man any longer? Cayton grunted. "I don't much like you, you know."

Stafford chuckled. "You're welcome. Now go on."

*Now?* He would much rather head to the opposite side of the room first. Perhaps exchange a few insults with Brook, whose disdain was at least comfortable, and glossed over a bit with shared grief. Maybe then he could manage a few moments with Lady Ella for some fortifying sunshine before he faced the dragon.

He took another step into the room when his cousin gave him a helpful prod. Melissa would devise some clever torture for him if she ever heard him call her a dragon. Like catch him in her claws and breathe fire in his face.

And she was, of course, never one to wait for the hapless knight to come to her. No, she strode across the ballroom with glinting eyes, wielding her fan like a sword. Or, no, talons. He had better keep his metaphors straight.

Stafford passed in front of him, angled toward his wife. "Just remember who you are—not who you *were*." With that bit of wisdom, he melted into the crowd.

Perhaps that would be easier if Cayton weren't still working that out. But he had changed enough to know where his own strength failed, and so he breathed a silent prayer for the Lord's strength to sustain him. For His wisdom to settle in his heart. And on his tongue.

Lady Melissa Harrington halted a step in front of him and made no attempt to smile. She was still as beautiful as she had been two years ago, when he had realized with no small amount of torment that she couldn't become his wife, or they'd end up destitute. Her warm brown hair was perfectly arranged, her dress the height of fashion.

But her eyes showed the truth. Deep brown, they sparked with long-banked fury and steely determination. And under it all, what had kept him at home, a coward, two years ago—pain. She lifted her chin. "I believe you owe me a promenade, Lord Cayton."

*The man you are—not the man you were.* He straightened his shoulders and offered his arm. "The garden? There is some warmth and light yet in the day."

"Fine." There was nothing soft nor gentle about her movements as she put her hand in the crook of his elbow. Her gaze remained straight ahead of them as he led her toward and out one of the doors that opened onto a stone terrace teeming with guests.

He wanted to look over his shoulder, to see if Lady Ella watched them go. He didn't.

The Duke of Stafford employed a skillful staff, trained under his and Cayton's firm-handed grandfather. Young men in livery stood at all the various entrances to the various gardens, trays of champagne and lemonade in hand. Some to the side of the entrance, a clear sign that all might wander that way freely. Some in front of the entrance, stating just as clearly that guests weren't welcome that direction.

Cayton headed toward one of the obstructed entrances, and the footman slid aside without a word. Yes, well trained indeed, and no doubt prepared by the duke for this, given that it had always been Cayton's favorite path. The hedges and trees blocked it from the rest of the garden, and soon a rainbow of blooms would spill their color into the world.

He waited until the babble of the crowd had muted before glancing down at Melissa, opening his mouth.

"Why did you do it?"

She never was one to wait for him to speak first. He took the time to draw in a deep breath, pray another prayer. "Do you mean marry her . . . or fail to talk to you about it first?"

"Everyone knows why you married her—money, pure and simple."

Money, yes. Simple . . . in a way. But pure his motives had certainly not been. He tilted his head up, tracing with his gaze the contour of the clouds still edged in purple and rose. "I'm sorry, Melissa. I chose the easy way, the one that shied from a painful confrontation."

"Would it have been painful for you?" She drew him to a halt and stepped in front of him, those dark eyes flashing . . . and troubled.

He reached up and rubbed at his neck, wishing . . . He didn't even know what to wish for anymore. Perhaps that the thing he had so easily labeled love had been strong enough to overcome monetary considerations. But had he even known the meaning of the word back then? "I was sincere. I intended to marry you. I was planning on proposing the morning after your debut, had a flowery speech all planned out. . . . Then my steward died, and I looked, really looked, at all the accounts and . . ."

"And I wasn't enough anymore." She folded her arms over her middle. It should have made her look sad, defeated. Strangely, it didn't. She merely looked as if she were fending off the cold his presence brought her. "I was a second daughter with a second daughter's dowry—not enough to shore up your estates."

The truth, plain and unvarnished. He wished he could deny it. Spreading his arms, his hands palm up, he could only say, "I'm sorry. It wasn't what I wanted, but I saw no other way. Your mother and brother would never have permitted a match if they'd known the state of my affairs, and I . . . I took the coward's way out. And was too much of one to tell you what I was doing, because I knew well you'd look at me and beg me not to do it, and I'd—"

She was in his arms—or he was in hers, more accurately. Her cheek was pressed to his chest, her arms tight about him, his still hovering there in the air. Afraid to wrap around her, but habit tried to pull them down. How many times had he held her like this, when she'd sneaked away from Whitby Park to meet him in Eden Dale?

But he wasn't that man anymore. There was no spark of pleasure, no thought of the future. Just that cold wonder that he had ever thought it enough to build a lifetime on. "Lissa . . ."

"I didn't know what to believe, Cay. I thought I knew you, but then . . . I began to wonder if you were more like Pratt than

I thought, quite willing to woo one young lady for your own pleasure when you were courting another the whole time."

A better blow she couldn't have aimed. "I am not like Pratt. Wasn't even then." But he had been too willing to believe Pratt was all talk. Too willing to turn a blind eye to the truth of his friend—and too happy to hide his own true nature behind what he deemed a fashionable facade.

"No, I know. I didn't mean . . ." She tilted her face up, and the setting sun caught a light of something dangerous in her eyes. Hope. "I know you tried with her. I was always plying Brook for information, trying to force myself to forget you. You tried, and you were a good husband. But you never loved her, did you?"

The conscience he'd silenced so effectively a few years ago screamed at him now. It hadn't been right, then, to hold Melissa and whisper about a love he didn't understand. And it wouldn't be right now either, when he knew without doubt he didn't love her. What did it matter if she said she loved him, when she didn't really know him? He put his hands on her shoulders and urged her gently away. "Much to my shame, no. I didn't love her. But—"

"And I know you've mourned her. I see that, and I realize you may yet need more time. But you are free again and—"

"Stop, Lissa. Please." He let go her shoulders but turned halfway away so she couldn't just put her arms around him again. "There is no going back."

"No, but there is going forward. We can—"

"No." He squeezed his eyes shut, ready to string up Stafford and Brook for forcing him to this. "We can't. I tried to love her, Lissa, as you said. I tried, but I certainly couldn't do it with another woman in my heart. I had to purge myself of my feelings for you. I *had* to. It would have been unfair to her to be dreaming of you while she was my wife."

Opening his eyes, he faced her again. He had to grant her that, this time. The right to look in his eyes and see him for what he was—a broken, weak, rather pathetic excuse for a man, who had nothing left to offer her. Who couldn't look at her without regret and guilt. Who didn't know how to show her who he really was. Who had broken her heart once for selfish reasons and would break it again, if he had to, for her own good. Because he couldn't be—or *pretend* to be—the man she'd loved.

That dragon's fury lit her eyes again. "And it was that easy for you? You could just . . . *forget* me?"

Sighing, he shook his head. "I'm sorry to hurt you, Lissa—sorry for doing it then and sorry if I do it again now. But I can't . . . I can't. And you deserve someone who can. Who can love you wholeheartedly."

For a long moment, she said nothing. Just watched him, her gaze unwavering. Then she made a curt nod. "So be it, then. I'll accept Kensington's proposal."

Was she trying to spark jealousy? Part of him wished he felt some—or felt something, anyway, other than relief at the thought of her married.

Well, there *was* something else. More guilt. "Kensington?"

She waved a hand. "An American, from New York. You wouldn't know him, but he's been in London all winter. Wanted to find a wife with proper breeding, he said, but one who could stand up to New York society." She lifted her chin, and a bit of a smile curled her lips. "I daresay I can put any of those uppity Yanks in their places—don't you think?"

"Melissa . . ." He had been half afraid she would wed long before now, seizing the first proposal to come along just to spite him. Afraid he would bear the guilt of *her* terrible marriage on top of his own awkward one. And yet he had hoped to hear the news that she had fallen head over heels for some perfect fellow who could give her a good life. His brows knit. "I want you to be happy. Do you love this Kensington?"

Not so much as a twitch in her countenance. "I like him quite well. And could love him quite easily, I think, if I let myself. But I . . . We'd so much between us, Cayton. I couldn't take that step until I knew."

Relief eclipsed grief. "Well then, now you can. I wish you all the best the world has to offer, Melissa."

Lips pressed together, she nodded and spun back toward the house. Though she went only two steps before she spun back.

He'd been expecting as much. No dragon was ever deflected so easily as that, and she came at him with a finger ready to drill its way into his shoulder.

*"How?"* A mere poke apparently not being enough, she shoved. "How can you say that so calmly and just let me walk away? Into another man's arms? Does it honestly, seriously, truly not bother you in the least to think of me marrying someone else?"

Gracious, he was tired. And the ball had only just begun. He lifted his shoulders, let them fall. "Honestly, Lissa . . . the thought of you finding happiness with someone only makes me glad. As I said—you deserve it, and you won't find it with me."

She took a step back, shaking her head. But the fury had simmered down somewhat, and nothing so terrifying as tears replaced it. "I just . . . I don't understand you. Not anymore, though I thought I did once. What are you doing, Cayton? Hiding from life, from all the things you once loved, closeting yourself away in a *nursery*. Your friends have scarcely seen you. You've not attended a single ball or fête aside from the ones your cousin forces you to at his home. You're wasting your life, and for what? Adelaide Rosten?"

His head was shaking long before she finished. Fire burning long before she spat out *nursery* in the way she had done. Proving his epiphanies right. She'd never known him. He'd never let her. And now he really was no longer the man that even *wanted* to be what he'd shown her. "You think I'm wasting my life *now*? It was then that I did so. Wasting my time with Pratt and Rushworth and their ilk, at the races, the clubs, the gaming hells. What did it ever gain me but too many memories I wish I could escape and debt that nearly ruined me?"

Melissa didn't look inspired by his change of heart. Exasperated, rather. "You were a typical young lord doing what they all do—you would have outgrown it, but that hardly means you have to spend all your time shut up in your house now, turning into a recluse like Uncle Whit."

His chin lifted a notch. "Would that I could emulate him. Lord Whitby has been one of the few men to whom I could turn this last year. He and Stafford."

"You never even *liked* Stafford!"

At least she had the good sense to keep the screech at a low volume, despite her slashing hand. The last thing he needed was the whole countryside murmuring about some dispute between its leading cousins.

He rubbed at his neck again—and realized he'd still missed a bit of paint. He could feel it there in his hairline. "We are family. Perhaps we weren't always friends, but that has changed. It has had to."

She breathed an unamused laugh and, shaking her head, backed up a step. "I never thought I'd see the day when the Earl of Cayton announced he preferred my uncle's reclusive ways to a life of society and friends."

Not a life she had ever shown any interest in—no, she was the type to respond to heartache by throwing herself with renewed fury into every crowd she could find. He had once tried to convince himself he was similarly disposed.

He could no longer. With pain came the need for quiet to soothe it. Quiet, color, and perhaps a few beautiful words. But he had never admitted to Melissa his painting habit. It hadn't fit the image of himself he'd worked so hard to craft as a young man. The image she had inexplicably fallen for.

They would have always been doomed, regardless of his marriage to Adelaide. He slid his hands into his pockets. "It seems we have exhausted all there is to say. For though you cannot understand me now, I cannot fathom going back to the man I once was. He holds no allure for me anymore."

The fire in her eyes died down, leaving her cold as stone when she crossed her arms over her chest. "So it would seem. Well then. I imagine my mother will send you an invitation for the wedding—if you don't come, I'll know it's not because you're full of regret."

She took a step away. He didn't follow. And he rather hoped she didn't turn back to see his smile.

Melissa turned down the path that would lead her from this secluded alcove, glancing only once more over her shoulder. "Good-bye, then, Cayton."

"Good-bye." A farewell long overdue . . . but he wasn't quite ready to thank Stafford for providing it. Drawing in a deep breath and letting it seep back out, he sank onto the cool wrought iron behind him.

Birdsong drifted his way on the breeze, along with the indistinguishable babble of crowds of people, and the first strains from the orchestra. His cousin would be opening the floor with Brook, both of them looking regal and blissful and gracious. He had sketched them so last year after their first ball as duke and duchess, trying to capture the smiles on their faces, the love in their eyes.

They were happy, and he was glad of it. Glad Addie would have their example to look to as she grew up.

"I would say I just happened upon you, just happened to overhear a bit . . ." Lady Ella's voice brought his head back up, around, to find her entering the alcove from the rear path. Her smile looked a bit abashed . . . but still there, pulling up the corners of her mouth as it always did. And now it grew a bit more mischievous. "But it would be a blatant lie. I was too curious, and no doubt now it will make you think less of me."

Were it anyone else, he would have been more than a bit annoyed. But for some reason, finding Ella had followed him just made a strange warmth grow in his chest. Chuckling, he stood and turned to her, held out a hand toward the bench in invitation, if she chose to accept it. "I am only surprised Brook and Stafford are not hiding there with you."

Relief in her eyes and her smile giving way to a grin, she sat, looking perfectly comfortable on the cold metal. "Brook *may* have offered me her new hat if I could report the encounter with accuracy. Though I daresay she didn't actually expect me to deliver."

"More the fool, her. May I?" He motioned to the spot beside her on the bench.

"Please." She scooted a fraction of an inch in the guise of giving him room, though she had nowhere to go . . . and Cayton didn't much mind the close proximity.

Though he should. He sat with a sigh and tilted his head up to watch the clouds dim. He had made such a mess of his life. Already he had hurt two fine young ladies—what made him think he'd ever deserve a chance with a third?

"I didn't realize Lady Melissa was seriously considering Mr. Kensington. Though I have met him, and they seem a good match. He has a strong but quiet personality."

A laugh slipped out. "A fine foil to hers indeed. I wish them well."

"So you said." She was watching him—even without turning his head, he could feel the steadiness of her gaze. "The question is, did you mean it, or were you just saying it because you deemed it in her best interest?"

He looked at her now. "More information for Brook?"

"Obviously." She had dimples. Two perfect little creases in her cheeks when she grinned—how had they escaped his notice? He needed to correct his drawings again. Dimples changed everything.

Cayton smiled too. "I meant it. I meant everything I said." But the smile couldn't hold for long. He let it go with another sigh and faced the sky again. "I wasn't a good man. Not as bad as those I associated with, I grant you, but not *good*. I don't know why she ever loved me. Why *either* of them ever did."

"Some women like the challenge of a man who needs saving. Others see the potential hiding under the layers of the world, and it is *that* they love."

"Hm. Which type are you?"

She laughed softly but with music enough to rival the orchestra. "Neither. Fall for a man in need of saving and you will be sorely disillusioned to find you are no savior. Fall for a man who is only potential, and you shall be constantly disappointed that he doesn't live up to it. No, my lord, I prefer gentlemen who already know redemption and who have sloughed off the ways of the world."

"Wise of you."

"And probably why I am unattached. But I am in no hurry—much as I would love to find the prince to complete my fairy tale, better to wait years for him than to wed too quickly and find my so-called prince is an evil sorcerer in disguise."

How could he help but smile at her? "An evil sorcerer?"

"Life is more interesting with a bit of fancy thrown in—don't you think?" She leaned back onto the bench and made a show of studying the sky as he had been doing. "What do you see when you look at the clouds, Lord Cayton? More rain on the horizon?"

"No." He hesitated, turned to study them too. And couldn't quite stop the truth from slipping out. "I see the spires of a castle, tinged in gold, barely peeking through those great tufts of lavender. Do you see its standard flying from that peak there? And then I see violet deepening it with every second, edging its way toward indigo. I see a sky ready to go dark with the softest kind of night, where stars will soon dance." He tilted his head, gaze on those imagined spires. He could do a painting for Addie's room of this, with but a few added touches. "It needs a Pegasus flying through the sky yonder, I think. Or perhaps a winged unicorn."

He realized he had said it aloud only when Ella clapped her hands together. "A winged unicorn, to be sure!" She gazed up at the sky as if she could see it as clearly as he did, and with the same shade of delight he imagined Addie someday feeling as she looked upon the painting and imagined herself flying through the clouds with her fantastical pet.

Melissa would have laughed, but not with delight. Adelaide— the only woman other than his mother to see his paintings in progress—would have patted his hand and declared it a fine idea, but she would never have seen it. Not until a work was done, and even then she never saw beyond the strokes on the canvas to the vision behind it.

He stood, held out a hand. "I believe you promised me a dance, Lady Ella."

"I didn't, as well you know." She put her hand in his, though, let him help her up. But then she frowned. "I will dance with you, Lord Cayton . . . but only if you dance with quite a few others first. And after. On the brink of an engagement as she may be, I daresay Lady Melissa is feeling territorial just now. And I don't much relish being the object of her fury—she is absolutely frightening when she's angry."

"You really are as wise as you are witty." He glanced toward the house, with its crowds of people waiting to swarm. Young women waiting to be given an introduction. Eager mothers waiting to shove him toward their daughters. The very idea made his head ache. He turned to Ella, bowed. "I can hear the music quite well from here. What say you?"

Her answer was a curtsy, and a return of the sparkle to her eyes. She placed her hand on his shoulder, her other still in his, and let him draw her into the opening stance of the waltz.

It was easy, *too* easy to fall into the rhythm, to gaze down into her lovely face and wonder. Too easy to let his heart go soft and yearning. Too easy to recall how perfectly happy Addie had been in her arms.

But he'd made the mistake before of letting his heart wander down the easy path, and look where it had led him.

Ella's brows drew down. "You're not plotting how to turn me into a frog, are you?"

His smile could last only a beat, a pulse. Then it faded away. "No. I assure you, I only do that to people who are very deserving."

A smile flit over her lips, but it was as swiftly gone as Pegasus in the clouds. She seemed to sense his internal pulling back. She went stiffer, her chin came up, and the light in her eyes dimmed.

He wished he could take back the spontaneous offer to dance. No, go back and undo their exchange in the garden yesterday.

Or perhaps think to ask Mr. Norton where Stafford was before just heading to the library the day before *that*.

Or better still, go back and put a different face to paper when he was trying to find an image of a smile. She surely wasn't the only laughter-prone woman he'd ever glimpsed. Why in thunder had his fingers and mind had to put her down upon the page? If he hadn't, he would have viewed her entirely differently upon an actual introduction.

The moment the music hit its cadence and came to a halt, Ella stepped away. She studied him for a moment, as if trying to puzzle out the riddle of what kind of man invited her to dance in a garden and then acted as though he'd rather have run the other way.

Perhaps she found her answer. For she stiffened, nodded a brief farewell, and turned toward the path from which she'd appeared.

Evans was right. The best, most worthwhile things in life were the difficult ones. Hadn't he and Stafford discussed that very thing in their study yesterday? The easy thing was seldom right.

Well, then letting Lady Ella Myerston walk away was the best thing, without question. Because it was far more difficult than it should have been.

# Six

"Y ou don't sound French."

Kira nearly dropped what she was doing and spun at that, the first words her new mistress had deigned to speak to her. But she granted herself only a brief pause and otherwise kept at her task of folding all the lady's clothes around tissue and placing them into the trunk with the same level of care she'd have given them were they *her* silks and satins rather than a stranger's.

The history Andrei had made her memorize about her supposed-self covered this. While her French was good, with only a hint of a Russian accent, her English bore testament to her roots. "My father was French. My mother Russian. I spent most of my growing-up years in Russia with her people before moving back to Paris."

Lady Pratt's only answer was a disinterested hum that made Kira wonder why she'd even bothered commenting. Darting a glance to her left, she verified that the lady was in the same position she had been ever since Kira entered the room—in a chair by the window, looking out at the busy streets of Paris. The rented flat gave only a mediocre view . . . but Lady Pratt probably saw little of it anyway. Her eyes had a haze before them, it seemed, making her look always within rather than at anything without.

Did Andrei know she suffered from some invisible torment? Was this why he had opted for espionage rather than a more heavy-handed approach? He could probably hold a gun to this woman's head and she would only blink at him.

Kira slid the last of the dresses into the trunk and stood. "I believe I smell tea." The English treasured nothing like their tea, *da*? Perhaps that would rouse her. "Will you join your brother?"

But the lady didn't stir. Though her hair was brushed and coiffed, though she wore a simple but elegant day dress, Catherine, Lady Pratt, had the look about her eyes of a woman who hadn't left her bed in half an eternity. "No. I don't want to get up."

And if the way her dress hung on her was any indication, she hadn't wanted to get up for things like meals for quite some time. "Shall I bring you something, then, my lady?" The title, so very English, still felt strange on her tongue.

The lady shrugged. "Do as you please."

Doing as she pleased would involve stalking from this modest flat and to the other side of town, to where her own house had a better prospect and servants waiting to attend *her*. But no—if she didn't do this, they wouldn't be her house or her servants for long.

She smiled, dipped her knees in what was more plié than curtsy, and moved silently from the room.

The flat was small, and Kira had no choice but to pass by the parlor to get to the kitchen. She glanced inside as she did, expecting to see Lord Rushworth, but it was empty. Perhaps he had taken his tea elsewhere today.

"Lareau—come here."

She jumped and came to a halt, searching the room again. Lord Rushworth *was* there, in a chair tucked into the corner. Edging into the room, Kira dipped a quick curtsy again. "Forgive me, my lord. I did not see you there."

Rushworth offered the bare outlines of a smile. "No need to apologize for a skill I have hewn so carefully over the years." He pointed to a chair. "Sit. I take it my sister declined joining me for tea again?"

She had dined with princes and dukes. She had laughed with the richest men on the continent. But somehow it felt completely wrong to lower herself to that cushion across from him when in the drab grey dress of a lady's maid. What choice did she have though? She perched on the very edge of the chair and folded her hands primly in her lap. "She did, my lord. I was going to fetch her some from the kitchen."

"Don't bother, she won't drink what they make her." He turned to the pot on the table at his side. "But I know how she takes it. She may at least have a few sips if I make it."

Kira tried to imagine one of her brothers making her a cup of tea, but the image wouldn't come. Boris, if trying to pull her from a mood, would poke her in the side and try to jest her from it. Evgeny would instead ask her to do something for *him*. Reasoning, he would say, that if she helped someone else, she would think less of her own woes. And the younger boys . . . They probably scarcely remembered her.

Sometimes she missed her family. Sometimes. Until she remembered the look in their eyes when she told them she would join the ballet. The disapproval. The disappointment. The judgment. Because they all knew what other life most ballerinas embraced. And they had apparently also known she wasn't strong enough to resist it, though she had promised them she would.

Rushworth glanced up at her. "We leave at first light. Is Lady Pratt packed and ready?"

"*Oui*, my lord." She nearly rolled her shoulders back but caught herself just in time. And lowered her chin too.

Rushworth breathed a laugh that held no amusement. "You needn't keep pretending to be French. My sister, when she rises from this morass, may appreciate the pretense—French maids being so very in mode—but I assure you, it is the fact that you are Russian that got you this position."

Now her spine snapped straight before she could stop it, and her chin came back up. Her brows pulled heavy and questioning over her eyes. "I do not understand."

"Oh, but I think you do. That is just the thing." Leaning back in his chair, Rushworth rested his chin on his hand and made a show of studying her. "What think you of Tolstoy?"

"Tolstoy?" What in the world did he have to do with anything? But Rushworth didn't so much as blink, so she moistened her lips and tilted her head. "He is the voice of Russia. My family traveled to his funeral a few years ago and wrote to me about it—he was to be forbidden a Christian funeral, being still excommunicated from the church, but the people . . . the people would not have it." Her eyes slid shut at the description of all those bodies pressed together. Thousands of people, all there in defiance of the very church they so loved. "They sang the chants anyway. And the police who were there to stop them joined them instead."

"Mm. I have read about his last moments. Have you?"

She opened her eyes again, trying to divine where he was headed. But the man's blue-green eyes made not a flicker to tell her the thoughts behind them. His dark blond head gave nothing away in its angle. Kira shook her head.

Rushworth nodded. "He wondered about the peasants' deaths. A familiar refrain with him, I understand, this idea that no one understood life and death so well as a Russian peasant. From what I can tell, everyone else agrees. Do you?"

"I . . ." She had to pause, shrug, clear her throat. "I have never thought of it, my lord." But she remembered the way Babushka had crossed herself when Mamochka had died. The way she had gathered Kira and all her siblings, the new babe in her arms, and told them that their mother was a spirit now, and they would put bread on her grave that Easter, and the birds would come and assure them that her soul was flying in the heavens with God.

The babe flew with Mamochka now too. She'd not lived to her first year.

Rushworth's eyes narrowed. "You needn't tell me. But my sister . . . Kitty needs someone who understands these things. It has been six months since her baby died, and still she stares out the window as if waiting for him to toddle down the street."

"That is what holds her prisoner?" She shifted, darting a glance at the cup. How long did they steep their tea? And why did Rushworth think *her* the right one to help his sister grieve? She had never lost a child. And rarely a sibling. Only two of them had died, her two sisters—far fewer in her family than any of their neighbors could boast.

"An excellent choice of words—and yes." He leaned forward again, poured the tea into a cup, and dropped a cube of sugar into it. "That is what has rendered her nearly comatose. She handled it well enough when her husband was killed. I never would have thought . . ." Rushworth shook himself and pulled a plate forward. "If you don't feel up to the task of serving such a mistress, now is the time to say so, before we leave Paris."

If only she had such luxury. Kira forced a smile. "I will serve Lady Pratt as well as I know how, my lord. I cannot guarantee to help her heal, but . . ."

"You will do well enough, I am sure. Princess . . . Forgive me, I will probably mangle her name. Alyona Vitalova? Is that right? She spoke very highly of you and assured me that you came from sturdy peasant stock."

Kira barely kept from snarling. Andrei had brought his precious *princess* into this? Had, what, listed her as a reference? "Did she?"

"Mm. I, of course, then had to question why she was letting you go, but now I see her point." His lips twitched into a smile as he set the cup onto the plate. "I daresay any young lady would think twice about having such a lovely maid when she is on the cusp of marriage."

Usually she would have been listening for suggestion in such a statement—just now, she could hardly see past the rage clouding her vision. They claimed she had been lady's maid to Princess Alyona? And what had Andrei told his darling when he asked her to meet with this man and talk of Kira? That it was how they could be rid of her? For surely Alyona knew of Andrei's relationship with her, everyone did, and no doubt she liked Kira no better than Kira liked her. She had probably taken pleasure in claiming she had been her servant.

"I see I have touched a nerve. My apologies." He didn't sound repentant as he arranged pastries around the teacup.

"Think nothing of it." But she couldn't convince her fingers to relax, and the pain in her knee made a sudden throb.

He nudged the plate toward her. "See if this tempts my sister."

The words that sprang to her tongue were Russian, so she bit them back and stood, reached for the plate.

"Do you read Russian?"

Her fingers paused, the anger still simmering. *"Da."*

Rushworth's lips still wore that little half smile. "Forgive me if the question has offended you—though I'm under the impression that much of the Russian populace is illiterate. Am I not correct?"

And what exactly had the princess told him about her family, their "sturdy peasant stock"? Surely not that her grandfather had been a huntsman before the serfs were freed, one of the highest male servants on a vast estate. Certainly not that her grandmother had been trained by her master as an opera singer, had risen to fame before her master had deemed her too old for his harem and had married her to Dedushka, giving her a generous dowry. And so, not that they were among the most educated and well-off of the peasants. Heaven knew that wouldn't suit the princess's fancy.

Kira forced a smile. "I can read and write Russian, German, French, and English."

Though he made an impressed face, the emptiness of Rushworth's eyes somehow spoke of suspicion. "Can you, now? You must have been in someone's favor growing up."

"My father taught us all. He was the one who had special favor as a boy." Probably because he was their old master's son, not Dedushka's, but that was a topic never raised, a question never asked. Babushka didn't speak of her life before her marriage. If ever it came up, the pain filled her eyes far too quickly.

"Well, it may be of use to me, if you would agree to translate."

Her suspicion flared too—what need would he have of a Russian translator, unless it had something to do with his dealings with Andrei? But she granted herself only a moment's hesitation before nodding. "Of course, my lord."

"Good."

Well then, perhaps this would be easier than she'd feared, and she would find the information Andrei sought within a week or two. Buoyed by that happy thought, she picked up the plate and cup and turned toward the door. "I had better take this to Lady Pratt."

Rushworth made another humming noise that sounded somewhat thoughtful. Rather than wait to see what else he might have to say, Kira headed for the door. She made it to the threshold before he called out, "Just a moment."

She paused, turned halfway around. And wondered again as she had wondered last night when word came that she had been hired what she would do if her new employer made advances. She was in no position to resist, not when she couldn't return empty-handed—but she was in no position to give in either, not when betraying Andrei meant a fate worse than death.

Rushworth's eyes were narrowed. "You put me in mind of someone. I cannot quite place who."

At that, she smiled—she had already anticipated being recognized. "Are you a fan of the Ballet Russe, my lord? I've been told I bear quite a resemblance to one of their ballerinas."

"Hm. I suppose that could be it. I did take Kitty to a performance when we got to Paris several months ago, hoping it would draw her out." He made a face and leaned back in his chair, picking up a book that had been sitting facedown on the table. Tolstoy's *The Death of Ivan Ilyich*. "It served only to remind her of how our cousin used to prattle about her love of the ballet from her days in Monaco. And our cousin is not Kitty's favorite person."

Kira held her place another second to see if he said more—she obviously had no commentary on their cousin.

But Rushworth waved her on. "Do let me know if she eats anything, will you, Lareau? And otherwise, have her ready to leave at first light tomorrow morning."

"Yes, my lord." She hurried out of the room and back to Lady Pratt's bedchamber, where the lady still sat staring out of the window. Kira slid the tea and pastries onto the little table near at hand. "Here you are, my lady. Your brother made your tea himself."

Lady Pratt actually reached for the cup, though Kira half expected her to send it flying through the room rather than drink it. But no, she raised it to her lips and took a slow sip. She even glanced—for half a moment—at Kira. "And what did he say to you? Did he tell you about Byron?"

"Your son? *Oui*, briefly." But how was *she* to provide any comfort? When a child died in her village, everyone would merely cross themselves and say either *"One fewer mouth to feed"* or *"He's with the angels now."* Of course, those mothers usually had a brood of other children at home and scarce supplies with which to care for them. Perhaps it was different if one's arms were then empty. And if one's larder was full.

Lady Pratt's gaze fell to her cup, as if the liquid within held answers. "He grows frustrated with me. Before it was always enough that we had each other—Kitty and Cris against the world—but he doesn't understand. He's blind to everything but . . . he can't understand." She looked up, eyes empty but for the tears. "Have you ever lost a child?"

More like feared one—nothing put an end to a ballerina's career as quickly as a squalling babe. Or, apparently, an injured knee. Folding her hands before her, Kira shook her head. "Not of my own. Though I lost two sisters growing up."

"Two of them?" Lady Pratt blinked. "Your poor mother."

"She had six other children—and counted herself blessed to lose only one. The other died after she did. Half our children die, my lady. Russia can be a cruel land."

"Half?" The lady looked ready to burst into tears at the thought. "How do you survive it?"

"With the knowledge that little ones go straight to heaven, which spares them a world of suffering." Words that meant nothing to this new mistress of hers right now, she could tell.

Indeed, Lady Pratt turned her face away. "You're religious?"

Kira shook her head. "I have not been to church since I left Russia." She had tried it, a few times, but the churches in Europe weren't the same. They had long benches where one was expected to simply *sit*. Sit and listen. How could one worship that way? "But faith is a different matter—I have heard it said that every Russian has faith, and I cannot argue. If we believed in nothing greater than ourselves, then we would give up rather than face the hardships that take us from one point in life to another."

A breath of a laugh slipped from the lady's lips. "That would be the simpler way. To just give up. Let go. Because really, why do we bother?"

The question scraped and scratched at everything Kira believed. How could anyone look at the impossible and not fight it? How could anyone just lie down and accept defeat? "We bother because if we do not, we are like the rest of the world, letting circumstances rule us." She shook her head and sent her gaze out the window, to where the world went on. Always on, telling her what she could and couldn't do. "I do not know about you, my lady. But I will not be ruled."

Something flickered in Lady Pratt's eyes, though it was nothing so bright as hope or determination. More like . . . resentment. "An odd thing to come from the mouth of a servant."

No more odd, probably, than the smile Kira could not tamp down. "But I am staff, not serf. I can leave whenever I please."

The lady put her cup onto the plate with a clatter. "And where would you go without a recommendation?"

"Anywhere." But for all her brave words, she *couldn't* leave, could she? Kira drew in a deep breath and forced her smile to soften. She curtsied. "But I want to be here. It is my great hope that I can serve you well, my lady."

Lady Pratt loosed a dismissive snort of breath and turned her face back to the window. "Go away. Come back after supper to help me retire."

Another curtsy made her knee ache, but Kira gritted her teeth against it and slipped from the room. She peeked into the parlor just long enough to report to Lord Rushworth that his sister had taken a bit of tea and nibbled on a pastry, and then she headed to the cramped little room in which she would only stay one night.

She hadn't bothered unpacking for her short tenure. Had scarcely looked at the plain, bare walls. The plain, bare chair. The plain, bare blanket on the bed. She didn't look now either. She merely moved the chair around so that she could grip its plain, bare back like a barre. Stripped off the ugly white apron and the heavy, cumbersome dress she was expected to wear, tossed them onto the bed.

Then she closed her eyes, summoned music into her mind, and drilled. *Rond de jambe en dehors*, closing back into fifth position.

She would not be what circumstances made her.

*Attitude* on her inside leg—her good leg—*devant. Fondu* on her supporting leg—her bad leg.

She would ignore the pain, ignore the weakness until it turned back into strength.

Arm sweeping out to second position. *Retiré* and straighten that bad knee, stretching it past relief and into new pain. Arm to fifth position *en avant*.

She would not be ruled.

# Seven

Ella turned to her left, then to her right, tightly gripping the wooden handle of her umbrella. But it was no use. Heaven only knew how she had managed it, but she had lost the castle . . . again. Perhaps some crafty fog had sneaked up and swallowed it whole. Perhaps the rain had washed it away. Or perhaps the wooded path she had chosen for her morning promenade had led her into a fairy world outside normal time, and she would be trapped there until some handsome prince saved her.

Not likely to happen before the umbrella lost the battle to wind and rain and she got a thorough soaking.

*Ah, well.* She examined the trees nearest her, searching them for some familiar marking. Unlikely, though—her mind had hardly been on the details of the trees as she wandered into the wood. Instead it had been on the handsome prince-turned-grumbling-earl who had scarcely said two words to her in the past week.

She usually wouldn't mind losing herself in the Staffords' wood, but the air was dreadfully chilly, and no one would be looking for her yet. Brook had been confined to a chaise in her private sitting room this morning, ill—no doubt a result of her happy condition. And though she knew Ella had gone for a walk, Brook was not one to worry if she failed to appear at the expected time.

Unlike Ella's brother, Brice, who would deliver an exasperated lecture if she happened to wander back in ten minutes later than he'd expected her. Which, now that she thought of it, wasn't entirely dissimilar from the exasperated lecture Brook had delivered last night when she caught Ella in the library again, a slew of books on jewels arrayed on the table before her.

Honestly, what had her friend expected? Brook herself would certainly never have so easily accepted a command to let something go. Why did she think Ella would?

And she had learned much about all things jewel-related this past week. Now she had only to begin the quest for information on India. She'd heard her sister-in-law, Rowena, mutter something about "the tiger's curse" last fall when arguing about the Fire Eyes with Brice. Surely she could find information on that somewhere or another. Once she found her way back.

Infernal castle, disappearing as it had done. Well, there were only so many paths through the wood, and most of them surely led back to Ralin Castle—where else would they go? She spun on the path to the right, estimating that she had at least half a chance of emerging back into the garden within a few minutes.

But instead she stood, those few minutes later, at a river. "Drat." It looked lovely, granted, with the rain bringing it to life with a thousand ripples, and with its bordering grasses bowing and curtsying in the wind. But her feet were cold and wet. And her hands were cold and wet. And before too long the rest of her was sure to be cold and wet too.

It shouldn't have reminded her of Stella. It hadn't been raining the day her oldest friend had raised her gun and taken a shot at Brice and Rowena. It hadn't been raining that night when Brice had realized she was the one behind the weapon, when poor Old Abbott had been forced to restrain his daughter while the authorities came. It hadn't been raining when Brice returned to Midwynd and told Ella what Stella had done.

But it had felt like it as she sobbed out her sorrow and regret in her brother's room. It had felt grey and dismal while she'd clung to hope, insisting that young Mr. Abbott—Stella's own brother, who had taken the bullet in Brice's stead—would survive the head wound.

The library had given Ella hope that day, as she sorted through medical books, desperate for facts to back up her faith. She'd found them. She always found them when she prayed to the Lord for a reason to believe. He wanted His children to have faith in the impossible. To hold to hope. To sing praises to Him when chained in the darkest, dankest prison. Or caught out in the pouring rain. And young Mr. Abbott had survived, proving her faith was not misguided.

If only that had eclipsed her terrible guilt of not having seen what his sister was capable of.

A thrashing sound broke through the curtain of falling water. Ella spun to face it, but she couldn't quite tell from where it came—or what was making it. They hadn't any bears in England, though she had to remind herself of that, given the size of the sound. No wolves either, had they? They were far too civilized a land for such beasts.

Though one never knew when a traveling circus might have lost some ferocious creature. It could be a dancing bear gone rogue. A lion escaped from its tamer.

No, she saw when a dark form emerged from the trees—it was far worse. A scowling, obviously angry earl who refused to play the part of handsome prince. And whom she couldn't help like despite it . . . or perhaps, in part, because of it.

Cayton tromped her way with fury coming off him in waves. "Blast it, Ella, what in thunder are you doing all the way down here in the rain?"

He was drenched, his grey overcoat gone black with the rain dripping from its hem. Under the hat brim dripping rain, his brow was as thunderous as the heavy clouds overhead. And he had called her Ella—not *Lady* Ella.

She tried, really she did, to keep from grinning. "At least I had the sense to bring an umbrella with me. What in thunder are you doing out here without one, Lord Cayton?"

His scowl only deepened. "Does your brother let you use such language?"

Men—so hypocritical. "Is *thunder* now a curse word? I thought it a weather phenomenon—and a rather appropriate one just now."

He stomped to her side and took her elbow. Not exactly gently, though more insistent than rough. "I didn't think I would *need* an umbrella to find a young lady who 'may have taken a wrong turn in the garden.' My cousin failed to mention that your detours took you to the blasted river rather than just the gardener's shed." He tugged her back up the path. "You are nearly off Stafford land—do you realize that?"

And how would she, unless there were a sign declaring such? "I would have found my way back, eventually. All roads lead to Ralin Castle around here, don't they?"

They stepped over a sodden branch, and his head collided with the umbrella. With an incomprehensible mutter, he abandoned her elbow in favor of wrenching the umbrella's handle from her hands and holding it a good six inches higher than she had been doing.

She had to press her lips together against a laugh that he would no doubt not appreciate. "Sorry, my lord. I did endeavor to grow taller, but for all my stretching and straining, I seem to be stuck here."

His answer to that was a grunt. Then he sent her a scathing glare. "Haven't you the sense to wait until it's done raining before you set off on an hour-long walk?"

She could understand his anger, given his soaking. Really, she could. What she couldn't quite wrap her mind around was the way he'd been scowling at her every time he happened across her path this past week, when she was quite sure he didn't dislike her. A man who picked her dandelions, spoke of unicorns, and asked her to dance in a twilight garden couldn't possibly dislike her.

But what did she know? She'd thought Stella to be kind and rational, after all.

Ella shook her head. "Now you sound like my brother."

"Who apparently needs to do a better job of keeping you in order—perhaps it's time you go home so he can have another go at it."

*Of all the . . .* "Excuse me, Lord Cayton, but it is hardly up to you to decide when I go home. And my brother knows better than to try to force me into order. It would never work—it's far too boring."

Was that a laugh or a grunt? Amusement or derision? She couldn't quite tell, and he didn't look her way again, just kept his gaze focused on the path.

She, since her hands were now free, picked up her skirt to step over a puddle. "You needn't have come looking for me. Brook knew I was out, and she knows I find my way back eventually."

Definitely a grunt this time.

Ella sent her eyes to the cloudy heavens. "How did you even find me?"

"The paths are muddy, my lady, and you not so slender that you fail to leave a print."

He had to be *trying* to sound so crotchety. He *had* to be. "My, you are charming. Careful, or I may fall at your feet in adoration, and then you'll have to carry my not-so-slender muddy form back to the castle."

Another laugh-grunt, and he glanced down at her, sweeping his gaze over her figure. Which was neither too round nor too thin, thank you very much. She might have a propensity for sweets, but she was also rarely idle.

Cayton shook his head. "Does nothing offend you?"

She gave him her cheekiest grin. She *had* been right. This time. "Nothing that I've found yet, though we may discover something if you keep up your current method of interaction when you are unable to avoid me completely."

A muscle in his jaw pulsed, proving that he was clenching his teeth against a response.

Grin still in place, she tucked her hand around the arm holding the umbrella. "Not that I can blame you, of course, for avoiding me. It's dangerous business, exchanging a few words with a young lady. Treacherous indeed when outside in a garden. Or in a nursery with a few happy toddlers. But especially, my lord . . ." She leaned closer, pitched her voice down. "Especially out in the wood in the rain. Why, my brother found himself married thanks to just such a thing. You ought to have run for cover when you saw where my footsteps led."

"Well, it isn't too late." He angled a wry look down at her, eyes beginning to sparkle, even if his lips were still turned down.

She moved her left hand atop her right to secure her hold on his arm. "You could try it, but this is one case where I would definitely chase after a man."

"Hmm." He turned his face away again, those brows returning to their nearly perpetual scowl. "I'll deliver you back to the castle, my lady, but do cease the flirtation. It only proves you young and naïve."

"Naïve?" It sliced, for a moment. How often had Brice applied that word to her? But when he said it, it was only frustrating, not hurtful. She wouldn't be hurt, though. She *wouldn't*, because he was obviously trying, for whatever ill-placed reason, to hurt her. And she refused to be bullied in such a way. "Those who call me naïve do so because it makes them feel better about their own ill humor, to think that I am only cheerful because I don't understand the world. But I assure you, my lord, I do. And I choose to greet it with a smile anyway."

"Senseless, then."

That offense she claimed a moment ago never to feel pulled taut within her. Until she saw the way his nostrils flared, the way his jaw pulsed. He *was* trying to be off-putting. And not because he disliked her.

Well, it only made sense. "You are so transparent, Lord Cayton. Changing your behavior toward me so abruptly after that conversation with Lady Melissa. Though do allow me to point out that it's your own fault we find ourselves in such mutually displeasing company right now."

"We'll be mutually rid of it soon enough." They'd reached a fork in the path, and he turned them toward the left.

She would have gone to the right. And where would that have taken her? Perhaps she'd explore it on a finer day. She followed, lagging half a step behind for a moment. As she caught up, a strange smudge at his hairline caught her eyes. Blue? Why would he have something blue caught in his hair?

Silence held for a long moment, a silence full of rain drumming on her umbrella and tree limbs swaying with water and wind. A silence full enough to wash away the pretense.

Cayton sighed. "I had a letter from your brother yesterday."

"You *what*?" She came to a halt, tugging him to one too. Brice always did have an uncanny way of sensing things, but *really*. How would he know from hundreds of miles away the very moment she found a man who made her like him despite herself? And why would he have written to *him* about it rather than *her*?

Cayton looked down at her, his gaze now empty of all the put-on distemper. And of the rain-induced real temper. Empty of . . . everything, it seemed. Which left him looking hollow and lonely.

"We've been corresponding since Adelaide died."

Now Ella frowned. She hadn't been aware that Brice *knew* Cayton, other than in passing. But he knew him well enough to write to him regularly?

And yet had never once mentioned him?

Cayton pulled her back into motion. Because he wanted to get out of the rain, or to avoid meeting her eye again? "We were both at Whitby Park one day last year—I believe the rest of you were at Lady Pratt's house party."

Ella's stomach turned at the mere mention. "The day that maid was attacked at Delmore. Brice arrived back there shortly after the constable."

"Right." He dragged in a ragged breath. "His return was delayed because he was praying with me."

That certainly sounded like Brice. Though she failed to see Cayton's point in bringing it up now. "Then you got a taste of his unusual ability to pray for what he ought not to know."

His next snort of laughter sounded actually amused. "And since then, his ability to write with advice far too apropos."

*Apropos how?* "So in his letter yesterday he must have reminded you not to act like a complete idiot just because you don't trust yourself to be better than you once were."

"If only it were so simple. No, my lady, in his letter yesterday he wrote that he had a bad feeling that trouble was on its way, and he asked that I keep him apprised if I heard anything from certain sectors."

Trouble—the Fire Eyes. That was the only trouble that Brice would be concerned with just now, and the trouble he certainly didn't need to worry with. But that only made her frown again. And stop again, this time at the edge of a puddle that soaked through her shoes. "Lord Rushworth? But why would Brice think . . . ?"

Cayton had turned to face her, meeting her gaze straight on. "You know more than your brother thinks you do, don't you."

She couldn't quite manage a grin. "Of course I do—because I'm *not* naïve, Lord Cayton—much as everyone wishes I were. I know my brother is far too involved in the business over which Brook was kidnapped. And I know . . ." What was that flicker in his eyes? "What?"

He swallowed and looked away, off into the rain-silvered forest. "Your brother is right that trouble is coming. You should go home to Sussex."

"And what makes you or him think said trouble isn't headed *to* Sussex? That's where it was last—"

"Because Rush will be seeking me out, and when he doesn't find me in Yorkshire, he'll know just where to come." Not meeting her gaze again, Cayton pivoted and opened his stride to eat up the muddy trail.

Ella stood stock-still for a moment, letting the rain pound her, before she darted forward to keep up. "Wait just a dashed moment. Why would Rushworth seek out *you*?"

"Why wouldn't he?" Cayton's fingers were nearly white around the handle of the umbrella. "We have been friends all our lives. Rush, Pratt, and Cayton. The three young lords of North Yorkshire."

And did he think that she had forgotten so quickly the horror that she had overheard in his voice last week, when Melissa had said she'd wondered if he were like Pratt? "And he thinks you still *are*?"

He halted again. "You may know more than your brother would like, Lady Ella, but you know far less than you think you do." Even now, his eyes were empty. Not angry, not determined, just hollow. "I know Rushworth better than anyone but his sister, now that Pratt is dead. I knew their resentment for Brook long before she realized it . . . but I said nothing. I knew Pratt had grown impatient and was going to go to drastic measures to get something from her—though I didn't know what at the time—and I said nothing. In his eyes, I have never betrayed his trust before . . . so why should I start now?"

Because the hollowness bespoke pain too deep to show. Because the very fact that he said such things to her meant he was aware of his prior failings and hated himself for them. Perhaps she wasn't the best judge of people, but there was no mistaking that. There couldn't be.

And yet—he'd *known*? He'd known Pratt was going to hurt, to kidnap one of Ella's dearest friends, and he did *nothing*? She had never understood people who chose silence when evil men were at work. She never had, and she never would.

Perhaps her thoughts were reflected in her eyes, for there was a flash of something in his—pain, regret?—before he nodded and turned once more.

Not walking now. Not striding. Trudging.

Ella drew in a long breath, let the rain wash that away too, and then darted after him. "You are different now."

"A happy assumption. Untested and untried."

The mud sucked at her shoes. A rivulet of water dripped from the umbrella's edge onto her shoulder. She would have to move closer to Cayton to be fully under its protection, but could he make it any clearer that he didn't want her there, by his side? She ought to obey good sense and his silent demand and steer far clear of him.

She couldn't. Not seeing that pain within him. "You are different. You said so to Lady Melissa—that the things that once held allure do no longer. I am sorry you suffered the loss you did, my lord, but it has made you stronger. Better."

"You know nothing about me. Why are you so determined to believe in me?"

An excellent question. And try as she might to find answers other than the cliché attraction, only one made itself clear. She sighed and folded her arms over her chest. "Someone has to."

The hitch in his gait bespoke some emotion catching him unawares, though Ella couldn't be entirely sure which one. "And why would that someone need to be you?"

The edge of the wood came into view, with the manicured lawns of Ralin Castle beyond it—and the familiar form of the Duke of Stafford striding their way. An umbrella in hand, proving he had better sense than this misanthropic cousin of his. "I haven't the foggiest notion, Lord Cayton. I suppose we'll have to figure that out."

He looked at her as if she were daft—and maybe she was. The more sensible, logical thing would be to shrug off all thoughts of this man who wanted nothing to do with her and focus on the real issue that had brought her to Ralin.

She straightened her shoulders. Once she was dry and warm again, she would settle into the library with every book the duke had on Indian lore. Perhaps somewhere she would find mention of these supposedly cursed diamonds . . . or at least a better understanding of the culture from whence they had come. Surely thousands of pages of history would suffice to take her mind off one bad-tempered earl.

Stafford looked to be tamping down a grin when they met on the lawn a few yards from the wood's edge. "Found her, I see."

Cayton grunted. "You could have warned me that she's wont to wander off all the way to the river."

Making an impressed face, Stafford nodded at her. "You must have been walking at quite a clip. Let's find Whit and let him know you're accounted for. He headed south."

Lord Whitby was out searching for her too? Suddenly Ella felt more flushed than cold. "Oh, you were *all* out? I am so sorry, Duke—but Brook knew I was walking and that I always find my way back. Why did she send you after me? Please tell me the staff hasn't been inconvenienced as well."

"Only the three of us." Stafford chuckled, though Ella couldn't be sure whether it was over her getting lost or at his sopping cousin. "And Brook said she hadn't realized how chilly it was when she let you wander about on your own. But none of us mind braving the rain to find you. Right, Cay?"

With another grumble that didn't, so far as Ella could tell, contain any discernable words, Cayton shoved the umbrella back into her hands. "I'm going home now, if it's all right by you, Duke. Perhaps with diligence I may actually dry out before I see you tonight."

Ella's fingers curled around the handle—still warm from his touch—as her brows lifted. "Are you joining us for supper this evening, my lord?"

"No."

When he offered no more, Ella looked to Stafford, who was most definitely amused at his cousin's expense. "I'll be dining at Anlic tonight. The invitation was, of course, for us all, but with Brook feeling as poorly as she does . . ."

She had glimpsed Anlic Manor, a mere mile away, when they'd gone into the village, and it looked properly charming. She would have liked to see the interior, had she not apparently just been uninvited. "Perhaps another time."

"Perhaps." Stafford led them across the lawn, toward the carriage house, where Cayton's automobile would be parked. "Actually, Ella, I was thinking . . . if Brook holds true to form, she will be out of sorts for the next month or two and eager for distractions. I was thinking the two of you could go on a short holiday together. To Bath, perhaps, or even to Midwynd, so she could enjoy the beach for a while before the Season begins. You know how she loves the ocean."

She also knew that it was not coincidence that within the space of ten minutes both Stafford and Cayton had suggested she leave—though one with far more charm. An incredulous laugh slipped out. "Do you really think me such a fool, Stafford? You have not been a day away from your wife's side since you wed. Do you really mean to tell me you wish to send her casually away for a few weeks for no reason but for a distraction? And she in her condition?"

To his credit, Stafford held his grin in place. "Well, she *does* get rather testy in these early days when the sickness is on her."

Ella narrowed her eyes, first at the duke and then his wetter-than-ever cousin. "You two are conspiring to get us ladies out of the way, aren't you. And tell me, sir, what do you think your wife will say when she realizes what you're about?"

Stafford sighed. "That's why I was hoping you would assist me, if I begged enough. I can't have her at risk, Ella. Especially not now. Rushworth and Lady Pratt are on their way back from France, and—"

"And we all know Brook will not leave your side, if that's the case."

Wiping the rain from his face—a vain pursuit—Cayton said, "I told you begging wouldn't work."

Ella breathed a laugh. "Nor did your method of irritating me away. Has it never occurred to either of you that perhaps Brook and I can help? Help finish this business once and for all?"

Their lack of answer was answer enough. She'd half a mind to stomp in a puddle just to splash them with mud. "Rubbish. If we *all* want to take a trip to Sussex to discuss next steps with my brother, then fine. But you shan't go sending the poor, fragile ladies away while you burly, surly men try to be heroes in our absence."

Stafford snorted a laugh. "Well, no question which of us is *surly* . . . though I never thought of myself as *burly*. . . ."

Ella stopped, letting the men walk on ahead of her. They could laugh, beg, or insult all day long, but she knew there was only one sure way to win this fight.

Stafford paused, turned to look at her.

She smiled. "You go on ahead, gentlemen, I'll see myself to the house. Even *I* can't get lost between here and there."

The duke narrowed his eyes. "This conversation isn't over, Ella."

"Oh, I know." It was only just beginning. And she intended to have reinforcements when it commenced again. If anything could win Brook over to Ella's side, it was this. They'd just see what the duchess said when she learned her husband wanted to get her out of the way.

## Eight

Cayton knew the moment he turned up the drive of Anlic Manor that something was wrong—well, something more than the fact that he was sitting in soaking wet clothes and fighting off an internal itch that said he shouldn't behave like such a bore with Lady Ella, even if it was for her own good.

An unfamiliar carriage sat outside the stable, the driver flipping through something in his hand and then mounting onto the box. A hired coach, apparently. An *empty* hired coach, so whoever had arrived in it was now in his home.

"Please be Mother and Aunt Caro. *Please* be Mother and Aunt Caro," he muttered. They were the only people he knew who would arrive at Anlic without a word. And it was possible. They weren't due back from the Riviera for another month, but he wouldn't put it past them to have missed Addie and Abingdon and decided to cut their holiday short.

The other option set his teeth on edge and made him press the accelerator a bit more than he usually would up this final stretch. He parked with a screech and jumped out, tossing the keys to Gregory as the old man approached.

Cayton's eyes were on the house. "Who is it? My mother and aunt?" It couldn't be Rushworth already, could it? He would have returned home to Yorkshire. He would have had to go there first to realize Cayton wasn't at Azerly Hall.

Cayton should have had another three or four days to plan a meeting. To figure out a way to handle Rushworth. That was in large part what he and Stafford were to discuss tonight.

Gregory caught the key but frowned. "No, milord. Not Lady Cayton—folks I've never seen before, though they sure put Mrs. Higgins in a tizzy when they showed up saying they were expected. *She* weren't expecting them, clear as day. A gentleman and his sister. Rushford, was it?"

"Rushworth." Cold stole into his very bones, and he couldn't blame it on the rain soaking him through. "Blast. They are earlier than I expected."

Gregory's face eased a bit, at that *expected*. "Mrs. Higgins showed them in, of course, and is getting them settled."

"Very well." Nothing to be done about it just now. He nodded to the groom and headed out of the carriage house, back into the rain for the brief span between it and the rear door of the house. Hopefully Rush and Catherine were still being settled in the parlor and he could slip up the back stairs to his bedroom, change out of these sodden clothes.

Mrs. Higgins was entering the kitchen from the hall even as he entered it from the outside, and she descended on him with blazing eyes. "My lord."

Holding up a hand, he hoped she read apology in his eyes. "I am very sorry, Mrs. Higgins. I thought they'd be another week before they arrived."

Her expression softened. A bit. "And what on earth happened to you? Did you fall in the lake?"

"I might as well have done. Forgive me if I drip on the floor."

ROSEANNA M. WHITE

He looked over her head, toward the hallway. "You haven't shown them to rooms yet, have you?"

The housekeeper fluttered a hand at him, shooing him toward the back stairs. "Their servants are seeing to their trunks up there, is all. Go and change, my lord—and how long are they to be here?"

"I wish I knew." He should get a note off to Stafford post-haste. As soon, that is, as he was dry. With a nod to Mrs. Higgins, he dashed out of the kitchen and up the stairs. Through this hallway, where the family rooms joined with the one where the guest bedrooms were located, he saw no one else.

Evans awaited him in his room, the worry in his eyes turning to sharp amusement when Cayton stalked in. "Did your car get stuck in the mud again, my lord? Have to walk home?"

Cayton turned his back on his valet so the man could help him peel off the jacket determined to cling to his shoulders. "I very nearly did, at that, when Stafford asked me to find Lady Ella on her promenade. Apparently the young lady is an expert at getting lost."

Humming his acknowledgment of that, Evans managed to rid Cayton of the jacket and went to put it somewhere or another while Cayton unbuttoned his equally wet shirt. When his valet returned, he had apparently had enough of small talk, given the look on his face. "How did they know to come here?"

Cayton could only shake his head. "Perhaps they simply left earlier than his letter indicated they would."

"No, I thought of that and asked his valet when they left Paris. Dorsey said they didn't go to Yorkshire first, my lord. They came straight here."

His sudden chill had little to do with the temperature of his room. He discarded the last of his wet clothes and accepted the towel Evans offered. "He must have been in touch with

115

someone in Yorkshire, someone who mentioned I hadn't been in residence."

The question was, was it someone who had just mentioned it in passing . . . or someone deliberately keeping an eye on him for Rushworth?

The second idea lit a fire in his veins as he hurried into a dry suit of clothes. "Rest assured I'll get answers."

Evans smoothed the dry jacket over Cayton's shoulders, frowning into the mirror. "Be careful, my lord."

"I shall." But there was no point in dallying. He would slip down to his study to jot a note to Stafford and then confront Rushworth.

Though he had to confess, the continued frown of his valet didn't exactly inspire confidence. If Evans, who had known him for a decade, had no faith in his ability to confront an old friend now recognized as an enemy, what did that say about Cayton?

Much. And none of it good. His shoulders slumped a bit as he stepped into the hall. How long before these changes in him were secure enough that people could trust them? That *he* could trust them, could trust himself not to fall back into old patterns? How long until he could smile at a young lady without regretting it and fearing if she smiled back he'd only hurt her?

His study was at the base of the front staircase. He would slip down that way, staying out of sight of the parlor. He would—

Addie's scream pierced the air, and he took off at a run for the nursery at the end of the hall. Probably nothing. Tabby could have taken away something the little one shouldn't have had. Or said no to something she wanted. There were countless reasons a nine-month-old would scream.

But Rushworth was in his house, and the sound lit panic.

He charged into the room and nearly collided with a shaking figure trying to back out. A Rushworth—or she used to be—but not the brother. Catherine gripped the doorframe and turned wide, wet eyes upon Cayton.

Addie was on the other side of the room, safe in her nurse's arms. Tabby looked more frustrated than alarmed, which surely meant that nothing was wrong, not really.

The nurse dipped into a curtsy. "My apologies, my lord. The lady just stepped in to say hello, and you know how Addie can be around strangers. Just started screaming, she did."

A gasp drew his gaze back down to the woman beside him. No, not a gasp—a sob. Catherine pressed a hand to her mouth and squeezed her eyes shut, turning to the hall.

Not quite knowing why, Cayton stayed her with a hand on her shoulder. "Kitty?"

She shook her head and shrugged away from his touch, stepped fully from the room. It was then that he noticed how gaunt she had become since he'd last seen her. Her frock hung on her, her cheeks were hollow. When she shook her head, a lock of golden hair slipped free, and she didn't even tuck it behind her ear. So very unlike the meticulous, preening woman he'd known most of his life.

"I'm sorry." Even her voice was strange, filled with a pulsing ache. "I didn't mean to upset her, Cayton. I only wanted to see how she's grown."

"You've no need to apologize. She is wary of strangers—that is all." Of every one of them but Ella, it seemed. Though at the moment he would focus on the young lady before him rather than the one a mile away. "How have you been, Kitty?"

Whatever string had been holding her taut seemed to snap. Her shoulders sagged, her spine bent, her chin dipped down. Still, he didn't miss the tears that dripped onto her cheeks. "He keeps telling me I have to put it behind me. I have to move past it. As if there is anything left in the world that matters."

Addie's crying had ceased, and now she strained against Tabby, reaching for him. "Dadadada!"

His heart twisted within his chest. How would *he* feel if his child were ripped from his arms? And her Byron had been just the age Addie was now when he died. So lively, so interactive. So quick to rejoice in the presence of a loved one, so opinionated. At an age so very dear, when a child's personality really began to emerge.

He held out his arms so Tabby would bring her to him but didn't step away from Catherine. If he did, he had a feeling she would flee. His daughter nestled happily into his arms, though she buried her face in his shoulder rather than face the stranger.

The lady blinked rapidly and wiped the tears from her face. "When last I saw her she was the tiniest thing. Now look at her. So lovely."

Cayton rubbed a hand over Addie's back. "She is. I only wish Adelaide could see her. She would be so proud."

"She would be." Sniffing, Catherine folded her arms across her middle. "You have that, at least. Pratt, on the other hand . . . I loved him my whole life, but I was little more than a convenience to him. He didn't even care that we were having a child."

"Oh, Kitty." What was he to say? They had both lost a spouse, but that was where the similarities in their stories ended. "You were more than a convenience. And he would have loved his son."

Her eyes had gone unfocused, giving her a dazed look that was more than a little startling. How long had she been like this? It was no wonder Rush had gone to such lengths to try to stir her from such a stupor. Though Cayton had never liked the catty, backbiting, often duplicitous Catherine, at this moment he would have preferred that woman to this hollow shell who looked ready to crack and crumble.

"Do you think so?" She didn't look at him, didn't sound as

though she had the least drop of hope that his answer would be what she wanted. "Crispin always just snaps that Pratt never spoke of such things. Of his heart."

Pratt *hadn't* spoken of such things. Not for the most part. But still, Cayton had known Pratt well enough to read between the lines. He'd known, as Pratt surely had, that Catherine was the only woman he'd cared for on a deeper level.

Even if he would have readily tossed her over to get at the diamonds, had that been an option.

"I suppose your brother wasn't his chosen confidant for such thoughts, Kitty. But I assure you, he loved you. I always knew it. He spoke of you differently than anyone else." With hefty doses of cynicism and the occasional coarse reference to her willingness to go into his arms, but Cayton saw no need to mention that.

Honestly, he could hardly believe he had to mention any of it. She had seemed more bent on revenge than devastated after Pratt's death nearly two years ago. But perhaps that was because she had his son to live for. Now she had . . . nothing.

No wonder she stared into space and questioned what the point of her life had been. She had focused all her efforts for years upon marrying Pratt. And what had it gotten her but misery?

Catherine edged away. "Thank you, Cayton. Again, I'm sorry to have upset your daughter. I think I . . . I had better rest. The trip was difficult."

A man stepped from the adjacent hallway, where the guest bedrooms were located. Cayton recognized him vaguely as Rushworth's valet. Dorsey, wasn't it? "This way, my lady. Lareau's waiting to help you settle."

Catherine, eyes downcast, slipped toward the man. He reached out as if to guide her around the corner, but she shied away from the touch.

"Come to Tabby, Addie." Speaking at a hush, Tabby eased forward with arms outstretched.

Cayton transferred the girl back to the nurse's arms. Much as he could have used a few more minutes of holding her, it was time to confront Rushworth. Especially, he saw as he stepped toward the stairs, since the man was standing at the base of the staircase, his gaze on Cayton.

His old friend looked up at him as he'd always done. Eyes unreadable. Face a mask of emptiness. Both paired perfectly with his habitual silence when around any more than one other person. For the first months of their acquaintance as adolescents, Cayton hadn't even heard him speak—at the time he'd thought him little more than Pratt's shadow.

In recent years, however, he had begun to wonder who was the shadow and who the clever puppeteer. He couldn't quite manage a smile as he descended the stairs and stopped before his uninvited guest. He could only force a nod. "Rush. I am surprised you came directly here—I hadn't time to get a letter to you telling you I wasn't at Azerly Hall."

Not so much as a twitch of the lips, not so much as a blink out of turn. "And I hadn't the time to coddle your sense of privacy, my friend. It was no great secret where you were spending the spring, nor any great difficulty to discern it. Please." Rushworth held out a hand toward the drawing room. A rather audacious command, given that Cayton was the host, not the guest. "There is much to discuss."

Cayton stayed rooted to the spot. "I'm sure there is, but I must first get a note off to my cousin. He was planning on joining me for supper tonight, but obviously—"

"Perfect." As always, Rushworth's voice remained even. But a glint lit his eyes ever so briefly. "I was hoping for such an opportunity. Paris may have failed to stir my sister, but seeing

Brook again just might. Our cousin always did bring out Kitty's competitive side."

And *his* cousin would let loose his furious-duke side if Cayton let him walk blindly into such a situation. He shook his head. "Brook wasn't planning on coming, just Stafford."

"Well, in that case." Rushworth waved a hand toward Cayton's study. "Do send a note inviting the duchess as well. Tell them we're here and would like to have a conversation—that will surely convince Brook to join her husband. She can never turn away from a fight."

A fight he was none too keen on having in his house, with his daughter just up the stairs. "I really don't fancy getting involved in this argument between you, Rush—"

"I'll make it worth your while."

Cayton blew out a long exhale. Either way, a note needed to be sent. And best just now not to tip his hand—whatever hand he might have—until he and Stafford had planned their course of action.

Why had they not done so last week? Why had he been so content to focus solely on studying the Word with his cousin in the morning, pushing away all thought of what he'd known would be coming? Stafford had said something about the wisdom of putting on one's spiritual armor first, true, but . . .

He stalked to his study, grateful that at least Rushworth didn't follow. But what if Cayton wasn't strong enough for this? What if his faith wasn't great enough to let the Lord's strength work through his own weakness? He had, after all, far more experience in making a mull of things than in solving problems.

Pulling forward a piece of paper, he unscrewed the lid from his fountain pen, not even bothering to take a seat. He merely leaned over his desk and dashed off a quick note. *Rush and sister arrived already. They ask that Brook join you here tonight. If you don't come, we'll talk in the morning.*

It would do. He folded it, shoved it into an envelope, and went in search of Gregory's grandson, Ronald, to run it over to Ralin. The boy was half-duck, it seemed, always happy to go out in the rain. Perhaps because he knew the chef at the castle always had a biscuit or two ready to give him for his trouble. He found the twelve-year-old hovering in the kitchen, obviously hoping for just such a task.

With no other excuse for dallying, Cayton trudged back to the drawing room, where Rushworth stood before a portrait of Adelaide sitting in her favorite spot, under the little miniature pavilion beside the fish pool.

The man acknowledged his presence by motioning to it. "I am rather surprised you left this up—I assume it is a relic of her days as Miss Rosten."

Cayton shoved his hand into his pocket to keep from curling his fingers into a fist. "On the contrary, it was done just a year ago. She was actually expecting when she posed for it, though the artist didn't paint her so." He nearly had, but upon realizing he had no other good-sized portrait of his wife, he had thought it better to put her to canvas in her natural state.

Rushworth grunted. "A rather flattering representation, don't you think? I don't believe I ever saw your wife with such color in her cheeks."

Cayton dug his fingers into his leg. "She was always at her best here at Anlic." And who was he to accuse Cayton of a false representation—even if he had no idea Cayton was the artist? He cleared his throat. "But I daresay you didn't come just to critique the portrait of my wife."

"No." Rushworth turned and helped himself to a seat. In Cayton's favorite chair. He hooked an ankle over the opposite knee and steepled his hands, staring at Cayton long and hard. "You are seeing more of your cousin than you once did."

Another something the man shouldn't know. Cayton sat, forcing his stiff back to relax into the sort of pose he once would have adopted when speaking of Stafford. A bit belligerent, more than a little irritated. Because until he knew what Rushworth wanted, it was probably best not to shout out that he was on Stafford's side in this particular war. "He requested that we be friends. And who am I to turn down the duke?"

Rushworth's lips curled up a degree. "It is a useful connection, at that. And I am glad you have fostered it. I need your help, Cayton."

Shifting, Cayton made no attempt to hide his scowl. "If this has to do with that diamond business that got Pratt killed, I want nothing to do with it."

"A position I well understand. But hear me out." Both feet on the floor again, Rushworth leaned forward. "Pratt was killed because he was, as usual, too impatient. Too headstrong, refusing to listen to reason. Had he done as I suggested—but he never would, and because of that he got his due deserts."

"Deserts I do not wish to share."

"I assure you, neither do I." Was that worry that flickered through Rushworth's blue-green eyes? Cayton had never seen the emotion in the man to know how it looked on him. "But apparently our late friend accepted a good-faith deposit upon the Fire Eyes from his buyer. Which, of course, he spent on that ramshackle home of his. I had no idea at the time, but . . . Cayton, if I cannot deliver the diamonds to the buyer by June, my sister will be expected to pay Pratt's debt. A debt we haven't the funds to cover, and I dare not guess at how the man will extract payment."

Yes, definitely worry. It increased tenfold, until it couldn't

123

be denied. Rushworth shook his head. "I'll not lose my sister to this nonsense, no more than I'm willing to lose her to this blasted despair that has eaten her up."

Cayton's frown pulled deeper. "Forgive me, Rush, but I don't know how to help you. I could perhaps lend you a bit, but most of what's left that Adelaide brought to the marriage is tied up in the mills, and—"

"I did not come to you seeking a loan." Frustration flashed through the worry. "What I need is your help finding the gems."

He and Stafford had been right. Though it brought little comfort just now. "How am I to help with that? I know nothing about them aside from what was in the papers. Stafford has told me only that the diamonds are colored. Blue, is it?"

Rushworth looked at him as though he were daft. "Red. Far rarer than blue, which is why they're worth a fortune, even being relatively small. Your cousin has said nothing else?"

With a shrug, Cayton sifted through the few details Stafford *had* mentioned, trying to light upon something that Rush would deem useful but which Stafford wouldn't deem wrong of him to share. He settled on, "He mentioned only that Brook doesn't have them anymore."

"Ha!" Rushworth surged to his feet in a show of temper far greater than any Cayton had seen from him before. He strode to the window. "What they wanted everyone to think. Kitty saw Brook give jewels to the Duke of Nottingham, thought for sure he had them. But she gave him only rubies."

Dread sank in Cayton's stomach. He and Stafford had to have a talk, without question. "How can you be so sure?"

Rushworth spun to face him again. His face, again, blank and calm. "Last autumn my sister got to know the Duchess of Nottingham. The duchess told her where the diamonds were, and we've . . . seen them."

Not admitting to threatening the duchess or stealing the jewels, of course. That would be too much to hope. Cayton nodded. "And?"

"And they were fakes. Rubies. I cannot think the cowardly duchess would have tried to dupe Kitty—which means that my dear cousin, Brook, duped Nottingham."

Cayton drummed his fingers on the arm of the chair. "Or . . . she never had diamonds to begin with, but only rubies."

Rushworth snorted. "We had better pray that is not the case. And I would indeed find it difficult to believe. My uncle had them authenticated twenty years ago. My uncle had them hidden in a necklace. My uncle gave said necklace to Brook's mother, who in turn left the necklace to Brook. Therefore, Brook had the real Fire Eyes—and I daresay she does still."

What could he do but shrug? Cayton had never made any attempt to learn about this particular business . . . and would rather not do so now. "As I say, Stafford has told me little. I am afraid I am of no help."

"But you can be." Rushworth strode back to the chair and perched on the edge of the cushion. A plea entered his eyes, warming them, making his face vulnerable. Just another of his masks. "My cousin is unlikely to speak with me at all, much less hear my plea. Your cousin, however, is quite likely to trust you. You can learn what I cannot."

Cayton lifted his brows. "And risk Stafford's wrath? After I've worked so hard in recent years to avoid it?"

"As I said." Rushworth settled deeper onto the cushion and produced a small smile. "I'll make it worth your while. A third of the price the Fire Eyes will bring is enough to guarantee that even if your mills suffer or you place your bets on every losing horse at the races, you will still be able to live comfortably."

Able only to stare at him, Cayton let his mind flood with all the offhanded remarks Pratt had once made about the fortune that should rightfully be his. About exactly how huge it was. About all he could do with such funds, the improvements he could make on Delmore, the automobiles he could buy, the limitless pleasures that would be at his fingertips. Why in the world would Rushworth offer such wealth to Cayton? "I didn't realize we were such good friends, Rush."

The other man breathed a laugh. "I know when to admit that I need aid—and that time is now. I have found a few of the servants at Ralin Castle willing to feed me information for a price, but they can do little but observe. And there is, at the moment, nothing to observe."

Cayton's stomach twisted. Stafford would *not* be happy to learn that any of his staff had been bought. "Who is in your employ?"

Rushworth chuckled. "No, no, my friend—you are new to this, but the first lesson you must learn is that I protect them by never mentioning their names—a courtesy I will also extend to you. Suffice it to say that anything that goes on at Ralin Castle or Whitby Park makes its way to me."

Stafford was going to be in a rage. And Whitby none too happy either. Cayton kept his face neutral. "Do you mean to steal them, as Pratt did?"

"Of course not. I mean to inspire them to give them to me." He smiled. But the frigidity of his eyes made Cayton wonder by exactly what means he intended to *inspire* them.

# Nine

Kira sat with a sigh upon the narrow bed in the room she'd share with one of the maids at Anlic Manor, stretching out her leg. Just now, there was no point in hiding the wince at the pain in her knee. She probed it—it was swollen. No great surprise after so much travel. They had gone from train to boat to train to carriage, and during all of it she'd been expected to remain seated by Lady Pratt's side.

Perhaps, while the lady was at dinner with her brother and their host, Kira could slip out for a walk. It was still raining, but she hardly cared. She had to move the thing. It would never strengthen again if she spent her days on her backside instead of her feet. Of course, she should also use the time to poke about Lady Pratt's things. She'd spotted a box of correspondence. Magazines that might have pages tucked within them. And the lady was out of her rooms so rarely. . . .

Pulling her dress up above the knee, she indulged in a moment of self-pity as she verified with her eyes what her fingers had told her. Swollen. Ugly. And, oh, how it hurt. But pity wouldn't get her back on the stage. She tossed her skirt down again and stood. Lady Pratt probably wouldn't stay with the others as long as Rushworth would hope. If Kira was going to get in both a walk and time to read her employer's letters, she couldn't dawdle.

The door opened even as she reached for it, and though Kira jumped, the girl on the other side smiled. She looked to be near Kira in age, with a face that looked as swollen as Kira's knee— no doubt related to the belly protruding with a babe. She was probably about seven months along, perhaps even eight, and she extended a hand in welcome.

"My aunt said I would find you in here. I'm Felicity. You'll be sharing my room while you're here." She motioned at the tight space.

Kira smiled and took the also-swollen fingers in hers. "Good to meet you. K . . . Sophie. Sophie Lareau. Thank you for sharing your space with me."

"Oh, it's nothing." Felicity stepped back into the hallway, a hand upon her belly. "Are you going out?"

"I thought to walk a bit."

The girl didn't question her intentions to go out in the rain. Rather, she nodded, her eyes gleaming. "The Duke of Stafford's carriage is coming up the drive. I was going to watch them come in—we can peek out from behind the stairs and not be seen. Would you like to join me? Her Grace always has the most beautiful gowns."

Beautiful gowns . . . How Kira longed for her own. To feel silk against her skin. She probably shouldn't go stare at another woman's, not if she wanted to keep her focus. But she hated to be rude—and it might come in handy at some point to have a friend. She had never spied before to know for sure, but it seemed wise. "Thank you. I would love to."

Felicity smiled, proving herself pretty under the obvious strain of impending motherhood. "Follow me."

Kira did, unable to help but note the way the girl moved—with that unmistakable wincing step that bespoke pain. She frowned, trying to tamp down long years of training, but it was no use. Though she had left the life her mother had wanted for her, she couldn't forget what she'd been taught for so many years under Mamochka's tutelage. "It is your back paining you?"

Felicity glanced back at her over her shoulder, question in her brows. "Aye, and down into my legs."

Nothing terribly unusual there, though it could certainly make for an uncomfortable pregnancy. Kira smiled. "My mother was a midwife. I learned much from her." It had been a cruel irony that Mamochka had herself died giving birth, after saving so many other women. That all the tricks she had taught Kira had accomplished nothing.

And her family had wondered at her determination to follow her heart onto the stage. How could they have failed to understand? *Da*, death was part of life. But that hardly meant she had to live a life that tried and failed to fend it off every day.

Felicity's eyes lit. "Really? Perhaps you'll still be here when my time arrives. We've a midwife in the village, of course, but . . ." She leaned close, a smile playing at her mouth. "I never much liked her. Especially . . ."

They turned a corner and headed for the unadorned service stairs. "Especially?"

Sighing, Felicity turned half around as she continued moving. "My husband left—right after I found I was with child. Everyone's saying the babe scared him off, the thought of being a father—and the midwife, she's his mum's cousin." The girl's brows drew down. "The one thing we agree on is that the thought of a babe wouldn't have sent him running. So she thinks it was something *I* did."

Men could be such idiots. Thinking it their right to come

and go, to pick and choose when to be responsible. Kira made sure her smile was warm. "I daresay it was not that. Men can just be as skittish as a bird, *nyet*?"

"Not Stew." Felicity's face went hard before she turned it back to the stairs. "I don't know where he is, but I know he's there for a good reason, and that he's coming back. He wouldn't have just left."

Kira pressed her lips against a response. Men were always doing things their women thought they wouldn't. But there was no point in saying so to those determined to believe the best. Or to those already nursing heartache at the worst. "I am sure you are right."

They went up the stairs, and at the top Felicity pressed a finger to her lips. The girl paused a moment, looking both ways, then motioned Kira to follow as she darted out into the hallway. A few moments later they were both scrunched into the little closet below the stairs, peering through a crack in the door.

Kira hadn't felt so like giggling in months.

The butler shot them a look that mixed warning with amusement and seconds later reached for the front door. A footman hurried out with umbrellas.

The first to enter was a redhead, who stepped inside with a smile bright as the sunshine. Felicity leaned close. "That must be Lady Ella—Tabby's been going ever on about her, and Evans is teasing his lordship mercilessly."

Kira didn't know who Tabby and Evans were, but she smiled. "She is lovely." And had excellent taste. The pale yellow of her dress perfectly complemented her hair and the ivory of her complexion, and was in a style similar to Kira's favorite gown. She wore pearls around her throat and rubies in her ears.

Lifting a hand to her own ears, Kira couldn't help but wish for the gold and diamonds that had hung there so recently. She had them with her—she hadn't trusted her staff enough to leave them unattended in her flat for months—but knew well she couldn't ever put them on.

"Can you imagine wearing a gown like that?" Felicity breathed a wistful sigh, then chuckled softly. "Not that such a one would fit me now, of course."

A couple came through the door next, saving Kira the need to respond. Felicity softly breathed, "The duke."

For a moment Kira saw only the nearly-matching golden heads, the exquisite gown, the perfectly tailored suit. Then the duke looked up, and a vague memory stirred. She'd seen him before—she was sure of it. Not such an odd thing, really. She had met several English dukes on Andrei's arm and had no doubt glimpsed many more in the theater crowds.

But it was when the duchess looked up that Kira pulled in a gasp before she could stop herself.

"I know," Felicity whispered. "Simply gorgeous. What would you call that shade of green?"

Unlucky, that's what. Kira squeezed her eyes shut, opened them again, but that only made her more sure. The Duchess of Stafford was Brook Sabatini. Once welcomed into the palace of Prince Albert of Monaco as his granddaughter. Once thought to be the daughter of famed opera star Collette Sabatini and Prince Louis.

Once a ballet student that Sergei had let practice with the corps—at first solely because he wanted to indulge the royal household, but she had held her own. She had never performed with them, of course, but she had been there for practices. Been with them in the dressing room, laughing along with the other girls at the men paying them court.

Kira remembered when she had left, soon after Lord William's tragic death on the mountain roads—which was why

Brook's husband looked familiar. Lord William's son. Not the duke at the time, of course, just Lord Harlow. The prude of the family, the girls had always joked. As handsome as his father, though he never made any attempt to get to know the dancers as Lord William had done. They had all tried to tease Brook about him, but she'd insisted they were only friends.

How she would have liked to approach her now. To kiss her on the cheeks and laugh with her that "only friends" was clearly much more now.

But she couldn't. She couldn't let the duchess see her, much less speak to her.

And why did the circle of European nobility have to be so cursedly small?

An older gentleman entered last, doffing his hat and then stepping near to Brook. The hand he touched to the small of her back was protective, familiar.

"Lord Whitby," came Felicity's helpful murmur. "The duchess's father."

So she had found him. That was why she'd left Monaco, just a few weeks before the Ballet Russe headed back to Paris. To be reunited with her true father. Kira had spared her a prayer or two at the time, before their return to France.

Then she had met Andrei.

Her eyes slid shut. She had been a different girl when Brook knew her. Still untarnished by the world, still claiming that she'd remain so. They had blushed together at the jesting of the other dancers about their men.

Now look at them. The former princess was now a duchess, surrounded by a husband, by a beautiful friend, by a father.

And Kira was hiding under the stairs, pretending to be a maid so she could please her patron. Her fingers dug into the doorframe. "Do they come here often?"

"When they are all in the area, aye. Every week or so. His lordship and the duke are cousins, you see. And the duchess is cousins with your mistress and her brother."

Lord Rushworth's words came back to her. *"Our cousin used to prattle about her love of the ballet from her days in Monaco. . . ."*

Cursedly small world indeed.

∞

Ella followed the Staffords into the drawing room, looking about her with interest even as she reckoned that, had she a knife, she could have sliced through the tension in the air. Stafford and Whitby were both still a bit miffed that she and Brook had insisted on coming—even before the note had arrived from Cayton.

There had certainly been no dissuading the duchess then.

But just as obviously, Brook had no desire to be now in the same room as her duplicitous cousin. She walked stiffly, spine straight and shoulders back, her hand resting on Stafford's arm. Whitby was at her other side, his face in hard lines.

None of them noticed when Ella slipped off to the side. There were plenty of times in life when she enjoyed being the center of attention, but not tonight. Tonight she would rather observe and let the others forget she was there.

Her first observation was somewhat startling, given the changes in Catherine Pratt's appearance. Pity stirred in Ella's chest. As she sat on a sofa, the woman looked gaunt enough that she might indeed fail to leave footprints in the mud if ever she wandered off. When she turned a hollow-eyed gaze on her long-sworn enemy and blinked as though she didn't even see her, the pity turned to something deeper. Stronger.

Ella had never claimed her brother's ability to know just

133

what to pray . . . and it was true she had missed something vital buried deep in her oldest friend's heart . . . but she wasn't oblivious. Sometimes the Lord sounded an alarm within her to tell her to pray—and one was clanging like a fire bell now.

"You could have taken pity on us, Lady Ella. Stayed at the castle. Declined getting involved in this."

Cayton's voice sent a little trill dancing up her spine, whether either of them wanted it to or not. She turned, half a smile in place, to see he'd slipped into the room behind them and was scowling at the backs of his newly arrived guests. Or perhaps at his not-quite-as-newly arrived ones. Hard to say. "And miss the chance to make you think I came only to torture you with flirtation? Never."

"Ella. It's not a jesting matter." He sent her a second-long glance, full of serious things, before looking away again. "This isn't your business, and you oughtn't to make it so."

"It's as much mine as yours or Stafford's."

"In what world is that true?"

"In this one. My brother is involved—as is one of my dearest friends. That is as much a claim as Stafford has, isn't it?"

His only answer was a throaty growl, and then he strode away. Or stomped away, more like.

She could understand, even appreciate his worry. Really she could. But if he thought for a moment it was going to budge her . . .

Pressing her lips against a smile, she meandered over to the wall with the mantel, her eye drawn by the paintings hanging there. There was one of who must be the late Lady Cayton, though Ella didn't remember ever meeting her. And a smaller one nearby of Addie, done just a few months before.

Her ears strained toward the far side of the room, where Brook was greeting her cousins. Vague words, uttered in a polite tone.

Ella peeked over at them. Catherine's eyes still looked unfocused as she sat staring at the floor, and Lord Rushworth was frowning at her. At length, the lady's lips parted, and she at least looked up at her cousin. "How is your son?"

The ache was so encompassing that Ella had to splay a hand over her chest to try to push it down. Over the years, she'd heard Catherine Pratt speak in quite a few different ways. Overly sweet, catty, flirtatious, goading, angry, serious. But this tone had no name that Ella knew to apply to it. *Raw*, perhaps. It was the closest she could come.

Brook sighed. "He is well. Growing."

"Walking?"

Tears stung Ella's eyes, and she had to look back to the painting of Addie to blink them away.

Brook's hesitation lasted a heartbeat longer. "Yes. And chattering, though few words are understandable."

"Cris said you tried to come to the funeral, but he let no one in." How could a voice be stripped so very bare? It sounded like little more than an echo. "I was not sorry at the time, but . . . but it was good of you to try to come. Thank you."

Ella didn't dare to see how Brook handled such words. Not with her own tears refusing to be tamped down.

"We are family, Kitty. Whatever else is between us, I grieved with you over the loss of your son."

"I know. You are too good not to do." It didn't sound like a compliment.

Ella drew in a long breath and blinked until her eyes cleared. Rowena had tried to befriend Catherine last autumn, and it had proven a disastrous mistake. The lady was capable of cruelty and not to be trusted—facts that could not be changed.

But something had shifted. That wasn't optimism speaking, not hope. Not something she could misinterpret. Even Catherine

Pratt wouldn't have starved herself for six months simply to play on their sympathies. Even Catherine Pratt wasn't so skilled at deceit that she could feign this level of hopelessness.

Something had changed within their rival. They simply had to determine how to react to it, how to use it. Not that Ella wanted to use a mother's grief to her own ends—that wasn't what she meant—but . . .

"Catherine." Whitby stepped toward the Rushworths, motioning toward the empty cushion beside the lady. Ella watched from the corner of her eye as he said, "May I?"

Catherine didn't so much as blink. "As you wish, my lord."

Whitby lowered himself to the seat. "Rarely over the years have I had cause to speak to you two as family, and we all know why. But I will now. Catherine, you must pull yourself out of the morass now, or it will never let you go."

Ella turned her head their way in time to see the anger cover Catherine's face. "How dare you?"

"I dare as one caught in the same morass for far too long." Whitby's face somehow remained impassable and yet not unkind. "I know what it is to lose a spouse and a child."

Catherine turned her face away from him, nostrils flaring. "You found your daughter."

Brook shifted closer to her husband. Ella raised her gaze again to the painting of Addie. Whitby had never seen Brook at that age, sitting up with such delight. So far as she had seen, he'd had no portrait nor photograph to remind him of her. Was that perhaps in part the reason Cayton had commissioned one? Did the loss surrounding him, his own wife's included, make him determined to capture that early phase too?

He had found a top-notch artist. Most portrait painters captured only the detail—this one captured the heart of that sweet little girl. And she surely hadn't sat for whoever had done it, not

ROSEANNA M. WHITE

so still for so long. Yet still he had put to canvas the way that one lock curled just so around her ear. That precious dimple in her elbow.

Whitby sighed. "Eighteen years later I found her, yes. But that is an eternity to be without one's child, especially when the whole world insists she is dead."

Brook moved to the sofa and set a hand on her father's shoulder. Catherine didn't deign to look at him again. "You never believed them."

"And was labeled daft for it. I realize there are vast differences in our situations, Catherine. But the *feelings* . . . the feelings are the same, regardless of the eventual result of mine. I know that pain that surrounds you always. I know that darkness threatening to consume you whole. You mustn't let it."

"What does it matter if it does?"

Beside Catherine, her brother sighed and reached for her hand. "Please, Kitty. Please listen to him. How many times have I begged you?"

A throat cleared in the doorway, and Ella spun with the others to see the butler there. He bowed. "Excuse me. Dinner is served."

Everyone shifted, stood, ready to follow the summons. Even Catherine took to her feet. In the shuffle Ella nearly missed her quiet "I am not hungry. I think I shall—"

"No." Lord Rushworth's voice was muted, but his tone brooked no argument. "You will eat with us, Kitty. I insist."

A wise insistence, but Ella wasn't surprised to look their way and see that the lady's eyes had lost all feeling again, that her posture remained upright but somehow slack, as though a puppeteer's string held her erect more than her own will.

Lord Rushworth looked over his sister's bent head and directly at Ella. His gaze went soft, his lips hinted at a smile. He nodded, though he made no greeting across such a distance.

Ella offered that tight-lipped quarter smile that was as big as was polite after such a conversation in which she had no part. An acknowledgment, nothing more. And recalled the way Rushworth had flirted with her six months ago, during the one time they'd really been near enough to exchange words. It had struck her as odd then. As odd as that light in his eyes struck her now.

Cayton stepped before her. Scowling, of course. And practically hissed, "You are *not* smiling at him. Are you mad?"

No one but she could have heard the low accusation, but still. She sent her gaze to the ceiling. "The word is *polite*, Lord Cayton. A concept, granted, with which you seem rather unfamiliar."

"As *caution* is a concept unfamiliar to you." He turned, held out his arm. Though one would never call it invitation in his eyes. "Shall we go in?"

The others were already filing out the door. Brook on Stafford's arm, Catherine on her brother's, Whitby glancing over his shoulder at Ella and Cayton with a lifted brow.

She folded her arms over her chest. "I am surprised you would dare to escort me rather than leaving Lord Whitby to do so. What if I mistake your attention for interest and start planning the wedding, my lord?"

Cayton didn't budge, not so much as a twitching facial muscle. "Surely you are not *so* daft as to ever wish for a future with my surly self."

It *was* rather amusing to listen to him growl over absolutely everything. She made a point of giving him her most mischievous smile. "Don't be so sure. I have yet to test the limits of my reason."

He looked pointedly at his arm—in part, she suspected, to hide the laughter in his eyes. "Sometime tonight would be preferable, Lady Ella."

"Well, that's rather quick for a wedding, don't you think?" With a bat of her eyes, she slid her hand onto his arm and stepped near to his side. "I would prefer September. The autumn foliage would provide the perfect backdrop for my *auburn* hair when you paint my wedding portrait."

He'd led her one step but stopped at that, a single brow lifted. "Pardon?"

"October, then? It may be a bit cool. Do paints behave strangely in the cold? I've no experience with them. I was an absolute dunce at anything artistic."

She'd done it—she'd caught him completely off his guard, and the bafflement in his eyes eclipsed the surliness.

She deserved some sort of prize for that.

He shook his head. "Why would you think I have any more experience with paints than you have?"

Ella tugged him forward—Whitby was still lingering in the hallway waiting for them—but nodded toward the painting of Addie. "That, my lord, was done by someone who had spent entire days just watching her. And done, moreover, with love."

"I hardly think—"

"Plus." She grinned. "You had paint in your hair this morning. I didn't know at the time what it was, but now it becomes clear. Bright blue paint."

Cayton sighed . . . but tugged her a bit closer. "Cobalt. And I'm going to have to sack my valet yet—he's supposed to catch those things before I leave my room."

A chuckle tickled her throat. She'd been right. And realizing that he had such talent, that he indulged it in more than occasional poetic talk . . . Perhaps her instinct to like him wasn't so misplaced. Maybe, just maybe, it was Brook who was wrong about him, not her.

They moved at a leisurely pace toward the door, though Whitby preceded them when he saw they were coming. Ella angled her head to look up at Cayton's profile. "Why do you hide it, my lord? You have an admirable talent."

He snorted. "Wildons are not artists. They are empire builders."

"And what is the point of building empires but to have the leisure to explore the arts?" She shook her head.

He inclined his, his gaze straight ahead but his attention quite obviously hers.

She might as well push, then. "Besides which, you're not a Wildon. You're an Azerly. Cayton, not Stafford. And what of that side of your family?"

The arm under her fingers rose as he shrugged. "I never really knew my father's people. It was the duke who served that paternal function."

The duke, then, who filled his head with such utter rot about what was expected of him? She'd never met the man, but she suddenly didn't like Stafford and Cayton's grandfather one whit. "Well, if he failed to see and encourage your gift, then he was a fool."

Cayton started and turned wide eyes on her. "No one speaks so of my grandfather. He was a duke."

"As was mine, and my father. That makes them no less people, and no less apt to be wrong now and then."

"Well." He faced forward again. "Be that as it may, I was never of a mind to shout my habit from the rooftops. It didn't suit the image I wanted to portray."

The image Lady Melissa had fallen for—a young buck at his best in society, rousing the rabble and losing wagers at the races. "I daresay that image was no more pleasing to your grandfather."

A gruff laugh slipped out as they stepped into the hallway. "Ah, but that he could attribute to the wild ways of youth. My propensity for poetry and painting would have been far more worrisome."

"Poetry too?" She leaned a bit closer—and did at least keep her volume low. "I should have known. Castles in the clouds and winged unicorns."

The scathing look he sent her as they trailed the rest of the party into the dining room might have been a bit more effective had they not been talking about his inner artist. "Breathe a word of it to anyone and I'll . . ."

The dining room was brightly lit, the electric chandelier looking new and beautiful, dripping crystals. Ella grinned up at him. "You'll what, pray tell, my lord?"

"I'll think of something. I'm very imaginative."

She couldn't help but chuckle as he delivered her to a chair beside Lord Rushworth's, across from Whitby.

Brook sent Cayton a long-suffering look. "Are you being rude to Lady Ella, Cayton?"

He didn't look the least bit perturbed as he took his place at the head of the table, Catherine to his right and Stafford to his left. "I don't know what you could possibly mean, Duchess."

When Brook sat, the rest of them followed. "You had manners once. I saw them."

"No," Stafford said on a grin. "He could simply feign them."

Brook muttered something, but it must have been in Monegasque—Ella had no clue what she said. Though whatever it was made Stafford laugh.

Ella pressed her lips against a smile . . . and Lord Rushworth turned her way.

# Ten

A fruit tart sat before her, only half-eaten. Which was a shame. Ella would have liked to finish it, but it was difficult to enjoy her dessert when four sets of eyes kept glaring in her direction. Solely because she wasn't being outright rude to the man at her side.

What was she supposed to do, refuse to answer any of Lord Rushworth's questions? What purpose would that serve? Yet every time she replied to some inquiry as to the weather in Sussex or her family's plans for the Season, they all looked at her as though she had committed some crime—the Staffords, Cayton, even Whitby.

It was definitely enough to put one off one's sweets. And the tart was perfection, so that deserved a bit of mourning.

Brook only toyed with hers too. Her face had grown paler and paler throughout the meal. She now put down her fork, swallowed with what looked like effort, and turned to Rushworth. "Forgive me for acknowledging the invisible elephant, but I daresay we all tire of niceties. Why did you wish me to come tonight, cousin?"

Beside her, Lord Rushworth took his time swallowing his bite of tart and then dabbing at his mouth politely with his napkin. His posture was exactly what one would expect from a lord—perfectly upright and yet perfectly at ease. No strain to speak of discomfort at the question. No hunch to hint at defensiveness. No leaning forward to denote aggression.

Cayton had called him dangerous. And Ella had no reason to doubt him, but . . . but he did not *seem* dangerous.

Which perhaps made him all the more so.

His smile was gentle. Indulgent, even. "Of course. Perhaps if we are all ready to adjourn back to the drawing room? You look as though you could use a rest, Duchess."

Catherine was the first to push away from the table. "As do I. I'm going to my room."

Now Rushworth went tense. "Kitty—"

"You don't need me, Crispin." She tossed her napkin onto her barely touched plate. "Good night."

The brother sighed as his sister retreated from the room without so much as glancing at anyone. She hadn't said a word all through the meal, and had eaten perhaps one bite for everyone else's five. Ella said a silent prayer for her as she set down her napkin and stood . . . and added one for Brook when her friend's face went even paler upon standing.

Perhaps she should have indulged Stafford's request to get Brook away from all this. Had it just been selfishness on her part to enlist Brook's help in remaining? Ella hadn't thought it so, not when her whole purpose was to relieve her brother of this worry. But maybe she was no better at judging what was helpful than she was at knowing a person's hidden heart.

Lord Rushworth was watching her, a smile upon his lips and his elbow proffered. "May I escort you back to the drawing room, Lady Ella?"

She didn't even discern the danger in this man, who clearly had motives her eyes couldn't see. What did that say about her?

Still, she had no choice but to accept his escort. Though the rest of the party didn't seem to agree. She could feel their stares drilling into her as she tucked her hand into the crook of his arm. "Thank you, my lord."

He darted a quick glance at their scowling companions and led her out of the dining room with a grin. "You would think I had just committed a crime."

She couldn't help but chuckle at that observation. Even if that did earn her even sharper gazes drilling into her back.

Rushworth's eyes positively twinkled as he leaned down just a bit. "I must say, my lady, I didn't realize you would be in Gloucestershire, but a more pleasant surprise I couldn't have devised. I have long wished for the chance to get to know you better."

"Have you?" Not the ladylike response, to be sure, but the shock slipped out. Yes, he had flirted with her last September—once. But it was as unexpected now as it had been then. She would have sworn, had anyone asked her, that Rushworth would have been the type to be annoyed by her personality.

Much like his sister.

Yet his gaze was warm as he continued smiling at her. "I have. Do you know the first time I saw you?"

Ella lifted her brows and tried to think of a ball or fête or soirée they had both attended last season. Her *only* season. "I'm afraid I don't, my lord. I know we were in a few of the same places last year, but . . ."

"It was before that." He drew her down the hall, toward the same room they'd been in before, with Addie and the late Lady Cayton smiling down on them. "At Whitby's house party, before you were out. We weren't introduced, of course,

144

but I was there when you learned that Lady Regan had just accepted Lord Thate's proposal, though your brother was courting her."

That drew her brows together. She remembered the day, of course. The day she had first met Brook. The day the late Duke of Stafford had died and news of it had reached his grandsons. But she certainly didn't recall Rushworth having been nearby. "Forgive me, my lord—I'm afraid all I recall from that day is that announcement itself, and then the sad interruption when the news of the late duke's death reached us."

"Oh, I don't expect you to have noticed me. I had only just returned from the hunt, and . . ." They stepped into the room, and he glanced over his shoulder at the others who were hot on their heels. His smile looked resigned now. "I suppose this is a waste of breath. They would have already prejudiced you against me."

Now what in the world was she to say to that? Assure him that they hadn't—though of course they had? Demur and take the excuse to walk away? Put him in his place with a biting, caustic remark?

She never had perfected the art of the caustic remark though. She could tease with the best of them—it came of having a brother who teased her incessantly—but she suspected none of her scowling friends would much appreciate that reaction.

So she opted for honesty. A smile that was polite but not encouraging, and she slipped her hand from his arm as she said, "I make my own judgements, my lord." Faulty as they may often be. Let him imagine what he would about which she had made here.

His returning smile was a great deal warmer than hers had been. "I expect nothing less from a lady of your caliber." He turned back toward the door as she made for the couch . . .

Though his gaze seemed to snag on her as she moved, and his eyes narrowed.

She had always rather liked her profile, but really—it wasn't *that* intriguing, was it? But when she sent him a questioning look, he merely faced the others, refreshing his smile.

An odd man, to be sure. Ella took a seat on the couch and smoothed the skirt of her evening dress . . . and knew immediate guilt for dwelling on anything so trivial as whether or not Rushworth was enamored with her when Stafford and Whitby entered, Brook sandwiched between them.

She had a hand pressed to her stomach and absolutely no color left in her checks, even as she waved away the buzzing males with an insistent, "I am *well*."

"I knew you should have stayed home." Stafford's face was set in hard lines, and he ignored his wife's attempt to bat him away. "We can finish this conversation another time. Cayton, if you could have our car—"

"I am not ill, nor am I an invalid. I am perfectly capable of having a conversation." She speared Cayton with a glare that said if he obeyed his cousin, he would meet with pains of torment.

Cayton did an admirable job of not smiling. He skirted the edges of the room and perched on a chair on the far side, well away from where Brook sank slowly to a seat beside Ella.

"Are you really all right?" she asked her friend in a murmur.

Brook swallowed. *"Oui. Ça va."*

Ella frowned right along with Stafford and Whitby. When she lapsed into French, it usually bespoke a state other than "all right."

"I'll get right to the point." Rushworth, rather than sitting, stood before the mantel, in nearly the exact place Ella had before the meal. His expression was one of concern, his posture shouting consideration. "I know we have had our differences, cousin, and that you think Kitty and I had a hand in Pratt kidnapping you, that we have a stake in the diamonds—"

"I *think* it?" Brook's nostrils flared, but it didn't seem to be from emotion so much as a more physical feeling. "It goes well beyond my opinion. *Cousin.*"

No anger flashed. From where Ella sat, she saw not a flicker of *anything* in his eyes. Nothing but the same concern. He splayed his hands. "I know I will never convince you otherwise, and I shan't try. Especially since, at this point, I will be quite frank and admit that, yes, I need the diamonds. Not by choice but because of Pratt."

Ella shifted and wished she had opted for a seat on the fringes too.

Stafford folded his arms over his chest. "Even now you will blame it all on him, though he is dead? And is he responsible for stealing from Nottingham last autumn too?"

Now puzzlement dimmed Rushworth's eyes—for a moment, though he shook it off. "If you will allow me to explain. Duchess, did Pratt ever mention to you that he had already found a buyer for the jewels?"

Brook's nod was short, her breathing so even she had to be making an effort to keep it so. "He mentioned . . . a Russian princess."

"Indeed. But I don't suppose he mentioned that he had already accepted partial payment for the jewels?"

Brook pressed her lips together. Stafford gusted out a breath.

Rushworth braced an arm against the mantel. "I still have not been able to ascertain who this buyer is—but his men paid me a visit and made it quite clear that if we do not produce the diamonds in short order, my sister will be held accountable for the promise her husband reneged on." He straightened again, desperation burning now in his gaze. "So you see why I come to you. Doubt all you want about my person and my innocence, but you cannot doubt my care of my sister. You cannot."

"We don't have them." Her voice tight, Brook drew in a slow breath. "I am sorry, Rush. But we honestly don't. Perhaps you should just return the money—"

"Pratt sank it directly into Delmore, which should come as no surprise to anyone who saw the state of the place." He paced toward Cayton, pivoted, came back their way. "Perhaps had we realized before little Byron died and Kitty lost it all, we could have liquidated parts of his estate. But now—I am desperate, cousin. I cannot let harm come to my sister, but I fear what these men will do. And there is simply no way I can pay the debt from my own reserves."

"But we don't have them. And honestly, I haven't a clue where they are now." Brook rose slowly and then blinked too rapidly. "And even if I did—there are holes in your story, Crispin. You say you learned of it *after* your nephew's death. So tell me, why were you willing to steal from Nottingham beforehand?"

His eyes returned to their previous blank state. "I don't know what you mean."

"Then we are at an impasse, *non?*" She strode for the door. *"Excusez-moi. Je . . ."*

Ella leapt to her feet at her friend's first wobble. Stafford and Whitby were right there too, matching panic in their eyes as Brook's frame sagged. She never had a chance of striking the floor, not with her father and husband at her side, but their strong arms didn't keep her head from lolling and her knees from buckling.

Ella pressed a hand to her lips, rushing forward even though she knew well she could do nothing to help. "Brook!"

"Call for the doctor!" Stafford turned his frantic gaze on Cayton. "She needs to lie down."

Cayton was already charging into the hall bellowing, "Mrs. Higgins!"

For there being only five people in the room, the amount of chaos was astounding. Stafford swept Brook into his arms, Whitby swung wide the second of the double doors, both of them speaking at once—Stafford in French and his father-in-law replying in English. The duke charged toward the doors, the earl urging out of the way the servants flying toward them from every direction.

Try as she might to follow, Ella found herself at the rear of the gaggle of concerned people, and she gave up on the attempt to step into the hallway. From the looks of it, every female member of the staff was fluttering around Brook as Stafford carried her up the stairs. They would see she was comfortably situated, and Ella would give them a few minutes to do so before she went up. She would do just as much good down here, praying.

Her eyes slid shut. Her heart opened. Her lips moved as silent words spilled out.

She jumped away when a hand landed on her arm.

Lord Rushworth offered an apologetic smile. "Sorry to startle you, my lady. But you would be in less danger of being bowled over by the servants running about if you prayed in here."

Heat stung her cheeks, though she couldn't have said why. Certainly not at him seeing in a glance that she was praying—but perhaps at not having the sense to remove herself from the middle of the hallway to do it. Servants *were* dashing about, and given the way a particularly expectant one had a hand on the opposite wall to correct her balance, Ella suspected she had nearly collided with her.

Nodding, she let him guide her back into the drawing room

and to her seat. Her gaze on the doorway, Ella knotted her fingers together in her lap . . . and felt a new unease when Rushworth settled beside her.

"I am sure she was simply overtaxed. Had I known she was unwell I certainly never would have asked for this meeting tonight."

His tone was right, filled with humility and concern. But that couldn't negate that, as Brook had pointed out, he was a liar.

Ella must remember that. Must remember that he had tried to steal the Fire Eyes from her home last year, yet had just said he had no motivation for doing so until after that incident. She turned her head to look at him.

His eyes were riveted on her. But not on *her*. He seemed mesmerized by the sway of her earrings as she moved.

Touching a finger to them to stop the ruby pendulum, Ella lifted her brows.

Rushworth smiled and shifted his gaze that slight bit to her eyes. "Forgive me. They suit you so well, the perfect complement to your hair. Am I correct in guessing that they are part of the Nottingham rubies?"

Did he really want to talk about her earrings? It seemed odd . . . especially after a conversation not five minutes before about coveted red diamonds.

But these were just rubies. Not the Fire Eyes. Brice never would have let her borrow the things if they contained the Fire Eyes.

Would he have?

She pasted on a smile. "That's right. My sister-in-law's ears aren't pierced, so I've borrowed them while I may."

But they *weren't* part of the original set—only modeled after them. The original earrings had been stolen when Ella was just a girl. It had been such a big to-do—what with servants dismissed over it and Mama in tears for a solid week—that she still remembered it. Brice had only had the missing pieces redesigned last autumn.

Last autumn. When, by all accounts, he was in possession of the Fire Eyes. Red diamonds long mistaken for rubies . . .

Blast him to pieces! And he *had* tried to stop her from borrowing the earrings the first time, at the ball Rowena had thrown for his birthday in December.

"Well, I cannot imagine them looking any more fetching on any of the duchesses than they look on you, my lady. You've the complexion for them."

Ella brightened her smile and added a prayer to the one still whispering in her heart for Brook that Cayton return to them soon. What would this man do if he were certain she wore the Fire Eyes even now? Bash her upside the head and steal the things from her very ears?

"Thank you, my lord. How kind of you to say." Not knowing what else to do, she slid into the bright bluster that would hopefully blind him to the truth pounding away inside her head. A laugh. A wave of her hand. "I'd begged my mother for years to let me borrow them, but just because I have a habit of misplacing things for a day or two, she always refused. Rowena, however . . . " Here she grinned and darted a glance toward the door. "She is much easier to convince."

"And with fetching results." He leaned back against the cushion, eyes fastened on her face now with the same intensity they had focused on the earrings. "I find it charming that you would try for years to borrow them. I have always admired a person who knows what she wants and persists in her attempts to achieve it."

Never in her life had she felt so shallow and base for wanting to borrow a pretty bauble. "It became a bit of a jest—that's all." Not her initial wanting to borrow them, given that she had exaggerated that, what with the things having been missing most of her life. But since the birthday gala, when she had conveniently forgotten to return them time after time . . . *That* was a jest.

Rushworth smiled. "And I see you *haven't* misplaced them, so your mother's fears were for naught."

She laughed again. And willed Cayton to return. He would, surely. He must. *Someone* must. Surely someone would realize that she'd been left with Rushworth and come to her rescue. Even if they didn't all think him a threat—which they did—it was hardly proper to leave her unchaperoned like this. "In this instance I have proven her fears wrong. But I do confess, my lord, that I am always misplacing things, myself included. Though I maintain that life is more interesting if you allow yourself to get lost now and then. How else do we discover things?"

Something sparked in his eyes, highlighting how empty they usually seemed. "Indeed. Perhaps you should be an adventurer, my lady. Go off to explore what remains of the wilds."

"Perhaps if I didn't adore my family far more than new discoveries." Even if she did have the urge to shake her brother just now and demand some answers.

Though, to be sure, if he realized she was now in company with Rushworth, Brice would likely lock her up in Ralin Castle until he could bully her safely back to Sussex, and then lecture her endlessly on taking care and being reasonable.

"I have often wished to go someplace new. Shake the dirt of this place from my heels and see if perhaps a new locale would suit me better." His gaze went nearly wistful. Which looked odd on him. "Someplace warm and sunny and still a bit untamed."

Ella tilted her head, trying to study him out. "Why not go, then? Perhaps a change of scenery would do your sister some good."

Though she was watching him, she still wasn't quite sure how he managed to shift his bearing so subtly yet so completely. A blink, a movement of his shoulders, and he went from wistful would-be adventurer to a man who all but blended into the upholstery.

Just in time for Cayton to step through the door. "There you are. I would have thought you'd gone up with Brook." Thunder rumbled through his words.

She could have kissed him for giving her an excuse to spring to her feet. "I intended to, but there was so much commotion I thought I'd let her get settled first. How is she? Is she awake?"

Cayton shifted his gaze from her to Rushworth and back again. "Not as of a moment ago. But Dr. Fields is on his way, and apparently Lady Pratt's lady's maid has some experience with midwifery, so she is being found too."

"Midwifery." Rushworth stood, his face going dark. "The duchess is . . . ?"

Cayton lifted his brows.

Rushworth expelled a long breath. "I am merely concerned for how my sister might take such news."

"Well, perhaps you should go and check on your sister while I show Lady Ella to Brook's room."

"An excellent suggestion." He stood, nodded to Cayton, bowed to her. "My lady, it has been a true pleasure to see you again. And I wonder . . . I wonder if you wouldn't consider calling on my sister sometime while we are all in the area. She could do with some laughter and smiles."

Ella's back went stiff even as her brows arched up. "Forgive my bluntness, my lord, but your sister despises me."

His smile would have been charming had Ella not still feared he meant to bash her in the skull and steal her earrings. "Don't take it personally—she despises most everyone at this point."

"She despised me long ago."

He chuckled as he drew near, held out a hand to receive hers. "She used to be a jealous creature, despising any young lady she deemed too beautiful."

"You are too kind." She didn't really mean to put her fingers in his—it was just habit, ingrained for years.

A habit she wished she had broken when he pressed his lips to her knuckles. "I hope you believe so, despite the low motives your friend would ascribe to me."

He lifted his head, gaze tangling with hers, but didn't release her fingers. "As for my sister—she is not who she once was. Perhaps you can help her grow into someone . . . more like you."

Was he acting this way solely because he thought she might have the diamonds? No—he had begun well before he spotted the earrings. Which then begged a new question.

Cayton stepped closer. "If you're done flirting, Rush, Ella needs to be returned to her chaperones." His voice was as hard as ice. As cold as judgment.

Rushworth smirked in the face of it. "By all means."

Ella tucked her hand into the crook of Cayton's elbow when he offered it. But she wondered. She wondered if she dare try to use Rushworth's seeming attraction against him. She wondered if spying on one's brother could possibly prepare one to continue the game when it wasn't a game at all.

And knew without a doubt that every single one of her friends and family would object to her even asking the question.

At least . . . they would if they knew.

# *Eleven*

Cayton led Ella up the stairs and down the family hall, thankful that Mrs. Higgins had brought the Staffords here and not into the guest wing—where Rush was turning. Still, he didn't guide his companion straight to Brook. He instead mumbled something about giving the doctor a moment, since that man was even now trooping up behind them.

But he figured they both knew, as he steered her into what had been Adelaide's sitting room and switched on the light, that Brook had little to do with his thoughts just now, concerned for her as he may be.

He was more concerned for the trouble-finding redhead who spun to take in the room as if she hadn't a care in the world.

"Are you daft? Flirting with him?"

"I was *not* flirting with him—he was flirting with *me*." Clasping her hands behind her back, she wandered toward the wall with the enormous landscape painting hanging upon it. And wrinkled her nose. "You didn't do this one. Rather flat, isn't it?"

It was—and he had once intended to replace it, then didn't see the point after Adelaide's death. No one ever came in here anymore, though his mother had made some mention of putting it to use. If she did, then he would certainly replace the uninspired oil painting. But he would not be distracted with that now, not when Rushworth had been flirting so. "And you don't find that rather odd? Telling, even?"

"That you've allowed such a terrible painting to remain when you're so capable of replacing it with better? I daresay it's more oversight than oddity, but . . ."

"Ella!"

She turned to him again, lips smiling but eyes decidedly not. "You know, it usually takes a much longer acquaintanceship than we've enjoyed for people to feel comfortable chiding me as much as you've done."

That familiar guilt gnawed at him—until he reminded himself that if he was being rude, it was for her own good. "I'll beg if I must. Stay away from him. Please."

"Much as I do enjoy making a man beg . . ." She sashayed back to him, stopping a mere foot away. Close enough that she had to tilt up her face to meet his gaze. "I find it annoying how often I must remind people of this—but I'm not a fool, I'm not a child, and I'm not naïve. I know well that he's flirting with me because he thinks I have a connection to the diamonds."

The logical conclusion . . . but Cayton wasn't so sure. In all the years he'd known Rush, he'd never seen the man flirt. Ever. With anyone. "I highly doubt that's his only reason."

Why did her smile always have to be so quick, so bright? "Careful, my lord. That nearly sounded like a hint of an implied compliment."

Nearly, hint, implied—he snorted a laugh. "I'm not the one who needs to be careful. You acted all night as though he were any other doting suitor, but he's *not*. He's . . . I don't even know what he is, which is rather the point. He shows only what he wants people to see. He is . . . a chameleon. And we must ask why he chose to put on a face of charm tonight. Why he is so set on winning you."

She rolled her eyes and stepped away. "I would hardly call a few flirtatious comments being 'set on winning' me."

"In the decade we have been in society together, he has never once flirted with a young lady like he did with you tonight. Never. Once."

Ella lifted her arms, though her expression was more of frustration than helplessness. "What do you want me to do, Lord Cayton? Snub him? Insult him? Spurn him?"

"Yes. No." If Rushworth's heart *was* involved—odd a thought as that was—they certainly didn't need it broken. Who knew how volatile he might become. Cayton rubbed at the back of his neck and wished he had taken Addie to the Continent for the spring, with Mother. "Why can you not just see the wisdom in going home?"

Her snort shouldn't have sounded ladylike. Shouldn't have been endearing. But it was. At least until she muttered, "I daresay he would follow me."

He hadn't pegged her as quite so proud. "You really are sure of your charms, aren't you."

"What?" She met his gaze again, and hers went . . . amused. Of course. "Hardly. But I . . . I think he believes I have the Fire Eyes."

Cayton crossed his arms over his chest. "Why would he think that?"

"Because I just might." She reached up to her right ear and fiddled with her earring. A moment later she held it in her palm. "What do you think? Could they be in here? He was staring at them . . ."

"And you just . . . Have you no sense?" He spun for the door, checked the hall. It was still abuzz but focused about the room to which they'd taken Brook. No one was paying any heed to them. He pulled the door shut though. "You announce such a thing for anyone to overhear?"

For once, she didn't smile. "Sorry. I'm still frazzled." She held the dangling earrings toward the light and squinted at the jewels. "What exactly do red diamonds look like?"

He could only shake his head. "Why are you wondering such things to begin with? And why in my company? You scarcely know me. I could clobber you over the head and steal them."

"But you won't, because you're an honorable man who is on the correct side in this particular war." She shifted the gold, letting the jewels catch the light. "I'm at least certain of *that*," she added in a low mumble he scarcely caught.

Perhaps he would have made some response to that addition. But a red rainbow shot onto the wall opposite, stealing his attention. Ella didn't seem to notice it though. Not until he sucked in a breath and pointed. "Ella."

Holding her hand still, she looked up and over. Her eyes went wide. Taking in the dance of light, every shade of red from scarlet to jasper. "Well, I guess that answers that question. Have you any helpful advice, my lord, as to what I'm to do now?"

"Go home."

She sent him a glare that said *he* was daft and refastened the earring in her ear. "To my sister-in-law who will be having a baby any day now, you mean? When Lord Rushworth is sure to follow?"

"He couldn't have spotted them so easily." Except that he was probably looking for them everywhere. In every set of rubies, in anything either the Staffords or Nottinghams had touched.

Hope failed to glimmer in her eyes. "Let us pray he didn't. But until I'm sure of that, I'm certainly *not* going home. Brice and Rowena have been through enough since their marriage—they don't need this insanity visiting them again. We'll take care of it here. Now."

Worry redoubled and lodged itself between his ribs. "We?"

Ella planted her hands on her hips. "Would you have me march into that bedroom and hand them to Stafford while his wife lies unconscious?"

"Of course not." But why were they caught so thoroughly in the middle of something of which they had absolutely no part? He sighed and leaned against the door, his ears straining as always for sounds from the nursery. Wondering if the commotion had disturbed Addie.

Wishing Addie were safely in France with Mother.

Taking a deep breath, he whispered, "People have died over these jewels. Far too many of them."

"That's rather my point. I'll not have anyone I love pay that price."

Foolish woman. Another long breath seeped out as he tried to reconcile her figure—all brightness, innocence, and laughter—with the utterly serious look in her eyes. "Have you given any thought at all to the danger *you* will be in?"

She flashed a cheeky smile, but it did nothing to banish the very real shadows in her eyes. Proving that yes, she had thought of it. It just hadn't deterred her. "Let us hope he really does like me, hmm?"

Cayton sighed. "Have Stafford put them in his safe—it's impenetrable. And he won't think anything of it, they being part of the Nottingham rubies."

"You see, I knew you'd be full of logic and sound advice."

He pushed off from the door so he could open it again. Waved her out. "Go to Brook before her father thinks I absconded with you."

Somehow, she managed to chuckle even as she stepped past

him. "Oh yes, can't have that—then we'd be forced to a summer wedding, when I would so prefer September. Addie could carry colorful leaves instead of flower petals. It would be splendid."

He shook his head—and kept his lips firm until she'd slipped out. Then he had to let the smile come, just for a second. He let himself imagine, just for a second, that he could tease and jest and flirt like he used to do. Then he shut his eyes and leaned against the wall. She was too bright, too sunny, too good. Too undeserving of all the heartache that he would inevitably bring.

He would help her figure out how to handle Rush, how to escape this business that had found her. How to keep the Staffords and Nottinghams out of it. Then . . . Then he would bid her adieu. Finish the painting underway in the garret. And let her image on his canvas—and a clear conscience—be enough.

It would have to be. If he held her in any esteem at all, then he must do the right thing and keep himself and the misery he was sure to bring far from her smile. The last thing he wanted to do was dim it with his shadows.

⌘

Kira pressed herself to the wall, out of the way, ready to slip back through the door the moment the duchess's eyelids fluttered open. Which they would do soon, she was sure. So far as Kira had been able to determine, there was nothing really wrong with her that rest wouldn't fix. But of course Brook's husband and father weren't willing to take her word for it. She suspected they wouldn't take the physician's word for it either, though the older man was saying many of the same things she had said.

The doctor now closed his black bag and straightened, patting the duchess's hand. Her breathing hitched, her head moved slowly from side to side. Sure signs that she was rousing. The doctor looked to the duke. "You must see that she rests, Your

Grace. Challenging as I know it will be, she should stay abed for a few days, at the least."

The duke nodded, nostrils flaring. He had barely glanced at Kira as she pressed gently against his wife's abdomen, seeking evidence of a pregnancy gone awry. He barely glanced at the doctor now—his gaze stayed locked on his wife's face. "She was scarcely even sick last time."

"Each pregnancy is different. With this one, she will simply have to take it easy. At least through these first weeks."

The duchess let out a long breath. "How am I to do that with a toddler running about?" Her voice sounded faint, sleepy.

Lord Whitby took the chair the doctor had been in, lifted her hand. "He has a whole team of nursemaids. Lady Ella is here, she can help. And Stafford and I can keep the little imp entertained when he escapes from them. Now. I believe I strictly forbade you from ever scaring me like this again after your *last* bout of unconsciousness."

She turned her head toward her father—toward Kira—but still didn't really open her eyes. "I am only tired. I was dreaming . . . of the ballet. In Monaco."

Kira's cue to beat a hasty exit. She did so with a quick curtsy that no one even looked up to notice, her pulse quickening as she slid out into the hall.

She nearly collided with the redhead—Lady Ella—who laughed and steadied her. "I seem to be running into everyone of late. How is she?"

Kira looked over her shoulder. From here she could only see the housekeeper wringing her hands, not the duchess. "Coming to. Excuse my clumsiness, my lady. But I had better get back to my mistress."

Lady Ella tilted her head. "You must be Lady Pratt's maid—the midwife?"

"Daughter of one, but *da*." She dipped another quick curtsy. "Sophie Lareau."

The lady's brow creased. "Did Lady Pratt hear why you were being called to assist the duchess? Is she all right?"

Kira pulled out a small smile and fastened it into place. Given Lady Pratt's mutters after she returned to her chamber, the two women were certainly not friends. But Lady Ella's concern looked genuine—and appropriate. "She did not hear, thankfully. But I daresay she will be distressed when she does."

"I guessed as much. I understand she always compared herself to her cousin, so to see her not only with a healthy son but to know another child is on the way . . ." The lady shook her head and focused her gaze on the doorframe. Then she reached out to touch a hand briefly to Kira's wrist and leaned close. "Ask her . . . She will refuse, but if you would ask her to join me for tea in the village tomorrow. I'll come to call at two, if she wants to join me."

Kira bobbed her head. "I will tell her. Although . . ."

"I know." With a sigh, Lady Ella stepped away again. "She has never liked me and is not likely to begin now. But I do appreciate you giving her the invitation, Lareau. Thank you."

Kira offered a tight-lipped smile, another dip of her knees, and sped away while the lady entered. She needed to get herself—and her voice—far away from the duchess before the woman realized it was more than a dream of the ballet, that it was memory.

When she'd left Lady Pratt fifteen minutes earlier, the lady had already climbed into bed, claiming exhaustion from the travel. But a bar of light seeped out from beneath her chamber door, and voices came from within. Kira paused outside it and listened for a moment.

Lord Rushworth. His voice was hushed, but she caught a few words. "Certain . . ." and ". . . jewels."

Her pulse picked up. This was the first she had heard anything promising drop from their lips. Perhaps she could—

"Lareau, if that's you hovering outside the door, just come in."

She straightened and made mental note of the lord's powers of observation. She would have to be careful indeed. For now, she entered with her head down and a polite curtsy ready. "Pardon me. I only thought to check on Lady Pratt."

She was still in her bed, sitting up against her pillows with a scowl aimed at her brother, who had taken the chair by the window. "I was quite well until Cris decided to wake me up."

Rushworth scowled right back. "You were wallowing, not sleeping."

"And you are irritating, not helping me." The lady flicked a gaze to Kira. "I don't need anything. You can go away, and you can take my brother with you."

Something went hard in Lord Rushworth's eyes. He leaned back in his chair, hooked an ankle casually over the opposite knee, but there was nothing relaxed about his expression. "Before I share our cousin's happy news?"

Kira took a step forward before she could think not to, a hand up. As if she had any power to object—but she could not help herself. "My lord, please. Lady Pratt does not need to hear that right now."

"Lady Pratt needs to learn that life goes on."

The lady looked from her to Lord Rushworth, suspicion making her eyes even greener. "What? Is she . . . is she with child again?"

The curl of Rushworth's lips sent a shiver up Kira's spine. He made a noise that was caught halfway between a grunt and a laugh. "If it helps, she's so unwell from it that she just passed out."

"How in the world would that help?" The lady pulled her blanket higher. "Go away. Both of you."

Her brother didn't budge. "Life goes on, Kitty. If you would look beyond your pain for half a moment, you would see that. Remarry. Have other children. Put Pratt and his son behind you."

Gripping the blanket until her knuckles went white, Lady Pratt ground out, "*His* son was *my* son. Your nephew. How can you speak this way? How can you . . . how . . . *how*?"

"The better question is how *you* can be ready to give up on life. After all we have been through, all we suffered, what is this but one more obstacle? We can overcome it, Kitty. We can—if you but determine to try. Get out of bed, out of your room, and *do* something now and again."

Lady Pratt tugged the blanket up to her chin. "What am I to do? I have no real friends. No one who understands. No one who even wants to spend time with me. Everyone I once knew has gone on with their lives while I . . . I am adrift."

Kira cleared her throat. "Lady Ella has just invited you to join her for tea in the village tomorrow, my lady. She says she knows you will hesitate to accept, but she truly hopes you will."

Though Lady Pratt looked ready to snarl, Rushworth put both feet on the floor and sat forward, his eyes brighter than Kira had ever seen them. "She'll go."

His sister sighed. "Crispin—"

"Please, Kitty." That particular tone in Rushworth's voice was new, and interesting. A form of pleading Kira had never heard from him, but which sounded . . . vulnerable. "I have never asked you to befriend a young lady for my sake. But I'm asking now."

Lady Pratt stared at him for a long moment. "I don't know what you see in that insipid hoyden."

He winced, no doubt at her choice of words—*insipid hoyden*. Though Kira was unfamiliar with their meaning, the idea came through clearly enough. Lord Rushworth shook his head. "I do not really know what it is about her that intrigues me—but I would like the opportunity to find out. And that is far more likely to happen if you can convince her that you're not the villainess that her brother and our cousin would have told her you are."

"A tall order, brother." And one she didn't look up to handling. She slid lower into her bed and turned her back on Rushworth. "Have it your way. I'll go to tea. But beyond that, I make no promises."

Rushworth looked about to say more, but then he glanced at Kira. He nodded, stood. "It is a start. Good night, Kitty. Lareau."

Kira stepped aside to let him slip out the door, but she didn't immediately follow. She hovered there a moment, wishing she knew what to say to ease this woman's pain. Wishing she could do even a bit of the good Lord Rushworth seemed to think she could. Wishing, too, she could just find the information Andrei needed and get back to Paris, leaving this broken family to their own woes.

She had plenty of her own to contend with.

Lady Pratt pushed back onto her elbow and focused her gaze on Kira. "When did you see Lady Ella?"

"Outside the room where they took the duchess. I mentioned to one of the maids here that my mother trained me in midwifery, so . . ." And why did she feel as though she should apologize?

"Is the duchess all right?"

It was the first time Kira had heard the woman ask about anyone else. Odd, given that all evidence pointed to her not getting along with Brook. She edged closer to the bed. "She will have to stay abed for a few days, at least."

Lady Pratt breathed what might have been a laugh. "She'll hate that."

"*Da.*" When she'd known her in Monaco, the girl had been always racing from one thing to another—from the ballet to the palace, escaping her guards, taming wild horses. Not that Kira could admit to knowing that. "That is what her father and the duke said."

The lady sighed. "And Lady Ella. How did she seem when she issued this bizarre invitation?"

That Kira could answer with no hesitation. "Concerned for you, my lady. And genuine."

Lady Pratt rolled onto her back, her gaze on the ceiling. "She is either out for information or . . . or actually interested in Crispin. Which would be odd, given her brother's opinion of us. Unless she is the rebellious type, I suppose. Is she, do you think?"

Kira spread her hands, shrugged. "I saw her for but a few seconds. Spoke but those few words."

"Well, I suppose I shall find out tomorrow, shan't I."

"Indeed." And Kira could be alone in Lady Pratt's room, able to poke through all her things, as she hadn't had time to do tonight. Able to find whatever information on the diamonds she might have. She smiled. "Indeed you shall."

## Twelve

Ella slid into a chair at the small table draped in white linen, telling herself to look around her rather than at her companion. The tea room wasn't nearly as grand as the ones in London to which she was permitted to slip away unchaperoned—no orchestra, no dancing, no high-arching windows. But it was lovely, all fair, bright colors and copious amounts of light, and Brook had assured her when she first arrived that the food was delicious and the establishment well-respected.

And so, Brook hadn't batted an eye from her chaise when Ella had said she would take tea here this afternoon. Brook never thought to wonder at someone wanting a taste of independence. Whitby, on the other hand, had narrowed his eyes at her and had been about to ask more questions when little Abingdon had saved the day by squealing his way into the room, having escaped from his nurse. Again.

And now, across the table from her, Catherine released a sigh that begged to have attention paid to it, so ripe was it with incredulity. She looked around with what seemed to be a critical eye. "I have not been to a tea room in a year or more. I used to love the Corner House in London."

167

Ella smiled. "We always favored the one at Fenchurch."

"Of course you did."

It was, at least, the Catherine she'd expected to see. Caustic, cold, calculating—and slightly less disturbing than the broken one she'd seen last night. Though Ella did have to wonder why she had accepted the invitation when she clearly didn't want to be here.

Catherine turned back to their table, her stare going blank again as she took in the cups and plates and silver. "I'm really not hungry."

"An excellent excuse to have nothing but tea and cake, then." When a young woman approached with a smile and a request for their order, Ella took the liberty of ordering for them both. If left to Catherine, she suspected they would have gotten up and gone.

Once the waitress breezed away, Ella looked at her companion until Catherine actually glanced up from her napkin and met her gaze. "Why did you agree to come?"

"Foregoing niceties, are we?" Catherine leaned back against her chair and studied her with pursed lips. "My brother begged. He likes you."

Ella shook her head. *"Why?"*

A hint of a smile touched the corner of Catherine's mouth. "That's what I asked him. I never would have thought he'd fall for someone like . . . *you.*"

Perhaps she would have taken offense, had she not completely agreed. "I daresay it isn't me he likes. He no doubt thinks I can get him the diamonds." There—her cards on the table.

Catherine didn't so much as blink out of turn. "You would think so. But no. Perhaps he likes your good humor, annoying as some of us find it. He certainly never saw much of such a thing in our home." She tilted her head in a way Ella had seen her do before. Previously it had struck her as a cat studying a mouse. Today it looked like but an imitation. "But is that why you invited me? To talk about the jewels?"

"No." Ella unfolded her napkin from its seashell shape and smoothed it over her lap. "I know I cannot understand your loss. And that I'm not a likely friend in any case. But you're hurting. And I thought . . ." What *had* she thought? She'd lain awake half the night wondering. Convincing herself it wouldn't matter, that Catherine wouldn't even come. Yet here they were, and the question still had no answer. She could only breathe a prayer and see what words slipped out. "I thought perhaps it would help to get out for an afternoon. To be distracted with thoughts of how much you dislike me."

The woman's laugh sounded like a minor victory—even if it *was* at her own expense. "Thoughtful of you."

"You'll find I'm as thoughtful as I am annoying."

Catherine watched her for a long moment, amusement still playing around the corners of her mouth. Then she shook her head. "Perhaps you're not quite as vacuous as I thought. Though let's be honest—he can't possibly stand a chance with you, can he? Not hating us as your family does."

Ella shifted and willed the tea to arrive soon. She could just imagine what Brice would think if he saw her now. Or Brook and Stafford and Whitby, for that matter. "Honestly, my lady, I scarcely know him."

"I suppose you know Cayton much better, then."

Ella froze, not so much as lifting her brows. "Pardon?"

Catherine's chin tilted up just slightly, and her eyes hardened. Strange as it seemed, it brought a measure of relief. This was the Catherine whom Ella had met before. "You did quite a good job of flirting with our host at dinner. Granted, flirting with Cayton has always been an easy task, but I was under the impression that he's closed himself off since Adelaide's death. I daresay you're wasting your time there."

Ella grinned. "Not if my goal is merely to torment him with it. He has been so deliberately rude to me that I *must* flirt just to offset it."

Catherine shook her head. "As good a reason as any, I suppose. Though personally, I always preferred to do it because it irritated *Stafford*."

The waitress headed their way, wheeled cart before her and a casual smile upon her lips. Conversation halted while the girl set out their teapot and sugar and cream, the tiered tray filled to bursting with sweets. She left again with a promise to check on them in a few minutes.

Ella selected a scone and pulled close the pot of clotted cream. "Shall you pour or shall I?"

With a sigh, Catherine reached for the teapot. "Strong or weak?"

"Strong. Thank you. Biscuit?"

"No. Thank you."

Silence could be a pleasant thing, when one shared it easily with someone. This one was taut and unwieldy, and Catherine showed no signs of being inclined to break it. Ella took a nibble from her scone, waited for her cup of tea, and then set it down silently upon her saucer after she'd tested a sip. "Why does he lie?"

Now it was Catherine who froze, her fingers resting gracefully upon the lid of the pot. She could have been a still life painted upon Cayton's canvas. "Pardon?"

"Your brother." Ella trailed a finger along the gold-leafed rim of her cup. "He stood in the drawing room last night and told us he only wants the jewels to save you from the buyer who had already made a payment to your husband. We all know that's a lie, given the lengths to which the two of you went last year, before he supposedly learned of this. When you took advantage of Stella, called upon a monster from my sister-in-law's past, and nearly caused the deaths of two people who matter more to me than anyone." She delivered it coolly, evenly. She gave herself kudos for that, when it all raged inside as so much more than words.

"You want *honesty*?" Catherine leaned forward, closing the space between them. "I want nothing to do with those jewels anymore. They have taken everything from me. *Everything*. Perhaps I once thought they were worth it, but . . ." Tears clouded her throat and her eyes. "Your sister-in-law is right. The curse is more than a fable. And if I could end its hold on my family by letting this buyer kill me, I would. If it would settle the debts, settle the score, put an end to it all . . ." She shook her head, nostrils flaring. "But it wouldn't. Nothing will. He'll not stop—he'll *never* stop."

Ella's throat went tight. "The buyer . . . or your brother?"

A little snort of breath, a little closer in her lean. "Both, I daresay. You don't understand, Lady Ella. You *can't* understand. It's his only way out of this prison our father made for us. Me, I can get away through marriage, I can distance myself from the name. He can't. He is trapped there forever, in that horrid little house with all the terrible memories."

Ella's stomach went as tight as her throat. "How will the Fire Eyes change that?"

Now sorrow drenched Catherine as she sat up a bit, but with stooped shoulders. "It won't. But he cannot see that. I couldn't either, before. They would bring so very much money, you see. He thought if he could just use it to leave England, to get away from all this . . ." She shook her head. "I thought that was the answer too. But it follows you. It will always follow you, until it takes every single blessed thing you ever loved and destroys it."

Ella reached for her tea again, took another fortifying sip, and prayed for wisdom. For the right words. For insight. "If his goal is to leave England, why does he not just . . . go?"

Catherine tilted the pot over her cup with a sigh. "With what means? He just spent all our spare funds on that ridiculous trip to Paris—I told him we oughtn't to have, but he . . . It is my own fault, I suppose. I used to say how much I longed to go there. He thought it would help—as if anything can make me forget my empty arms."

The tea trickled warm and soothing down Ella's throat. She drew in a careful breath and noted the lady's clothing—well made, in the height of fashion, if a bit loose on her frame. "Forgive me, my lady, but . . . neither of you seem to be what one would call shabby." They were both, however, what one would call loose with the truth. How much of this was just a story designed to ignite pity?

It didn't feel that way. Which was either proof of the insight she had prayed for . . . or of the bad judgement she desperately prayed against.

Catherine added a cube of sugar to her cup and stirred. "Let me try to explain this to you. My great-grandfather committed the ultimate crime in the eyes of society—he let his debts get so far out of hand that he lost the family estate. He was forced to sell it to cover those debts and had barely enough left over to purchase the miserable little box we've called home since."

Ella set her cup back down. For an earl to sell his familial lands—that *was* terrible, especially in the century past. "I imagine that made things difficult for your family."

Catherine set the spoon on its rest but didn't lift her cup to drink. "They could only dig in. Tighten the purse strings. Live a quiet country life."

"There are worse things. North Yorkshire is beautiful—"

"A place can only be as lovely as the people with whom one lives." Green eyes going distant, Catherine wrapped her arms around her middle. "And my family never cared for anything but regaining what they'd lost. At whatever cost. Father was . . ." She paused, muscle ticking in her jaw. "There are no kind words to describe him. I daresay he was never a nice man, but after Uncle Henry came home with those cursed diamonds, after Pratt's father was killed when he had to renege on the deal he had struck with a buyer, when Henry ran off again . . . That is the only father I ever knew. Cold, cruel, and entirely fixated on how he'd been cheated."

Only when she felt a prick of pain did Ella realize she was digging her fingernails into her palms. "He sounds a bit like Rowena's father."

"I know. She came to me last year, thinking to commiserate—but thinking it Crispin who was the cruel one." Catherine shook her head, though her eyes remained hazy. "He is the only reason I did not spend my childhood bruised. He always took the punishment for me. Always. He protected me."

"I daresay that explains why he is so distressed now at seeing you close yourself off."

Catherine blinked and focused her eyes again—on the table. "The best day of our lives was when our father died. And yet, we still couldn't escape. Crispin was then Lord Rushworth, forever tied to that miserable estate. To the stain on the family name. He cannot escape it, not so long as he's in England."

Ella forced her fingers to relax. "And so, he wants to leave. Why not do it then? Sell the estate and go?"

No hint of amusement brightened the breath of laughter.

"Sell our estate for the second time in so few generations? It would bar England to him forever, yet not fetch enough to make a good enough life anywhere else. He needs more than it would bring, a windfall."

He could settle for a smaller home, a quieter life—but that was obviously not an option in Lord Rushworth's mind. And she supposed she could understand that. If he had received the brunt of his father's anger, all over their lack of means, then the last thing he would want would be to slide further into poverty.

Not noble motivation—but understandable. Ella drew in a slow breath, released it. "What if I can find them—the jewels? Should I give them to him?"

Brook would have screamed at her in three languages. Brice would have looked at her with horror and forced her from the room. But she had to know how Catherine would respond.

She shook her head wildly. "Are you daft? I'll not lose him too. I won't. He is all I have left, but—even *seeking* these awful diamonds has destroyed us. What would touching them do?" She leaned close again, voice hushed but feverish. "I've lost my husband. My . . . my child. I'll not lose my brother to them. I won't. You must promise never to tell him if you know where they are. Don't ever let them near him. Please. I know I have no right to ask you for anything, but *please*."

Not a game. Not a trick. As Ella looked into Catherine's desperate green eyes, she was entirely certain that this woman everyone assumed to be the driving force behind the search for the Fire Eyes was genuine right now. This woman who had been willing to turn their lives upside-down last year had seen how wrong she'd been.

This woman could be the strangest but truest ally they had. Ella pitched her voice low. "But what if he thinks I'm his best chance at getting them?"

The life, the energy that had lit Catherine's eyes during her plea drained away into dejection. "No." She rose from her seat, stumbling a bit on her first step. "Excuse me. I-I can't."

"Lady Pratt, wait." Ella paused only to toss money on the table to cover their unenjoyed tea and then hurried after her. She didn't catch up until she had emerged into the weak, watery spring sunshine. Catherine was trudging along the quiet village street, aimed not at the borrowed Stafford car that had driven them there through the afternoon drizzle, but rather back toward Anlic Manor, whose chimneys were just visible at the top of the rise. Ella hurried after her, waving away the chauffeur who had come to attention. She touched a hand to the lady's elbow as she drew near. "What will he do?"

Catherine didn't look at her, just shook her head. "Anything. You had better pray he is more than fascinated with you—if he loves you, perhaps you have a chance. Otherwise . . ."

Otherwise *what*? Though Catherine's pace increased, Ella matched her. "Catherine. What will he do?"

Strange how well the shaky laugh paired with the tears Catherine wiped away. "You don't know him. No one really knows him. My brother . . . he can be anything. He can be the kindest, sweetest man in the world, and if he loves you . . . If he loves you, he will give up his own life for you. You could be happy by his side if he loves you, Lady Ella. He would make himself into exactly what you needed. He would give you quiet when you needed quiet, laughter when you were down, he would take you to the grandest balls if you craved a crowd. He would do absolutely anything to make you happy, and doing so would make *him* happy. He would be a good husband."

Ella sidestepped a puddle, knowing her mouth was agape. "Are you quite serious? After warning me that he would do anything to get the diamonds, you try to convince me to *marry* him?"

"It is your best hope. Love him, and you'll be saved from hating him. Saved from fearing him."

It was a good thing she had taken no more than a bite of the scone—it may have threatened to abandon her stomach otherwise. "Do *you* fear him?"

Catherine looked over at her as though thinking she were daft. "Were you not listening? I don't *have* to fear him—I love him. We have shared the same horrors, the same hopes. It is just—losing a nephew is apparently not quite like losing a son. He cannot grasp that pain. He cannot understand where it has led me, but . . . but he is still my brother. My protector. And now . . ." She sniffed, lifted her skirt an inch or two, and sped up still more. "Now I must protect him. I can't let him destroy himself with the Fire Eyes. I *can't*."

"Catherine." They were slogging up the hill now, along the road, the sidewalk having ended three steps back. Mud sucked at Ella's shoes—not the ones she would have chosen had she expected a walk through the countryside—and the pale green of her tea gown would surely be brown at the hem before they reached Anlic. "What. Will. He. *Do*?"

Catherine sped up still more. "Unleash the monster. And no one wants that—trust me. We have to stop him. Convince him that you *don't* know where they are, that you cannot help him find them. Make him fall in love with you, distract him from this. It could work. I've never seen him take such interest in a young lady, and if anything can make him forget the diamonds, it is love. You're the type not to care about trappings, are you not? You won't care that our estate is struggling."

She may be their strangest, truest ally, but Ella was beginning to question Catherine's sanity. "You seem to be overlooking one vital bit of information—if he was telling the truth about this buyer to whom you owe money, he will *not* stop, no matter what. Even if he *did* fall in love with me"—an absolutely terrifying thought—"it would certainly not replace his love for you, and his need to protect you from this man. Unless he was lying. Unless there is no such man, that there has been no threat."

Catherine's step faltered. Her profile showed eyes squinting in thought, quivering lips. "I . . . I don't know. The buyer is certainly impatient—he has long been so. That is why last fall we . . . but since then, everything has been such a blur."

"He said that Pratt accepted money from the buyer—a good faith deposit—but that he sank it into Delmore."

Catherine's expression went even more thoughtful. "It sounds right. I don't know. If he did receive funds, they would have gone straight into the estate, everything did. Cris hated that. He hated Delmore nearly as much as he hated Rushings, but it was all Pratt thought about. He intended to use his portion of the money from the diamonds to finally finish renovating the place. Cris thought him a fool for that. Thought me one for wanting to marry a man just as obsessed with his estate as our father had been, but . . . but I loved him. I'd always loved him."

The wind brought a sweet, flowery scent to Ella's nose. The mud sucked at her shoes, and a bird twittered from the trees. She gripped her skirt, trying to make sense of it all. But her mind kept going back to those three words Catherine had rushed over. *"Unleash the monster."*

Cayton was obviously right—Rushworth was dangerous. The kind of dangerous that hid itself behind an unobtrusive personality and polite smiles. The kind kept carefully reined in until it suited him to let it loose. The kind that never showed itself in the man's eyes.

What was she to do? He knew more than that she knew the

location of the diamonds—he knew she *had* them. What was to keep him from kidnapping her as Pratt had Brook? Threatening to kill those she loved if she didn't hand them over?

Anlic Manor stood sentry at the crest of the hill, near enough now that she caught the bite of smoke from its chimneys. Inside those honeyed-stone walls, Rushworth no doubt waited for his sister's return, eager for an update on how tea went. And what would he say, what would he do if his sister returned in her current state, muddied and obviously distressed?

The breeze was cool but not responsible for the shiver that stole up Ella's spine. She moistened her lips and settled her gaze on the bare traces of a path into the woods. "Would you walk with me a little longer, my lady? I cannot help but think it would not serve us well to return to Lord Cayton's home upset."

Catherine sucked in a breath, huffed it out. "I suppose you have a point. Where shall we go? I am unfamiliar with the area."

Ella nodded toward the path. "Onto that path through the wood for a bit? I daresay it winds back around to the manor." Or to the river. Or perhaps even to the castle a mile distant, how was she to know? But the trees were not so dense that they would get lost in them, and the hour was early.

Catherine sent her an arched look. "That is not a path. It is at best a deer trail."

"Nonsense. That is what all the paths look like in this wood. I have explored many of them from Ralin Castle." She took off toward the trees with an open stride.

Catherine followed, though she lagged a few steps behind. "I am not one of those who enjoys traipsing through the forest, Lady Ella. And we're going to ruin our shoes."

"The damage is already done there, I daresay." And plunging into the cool green beneath the trees' canopy brought a return of peace, of hope, to her spirit. "Though that does remind me of my initial observation, which you never answered. How, if you live on such a budget, are your clothes always the height of fashion?"

"Come, Lady Ella, think it through. What is a gentle family's best hope of increasing their means—aside from priceless diamonds, of course?"

There it was—that same tone everyone always used with her, as if she were a child. Ella sent what she hoped was a quelling glare over her shoulder. "Marriage, but I fail to see—"

"And how does one attract a well-to-do spouse, if not by appearing to be well-to-do oneself?" Catherine waved a hand. "The wardrobes are an investment. Carefully calculated in order to present a certain image that is meant to result in *more* means. To convince society that the Rushworths have rebounded from what nearly ruined us."

"Right." Why was so much of life careful calculations and masks to hide the truth? She shook her head and focused on stepping over a fallen branch without its wily fingers snatching at her dress. Then she had to pause to await Catherine, who looked for a long moment as if that small obstacle might deter her altogether.

But at length she sighed and stepped over.

They moved in silence for a minute or two, this one not so heavy and awkward as the one in the tea room. But this one was moderated by birds singing and the crunch of leaves underfoot, the gentle rustle of the breeze through the newly-green ones above.

The path curved to the left, rolling gently down the hill. Ella followed.

Catherine cleared her throat. "How is Brook this morning? My brother said that last night, she . . ."

He had told her? Ella's brows drew together. But her tone of voice hadn't sounded angry or distressed. Just concerned—and trying not to be. "I was unaware that you cared about her well-being, Lady Pratt. If stories of your history can be trusted, you wish her ill rather than well."

"I do vaguely recall having energy for such trifling rivalries. But these days . . ." Catherine's sigh seemed to go on forever as the wind took it and echoed it. "I handled it all so poorly, just assuming she would be an enemy, like everyone else. Assuming it would always be me and Cris against the world. Had I just told her at the start what we were looking for and why—she would have thought it an adventure. She would have helped. Had I not forced her to hate me, I daresay she would have handed them over willingly."

"She doesn't hate you." Not that they'd ever spoken of it outright, but Ella knew Brook. "She is still hurt by your betrayal though. She thought you the closest of her new friends, and then . . ."

"I know." Catherine didn't sound remorseful or contrite, nor callous or stony. She sounded simply . . . tired. All the more so as the silence stretched again for a long moment. Then, "You didn't answer me. How is she?"

Ella sighed. "Poorly enough that she didn't argue at the command to stay abed—what does that tell you?" She glanced over her shoulder.

Catherine's brows had knit. "Is she . . . is she in danger of losing the child?"

"The doctor didn't think so. He will watch her carefully, of course, but he seemed certain that this was normal, and she simply must take it easy."

Catherine nodded, but that news didn't seem to ease *her* any.

The slope of the path grew more distinct, and Ella faced forward again to better keep her footing, ignoring the mumbles of discontent from behind her. Just ahead the trail forked, luring a smile back to Ella's lips. Which way to choose?

Her feet pulled her to the left, and after a dozen more steps the gurgle of water reached her ears. She didn't know how far this part of the river was from the one she had discovered yesterday, but she was far more ready to enjoy the view with the sun staking its dominance in the sky.

"Mind your step. Part of the path seems to have washed away over there." Catherine had lifted her skirts another inch, which only served to reveal that her shoes and stockings were thoroughly muddied.

"So it has." Ella lifted her skirts a little higher as well, and kept her eyes focused on the path in the search for drier or stonier spots.

A wink of light caught her attention and drew her feet toward the river. It came again as the leaves overhead shifted. Sunlight on metal, it seemed. "Do you see that?"

"Probably just a tin can or buckle washed ashore."

Probably. "Or treasure, lost by some highwayman of ages past. No doubt it's a ring to put those Fire Eyes to shame. A crown, pilfered from a visiting monarch."

Catherine breathed another laugh, though the victory of this one was swallowed up in curiosity as Ella drew nearer to the glinting metal.

It was a button—a row of them. Attached to . . . Her feet came to a quick halt. Not just buttons, a whole jacket, brown as mud and frazzled and frayed and . . .

"Oh, my goodness." Catherine grabbed her arm, pulled her back a step. "Don't. Don't go any nearer."

The earth was streaked all around, washed away here, piled up there, debris clustered where it was left by an overflowing ditch on its way to the river. But those familiar signs meant nothing. Not when her eyes followed their path up the row of buttons and to something whitish-grey, partially visible beneath a pile of rotted leaves.

Catherine must have spotted it at the same moment. Her fingers dug into Ella's arm, they both stumbled back. They both sucked in a breath and, as one, released it in a scream to shatter the sunshine.

## Thirteen

Cayton dropped the paintbrush onto the floor and dashed from the room as the sound pierced his consciousness, barely registering what it was or where it came from—aware only of the desperation and terror within it. He'd had the window open to receive the cool breezes and golden sunlight, and it brought the screams to him without hindrance.

The river. That was where they had come from. He flew down the stairs, praying with every footfall that it wasn't Tabby, that she hadn't taken Addie down there for an afternoon game. That his daughter hadn't fallen into the swollen waters. *Not that, Lord. Please, anything but that.*

"What is it?"

He noted, vaguely, the other steps falling in behind him, matching his sprint. Rushworth—that was the voice, but his weren't the only steps. There was a veritable horde of them following in his wake as he tore through the trees toward the continuing screams. He hadn't explored this edge of the property very much, always preferring to go the opposite direction toward the pond, but his feet either found or forged a path, heading ever toward that cry.

Not Tabby. That realization had settled at some point as he ran, but his feet didn't slow. Couldn't, not when his mind's eye began to piece together a different image. Red hair, fair skin, cider-brown eyes. But what would Ella be doing here? Had she wandered the mile from Ralin, on foot? On horseback it would be an easy ride. She could have fallen, broken something.

"Ella!" What was it about that girl, that she could not stay out of trouble? But he would have preferred a thousand times to track her through the rain, knowing that a soaking was the worst she could find, than this. Hearing her scream. Knowing that whatever it was, the danger must be real.

"Cayton?" Never in his life had the uttering of his name sounded so terrified, so ragged. He followed the sound of it past another stand of trees, ducked away from a bramble, and spotted the beacon of her hair. She stood by the swollen river, beside—for a moment he thought it Brook, but no. Catherine.

"Kitty! Lady Ella!" Rushworth surged to Cayton's side.

Catherine stood frozen in her place, face as pale as the clouds scuttling away overhead, gaze latched on a spot about five feet ahead of them.

Ella pulled away from her and ran toward them. Her expression of horror was one he had never bothered imagining on her face, so ill did it fit there where laughter should reign. She pressed a hand to her mouth, but it did nothing to muffle the sob.

A step away from him, her foot snagged on a tree root. He caught her, prepared to put her back on her feet, but she gripped his lapels and held on tight, burying her face in his chest in a way not unlike how Addie did when she wanted to hide from a stranger.

He didn't feel nearly the same though, holding her to him. The scent of lilacs came to his nose from her hair, and her back heaved with silent sobs under his hands. "What happened? What is it?"

Her grip tightened. "There's a-a *body*."

Gregory sidled past them, his face a web of wrinkled anxiety. "I'll have a look. Keep the ladies back, milord."

Rushworth followed the groom. "I'll bring my sister away." Yet it was Ella to whom his gaze returned, at least for a few steps, before the roots and mud demanded his attention.

Cayton's hands pressed harder against Ella's back. He wanted to ask her what she was doing in his wood, with Catherine. What she had seen. Whether she clung so tightly only because his were the arms that had caught her or if it were something more.

He said nothing. Just held her and kept his gaze on Gregory's progress.

As the groom stepped toward where Catherine's gaze was locked, Rushworth reached his sister, taking her by the hand and tugging.

She wouldn't budge, and her brother apparently decided he would do more good standing by her side than forcing her somewhere.

Gregory halted, sucked in a breath, and stooped down. He brushed at the leaves, scooped aside mud. Looked up, across the distance between them, to catch Cayton's gaze. "Anlic livery, milord."

"No." His eyes slid shut and clamped tight. There weren't that many in his employ who wore livery. And only one who had vanished in the last year. "Is it Stew?" *Please, Lord, not Stew.*

The very thought, the realization of how it would devastate Felicity—it didn't bear considering. But who else could it be? Unless someone had stolen a jacket at some point, but what were the chances of that?

The air tasted foul and thick. It made breathing a chore.

"Hard to say. There's . . . not much left. If you gentlemen will take the ladies inside and call for the constable, Ronald and I will guard the area."

Ronald? Cayton opened his eyes again and looked over to find that, indeed, Gregory's grandson had followed them down and now stood, pale and wide-eyed, a few strides away. "Ronald . . . you don't have to stay here. You can take the ladies up, and I will—"

"No, milord. I can handle it." As if to prove it, Ronald swallowed, lifted his head, and trudged toward his grandfather.

Ella shifted against him, tilted her face up. A shudder stole through her. "Who is Stew?" Her voice had the sound of an unused hinge, rusty and laborious.

He should release her now, since her grip had relaxed. But he couldn't quite yet. "Husband to one of the maids—Felicity. She was Adelaide's oldest friend and lady's maid, niece of Mrs. Higgins, my housekeeper. She . . . she is with child. Due in another month or so, I think."

Ella's lashes fluttered down, shuttering her expressive eyes against his gaze. "I think I saw her last night. Her husband is missing?"

"We all thought he had run off, scared at the thought of being a father. I don't think she ever believed that. But it would be better than this."

"Poor girl." Her head hung, her shoulders were sloped. She released his lapels suddenly, as if just realizing she'd had hold of him, and took a step backward. "Excuse me, my lord. I didn't mean—"

"You needn't apologize, Lady Ella. Not now." Were it a lighter reason that had landed her in his arms for the second time, he would have waited for a jest, a tease, some comment about forcing him to the altar.

As it was, letting go of him only resulted in her wrapping her arms around herself and pressing her lips together.

Cayton looked over her head, to the Rushworth siblings. "Rush, Lady Pratt—come. We need to notify the authorities."

This time Catherine didn't resist when her brother pulled on her, though her gaze remained locked on that spot beside Gregory for a long moment. She pressed a hand to her stomach as she came their way.

Rushworth was studying Lady Ella again, though she didn't look up to see it. Cayton got the distinct impression that had Catherine not been there, holding tight to his arm, Rushworth would have been fawning over Ella.

Cayton curled his fingers into his palm. Why now, of all times, did Rush have to take an interest in someone? And why *her*? Not that Cayton had any intention of fostering that spark that had lit in his veins before Melissa had reminded him of what a disaster he was, but was it not enough that he had to protect her from himself? Now he must protect her from his supposed friend too. He must; it was his responsibility.

Because if it weren't for Cayton, Rushworth never would have come to the Cotswolds. If it weren't for Cayton, Ella would not have visited last night, wearing the Fire Eyes. If it weren't for Cayton, she certainly wouldn't have just stumbled upon a body on Anlic land.

He touched a hand to her elbow to urge her up the path toward the house. "How did you happen upon such a thing, my lady? Did you walk here from Ralin?"

It took her a long moment and a dazed hum before she turned her face up to look at him. Her blink did little to bring her eyes back into focus. "I . . . no. No, the chauffeur may still be in the village. Perhaps. I went for tea. With Lady Pratt."

"You . . ." But what could he say, just now? It was hardly the time to chastise her for the company she kept—not with her in such a fright and the lady in question but a few steps behind. "Let's get you inside, hmm? You can rest for a few minutes, have another cup of tea, perhaps. I'll fetch the chauffeur after I've rung for the constable."

She made no response. Not as they picked their way back along the overgrown path, not as they came out into the side yard. Not until Tabby, Addie in her arms, stood from the stone bench by the fish pool and approached them.

The nurse's brows were furrowed. "What is all the commotion, my lord? Addie wanted to follow when we saw you run by, but . . ."

"I am glad you didn't." He angled their way, knowing her worry was reflected in his own eyes. He held out his arms for Addie, who reached for him with a happy squeal and pressed a small hand to his cheek once he held her to his chest. "Ladies Ella and Pratt found a . . . a body. In Anlic livery."

Tabby's face washed pale. "Stew?"

"I don't know who else it could be, but we'll leave it to the constable to decide for certain. I must go and ring him up." He turned back for the house, then paused. Ella still stood where he'd left her, staring at nothing. Seeing horrors, no doubt.

Addie clapped and lunged, halting his progress. "La! Lalala." Given her stretch toward the lady, *La* must be *Ella*. He headed her way. He could take Addie in with him—he'd used the telephone before with her in an arm—or he could have given her back to Tabby. This, however, seemed the better course. He stopped a foot before Ella and let his daughter lunge for her.

Ella's cider eyes cleared, her lips curved up, and her arms received the little one without hesitation. "Hello, my little sunshine."

There. Lady Ella would take care of Addie—and vice versa—

188

while he saw to necessity. He strode inside, heading straight for his study, where the house's candlestick telephone had its place of honor on his desk. He sat, lifted the receiver, and put it to his ear—then had to close his eyes as he drew in a deep breath and leaned toward the transmitter.

"Good afternoon, Anlic Manor," the operator said into his ear. "How may I direct your call?"

He squeezed his eyes tighter, suddenly glad Mother wasn't here, to have to go through this. Wishing Mother were here, to lend the staff her warm support. He was no good at it. "I need the constable, please."

⸎

Kira rubbed her palm over Felicity's back, crooning words in Russian that the girl wouldn't understand but didn't need to. Words never mattered in moments like these, anyway. But the sound of them could be as soothing as a hymn. A gentle touch could be a balm. Knowing there were people around her who cared would, at some point, give comfort.

The housekeeper and Ronald, a boy who looked about twelve or thirteen, had sat with Felicity for an hour or more, but duties had eventually pulled them away. And since Lady Pratt had closed her eyes against the world and seemingly fallen asleep, Kira had slipped back to the room she shared with Felicity, not wanting her to be alone just yet. Not so soon after the constable confirmed everyone's suspicions.

The dinner hour had come and gone, and Kira's stomach made muted protests—but she was accustomed to going without food now and then, when costumes pulled a bit too tightly across her frame. When one spent so much time without a corset on, one couldn't be too free with one's diet. Not that it mattered anymore.

But at the moment she could be glad that her stomach was used to being dissatisfied. She ran her fingers through Felicity's hair, which had long ago come loose from its bun, and handed her a fresh handkerchief when she sniffed.

"Thank you." Felicity's voice was a collection of a thousand tears, most of which had soaked into her pillow. But some still huddled in her throat, choking off her words. She was curled up on the narrow bed on her side, around her stomach. "I kept hoping . . . I thought at first something must have happened, but everyone kept saying he'd run off. So I hoped he had. Hoped he would come back. That our babe would know him."

Kira gathered the long brown hair together and separated it into three sections. "Of course you did. But terrible as this is, at least you know he did not leave you. Not of his own will."

"I know." Another sob cut her off, though she swallowed it down. "I can't think who would have done this to Stew."

Kira's hands paused, though she granted them that tell for only a second. Then she went to work braiding the long locks. Something to distract them both. "Was it on purpose, then?" She had heard only the whispers that it was Felicity's husband—verified by the items found with the body—nothing about how it had happened. It had, for a reason she couldn't quite pin down, made guilt surge at the fact that, while Lady Pratt had been out stumbling over this discovery, Kira had been going through her mistress's things, looking for some clue about the diamonds.

It just seemed so petty, in light of death.

Until she considered that her own might follow if she didn't do as she was told.

"Blow to the head, the constable said." Felicity curled tighter around her unborn babe. "And . . . and perhaps strangling. I cannot think why. Or by who. He had nothing but friends. Aunt Higgins always said Stew had never met a stranger, and that was the truth of it. Everyone was a friend, absolutely everyone. It was another reason . . ." She caught another sob before it could escape. "Some speculated he ran off with another woman. He was so charming, you see. And who was I to have claimed his heart?"

"The one he loved—that is who." Kira crossed the sections of hair again. "Could it have been an accident? Could he have slipped and fallen? Hurt himself that way?"

"No. I remember the night he left, saying he was meeting his cousin at the pub. It was raining. The ground was soft. That area has been cleared of stones, and the constable said that where the skull was crushed . . . it couldn't have been a branch."

Murder. She had no response to it, not here. Not when it was the beloved of someone she knew, not just a name with no face, with no connection to her.

"He was never really to meet his cousin—that's what Timothy said when I asked him next day, after Stew never came home that night. Whatever he'd been doing out there, he lied to me about it." Felicity reached for a ribbon on her stark bedside table and handed it over her shoulder to Kira. "It shouldn't hurt so after all this time. But it does."

Kira took the ribbon and tied it around the end of the braid. "It could have been for a good reason that he lied. Perhaps he was out trying to surprise you with something." It wasn't nearly as likely as that he had found trouble somehow, but that wasn't what a grieving widow on the cusp of motherhood needed to hear. She tightened the bow she'd tied and let the braid rest on the mattress.

A knock, tentative and quick, came upon the door. Kira patted Felicity's shoulder and stood to answer it—though she started when she cracked the door to reveal Lady Pratt in the hall. "My lady! I thought you were asleep. If you need anything, I—"

"No." Lady Pratt peered over Kira's shoulder, her brows furrowed and mouth pinched. "I just thought . . . I could not rest for thinking of what she must be feeling." She nodded toward the figure curled onto the bed. "Could I come in for a few minutes?"

Kira craned her head around to see Felicity's response. The girl's shrug didn't forbid it, so Kira opened the door wide to allow her mistress entrance.

The room hadn't felt cramped with Mrs. Higgins and Ronald in it when Kira had first come down, but now it did, with Lady Pratt's fine linen dress and gold jewelry taking up space. She sat gingerly on the edge of Kira's narrow bed, across from Felicity's. "I know there are no words. Not today."

Kira eased the door closed again but didn't know where to move within the closet of a room. So she stood there, between her bed and the door, and wished for just a moment for her salon at her flat in Paris, where she could entertain a dozen guests and not feel this crowded.

Lady Pratt smoothed a hand over her leg. "I know, because I was there not so long ago. My husband killed, a babe on the way. I know the terror and the ache. The anger. The sure knowledge that all that matters is gone—all but the little one, who you can't even hold yet."

Felicity rubbed a hand over her swollen abdomen. "What did you do, milady?"

"Swore revenge." The lady's lips curved up, sagged down. An echo of a pretense of a smile. "I didn't know the price would be so high, that it would cost me my son too. Now I have only my grief—first for the husband I scarcely mourned through my anger, and now for my baby. I would give anything to go back. Do it all again, differently. But we are not given second chances in this life."

Felicity's lips quivered. "I have been thinking that if I had just kept him home that night . . ."

"I know. Every day, I think that if I had only kept Byron with me that afternoon, perhaps the crib death wouldn't have snatched him. I should have let him sleep in my arms, as he had wanted to do. But I had guests coming. Things to do." Lady Pratt swiped at her cheek. "It is enough to devour me whole."

Kira's knee throbbed in commiseration. She didn't dare speak up and say how she mourned the loss of herself in much the same way. She didn't want to belittle the literal loss of life, of spouses and children. It wasn't the same.

But still, the regret was familiar. The sure knowledge that one could drown under the reality pressing in. That all one's dreams, all one had sacrificed for, all one had ever loved could be taken away in the blink of an eye.

Death was an inescapable part of life. She had always known that, as surely as she knew that the winter would be long and the summer too short. As surely as she'd known that there were questions not to be asked if she wanted to keep her babushka smiling. Still, she had always believed that in this age of freedom her grandparents celebrated, she could fight to keep what she had fought to earn.

But life could be as cruel as winter. A truth Babushka would be shocked to realize Kira had not known instinctively.

Lady Pratt sighed and turned to meet Kira's eyes. "Have you eaten?"

It felt weak, somehow, to shake her head. But she saw little point in lying. "But I am not—"

"Lareau, if you haven't learned it yet, I'm not often given toward thoughtfulness. Take advantage while the opportunity presents itself and eat. I can sit with her for a few minutes."

That, too, felt odd. Wrong. But Felicity didn't send her any gazes begging her to stay—and why should she, when they were barely even acquainted? With a nod, Kira turned, remembering too late that she ought to have curtsied as well. But Lady Pratt was paying her no mind.

It still felt strange to navigate the servant hallways. She had never been in a grand house in Russia, much less the bowels of one, and in France she had always been on the other side of those halls, the side where the serviceable had been papered over and plated in gold until function was superseded by beauty. Perhaps she should have felt more at home here, where wood was coated in nothing but flat paint, like the small house she had once called home.

She didn't.

But the kitchen was warm and fragrant when she entered, and that was something she missed from her growing-up years. The heat from a hearth and a stove, the air colored with the scents of cooking and cleaning up. It was only missing the bustle of mothers and grandmothers, the shouts of brothers, the rumbling laughs of fathers and grandfathers.

The only one in residence in this kitchen just now was Dorsey, Lord Rushworth's valet. Kira had scarcely exchanged five words with the man up till now, but he greeted her arrival with a handsome grin and a wave toward the counter, where bread and meat and cheese were laid out, along with vegetables and fruit.

"The cook left food out for everyone, what with the uproar."

Kira nodded and returned his smile, heading for the counter. "Quite a day, *nyet?*"

"That is was. Are you fetching something back for the maid, or will you join me here at the table?" With his foot he scooted a chair out across from him in an invitation that any one of Kira's brothers could have made.

It teased a smile to her lips. Mamochka would have scolded

her sons for putting their mud-caked boots onto a chair, and no doubt Dorsey wouldn't have done it had the cook or house-keeper or Lord Rushworth been present. She had, in their limited days together, never seen Dorsey be anything but decorous.

Getting a glimpse at the boy beneath the elegantly-clad man was more refreshing than it should have been. She fixed herself a quick plate and took the chair. "*Spasibo.*" At his raised brows, she added, "*Merci.* Thank you."

"Ah." He grinned, and looked ten years younger than she had thought him. "Quite welcome. We've not had the chance to really speak thus far, but I've been meaning to give you a proper welcome to the Rushworth household."

Not that she intended to be a part of it any longer than she must. But she nodded. "Have you served Lord Rushworth long?"

"Half of forever, it seems." He raised a slice of apple to his lips and bit. "About twelve years, if we're counting actual time."

Twelve years. Twelve years serving and bowing and handling other people's things instead of one's own. Kira shook her head. "Twelve years ago I was in short dresses, tumbling about my babushka's knees."

"You saying I'm old?" He didn't seem it as he laughed. He seemed more likely to chuck that bit of apple at her head. That's what Boris would have done, anyway, had it been her brother across from her. "I feel it sometimes, at that. But as positions go, it's been a good one, and Lord Rushworth knows I don't intend to serve him forever."

Her brows lifted. It seemed a strange statement in light of how long he'd been doing it already. "No? What else do you plan to do?"

Dorsey tapped the half an apple slice against his lips, his eyes distant. "Who's to say? I'd like to see a bit of the world. Africa, maybe. Go on safari."

Dreams, then. She was tempted to discount them as nothing more—but everyone in her village had thought the ballet just a dream of hers. Dreams could be powerful things. "You have a fondness for wild animals?"

His grin was quick, bringing his blue eyes back into focus. "I have a fondness for open spaces and no one to tell me how to run about in them. I get on right well with his lordship, but he does like to dictate my every minute."

She wanted to press, to ask what things Rushworth might have dictated, and whether any of them had to do with diamonds. Instead she said, "And yet he knows you intend to leave service and does not mind it?"

The blue eyes sobered, went . . . not hard exactly. Not cold. More like . . . flinty. Hard *and* cold, yet capable of producing sparks. "No. Not so long as I do my job best I can until then. Loyalty and precision, that's what it's all about with Lord Rushworth. But he knows things change. So long as I do my part until they do, he doesn't mind me having other goals."

"So you will someday go on safari." The *someday* still niggled at her. How would a valet afford to do so?

Perhaps he heard her silent question. He sighed. "I've been saving for years. I can get there, I daresay. Though I won't be living like a king when I do. Probably end up working for some long-mustachioed lord over there who hunts for lions like Lord Rushworth hunts for freedom."

"Freedom?" She didn't mean it to sound scoffing, but it must have.

Dorsey's eyes went back to flint. "Don't let the title fool you, Lareau. He's had a hard go of it."

She stretched out her aching knee under the table. "My father always says that suffering is no respecter of status. It visits rich and poor alike."

"Aye." The softness came back, and the smile. "Though to be sure, certain types of suffering visit one more than the other, and I wouldn't mind trading which ones I've got, trying the other on for size. How about you?"

She thought of her flat, of her things, of the jewels she'd brought with her to keep them from being stolen. Of wondering how long home would be home. Wondering, sometimes, if she even had a home. She had spent most of her life wishing for what she couldn't have, and the rest afraid she'd lose what she'd gained.

Not so different, really, those two. She sighed and toyed with her food. Her stomach was still empty, but it had nothing on that deeper ache inside. "I have tried enough to know that none of them suit me."

Dorsey laughed and raised the glass of water that had been beside his plate. "Hear, hear."

Kira took a bite of her sandwich, promising herself a walk later. Preferably to some tucked-away corner of the property that would allow her to stretch and plié, to dare an arabesque on her bad leg. To force the knee to strengthen again.

Dorsey polished off his remaining apple slices, but he didn't then get up. Instead he leaned back in his chair and folded his hands over his stomach in contented repose. He had the look she always associated with the English—that wave of brown hair over his forehead, the easy blue eyes, the straight, narrow nose. All Western, those features, with none of the Eastern influence that could sneak into Russian eyes and noses and cheekbones here and there, courtesy of the Mongols who had held the land in their fists for five hundred years.

His smile was carefree and friendly. "Can I ask you a question, Lareau? You don't have to answer if you would rather not."

She finished chewing, letting her raised brows invite the question, along with a slight nod.

Dorsey narrowed his eyes at her, but in a way that made him look as though he were concentrating, not cross. "What brought you to service? You're a beautiful young woman. I would have thought the men would be clamoring to make you their wife."

An echo of what her family had said so many times—"*You can have your pick of the village boys. Let go these foolish dreams and do what you should, Kiraka.*" She shook her head to clear it of those voices. "I was not interested in a husband and family. I wanted to see some of the world. Make my own way."

She hadn't known his grin was so quick, but it flashed again, bright as the laugh that followed. "I can hardly argue with that, can I?" He leaned forward again, eyes teasing. "How do you feel about Africa? I daresay life on safari would be easier with a pretty girl at my side."

Kira just took another bite of her sandwich and chewed it, holding his gaze without flinching. It was, she'd found, the best way to show a man that she wasn't going to be swayed where she didn't want to go.

Dorsey chuckled, shrugged, and stood. "Can't blame a chap for trying. And don't count me out yet, Sophie Lareau—I'm a good bloke. You might just tumble straight into love with me."

She sent him on his way with a good-natured roll of her eyes. He could be the best "bloke" in the world, whatever that was, and she highly doubted her heart would be in any danger of falling for him. Her purpose here was too clear. Find out where the Fire Eyes were. Get back to Andrei. Reclaim her position in the ballet.

After a few more bites, she shoved her plate away and stood. She hadn't found anything of interest in Lady Pratt's things today and didn't dare go back up now, when the lady could return to her room at any moment. But she could work on her knee. Best to ensure that when she went back to Paris with Andrei's precious information in hand, she was strong enough to recapture her life.

# Fourteen

Ella clawed her way from sleep with talons and heaves, desperate to leave behind the dark images that chased her. In her dreams, it wasn't some stranger lying there under a season's worth of mud and leaves and sticks. It was her father. Young Mr. Abbott. Then her brother. And then, as she denied that possibility too, Cayton.

She ripped herself from the dream and to the light of day, which streamed through the window brightly enough to confuse her for a long moment. Her pulse still hammered, and her breath wasn't quite steady. But the light helped. Bright and warm and free.

Too bright and warm for her normal hour of waking. She scrubbed at her eyes until the haze of fear cleared from them and then pushed herself up. Her nightgown and sheets were damp from terror, and the clock on the mantel told her it was already midmorning.

The price, she supposed, of jerking herself awake at least five times last night, and then lying there whispering prayers rather than going directly back to sleep. She untangled the sheets and scooted to the edge of her bed, praying again that those at Anlic Manor had found more peaceful repose than she had.

The thought of breakfast made her stomach turn, and the thought of ringing for the maid the Staffords had provided for her made her heart ache. She didn't want a stranger in her space and offering words that wouldn't help. She wanted someone who *knew* her. Someone who would draw her close and hold her.

Someone who smelled of oil paints and turpentine.

Sighing, she shoved to her feet and shook away thoughts of Cayton. She ought to be embarrassed at having thrown herself into his arms yesterday. Except that she wasn't. Couldn't be. She'd needed the arms, and his had come around her easily enough. He'd held her there, exactly like she'd needed him to, and . . .

Her eyes narrowed the closer she got to her dressing table. Her hair pins were scattered about—perhaps not unusual for *her*, but she had watched the maid put them away last night. And a gold chain was half-out of her traveling jewelry case. Odd indeed, given that she hadn't worn any jewelry yesterday to put away, and again, the maid kept things tidy.

Was it residual unease that wracked her, left over from the dark dreams? From yesterday? She didn't think so. It was rather a whole new twist in her stomach.

Someone had been in her room. Last night . . . during one of her bouts of intermitted sleep. Someone had been right here, while she tossed about her bed, and they had pawed through her things. Not seeing to them, not like the servants always did, but carelessly searching them.

She opened the lid of the jewelry case. It would look like a jumble to most people, but she knew where everything was in it. Mostly. She certainly never kept her earrings in the same compartment as her bracelets, but there was one of the red-orange crystals, tossed among the gold. And the necklace that was half-out, and another necklace dangling between two compartments.

Her hand may have gone cold as she righted it, but it didn't shake. It didn't shake.

Someone was looking for the Fire Eyes—someone knew she had them, and must be in the employ of Rushworth. He had . . . had hired someone to pilfer her things. After he'd taken her hand yesterday afternoon, as she stumbled her way back into the Stafford car to come home. After he'd looked so sympathetically into her eyes and said he prayed she could rest well, after he'd thanked her so sweetly for spending time with his sister.

Letting the lid of the box snap shut, she curled her fingers into her palm. He wished her to rest well indeed—so he could send a thief into her room while she slept. She should have kicked him in the shins.

Feeling grimy from more than the nightmare-induced sweat, Ella stomped into the newly remodeled water closet and took a long shower. To avoid ringing for the maid, she slipped into a simple Paul Poiret day dress and twisted her hair into a bun that would probably not last the rest of the morning. But she wasn't looking to impress this morning. She was looking to . . .

She didn't rightly know what she was looking to do, but she had best start by shedding the foul mood that still had her in its claws.

Breakfast would no doubt already have been put away, and though she knew they'd expect her to ring for something, she was still in no mood for people. So instead she sought the out-of-doors. She would take a stroll through the gardens.

But no. Every time she glanced up at the windows of the castle, she wondered if the would-be thief was behind the drapes, watching her. Better to wander a little farther, to escape any prying eyes for just a few minutes. She wouldn't go far, would keep the castle within sight—and earshot, if she ran into trouble.

The sun was even warmer and brighter without her window

interfering with it, and the brisk pace she set past the paddocks left her nicely flushed. Her stomach growled—proof that it was no longer quite so twisted and sour.

She headed briefly into the trees, careful to stop before they could obscure her view of Ralin's turrets, much as she would have preferred getting herself good and lost. Alas, no knight, neither in shining armor nor tarnished, was likely to rescue her today. "Just as well," she said to the sparrow perched in a limb above her. Though she wasn't quite sure *why* it was just as well. Even surly Cayton appealed to her, rudeness and all. But then, she knew well the rudeness was a front. That he was *trying* to put her off. Which was, in a convoluted way, rather sweet. He wanted to protect her from himself.

Her gaze settled back down to earth, where a few spring wildflowers were just beginning to open their petals. *Himself* was the least of their concerns just now. They would do better to protect themselves from Rushworth.

Silently promising the birds and trees that she would explore again another day, she turned back toward the safety of lawn and paddock and castle. She drew in another long breath of fresh, sunshine-washed air. And saw again those telltale pins and necklace chain.

To be thorough, she ought to ask her maid. Perhaps it was something as simple as her noticing an item left out and trying to tidy it up without waking Ella this morning, but being unable to do so in the dark.

The tension in her shoulders didn't ease at that thought, though. She would ask the woman, but she fully expected a blank look and a quick denial.

Then again, whoever *had* searched her jewelry was sure to greet any questions with the same. But someone had. And it could be anyone, absolutely anyone at Ralin Castle. Which, if the house of Stafford employed as many people as Nottingham did, meant well over a hundred.

She would tell Stafford as soon as she got back to the castle. And Brook, of course. She would talk to Brook first—she probably knew the female staff better than Stafford did, and if Rushworth were going to hire someone to search her room, wouldn't a girl make more sense? No one would bat an eye at some under maid slipping in, but a man in that wing of the house would garner unwanted attention.

"You're trying to convince yourself, Ella. You might as well admit you want to think that because it would frighten you less." Having no rebuttal for herself, she huffed out a breath and increased her pace.

Ralin loomed large, if a bit distant, beckoning her back. It may have been the first time she'd gone on a promenade without getting the least bit lost. "I'll have to write Brice to tell him."

"Tell him what—that his sister talks to herself?"

The voice didn't startle her so much as fill in one of those aches inside with a happy *Yes*. She turned until she spotted Cayton, leaning on a horse pasture fence. He wore no hat, which meant his hair was wind tossed, and his clothes were mud spattered. He must have been riding with Stafford this morning, not just studying the Word in the tower office. She gave him as much of a smile as she could muster. "He knows that already. Where's Addie?"

His eyes went soft, though it did little to ease the shadows under them. "Still inside with Abingdon and their nurses. I saw you walking this way when I dropped Troubadour back at the stable and thought I'd see how you are this morning."

After yesterday, he meant. "Ducky." She evened out the hitch in her stride that his appearance had caused and kept moving toward the castle.

He fell in beside her. "Was that sarcasm? From Lady Ella of the Laugh?"

"Well, you looked far too agreeable, so I figured I'd better take up your role, since you'd neglected it."

A grin touched the corner of his mouth before it flitted away on the breeze. "You look tired."

"So do you."

"Because I slept as poorly as you appear to have done." He walked at her side, yet not close enough to touch. He didn't offer his arm. "Stafford said Brook got rather ill yesterday when she learned of it all."

Poor Brook. Ella sighed and nodded. "The very thought of it, I suppose . . . and Stafford said that the constable verified that it was that Stewart fellow?"

He took her sigh and deepened it. "Felicity is in a shambles. Rightly so. And everyone else feeling like utter dunces for insisting all these months that he'd run off."

Silence walked between them for several yards. Until she drew in a breath and said, "Someone searched through my things during the night. My jewelry case."

His stride faltered, and he picked it up again in rhythm with hers. "Thanks to Rush, no doubt. Looking for the diamonds. You *did* have Stafford put them in the safe, didn't you?"

"I'm not an idiot." Though she felt far more like a crab than she usually did. "I haven't told him yet. I haven't seen *anyone* yet this morning, I was in too foul a temper."

"Mm."

She looked over at him, eyes narrow. He had sounded . . . Yes, he *was*. Amused! "Is something funny?"

He didn't have the courtesy to hide his grin. "Yes. You, in a foul mood. It suits you so ill that I can't quite help but find it absurdly amusing."

She wanted to be angry at his grin, his chuckle. His teasing. Shouldn't she be, given the mood under discussion? And yet it made the shadows edge back, let a little more of the sunshine filter in. Made her consider smiling in return.

They passed by the paddock where trainers were putting Oscuro through his paces, no doubt preparing him for some race or another coming up. She watched the horse's muscles flow as he ran at the end of the tether, a symphony in black coat and power.

Only once they were by did Cayton draw in another breath. "Ella." His voice was barely audible over the sounds of the vibrant estate. "What were you doing there yesterday? With Kitty?"

She saw no point in hiding the truth now. "I told you yesterday, didn't I? We took tea together. In the village."

He came to a halt, which drew her to one too. When she looked over at him, his face was a work in negativity. Shock, rebuke, perhaps a bit of fear. "I thought perhaps I'd heard you wrong. Have you gone daft?"

Well, at least he was concerned about her well-being. That was something. And look at that, her mood was improving by the second. She fluttered her lashes and put on a mockingly demur smile. "Not yet. But you can ask me that again if I obey *Kitty's* advice and let her brother court me."

Cayton blinked at her and folded his arms over his chest. "On behalf of your brother, the Staffords, and everyone else who knows you even a bit, allow me to say, 'Don't even consider it.'"

She pushed out her lower lip in an exaggerated pout. "But don't you want to know *why* she thinks I should?"

He blinked again.

She leaned closer and let the ridiculous expression fall from her face. "Because, you see, if I love him, she says, then I won't have to hate him or fear him."

Now Cayton's brows knit. "She actually said that to you?"

"She did. She seems to think that my only hope of avoiding some foul fate as a result of the diamonds is to make certain he's in love with me."

Cayton muttered something under his breath and turned back to Ralin. She wasn't sure what the something was, but it had the tone of the vicar's last sermon on the dangers of sin leading straight to Hades.

Ella scurried to keep up with his renewed strides. "She also said something about how he would 'unleash the monster' to get them. That he would stop at nothing. Cayton, we know crimes have already been committed in their pursuit of this. Surely we can find evidence of them."

"I don't know. I don't know what he might have done. And I'm certainly no detective to figure it all out." His brows had pulled down again into that perpetual glower of his. Her fingers itched to smooth it away. He shook his head, as if in opposition to that thought.

Ella sighed. "So you'll just sit there, with him under your roof?"

He turned the scowl on her. "No, I'm not just *sitting there*. But in the entire *two days* since his arrival, I haven't exactly had the chance to catch him in a crime and turn him in, have I? I've been a bit distracted with finding my footman in a ditch. Which even your imagination can't link to this diamond business, so I do beg you to have patience, my lady, as one trouble momentarily derails another."

"You don't give my imagination enough credit."

He rolled his eyes and increased his pace.

"And it's not about what you've already done in those entire two days. It's about what you intend to do."

He turned his face away, toward the nearer paddock. "I don't know yet. But something, rest assured."

"And he's back to surly," she said to a passing bird.

"And she's smiling about it," he growled to a squirrel.

Indeed she was. Just to needle him, she moved to his side and tucked her hand in where the crook of his elbow would be, had he bent it for her like a gentleman. Which he didn't, so she mostly just held onto his arm. "One of these days, we'll both be in a good mood at the same time."

"More likely a foul one, given all on our horizon."

That probably *was* more likely, but such thoughts would do nothing to help them. So she grinned. "If not before, then certainly on our wedding day. You won't be able to scowl when you see Addie with flowers in her hair."

His sigh could have blustered down the house around the hair of the three piggies' chinny-chin-chins. "Must you continue with that ridiculous jest?"

"Oh," she said on a laugh, all but hugging his arm to her. "Oh yes, I must. You look so delightfully irritable when I say such things."

And delightfully exasperated when he turned those deliciously green eyes on her. "Why in the world do you find my irritation delightful?"

"Because you're rather handsome when you scowl." Gracious, when had she turned into such a flirt? Perhaps it came naturally, having watched her brother make a career of it before his marriage. But at least she'd managed to surprise Cayton.

He shook his head, but he didn't look away quite fast enough. Not if he intended to keep her from seeing the quick flash of pleasure in his eyes. "You're an odd duck, Lady Ella. But then, I'd always heard that redheads had unpredictable emotions."

She let go his arm so she could slap him on it. "You are supremely lucky that I'm willing to put up with you for the rest of our lives."

Rather than laugh her off or scowl at the continued joke, he sighed again. "No, you wouldn't be."

His voice pulsed with ache, with insecurity and self-recriminations. Far more of them than she could soothe away in the remaining few minutes of their walk. Possibly more than she could soothe away in a month, a year.

But as she let her gaze wander over his profile, as she noted the tic in his jaw and the exhaustion around his eyes, something resonated inside her.

She *wanted* to soothe it away. Today, tomorrow, next month. Next year. She wanted to make him laugh when he was surly and listen to him talk about castles in the clouds when he was happy. She wanted to watch Addie grow and see the light in his eyes as he did too, beside her.

Good gracious, was it possible that she was falling in love? With a man who seemed to think that if he liked her, he had better push her away, using whatever insults the task required? With a man Brook barely tolerated, of whom her brother would likely not approve? A man with skeletons in his proverbial closet . . . and half-buried on his land. A man with trouble dogging his steps.

Well, there was trouble dogging hers just now too. How better to face it than with a friend by her side? She could be that to him, even if neither of them was ready for her to be anything more.

"I should get home." He put more space between them, angling toward one of the side doors of the castle. It was the one that led most directly to the nursery, she was fairly certain. "I may . . . I may discontinue my morning studies with Stafford until this blows over. Until Brook feels better."

Until Ella was gone? She linked her hands behind her back and followed him. "You think that wise? I should say that now more than ever the both of you could use that time of edification."

"I frankly don't know *what* is wise right now." His mumble was directed away from her, so that she barely caught it.

"Well, I am certainly not your tutor, to insist you study. And I imagine I shall see you now and then when I visit Lady Pratt, anyway."

That brought him to a halt, though his pivot back to face her was slow. And his face was a thunderhead. "You're jesting again. Please tell me you're jesting."

"I think . . ." How to put words to the impressions she had formed yesterday? Words that would actually convince him she had a bit of insight and wasn't an utter fool? "I think she is too desperate with grief to want more of it—and she is convinced the diamonds will bring more. I think she could help us, if we ask her the right questions."

He shook his head, so slowly it looked painful. "Please don't. Please."

The last thing she wanted to do was give him more reason to worry, to sorrow, to regret. But she couldn't shake the feeling that she *should*, no matter who argued with her. That no matter how many times she'd been wrong when it mattered, this was something different. A whisper from the Lord, not an assumption or judgment of her own.

Hoping he could see the apology in her eyes, she said, "I'm sorry, Cayton. I don't mean to cause you any trials. But I must trust what I feel to be the Lord's guidance—even if no one else believes me."

He worked his jaw for a moment, as if struggling to get his mouth around the proper words.

Before he managed it, a figure moved into sight at the edge of the gardens. One with gleaming blond hair and a jacket far too heavy for the lovely spring day, which of course meant it was Brook. "Ella?"

Ella waved. "Good day, Cayton." She knew well he'd say nothing more now, with Brook's attention on them. "Tell Addie I said thank you for taking such good care of me yesterday."

His answer was a breath that may have been a laugh, a lift of his hand that may have been a wave. And then he vanished behind the hedges while she headed toward Brook.

Brook was already sitting back down, her exhale shaky enough to prove she still felt nauseated. A cup of tea steamed on the little wrought iron table beside her.

Ella frowned. *"Tea?"*

Brook closed her eyes. "Mrs. Morris assured me that nothing cures an upset stomach like a good cup of tea."

"Assuming you *like* tea. Which you don't."

"The very smell may do me in—though my coffee did as well. Would you be so kind? I don't want to hurt Mrs. Morris's feelings."

"Well, just to be a friend." And perhaps to calm the beast gnawing away at her insides. She plunked in two cubes of sugar, gave it a stir, and took a gratifying sip. "Oh, this is lovely. I'm famished—I missed breakfast."

"Me too." Brook opened an eye a slit. "You've shadows under your eyes. Oh, *je suis désolée!*" She sat up straighter, though the way her face washed pale, she probably shouldn't have. "You probably had an awful time sleeping! And here I've been moaning all morning, without giving you a thought—what a terrible friend I am."

"Nonsense." Ella took another sip and reached for one of the biscuits. Perhaps not the healthiest breakfast, but it would do in a pinch. And she was feeling rather pinched. "I only just rose and headed directly outside—I was in far too foul a mood to make anyone suffer my company."

Brook's lips twitched as she eased back again. "Sorry I missed it. Ella in a foul mood. . . . I can scarcely imagine."

"The rest of the world is filled to bursting with ill-tempered people. It's my solemn duty not to be one of them."

"Hmm. Speaking of ill-tempered people . . . Cayton?"

Ella darted a glance toward the castle wall, as if she could see through it to the nursery. "He was asking how I am today. I was a bit upset when last he saw me yesterday."

"I should think so. You should have waited until you were back here to go for a promenade, Ella. What were you thinking?"

She still hadn't confessed that she'd been walking with Catherine. Perhaps she should, but . . . She shrugged. "There was a path."

"And so you must explore it. But it is not safe to be wandering about with *them* in the neighborhood. I ought to insist you at least carry a weapon when you go out of doors."

Ella shook her head, her stomach rebelling at the thought. "I've had enough of guns for one lifetime, thank you."

Brook's lips twitched. "I won't tell you, then, that I have one on me even now."

Her appetite fled. "Brook! In your own garden?"

"I was once accosted in my own stable, remember. I'll not take chances, not while they're here. And neither should you. I've another holster that straps to your leg, you can—"

"No! No, I can't. Not after Stella . . ." She shook her head.

"I know. And I'm sorry. But I worry for you, Ella."

Ella forced her fingers to relax around the teacup's handle. Forced herself to smile. "You oughtn't—you need to rest. I'll take care, I promise you. And I'll entertain myself in a properly boring way. Perhaps I'll set myself up in the library and . . . and write a novel!"

Amusement kindled in Brook's eyes. "A novel."

Warming to the idea, if only as an excuse for the research she'd barely begun on all things India related, she bounced a bit on her seat. "Yes! Why have I not thought of this before? I've had stories running through my head often enough, of course, it's high time I put one to paper."

Brook grinned, though it still looked a little green around the edges. "I'll make sure stacks and stacks of it are delivered to the library for you. Do you need a typewriter?"

Reaching for another biscuit, Ella waved that away. "Not yet. Notes, you know. I'll have to take mountains of notes, and I can't imagine typing those. I'm far too slow on a typewriter. Perhaps I should take a correspondence course to improve my skill."

Brook closed her eyes again, pressed a hand to her stomach. But still smiled. "A fine, *safe* pastime. I'm glad you're here, Ella. Even if I'm too sick to do much of anything for the next few weeks and sleeping as much as I'm awake, I'm glad you're here for those moments I'm up. Very selfish of me, isn't it?"

"Not given that I'm glad of it too. Even though . . ." Her confession about her things being searched got no farther than the tip of her tongue. But it was no fault of her own.

Brook, a hand clamped over her mouth, shot out of her chair and vanished.

*Poor thing.* Ella sighed and finished her biscuit.

# Fifteen

Cayton signed his name to the last of the correspondence needing his attention and handed it with a cursory smile back to the steward. "I believe this is the right move, Mr. Thomas."

The older man received the paper with a nod. "I at once hope you're right, my lord, and pray you're wrong. Thus far, stretching ourselves has paid off, but if war should *not* come . . . And yet I cannot pray for war."

"Nor I. But even if it holds off, the increase in the navy will not disappear, not now." And he had worked—actually *worked*—to get those military contracts for Adelaide's mills. It was now Rosten cloth outfitting all those new sailors on the dreadnoughts.

Germany may have given up racing them on the naval front, but they wouldn't just back off. Not entirely. "Everything my cousin tells me, everything my friends mention in their letters, says that war is imminent. I don't want such things to occur simply for my profit, but . . ." But *someone* would have to provide the cloth for all those uniforms if war was declared—and it might as well be him.

"Quite so, my lord. And if I may say so . . . ." Thomas straightened and gave him a small smile. "Mr. Rosten tried for years to get such contracts. He would be glad and proud to know you have succeeded."

It shouldn't have made Cayton's chest go tight. He'd scarcely known the late Mr. Rosten, and it wasn't his wife's grandfather's approval he'd always craved—it was *his* grandfather's, in place of the father he scarcely remembered. Still, the thought of anyone being proud of him . . . of perhaps his mother looking at him, when she returned from the Continent, with respect along with the never-faltering affection . . . He cleared his throat and nodded. "Thank you, Mr. Thomas. I appreciate that."

Mr. Thomas, apparently no more comfortable with the words than Cayton, edged toward the door. "I'll stop on my way out to pay my respects. Terrible shame about Stew."

"Indeed—thank you. Felicity and Mrs. Higgins will be in the kitchen." Cayton rubbed at his eyes. Locals had been dropping in all morning. Mrs. Higgins had made her a comfortable seat in the kitchen, which was where all the traffic directed itself.

He hadn't felt so much the outsider at Anlic in over a year. But he was quite clearly the newcomer today. The only one who didn't know how everyone in town was related and how long they'd known Stew and Felicity and what their opinions had been on his disappearance. Cayton had spent most of his childhood in this neighborhood, but not among the crowd now coming through the servants' entrances.

Adelaide would have known them all. Adelaide would have stationed herself right beside her oldest friend, their hands knit together, and made things better. Or at least sufferable. Adelaide had been so ill through most of her life that this village had been her whole world—she'd never had the strength to wander from it.

All Cayton could do was assure Mrs. Higgins that everyone could take as much time as they needed and that the manor was open to any who wished to stop in.

Having no other reason to linger in the study, he stood. Addie was down for her morning nap, otherwise he would fetch her and take her outside. Watch her crawl through the gardens on hands and feet, bottom pointed straight up. Hear her delighted squeal every time a bird or butterfly flew by. Feel that warmth of her perfect smile as she looked at him with perfect trust.

His paints would have to do, for now. Perhaps he'd sketch Ella with a frown on her face, just to memorialize the rarity. Maybe if he sketched it enough, he'd stop seeing her smile every time he closed his eyes.

He turned toward the doorway.

Rushworth filled it. Just hovered there, not coming in but blocking the way out. He didn't smile. He didn't frown. He just looked like his natural state—a blank mask.

The very thought of this man paying court to Ella made invisible spiders crawl up his spine. The same way they would have, he assured himself, had he heard Rush was fond of *any* female for whom Cayton had some small esteem. He cleared his throat. "Do you need something, Rush?"

This was usually where the man would draw out a smile mask and put it on, just so, over his empty countenance. He didn't bother with it today. Instead he moved a step into the room without looking as if he'd moved at all. Hands clasped behind his back. Posture perfect.

Invisible. Or he would have been in a crowd, anyway. "A moment or two of your time, if it's not too much bother."

Perfectly polite. Invisible. Cayton leaned onto his desk. "Of course."

Rush, never one to rush, took his time perusing the room. He glanced over the titles on the shelf—all remnants of the late Mr. Rosten, as Cayton made it a point never to leave his favorite tomes out for the world to see. He studied the ancient landscape on the wall, bearing the same signature as the one in the sitting room upstairs—Cayton had a better one drying at Azerly Hall that he would frame and bring with him on his next trip. Rushworth ended up by the window, looking out at the late-morning beauty that the Cotswolds wore so well.

Just when the silence began to itch, Rushworth said, "Lady Ella has the Fire Eyes."

Cayton wished for the silence back. And decided to play stupid. "I thought you said Brook had them—why would she give them to Ella?" *Lady* Ella, he should have said.

Rushworth caught the slip. Of course. Half a glance over his shoulder proved it. "I was mistaken. Apparently Nottingham and his wife played us for fools deliberately." He didn't twitch, didn't sneer, didn't move a muscle beyond what his mask-face required for speaking.

So how could Cayton feel the anger pulsing from him? He would have to write to Nottingham after Rushworth left the room. Warn him.

"He had them made into the Nottingham ruby set. Rather brilliant, really." Rushworth turned from the window, though the only things left in the small room to study were the obsolete sconces on the wall. He studied them. "Lady Ella was wearing them the other night."

Cayton swallowed. Folded his arms over his chest. "How can you be certain?"

Rushworth sent him a glare as sharp as an arrow. "Do give me a bit of credit, Cayton. This is my life's work."

"So."

"So." He turned his whole body to face Cayton. "I had her room checked. They weren't there."

Cayton had already known that. It shouldn't have made the fury and fear bubble in his veins like this. But it did. Cayton tilted his head. "She probably had Stafford put them in the safe." It was logical—Rushworth would have thought of it already.

He obviously had, given the dip of his head. "You can get them for us."

Cayton let slip a bark of a laugh. Straightened. "No I can't."

"Of course you can. You all but lived at that castle."

"Ah." It was easy to dredge up the old resentment, just so he could put it on display. "But I was never to be the duke. And so the duke carefully kept from me anything that only the duke should know. Like the combination to the safe."

"Combination." Rushworth half-turned away. "A key would have been simpler to lift."

"Hence why it's a combination. Three of them, actually. Grandfather had the thing remade just before his death, and he was a bit paranoid about theft, given that his stewards abroad had been pilfering from him. You can be sure that my cousin is the only one who can get into it." And probably Brook. But he would do his best to direct any attention solely at Stafford—it was what his cousin would want. Especially now.

Rushworth's fingers curled into his palm. "So we must convince Stafford to open it. Or Lady Ella to give them to us."

*Convince* had never sounded like so ugly a word before. Cayton's throat went dry. "I won't be party to hurting them. To hurting anyone."

The smile mask reappeared. "Of course not. I'm no monster, Cay."

Cayton lifted his brows, Ella's quote of Catherine's words

ringing in his ears. *"Unleash the monster."* They'd have to make sure he didn't. "What then?"

Rushworth's fist tightened. "You must court her."

*"What?"*

Placid-faced Rushworth looked no more pleased about it than Cayton felt. "I saw how she looked at you the other night. How she ran into your arms yesterday. She is wary of me, too wary—but you could gain her trust. Convince her to let you hide them better, if she knows she has them. Convince her to wear them again, if she doesn't know. Once they're out of the safe . . ."

They would never, so long as Rushworth was in the area, come out of the safe again. The castle could crumble around it and that thing would remain impenetrable. The diamonds untouchable.

Cayton shook his head. "No. She is a sweet girl, Rush, I won't do that to her. And you can't want me to do so—I saw how you looked at her too."

The fist went loose, his face slack. "And hopefully she will call on Kitty again, and I will have a chance to get to know her better. To convince her I am not what Brook and her brother have told her."

Except that he *was*. Just as Cayton was everything they would warn her against.

"She will naturally contrast us. Pick a favorite. Trust the favorite."

Cayton shook his head again, more emphatically this time. "No. She'll not trust either of us—for all the stories she's heard about you, Brook has probably told her even more about me. About how I courted Lady Melissa and then tossed her over for Adelaide. The duchess despises me, and she'll never let me be alone with her guest."

"Oh, but her guest wanders off so very frequently. Be there."
Leaning in just a little, Rushworth blinked. And suddenly his
eyes were filled with all the things Cayton never wanted to see
in them. Hatred. Greed. And a yawning black nothingness that
looked ready to swallow the world. "Be there, Cayton. And I'll
be here, and between the two of us, we'll get them from her."

"No." He was probably sounding far too little like old Cayton. But he couldn't help it. "And again, no. And what's more,
*no*. Besides which—how can you? Or do you simply want the
diamonds more than you could ever want her?"

Rushworth's eyes, usually a placid blue-green, simmered.
"In a perfect world, I'd have both. She would fall in love with
me, give me the diamonds, and then we'd run away together.
I would give her the world, and she'd give me her heart. But I
know well how imperfect this world is—and if I cannot have
both, I will at least have one."

Cayton clenched his jaw until he felt the muscle twitch.

Rushworth smirked. "We both know she would choose you
over me at this point. But we also both know you can't get
close to a lady without hurting her. So you'll hurt her. And
perhaps . . . perhaps I'll get to pick up the pieces."

Though it felt redundant, Cayton shook his head. Again.
And knew he'd never be able to hide the tightness of his throat
when he croaked out, "I won't do it. I already have two broken
hearts on my conscience, I cannot live with another." Because
Rushworth was right—he would hurt her. Of course he would.
If he got close enough. But he wouldn't. He *wouldn't*.

Rushworth turned away, making a *tsk*ing sound like Cayton's
tutors used to do when he mangled a translation or equation.
"Cayton, Cayton. I *am* disappointed in you. I thought you were
made of sterner stuff than this."

His arm hurt. Cayton realized only then that he had been

digging his fingers into his biceps. He didn't bother loosening his grip. "Sorry to disappoint you."

"Not as sorry as I. I hate to stoop to this, but you leave me little choice." He turned again. The mask firmly secured over his eyes again. "You will do as I ask. If you'll not do it for the fortune I would give you, then you will do it because I know the name of the hotel where your mother and Lady Abingdon are staying in France. You will do it because cars hurtle so easily off cliffs on those Riviera roads. You will do it"—he took a step nearer, eyes as unblinking as a snake's—"because your daughter is still so young. And babes so easily stop breathing in their sleep."

Everything inside him—every single thing—turned to ice, slicked over with terror. "You wouldn't."

But he would. He saw that he would, and it took every last ounce of control he had to keep from reaching into his desk drawer and pulling out the revolver that old Mr. Rosten had kept there, from aiming it at Rushworth's chest, and from composing his excuse for the authorities: *He observed that babies die in their sleep.*

Cayton would go to prison. Addie would be an orphan, raised on a trust and the charity of his cousin.

His fingers bit harder into his arm.

"Don't force me to it, Cayton. I would rather not see another adorable little cherub succumb to the crib death." He stepped closer, close enough that Cayton had little choice but to look into the dead depths of his eyes. "I'll do what I must. And I'll know if you don't do what *you* must. Remember that—I have eyes everywhere."

He left. Just pivoted, unhurried, and took his usual calm, easy steps from the room.

Cayton held himself utterly still until the footsteps retreated down the hall, until he heard a door open to the outside, until it closed again. Then he exploded. Out the door, down the hall, up the stairs, and into the nursery.

Tabby surged from her chair when he burst into the room, her eyes wide. "Milord! What is it?"

Addie slept. Just sleeping, perfectly at peace, as she always did. He could see from here that her side rose and fell, that her parted lips pretended to suck, even though her thumb had slipped out of her mouth. But it wasn't enough. He had to lean over the side of the crib, set a light hand on her side, brush back that one dark curl that circled her ear.

She was well and perfect and beautiful and happy. But she was fragile, so fragile. A wisp of a thing in this terrible, enormous world full of poisons and violent men who could speak of murder without even blinking.

"Milord?"

He traced Addie's petal-soft cheek, and her sleeping lips grinned at him. Love surged so strong it nearly knocked him back a step. So many things he had done wrong in this life, but if ever he needed proof that God could forgive him, there it was. A gift beyond any other. He eased away and turned to face Tabby.

Fear echoed the swell of love. "You mustn't let her out of your sight, not unless she's with me. Or Ella or Brook." *"I have eyes everywhere . . . I had someone search her room."* He swallowed. "Whether here or at Ralin."

Tabby nodded, but her brows had drawn in. "What is it, milord?"

*"I have found a few of the servants at Ralin Castle willing to feed me information."* That was his way, it seemed, as it had been Pratt's. Buy off servants.

Cayton forced a swallow. "I know she is not your babe. I know that your love for her cannot compare to the love for the child you had to leave behind to care for her." He had wondered, at first, how she could even do it—leave her own daughter in the care of a sister before she was weaned so that she could nurse Addie. He had wondered, but he had been too numb with grief to really care. And too desperate. "But you are family, you and Evans. You know that, right?"

He could see in her worried eyes that she wanted to question him more, but instead she nodded. "I know. *We* know. You've always been most kind, milord—caring for us and our mum, giving us so much time off when we're in Yorkshire so we can visit her. Letting my husband work at Azerly. And this position will provide for my little Millie for years to come. Addie might not be my own, but she's as close as she could be. I'd protect her at any cost, milord. I would."

Unless, perhaps, someone threatened *her* child, or her mum, or Evans, or the husband she hadn't seen in a month— because of Cayton. He backed up a step, his blood too high to let him remain still for long. "If he comes to you—Lord Rushworth, or Lady Pratt, or anyone else. If they come to you and threaten you or try to bribe you, come to me immediately. Will you do that? Because I promise you that we will neutralize any threat, and their bribery isn't worth much. It's all based on what he might get if he steals something. If he sells it. But he won't."

"Milord, I would never, *never* betray you!" Now just enough anger colored her tone that he believed her. "My mum raised me better than that."

"I know. I just . . . Addie." He looked to the crib again, where their conversation hadn't disturbed his daughter at all. "If anything happened to her, I would . . ."

"I know." And because she did, a bit of the terror eased back.

ROSEANNA M. WHITE

"But it won't happen. Not on my watch. You take care of this
threat, milord. I'll take care of her."

"I'd hate to lose another adorable little cherub to the crib
death." Cayton blinked, turned to the door. By *another*, had
he meant . . . ? "Thank you, Tabby. Now I must . . ."

He didn't know what he must do, but it started with him
flying from the room and ended with him at the door to Catherine's, ready to bang upon it, though he hadn't collected any
words to toss at her.

The door opened before his fist could connect with the wood.
A maid stepped out, her scowl so fierce that it pushed Cayton
back a step. He didn't know her name and had never looked
closely at her, though clearly she was Catherine's lady's maid.

She hissed at him in an undertone laced heavily with . . .
Russian? "Quiet! She spent the whole night sobbing after com-
forting Felicity and is only just now able to sleep!"

From the looks of her, the maid hadn't caught a wink either.
Her dark curls were frazzled under her cap, blue eyes ringed
with shadows, and she'd obviously lost all sense of manners.

Manners were greatly overrated anyway. He drew her away
a few steps with a hand on her elbow that may have been more
insistent than he intended. "How long have you served her?"

"*Pardonnez-moi?*"

The French sounded French, like Brook and Stafford's always
did. But the English had definitely been Russian flavored. Cayton
pitched his voice lower. "Were you there when her son died?"

The maid's face relaxed. She shook her head. "Just since
Paris. I am not certain what became of her previous maid, but
I was hired in Paris. A week ago."

He deflated, but only a moment. Perhaps it was better that
she had no attachments to them. "Do you know—or you can
listen, pay attention. Rushworth just said something to me that

223

made me think he . . . he may have had a hand in his nephew's death."

Stated so baldly, it sounded impossible. Who would kill their own blood kin? The beloved son of his beloved sister?

But the maid didn't erupt with a quick denial of the possibility. She pressed her lips together and looked at something over his shoulder. "That would be . . . That would destroy her. Completely. How did the boy die?"

"Crib death."

Her scowl returned, directed now at the wall rather than at him. "Are there drugs, do you know, that could . . . that could . . . What is the word? *Imiter*."

"Imitate—mimic."

She rolled her eyes. "A cognate, of course. Forgive me. I am not usually so . . . I have not slept."

"Understandable. And I don't know . . . but I daresay there are. Drugs. There are drugs for everything these days, it seems. Opiates and narcotics and . . ." He waved a hand. His grandfather had labeled the lot of them either hokum or poison, which meant that Cayton had grown up without any exposure to even medicinal drugs. He'd never considered rebelling against it.

The maid let out another hissing breath. "I will listen, *da?* To him. To her. What did he say?"

Cayton repeated it, wondering how weak it sounded to this stranger's ears, even though it contained a threat against his daughter.

Apparently not so weak that she dismissed it. Her eyes darkened. "If it is true, if he did this thing . . . she will never forgive him. Never."

If it was true, if he did this thing . . . then Rushworth was more than a thief and a liar and a briber. He was a murderer. And none of them were safe from him. He rubbed at his eyes.

"Listen, yes, please. But don't ask any questions. Don't . . . don't put yourself in any danger. Any more than you're in by mere proximity, I mean."

The maid nodded. At which point Cayton realized that she wasn't just *the maid*.

He cleared his throat. "Forgive me—I'm Lord Cayton."

Her eyebrows, which suddenly seemed far too perfectly plucked for *the maid*, arched. "I know who you are, my lord."

He returned the expression. "Would you be so kind as to return the favor?"

"Oh. Apologies." Her face fell back into exhaustion as she attempted a curtsy that resulted in a knee seeming to give out. She braced herself against the wall. "Sophie Lareau."

The name didn't fit those harsh consonants, the Slavic vowels. Didn't fit the bone structure of what he finally noted was a face too starkly beautiful for Catherine to ever want beside her. But who was he to argue with a woman's name? He sketched a bow. "Forgive me, Sophie Lareau, for dragging you into this."

She laughed a little, *sans* all amusement, and said, "*You* are not the one who did so."

The way she said it left him wondering who had.

## Sixteen

"Delmore." Ella felt decidedly scholarly, sitting as she was in the library of the castle, surrounded by veritable stacks of books on India—geography, culture, legends, myths, and the Hindu religion. The late duke had apparently seen it as his duty to collect all works he could find on any place in which he had holdings. Having counted on just that, she silently thanked him. And tapped her pencil against her lip as she tried to keep from watching Cayton too closely. "Catherine said that he hated Delmore nearly as much as he hated Rushings, that he resented the money Pratt would have put into it. It stands to reason that he would resent the money *Catherine* put into it too. But she could hardly avoid it, so long as she held the estate in trust for her son."

Cayton paced the library much like she imagined one of the tigers she'd been reading about paced the jungles. Stealthy, primal. Ready to pounce on any unsuspecting creature in his path.

Though the image was rather ruined by the giggling toddler he held on his hip, who squealed in delight every time he executed a pivot.

"Is that enough reason, though? To kill one's own infant nephew?"

"Is *anything* enough to do so?" Ella pulled her feet from the chair across from her where they'd been resting—which would have horrified Mama had she been here. She felt around for her shoes under the table, but they seemed to have scampered off under their own steam. "For a reasonable, healthy person, no. But I somehow doubt he could be classified as such."

Cayton made a disgruntled humming noise. Addie stroked his cheek as if to comfort him and rested her head on his shoulder.

Ella stood, hoping he wouldn't notice her lack of footwear. She had been relieved to see him driving to the castle this morning, and more than a little surprised when he'd found her in the library rather than seeking out Stafford. At least until he said that Stafford was dealing with a little boy who could not understand why he had to let his mother sleep and would not stop screaming at the nurse.

She would go up in a bit, see if she could lend a hand. For now, she would rather see if she could lure Addie from her father's arms. On his next pass, she held out her arms, wiggled her fingers.

"Lalala!" Addie lunged her direction.

Ella caught her, knowing well her grin was impish. She kissed the girl's head and looked back up at Cayton, who stared at them in complete bemusement. "Jealousy then?"

He blinked, much like he had yesterday. Where had he learned to blink like that?

And were those her shoes over by the window? How had they gotten over there? Ella sighed. "Catherine said something else at tea. About how it had always been the two of them against the world. Perhaps he resented the intrusion of someone that she arguably loved more than him."

"I don't know. None of it makes any sense—maybe he was just saying it to scare me, maybe it really was the crib death." He pulled out the chair she'd abandoned and sat down with a loud sigh. Then frowned at the table. "What in blazes are you doing, Ella?"

Addie reached for one of Ella's curls and gave it a tug. Ella tapped her nose and reclaimed the hair, distracting her with the shiny but virtually worthless glass beads she'd put on that morning. "Writing a novel."

"No you're not. You're researching the Fire Eyes."

Ella widened her eyes just to watch Addie imitate her. "Why does he ask questions to which he already knows the answer, sweetling?"

Addie lifted the necklace to her mouth and tasted it. Apparently it was delicious, as she kept on gnawing.

"Is that what you told Brook? That you were writing a novel?"

"I told her I *might* write a novel—which could happen, I'm getting all sorts of ideas. This, of course, I said was research—which it is." She could take the chair beside him, but he would probably surge to his feet to pace again in another moment. She opted for leaning against the edge of the table.

Cayton did that blink again. "And my cousin's wife, who is notorious for being overly bookish, thought nothing of your particular choices for research?"

Ella grinned. "She may have had to dash back out to lose her dinner before she saw them all." Though given the diamond book incident, it really was a wonder she hadn't been more suspicious.

"And my cousin?"

"Oh, he knows exactly what I'm about." She really *wasn't* being underhanded about it. If Brook hadn't had to flee the room in search of a lavatory, Ella would have duked it out with her again. "But he's fully set on coddling Brook while she's unwell, so . . ."

His lips twitched. He didn't smile. "Last question—what do you have against shoes?"

Ella smiled for him. "They pinch. Now, a more important question. Have you ever painted a tiger? I need such a one, I think. For inspiration." She reached over him with the arm not fully supporting Addie and pulled forward one of the books that was open to a photograph. A fierce tiger stared off the page, terrifying but too black-and-white. "It's just begging for its world to be colored."

Cayton directed his gaze toward the picture. "Must it be a painting? I could have a pastel drawing to you by tomorrow. It wouldn't have to dry."

"Whatever you want to do." Hopefully he didn't hear in her voice that she just wanted something he had created, something that she could look at and know he had done. For her. "As for Lady Pratt's son—I read what I could find about crib death when it happened. He was older than most victims. And very few cases occur during a daytime nap, as his did. It happens, but . . ."

"You read about that too?" Cayton set the tiger book away from him again and angled his frown her way.

"Of course I did. As I keep insisting to everyone, my optimism is not blind." If only there had been a book to warn her about Stella Abbott's true nature. She traced the curl that hugged Addie's ear, returning the grin the wee one gave her, even if it did seize up a bit. "We'll not let anything happen to Addie. Will we, sweetling? If it comes down to it, I'll simply give you the diamonds to give to him. They are not worth any more lives. Certainly not an innocent child's."

"But that wouldn't stop him, and he *has* to be stopped. If he really did this . . ." Cayton shook his head and rubbed at his eyes. "That kind of monster is never truly appeased."

"How does he mean you to get them, then?" He had only gotten so far as to explain the threat, and why he took it seriously. Though perhaps Rushworth meant Cayton to figure it all out on his own.

Cayton's sigh suggested otherwise. "That is why I sought you out. Would you sit? Please?"

His tone was so frightfully cordial that anxiety snaked up her spine. She pulled out the chair beside his and sat, Addie settling in her lap. "Why do I feel as though I've done something wrong?"

"It's not that at all. It's just . . ." He kept his gaze latched on the tiger. "Rushworth seems to think that if we both court you, the natural outcome will be that you'll favor one of us simply by comparison, and therefore trust that someone more. So that said someone can then convince you to wear the earrings again so they can be stolen."

She wasn't sure what he expected her reaction to be, but given the tension in his shoulders and the way he refused to look at her, he must be steeling himself for something explosive. Perhaps he thought she'd launch into a French diatribe, like Brook would do.

As entertaining as that might be, she settled for a hum. "Not exactly how I envisioned my first courtship happening, I confess. But all right, then. We play his game, you pretend to court me." Her voice didn't even catch on *pretend*. She deserved credit for that, didn't she? When what she really wanted to do was rip that word to shreds and feed it to the tiger.

He looked over at her, disbelief darkening his eyes. "He said he has servants here in his pocket who will report to him if I don't."

"I daresay he does." Which made her look over her shoulder. The library *seemed* impenetrable, but was it? Had they already said things that would haunt them?

Cayton followed her gaze. "We have no worries in the library, I assure you. I have tried, and failed, to eavesdrop on my family in this room many a time. There are no servant halls that connect to it, and the doors and walls are too thick, unless the occupants are shouting."

A measure of relief stole through her. Ella intercepted Addie's hand when she abandoned the necklace and went for her hair again. She tickled the girl's belly to distract her, nearly getting lost in that laugh that seemed to come from the baby's very toes. It gave her enough strength to meet Cayton's too-serious gaze again.

Heaven help her, she wanted his courtship to be real.

Ella made certain her smile was dull with cynicism. "So then. You'll join me here from time to time? It will give an appearance, even if the room is impenetrable. Then we can take a few promenades through the gardens and smile and laugh where we can be seen. To whomever is watching, it will look like a courtship. But it will give us time in actuality to discern how to catch Rushworth in his crimes."

Addie lunged for the floor, so Ella put her gently down onto the rug. On her feet, though her knees immediately bent and her hands found the floor with a happy slap, those knees then straightening again. Off she went toward the window in that adorable bottoms-up crawl.

Cayton's gaze followed his daughter. "I suppose that will have to do. But it pains me, my lady. I am not ready even for such pretense—and you certainly deserve something more than one pretender and one criminal seeking your attentions for the lowest of reasons."

"Careful, or you'll turn my head with such flattering re-marks." She stood to follow Addie. And avoid Cayton's eyes.

Would it ever be real? She knew he wasn't ready now—it hadn't even been a year since Lady Cayton's death. Of course he had to grieve her. But when this was all over, when he was healed . . . ? They would at least know each other better after this faux suit. Know, perhaps, if they had anything worth wait-ing for. Worth pursuing later.

Cayton's stony countenance, when she glanced back at it, said, *"I'll never let you find out."*

It was too late for that. He'd already given her a glimpse of his true self, of the man who painted fairy tales into the clouds. How was she *not* to fall in love with him? When he so needed someone to draw the real Cayton out of him, to make him smile?

She would just have to try to make the false as real as she could. To peek wherever she could into his heart.

"I'm sorry this is necessary, Lady Ella." His stood, all rigid muscles that shouted *"Keep your distance!"* "And I . . . I do hope you remember at all times that it's solely for appearances."

Had he read her mind? Did she wear her thoughts on her sleeve? She flashed a grin. "Do you think me so desperate for attention that I would read fact into fiction? I assure you, my lord—I'm not. I'm a duke's sister, you know. I have men flock-ing to me. Falling at my feet, as it were. I certainly won't fall prey to a suit that I know well is for show. *Charming* as you are. Though let it be noted you do know *how* to be so—you were when first we met."

That was, what, a century ago? Because nothing could change that much in a week and a half.

His shoulders hunched again. It looked defensive—strange how it seemed to result in him being *offensive*. "Before I real-ized you were all fluff and nonsense, you mean?"

A few choice names vied for a place on her tongue. He had aimed that arrow carefully, but she wouldn't let it strike. She grinned as she spun a globe absent-mindedly. "There you go again with that flattery. All but shouting that I'm blindingly beautiful, if it made you overlook my . . . *nonsense*. Well don't worry, Lord Surly. Pretty as your face is too, I'm not blinded. Except by Addie, of course."

The little one touched a chubby finger to the globe, slowing its rotation. Once it stopped, she turned and crawled toward her father with a hello-again squeal. He picked her up, studying her instead of Ella. "So long as we understand each other."

"I daresay we do." Better than he might wish.

His larynx bobbed with his swallow. Quieter, he said, "I don't want you to get hurt, Lady Ella."

She reached over, wanting to smooth away that furrow in his brow. Smoothing down only, of course, a wisp of Addie's hair. "It's life, my lord. Pain is inevitable. But I'll not live in fear of it."

He backed away. "I had better go and find Stafford. Let Addie and Bing play, if he has calmed down. I . . . I suppose I'll be back down. After."

She took a step back too, folded her arms around her middle, and wiggled her fingers at Addie. "Do try to look a bit happy about it, will you? I'm a young lady, not an executioner. For that matter"—she pulled out some mischief to sprinkle into her smile and extended her hand—"pretend you like me."

Amusement and rebuke both gleamed in his eyes, but he took her hand, raised it to his mouth, and let his lips linger on her knuckles a moment too long.

A game. But it wasn't a game. And she knew as she looked into his eyes that he knew it too. Knew it and hated it and hated himself for *not* hating it.

She never realized how much she liked the complicated, conflicted sort. It was no doubt cliché of her, just like being struck so quickly by his handsome face and falling for his adorable daughter. But some things, she supposed, became cliché for a reason.

He charged out of the room as if the doors might try to eat him on the way out, leaving the library far emptier than it had seemed before he came in.

Ella sank back down into her seat at the table and pulled a book forward again. She feared she was already lost where it came to Lord Cayton, but now it was time to lose herself in India again. Such a different world it all seemed.

What had Rowena and Brice said the name of the tiger god was that time she'd overheard them speaking of the curse? She pulled out a book on the various Hindu gods and scanned through the index, flipping to the entry on each familiar-sounding name until she found it. *Dakshin Ray*. Her eyes ate up the few scant paragraphs about him.

It seemed he wasn't a deity to be revered like most of India's others. Not like Vishnu, the sun god, nor Parvati, goddess of fertility. Dakshin Ray instead appeared to be some higher form of the tiger. A god that no one wanted to see—because to see him was to see the fearsome beast prowling through one's village, attacking one's children. Dakshin Ray was a god to avoid, to fear, rather than to revere.

Her gaze darted to the book on Indian animals, still open to that hard-eyed tiger that stared down the camera. She shivered at the thought of being near enough to such a beast to take a photograph like that.

She pulled out another tome on myths and legends. It was a monster of a book, every bit as intimidating as a tiger. It would take her forever to sift through it.

*Lord, don't let me stray from your path. Not with all this, and . . . and not with Cayton. Nor with Catherine.*

She turned back to the tiger book. It would tell her where they lived, somewhere in that chapter. And then she'd have a place to start.

# Seventeen

Kira darted a look over her shoulder, hushed her very breathing. Lady Pratt was visiting with Felicity again, which surely meant she would be gone for a little while, anyway. Hands still hovering over the garments she must yet tuck away into a drawer, Kira strained her ears for any telltale footsteps.

The only ones she heard were those of Dorsey in the next room, and his whistle as he saw to Lord Rushworth's things.

Abandoning the clothing still sitting on the chair, Kira sifted through the drawer to the slender box Lady Pratt had instructed her to put in the bottom. It was the perfect size to contain papers—papers that could very well reveal something about the diamonds.

Setting the box on the floor, Kira lifted the lid off and picked up the sheet of paper on top.

*My Kitty-Cat,*

*I miss you. Blast this infernal mud for making the travel so difficult between Rushings and Delmore. If it doesn't dry up soon, I shall risk it and come to see you. The sicker Mother becomes, the more I wish for just an hour in your company. I'm already plotting how I shall arrive late in the*

*afternoon, so your brother is obligated to offer me a room*
*for the night. Please don't play coy this time, Kitty. Please.*

The signature read simply *Pratt*. Kira touched a finger to
that dash of masculine letters. The lady's late husband, though
obviously this was sent long before Catherine became Lady
Pratt. According to the date at the top, it was before Brook
even returned to England from Monaco.

No mention of anything relevant. Kira set it carefully aside,
then frowned at the item beneath—a lady's magazine. She lifted
it out, her fingers following the guidance of the little slip of
ribbon inside it, opening to an advertisement.

It took her a moment to realize that the beautiful figure depicted, in the height of fashion and glowing with health and
beauty, was Lady Pratt. The artist had depicted her perched
upon an ornate chair, with a gleaming silver tea service at her
side. In her fingers was a cookie, a tiny nibble out of it, and the
caption proclaimed, "Fuller's Biscuits are the only biscuits I
serve with tea."

Kira lowered the magazine, flipped back to the front to see its
date—a year ago. Her gaze went unfocused. Who was this woman
she served? A celebrity, to pose for adverts? A widow, mourning
the loss of her husband? A mother, lost without her child.

Footsteps.

Sucking in a breath, Kira replaced the magazine, the letter,
the lid onto the box, and slid it back into the drawer even as
the doorknob turned. She reached for the clothing still waiting to be put away and was slipping it into its place when the
door opened.

Lady Pratt didn't let go the handle or come inside. She just
lifted her brows and said, "Come on, then. Felicity needs to
take a walk and said you ought to join us."

Surely the most charming invitation Kira had ever received. She forced a smile and straightened. "Thank you, my lady. I would love a walk." And some time to ponder where, amidst lost fame and too much grief, Catherine stored her information on the diamonds.

Felicity was waiting for them at the base of the stairs and led them out into the sun-kissed garden. "The weather has warmed." She turned her swollen face up toward the sunshine. "Perhaps it will stay so. That would be nice. I like to think that perhaps this little one will be born into sunshine. I always heard stories of how it was raining terribly the day I was born."

Lady Pratt smiled—it was the first time Kira had seen her do it, and she nearly tripped over her own feet. How pretty the lady was when she wiped the distemper from her face. Even lovelier than that artist had made her out to be in the magazine. "I was born in the dead of winter. It was snowing, I was told."

They both looked to Kira. She let her lips tug up too. "I was born on Easter. The best time of year in Russia, the most joyous. My mamochka always said that I was the perfect celebration of life eternal."

"But that's this weekend!" Felicity linked her arm through Kira's, smile rivaling the spring day in brightness. "We shall have to celebrate. Isn't that right, Lady Pratt?"

Lady Pratt didn't look quite so enthusiastic about the idea as Felicity.

Kira shook her head. "It is not quite that soon. Orthodox Easter is a different date than yours, not until April. And of course it varies by year so is not always on my birthday. We have two weeks yet."

"Then in two weeks we shall celebrate!"

Kira grinned at Felicity, happy enough to give her a reason to smile again, something to get excited about, to push the other from her mind. "What do you do here for Easter? I found Paris to be very different from Russia."

"Oh." Lady Pratt waved a hand. "Just church, of course. Simnel cakes, and some people decorate eggs. And a nice dinner, usually, with one's family." Her eyes faded. Just like that. "I suppose we will be here for Easter this year. That will be odd."

"I saw an Easter parade once." Felicity pressed a hand to her ribs, on her right side. She didn't seem to think anything of the action, but Kira frowned. "It was delightful. There was a band, and everyone in their finery. Utterly charming."

She would ask her about her ribs, and whether they were paining her, later. Perhaps it was just discomfort from not having gotten enough exercise the past few days. "You have seen nothing until you have seen Easter in Russia. In every village, there is a procession of the icons."

"Well, that sounds a *bit* like a parade." Felicity's hand was still at her rib, rubbing in circles.

"Then . . ." Kira turned her gaze straight ahead now, so that she could see Lady Pratt from the side of her eye. "Then we go to the cemetery. We bring bread and scatter it on the graves of our loved ones who left us behind."

The lady's step slowed. "Bread. Why?"

"Because it draws the birds. And the birds are symbols to us, reminders of how the souls of those we love are not trapped in the ground with their bones. They have flown to heaven. We leave bread out in the kitchen after someone has died too. Our way of remembering their souls are on that journey—everyone needs bread for a journey."

Lady Pratt wrapped her arms around her middle and headed for a little bench tucked under a lattice arch beside a small stone pool. Lord Cayton did have a lovely home—though Kira's mistress didn't seem to see much of it as she sat with that unfocused haze over her eyes again. "Why can they not carry us with them?" Her shoulders hunched. "Not, I suppose, that I deserve heaven."

"Who does?" Felicity sat too, right there beside the lady. Never stopping to think, apparently, that Lady Pratt might disapprove of sharing a bench with a maid. Though Lady Pratt made no objection, so perhaps Kira was too quick to judge. "I rather thought that was the point of Jesus's sacrifice."

"Nothing in life is so simple as that." Lady Pratt unwound one arm from about herself and reached up to touch a finger to an unfurling leaf on the vine growing up the lattice. "Perhaps He lived, He died, He rose again—but He still has expectations of us, does He not? That is what all those preachers drone ever on about. What we must *do*."

"My father always said it was like marriage." There was no room for Kira to sit, and she didn't want to anyway. She wandered to the half wall of stone and stretched against it. "It takes only a moment to marry someone, but an entire lifetime to have a marriage with them, *da*? Faith, he says, is like that. It takes but one moment to confess it, and a lifetime to live it out and understand it."

The words, her father's words, came so easily to her lips. Strange, since she hadn't paused to think of them . . . ever. Certainly not since leaving for the Imperial School, and then for Paris. Faith, she had thought, was just a thread in the tapestry that was life. Woven in, about, throughout, but indistinguishable from all the rest, really. One thing among many. Unimportant on its own.

Papka would no doubt disagree.

"It never seemed worth it." Lady Pratt's hand fell back to her lap. "So much work, being righteous, and for what? The empty thought of a reward waiting when we die? I should rather have a life worth living now."

"In Russia . . ." She paused, not sure they really wanted to hear any more about Russia. But Felicity looked at her with eager eyes, and Lady Pratt . . . Well, Lady Pratt looked at her, anyway. "In Russia, many believe that heaven exists somewhere on earth. That it is . . . trapped, perhaps, beneath this world we know. There is a legend of a city—Kitezh, it's called."

"Kitezh," Felicity echoed, though her lips formed only awkwardly around the name.

Kira smiled. "When the Mongols invaded, the city—the holiest city in all the land—was swallowed magically by a lake at the height of the siege, drowning all the Tatars."

Lady Pratt snorted. "And its inhabitants too."

"*Nyet*. That is the point of the legend. That the city still lives, under the waters—but only the truest of the faith can see it. On the summer solstice, we still go there. Gather around the lake and listen for the church bells. Hoping, praying that it will resurface."

She had believed, once, that it would. Back before her mother died, before she realized how much it cost to dream. Back when she thought anything could happen by sheer will and faith.

Felicity's smile was unfettered, even if her eyes still bore the lines of yesterday's perpetual tears. "Did you ever hear them? The church bells?"

"Once. When I was seven." Evgeny had scoffed, had told her it was only the bells of a horse driving by. But Babushka had shushed him, had clasped Kira's shoulder. Had said, "Of course you heard them, *doushenka*. Never doubt it."

When had she begun to think her brother was right?

"What *are* you doing, Lareau?"

"Hmm?" She froze, straightened, and realized that she'd been stretching out her leg, using the low wall as a barre. Heat rushed her cheeks. "Forgive me, my lady. I . . . I have a knee injury that still bothers me when it is damp. I was stretching it."

Felicity finally stopped rubbing her rib. "That was the loveliest stretching I've ever seen. As lovely as your walk—you're so graceful, Sophie. I bet you're a perfect dancer."

Lady Pratt's face didn't ease—it was a thundercloud obscuring Felicity's moment of cheer. "A grace wasted on a maid, don't you think?"

Kira straightened, blood heating. As if a person could be labeled so quickly—and worse, it applied to Felicity as well.

But Felicity chuckled. "Oh, milady, you obviously have no idea the fun we have belowstairs. I met my Stew at a dance in the village. Before Lord Cayton hired him on here. Everyone was there, crowded in. Adelaide—she'd just become Lady Cayton then—lent me a dress. It was . . . magical."

Her face looked touched by that magic still. As if she were in that moment again, looking out across the crowded ballroom into the eyes of the man she would love. Untouched by the loss that would find her.

Lady Pratt reached over and touched Felicity's hand, as softly as she had the newborn leaf. "Perhaps, if we are still here, you and your aunt can arrange some dancing for Lareau's birthday. Surely someone has an instrument—or . . . or I play a bit. The piano. I am not very good, but . . ."

Felicity came gently back to the present. "That would be lovely."

Kira drew her lip between her teeth. Lord Rushworth had it all wrong—it wasn't a Russian peasant his sister needed to draw her out of her grief. It was an English one.

Kira could learn a few things from her too.

⨭⨪⨭

Ella's mind was awhirl with scents she'd never smelled and stories she'd never heard and colors she was fairly certain she'd never seen. All those books painted an image, with their words, of a world that seemed so far from hers. A strange thing to contemplate as she stood dressed for tea, ready to walk to the village that may be the epitome of English villages.

Or she would have been ready if there weren't a duchess standing in her way. Focused on imagining a jungle path before her, Ella had nearly plowed into Brook.

"You really needn't take tea in the village again, Ella." Brook steadied her with a smile, her eyes quick as always to note that Ella wore walking shoes and had her handbag in hand. "I promise I will do my utmost to keep from running out on you if you want to join me here instead."

Ella chuckled, since Brook had yet to make it through a meal since the disaster at Anlic Manor. "Forgive me if I doubt your success, just now. But it's not that. I got in the habit of going to a tea room in Brighton over the winter, to give Brice and Rowena some time to themselves, and Mama usually took it with a friend in town while I was there. I got rather fond of the solitary time to attend my correspondence. Unless you mind?"

By way of answer, Brook stepped out of her way. "I begrudge no one their independence, as you well know. But do take the car. Or the little carriage. I don't like you walking alone given the undesirables in the neighborhood."

"On a day like today?" Ella waved a hand and stepped toward the door. "It's far too lovely. I need the walk as much as the tea."

"I don't like it. Do you at least have a weapon?"

Ella sighed. "Brook, it is a well-traveled road. And I shan't leave it—I promise you. I will be in no more danger than I would be with a loaded weapon that I am not comfortable wielding."

Brook didn't so much sigh as grumble. "Stubborn girl. Let my father walk you, then—he offered."

Ella sighed. She had no objection to a promenade with Whitby, but . . . "Where is he?"

"Outside, waiting to intercept you if you tried to slip away." With a grin, Brook stepped out of the way. "Have a good afternoon, Ella—and don't walk back without Papa, either."

There was no point in arguing. Ella hurried through the grand front doors of Ralin Castle, down the stone steps, and all but skipped her way along the gravel drive. This was a day that made one forget it had been raining so recently—and that the rain had washed away the soil and revealed horrors. This was a day that made one think happy thoughts like *Cayton will take a walk with me again tomorrow* and *I can pretend, for now, that it's real.*

"You don't fool me for an instant, you know. And frankly, I'm shocked you've fooled Brook."

Ella grinned and looked over to find Whitby emerging from the lawn. He fell into step beside her with a lifted brow.

Ella attempted to match his expression, though she suspected she didn't wear it so well. "How have I fooled Brook?"

The brow lifted a little more. "You are not simply walking to the village for tea."

A warm, painfully tender pressure squeezed her chest. It had been too long since she'd had a father give her that look. Mama tried to keep her in line, it was true, but Ella had always been Papa's little girl. Which meant he had always known when she was out in search of mischief.

Much, apparently, like Whitby did. Though to be sure, her mischief was far subtler than what Brook had done. "As a matter of fact, Whit, I *am* simply going for tea." She gestured toward the road and the village. And was even quite sure that she'd head the right way, there being only two choices. "And please don't launch into a lecture about carrying a weapon with me, like your daughter just did."

Whitby shook his head and kept pace beside her. "Not I. And you may in fact be going to tea, but I sincerely doubt you're taking it alone. And since tea rooms are generally heralded as acceptable meeting places for young ladies and any acquaintance with whom they desire to meet, I don't understand why you feel the necessity to be sneaky about it."

"Because it's so much more fun to pretend I'm mysterious." And, really, she had no idea if Catherine would join her for tea. She'd sent an invitation home with Cayton that morning, but she hadn't heard anything back. "And I most likely *will* be alone, unless I run into someone there."

Whitby snorted. "'Run into someone,' she says. We both know who that someone is."

"We do?" Well, that was baffling. How in the world would Whitby have figured out that she was meeting with Catherine?

He sighed and released his hands from their habitual holding place, clasped behind his back. Apparently so he could reach over and nab hers, then draw it through the crook of his elbow and set it upon his forearm.

She used to walk with Papa like this, too, around Midwynd's gardens. It had always made her feel so grown up.

She *was* grown up now. But with no father to look at her like this, with concern and affection all jumbled together.

How blessed she was, though, to have a friend who would lend her a father for such occasions.

"Ella," he said. Softly, slowly. "I know Brook has her issues with him, and perhaps that's why you feel you must act this way. I like Cayton quite well these days, but—if he's going to court you, it needs to be in the open. You shouldn't be sneaking off to meet him."

"Cayton!" She didn't know whether to blush or to laugh. "I'm not meeting Cayton." Though to be sure, she wasn't eager to confess to Brook the faux suit that she wished was real.

Whitby's expression didn't change. "Did you know that my niece snuck off to meet him when she was in Yorkshire? At my house, under my very nose? And I didn't realize. I'm shamed to admit it."

And he certainly knew how to make her happy heart stumble. "Brook mentioned it. But I'm not meeting Cayton."

"She would take the governess's cart, say she was going into Eden Dale for tea. Her mother thought nothing of it, so why should I have?" Whitby shook his head. "Cayton and I had a bit of a chat about that once I figured it out, I can assure you. I never imagined I'd have to have the same chat, again, over you."

Though really, it was rather amusing that he just assumed she and Cayton were . . . *she and Cayton*. If only they were, for more than pretend. Ella pressed her lips against a smile. "You needn't have that chat, I assure you. The only place I sneak about with Cayton is in the garden at Ralin, and that is hardly sneaking, given that anyone who cares to look can see us." Including, hopefully, whomever Rushworth was paying to watch them.

Whitby's glare shifted, turned questioning. "I did see you, as a matter of fact. Yesterday, and again this morning. Hence my deduction as to this." He waved at the road.

Ella gave his arm a squeeze. Perhaps she ought to begin calling him Uncle Whit, since he gave her the same treatment as he did his nieces. That was a lovely thought. "What you saw was playacting. Rushworth is watching us and seems to think Cayton can get the Fire Eyes from me."

"From *you*?"

What did the men talk about all day? "I apparently, quite by accident, borrowed them from Brice and Rowena. They're in Stafford's safe now." She cast a glance over her shoulder, back to the castle. "Don't tell Brook quite yet, will you? She is so overwrought just now. . . ."

He grunted again. "Don't tell her you have the diamonds, or don't tell her Cayton's courting you?"

"Pretending to."

"Hmm." He led her around a pothole. "Does he have people watching you in the tea room too?"

Laughter slipped out. "I am *not* meeting Cayton! I'm meeting Catherine."

His stride hitched, nearly stopped, stumbled on. "I beg your pardon?"

"Catherine. I'm meeting Catherine, Whit."

He said nothing. Just led her on. Around a bend, up a knoll, back down it. And still said nothing. Until Anlic Manor came into view and he finally looked at her again and asked, "Why?"

He had taken so long to frame a one-word question that it seemed only fitting she give her many-worded answer some thought too. Though not quite that long of a thought. "Because she needs to see that the world is more than she thought it. And I can't shake the feeling that I'm to help her."

"Oh, Ella." He patted her hand. "That is a big task. The Rushworths . . . they have always been what they are, the whole family. Brook thought she could be a friend to her once too. But look how that turned out."

And Rowena had thought the same. But Ella wasn't blind to the truth like Brook had been, or searching for common ground like Rowena. "I don't mean to accomplish anything on my own. I just mean to follow the Lord's guidance."

"I can't argue with that, much as I might wish to do." He nodded toward the driveway of the manor—and to the blond figure meandering toward its end. "But I will say this—I'd rather you were meeting Cayton."

Ella only chuckled her response, not wanting to say any more as they drew nearer, lest Catherine overhear them. She said a silent prayer of thanks that the woman had come out again—and another for wisdom.

Whitby made a quick, curt greeting and left Ella standing there with Catherine, saying little as he headed up the driveway toward the manor—no doubt prepared to watch for her return from the village and walk her back to the castle again.

It was good to have a father around, even if he was borrowed. Ella smiled at Catherine. "You came. I'm surprised."

"I came with a counter-offer, actually." Catherine inclined her head toward the manor. "Cayton apparently doesn't take tea—his daughter is napping now, so he vanished to somewhere or another. But Cris and I were planning on having some together. You could join us."

"Oh." Not what she had planned, not at all what she had planned . . . but aside from the unease that was to be expected, she heard no clanging alarms in her spirit. She put on a smile. "All right."

## Eighteen

Cayton took a step back, surveying the canvas with a critical eye. Morning light would have been more useful for determining whether he had the shading right, but morning only came once a day and never lasted long enough. He squinted at the flow of the unicorn's mane. It looked right, wind-caught. He would have to add a kiss of moonlight to the locks, but he *would* wait for morning for that. He wanted a kiss of it, not a torch.

The cloud castle had given him a bit of trouble, but it was turning out better now. Wispy here, voluminous there. And his princesses were lovely as they ran up the star-studded cloud steps. Their dresses, too, trailed off into wisps of vapor in the trains.

He smiled a bit as he bent close to add a touch more black to the lowlights of Addie's hair. He had used his imagination, and photographs of himself and Adelaide as children, to guess at what she'd look like in a few years. He didn't want her deciding at age five that she didn't want the painting in her room any longer because he'd painted her as a baby in it.

The other princess he probably shouldn't have put in at all.

But she'd been there, in the story. He was just the brush that told it.

"Anything else you're keeping from me, Cayton?"

Cayton spun, brush still in hand, so shocked at hearing a voice other than Evans's up here that he couldn't place it until he saw Whitby standing, bizarrely, in his garret doorway. A flash of familiar jacket behind him explained, at least, how he'd come to be up here. "Evans, I'm going to sack you yet!"

His valet's laugh trailed him down the hall, leaving him alone with his cousin's father-in-law. "Whit."

Whitby had been a recluse himself. He ought to have appreciated Cayton's wish for secrecy and understood that this room was off-limits. But he stepped in, neck craning this way and that to take in all the drawings and paintings and pastels and brushes and pads of paper scattered about. "Not a passing fancy of yours, it seems. You've been doing this a very long time."

"Don't tell Stafford, would you? He'd laugh about it."

Whitby sent him a look the very color of Mother's when she rebuked him for going to the races. "I believe you have one duke confused with his predecessor, my lord. This," he said, motioning at one of his better paintings of the fish pond at dawn that was drying near the window, "is nothing to laugh at." He moved toward a stack of canvases leaning against the wall. "May I?"

They weren't his best work, but they weren't his worst. He hadn't wanted to gesso over them—not yet anyway—but had no place in either of his homes to put them. He shrugged. "What brings you to Anlic, my lord? Tea? I believe the Rushworths are having it downstairs." Not that he could imagine Whitby wanting to partake with *them*.

"I know, Ella is with them. I walked with her."

Cayton's fingers went tight around the dainty brush. He had just walked with her a few hours before, once he'd pried her out of the library, and had told himself to dismiss her from his mind again until the next day.

The second, red-haired, princess laughed at him.

"Did you try to talk her out of it? Tea with them, I mean?" Whitby snorted a laugh. "Would it have done any good? My daughter has rubbed off on her too much, I think. When first we met, Ella could be swayed most anywhere—these days her smiles are all stubborn. But . . . " He flipped the first canvas toward him, revealing the second behind it. His take on Arthur and Excalibur, he believed.

Too cliché to display, even if it *had* turned out well. Except that he had used his memories of Stafford as a lad for Arthur. And he *certainly* wasn't going to admit to *that*, ever, in public.

Whitby didn't seem to care that it was an overdone theme. He studied it rather intently.

"But . . . ?" Cayton slipped his brush into a jar of turpentine.

"Hmm? Oh." Whitby looked up, down again. "But I didn't realize she was coming here to meet Catherine. I thought she was headed to the tea room to meet *you*."

Apparently Rushworth's spies weren't the only ones who noticed their promenades. Cayton blew out a breath and rubbed at the back of his neck. "It's just a front. To convince—"

"That's what Ella said." He eased the Arthur painting forward too. The next one was a landscape, with Ralin Castle in the distance. "Do you really expect me to believe it?"

Did he? Cayton stared at his canvas rather than his uninvited guest. He could still remember, all too clearly, the day that Whitby had shown up at Azerly Hall—uninvited then too—back before he'd met up with Adelaide again, when they'd all assumed he and Melissa would marry. Melissa hadn't even been in Yorkshire at the time, but Whitby had just found out about their trysts and been none too pleased.

That was when Cayton had decided he'd winter in London that year, where he could still call on Melissa. Without hard-eyed, threatening uncles watching.

He hadn't realized Whitby considered Ella as part of his family too. Though he supposed he should have. How was one to see all that bright, smiling innocence and not want to protect it? "Whit . . . you needn't worry. About Ella and me, I mean. I'm not . . . I have no intentions, noble or otherwise. It is only a farce, for the sake of keeping everyone safe. She understands this."

Mostly. Perhaps. Maybe. Though he couldn't quite tell where amusement ended in her gaze and something deeper began. What was jest and what was . . . more.

It couldn't be more, so it wouldn't be. End of story.

"Mm." Whitby flipped that canvas too, and then let out a bark of laughter.

Cayton leaned forward to see what he had revealed. His lips curved up. This one had been a continuation of his Arthur theme, but rather than have Brook be Arthur's Guinevere, he'd made her instead the evil Morgana, her rage letting loose a terrifying torrent of rain and blackest clouds.

"Brook would love this. I always say she is sunshine or tempests, but nothing in between. I wonder what she's shouting there."

Cayton slipped one hand into his trouser pocket. "I couldn't tell, it was in Monegasque. Something ferocious."

Whitby chuckled and eased the paintings in front of it to the side, crouching down to study this one head on. "She doesn't often show you her soft side, does she."

"Has she one?"

Whitby grinned. "Had it been she you hurt, she would have forgiven it long ago. But it was Melissa."

"I know. I understand. For that matter, I completely agree with her." He turned back to the painting underway, but his fingers didn't know what brush to reach for. What paint to daub it in from his palette. "I was a complete blighter. I'm lucky she lets me in her home, much less . . ."

"Cayton." Whitby straightened again and turned from Brook-Morgana. "I was not thrilled, three years ago, with the idea of you courting my niece. The company you kept, the rumors I heard—and then when I realized how the two of you were carrying on . . ."

His neck felt hot beneath the hand that had taken to rubbing at it again. "I know. I *know.*"

"Then when you tossed her over for Adelaide—well, I was quite happy to loose Brook and all her fury upon you."

Brook had been sickeningly polite then, when she first met the shy, quiet Miss Rosten. So very polite that he had wondered what foul tricks she was plotting for him to stumble into. Lucky for him, she and Stafford had fought that day, and all her ferocity was directed at his cousin rather than him.

Ah, memories.

Whitby took a step closer. "But you're not that man anymore. The Cayton I have seen grow and evolve this past year . . . He is a man I can admire. A man I am proud to know. I man I would have welcomed into my family." He nodded toward the cloud-castle painting. Or rather, to its redheaded princess who had Addie's hand clasped in hers.

Cayton sighed. "Ella isn't in your family."

"She might as well be."

"But I'm not . . . we're not . . ."

Whitby moved again, until he stood shoulder to shoulder with

Cayton, regarding the unicorn with its spreading wings. The night sky twinkling behind it. The two beauties running up the clouds. He'd have her forever here, at least. Paint on canvas. Enough.

"You have changed, Cayton, so very much. But you have changes yet to experience. You have yet to learn how to embrace the gifts God gives you. How to hope again."

He knew full well how to embrace the most important gift— by scooping her up and tickling her tummy until she let loose a giant, baby belly laugh.

Other gifts . . . that was too much to expect. Life had only so much joy in it, and Addie was all of his. "Addie is my hope."

"Part of it. But not all, I think. You need her," he said. "You need her laughter. You need her hope."

"No." He turned away, not letting himself think of that laughter filling one of his rooms downstairs, weaving its magic around Rush and Kitty, prancing up the stairs to weave itself into Addie's dreams. "I would destroy it."

❦

Kira replaced the last of the letters in the box, unable to keep herself from casting a glance over her shoulder, even though she knew Lady Pratt would still be down in the drawing room, having tea with her brother and Lady Ella.

The letters were useless. From a collection of acquaintances chattering about nonsense like new wardrobes and who they suspected was involved in an affair with whom.

Exactly the kind of nonsense Kira was accustomed to reading in her own correspondence. Nonsense. Emptiness. Nothing.

There remained nothing else to search through, not here. Not in a borrowed room in a friend's home. If they left and went to Yorkshire, to Rushings, then perhaps she would have better luck. Or perhaps in Lord Rushworth's room.

254

She didn't dare search in there. Not with so many people about, and Dorsey always coming and going. Given the way the valet smiled at her, she could probably flirt her way out of many situations—but not that one. She had absolutely no legitimate reason to go poking through the lord's chamber, and well he'd know it.

Maybe sometime they'd all be out at once, Dorsey included. She'd keep alert for such an opportunity.

On the bed she'd left an evening gown for Lady Pratt to don for dinner, if it met with her approval. That had been her pretense for coming in here. She'd lined up the items for a bath, too, if her ladyship had the desire for a soak, and set out the one book she'd found among her things—some novel Kira had never heard of. Things she might have been tempted by on a spring afternoon, had her life been her own.

The hallway was dim and cool and quiet, the back stairs squeaky when she stepped down them. Voices came from the direction of the kitchen, but she avoided those. She would slip down and into her shared room and do her exercises—Felicity would hopefully be with her aunt or others of the staff for a while yet. She had rested after their morning walk.

She'd still been rubbing at her ribs though. Claiming the babe was making her uncomfortable, but she had let Kira prod a bit at her abdomen. It had taken all her years of practice, first as a midwife in training and then upon the stage, to keep her face clear. The babe was in the right position, and growing enough that he *could* be kicking her so high. Except that she had felt the feet pressing on the opposite side, down farther. And Felicity's face and hands were so swollen. And Kira had caught her, a few times in the last couple days, rubbing at the bridge of her nose as if she had a headache.

From the crying, Felicity had said.

Kira prayed it was so. And feared it wasn't. Headaches, swelling, pain in the right-side ribs . . . She would keep an eye on her. And perhaps tell Felicity to see the midwife in the village and get her opinion.

She listened for a moment outside her door but didn't hear any rustling from within. Still, in case, she knocked lightly before she entered. Then came to an abrupt halt a step inside the door.

Someone was there. But it wasn't Felicity.

Lady Pratt sat on Kira's bed, an unfolded piece of paper beside her and a box in her hands. No, not *a* box. *The* box—the one holding the jewelry she hadn't wanted to leave in Paris.

Heat bubbled up, sure and fast. "What are you doing?" The words came out in Russian. She had to try again to manage the English, and even then they were so anger-laced that she doubted they were coherent.

Lady Pratt lifted a necklace heavy with sapphires and dangled it before her. "My very question, Sophie Lareau. What are you doing? Here, working as a maid? Running from whomever you lifted these?"

She had been accused of many things in her life—most of them, unfortunately, true—but never thievery. She flew toward Lady Pratt and snatched the box away, and the necklace from her fingers. "They are mine, and you have no right to go through my things."

Lady Pratt's expression didn't so much as shift. "I have every right to know if I'm harboring a criminal. Those aren't paste—no maid could ever afford them. Nor could a midwife's daughter."

Kira dropped the necklace back in the box, not caring if it tangled with the bracelets and other necklaces, if the earrings dripping diamonds wrapped around it. She snapped the lid shut. "I was not always a maid. And I am not a criminal."

"What were you then, Sophie Lareau, who moves with such grace and hides jewels among her layers of coarse cotton? Some man's mistress?"

Her teeth hurt from clenching them. Her chest hurt from the pounding within it. Her eyes hurt from trying to not see Babushka's disappointed eyes. She pulled open the drawer and tossed the box back into it. "It is no business of yours what I was."

Paper rustled. "My French is not so poor that I fail to understand this. 'My darling. I miss you. I miss your arms around me . . .'"

Kira spat out her opinion of her employer—but in Russian, so she would catch only the sentiment—and snatched the paper away.

A letter. From Andrei, though he had signed it with only an *A*.

But she'd *had* no letter from Andrei among her things, so . . . She checked the date at the top, grabbed the envelope from the bed. Part of her wondered how he'd known where to write to her. Part of her knew better than to ask such a stupid question.

She read quickly through the letter, knowing he wouldn't be so foolish as to put anything incriminating in it, but needing to make sure. It was all a bunch of nothing. How he missed her, how he'd eaten at her favorite café the other day and thought of her, how he'd seen the ballet and it wasn't the same without her —a statement that could have implied "without her by his side in the audience," not necessarily "without her on the stage."

Then a sentence in Russian. *I expect an update soon.*

She had the overwhelming urge to ball up the letter and toss it in Lady Pratt's snide face. "Get out of my room."

Lady Pratt leaned back against the wall at the head of the bed, arms crossed. "I'll have an explanation first, thank you."

"You already guessed it, and it is as simple as that. Yes, I was

257

a man's mistress. But he plans to marry, and I will not . . . I will not carry on so with a married man. So I left."

Lady Pratt snorted and pushed to her feet. "So funny, the lines we draw for ourselves. That you consent to such an arrangement, but not if he's married. Does that make you feel more righteous? More likely to see your precious Kiev resurface?"

"Kitezh. And who are you to judge me? I saw your wedding announcement among your things, and your son's birth announcement seven months later."

The lady's eyes flashed, dark and menacing. "Going through my things too, are you?"

Kira lifted her chin. "It is my *job* to order them."

Lady Pratt made no immediate reply. She just stood there, making the room shrink with her expensive perfume and her silk tea gown and her perfectly coiffed hair. Then she leaned close. "I loved him. Whatever my mistakes, they were born from love. Not some . . . monetary arrangement. So yes, I will judge you. And I will warn you—don't get any ideas about finding another such arrangement here."

Kira stood straight, her feet in second position, her spine balanced and ready to move. To bend, to lean, to leap away. Though Lady Pratt seemed more the type to attack with vile words than with her claws, one never could tell. Kira stood straight, and she held her head high. "You need not worry, my lady. I will never stoop so low again." She would never need to, not if she went back to Andrei with the information he needed. Not if she handed him this arrogant, hard-hearted woman on a silver platter.

Babushka's imagined eyes swelled with imagined tears. *"Do what you should, rebonok. Do what you should."*

Lady Pratt lifted a single finger, pointed it at her, drilled it into her shoulder. "If you tried it, you would regret it. Lord

Cayton is too reliant on the good graces of his sainted cousin to ever risk such an arrangement, and my brother—" Another flash of lightning in her eyes. "Steer far clear of my brother. The last pretty little maid of mine he dallied with ended up dead."

Ice replaced the remnants of fire in Kira's veins. She stepped away from the pressing finger and pointed her own at the door. "Get out of my chamber. And keep your threats to yourself."

The lady pushed past, all haughty indignation. But then she stopped in the doorway and turned back, and her face was softer than Kira had expected. "Lareau . . . it isn't a threat. I don't much like you and certainly don't trust you, but I don't want to see you hurt or killed. I don't want to see anyone else hurt or killed."

Not knowing how to respond to that, Kira said nothing. She just waited for Lady Pratt to leave, and then she folded up the letter and stuffed it into the drawer with her jewels. She closed the door. Pulled a chair into the scant open space. Closed her eyes and summoned the echoes of music.

*Rond de jambe en dehors*, closing back into fifth position.

She would not let a foul-tempered woman—or her unexpected softness—derail her.

*Attitude* on her inside leg—her good leg—*devant*. *Fondu* on her supporting leg—her bad leg. It didn't hurt so much today. Improvement. Progress.

She would find what Andrei needed, somehow, and she would get out of this place and go home. Smell the baguettes baking and order up her café au lait and . . . and never bother with a man again. Not with Andrei. Not with any other dukes or princes or merchants with more money than morals.

Arm sweeping out to second position. *Retiré* and straighten that bad knee, stretching it into new pain—but it was a pleasant, working pain, not the scream of injury. Arm to fifth position *en avant*.

*"The last pretty little maid of mine he dallied with ended up dead."* Kira's body continued its drill, habit taking over from thought. Her mind kept replaying those words.

She had wondered, yes, when she first met him, whether she'd have to worry with parrying his advances. But in all honesty, he didn't seem the type. Or hadn't. Now she wasn't so sure. She wanted to dash out now and find someone to answer her question, but she would never regain her role in the ballet if she cut even such basic practices short. She finished the drill, did it again.

Then headed for the kitchen. Dorsey wasn't there, but she spotted him just outside. "Dorsey."

He turned, eyes sparkling, when she stepped out into the warm, clean air. "Come looking for me, sweetheart? Changed your mind about the safari already, obviously."

A smile asked her permission to appear, so she let it. "Africa is too hot for me, I think. I am built for Russian winters, not perpetual summers. But I do have a question for you."

He took her hand and made a show of kissing her knuckles. "Ask me anything, lady fair."

Her smile stayed in place. He may not have the polish of the crowd she had taken to, but he had the charm. "It is . . . I feel silly asking, but Lady Pratt said something, and I . . . have I anything to worry about? From Lord Rushworth? As a woman, I mean. She said something about a pretty little maid he . . ."

"Nah." Dorsey squeezed her fingers but didn't let them go. "He's too quiet a sort to make advances. Hannah was the one what made it clear she fancied him. Besides which, right now all his energies are focused on courting that Lady Ella." Dorsey wiggled his brows. "Pretty girl, I grant. Though not so pretty as you." He kissed her fingers again. Winked. "It's his valet you have to worry about."

Kira laughed—and tugged her fingers free. "I think I can handle you, Mr. Dorsey."

"Don't be so sure. I always get my girl." His grin was infectious, his eyes more confident than they had a right to be.

Kira shook her head and took a step away. "Then get yourself one who likes the heat of Africa."

His laughter followed her around the corner of the house. She followed the sidewalk through the garden, not sure where she was headed. Not sure what would make this disquiet inside calm and fade away.

At the front of the manor, well out of earshot of the house, she spotted a trio that only made the disquiet quicken. Lord Cayton, Lady Ella, and Brook's father. What was his name? Whitby.

She ought to tell Lord Cayton what Lady Pratt had said. But she ought to wait until the two visitors from Ralin Castle left, oughtn't she?

Perhaps she was staring too intently as she wondered, because Lord Cayton turned, caught her gaze, and motioned her over. Since she could hardly pretend not to have seen him, she trekked over the lawn to where they'd positioned themselves under the spreading boughs of a beech tree. And told herself that, despite her internal squirming, Lord Whitby couldn't recognize her simply because his daughter would have.

"This is her maid," Cayton was saying. His voice was hushed, and he didn't bother with a smile of greeting. "We were just discussing how Lady Pratt disappeared during tea. Was she all right, do you know?"

Kira didn't know which of them to let her gaze rest on. Following his lead, she spoke softly. "She seemed well enough. Perhaps she wanted to give her brother time with the lady?"

The lady didn't so much as flush at the suggestion. She just edged a little closer to Cayton and tossed a grin Whitby's way. "She left us alone for at least half an hour—my chaperone ought to have intervened."

Whitby grunted. "Your chaperone who wasn't even invited to tea. By any of you."

Cayton tore his gaze away from Lady Ella—Rushworth obviously wasn't the only one taken with her—and put it back on Kira. Frowning. "Did you need something, Lareau? Have you . . . ?"

She looked to his companions, away.

His frown eased. "They know everything. You can speak freely."

Hardly. But she supposed she could tell them this. "Lady Pratt said something about a maid Lord Rushworth dallied with who ended up dead. His valet said her name was . . . Anna?"

"Hannah?" Lady Ella's face washed pale, her eyes went wide. "Hannah, from Delmore?"

Cayton only blinked. Lord Whitby's mouth thinned to a grim line. "The one attacked and killed at the house party last year."

Not until he said it like that, so starkly, did she realize that some part of her had hoped that "ended up dead" was by coincidence. A fever. A carriage accident. Something other than murder.

"What did the constable determine about that? I scarcely remember it—Addie had just been born, Adelaide buried . . ." Cayton shook his head. "That month is a haze for me."

"Nothing was determined, really." Lady Ella delivered it calmly, but her expression hadn't cleared. "Their prime suspect was the valet of some baron I scarcely know—they were seen talking the day before, I understand. Then he vanished during

262

the investigation, which threw the suspicion his way. Did they ever find him, Whit?"

"Not that I heard. Though I confess with much gratitude that I haven't had much cause to talk to the constable in the last several months." He looked beyond them all, down the road. Perhaps to his son-in-law's castle. Perhaps beyond even that. "I can talk to him, though. We're on good terms, and I'm certain he would be interested in anything new we can offer him. I daresay the information that Lord Rushworth was involved with her would qualify as news."

Cayton pulled away from Lady Ella. "You should discontinue these teas."

"Do stop trying to dictate to me, my lord." Her voice was mild. Her eyes were flint. "If you would prefer we not enjoy our tea here, in the safety of your home where you can join us whenever you wish or post a trusted someone within earshot at all times, then I suppose we'll simply go back to the tea room each afternoon."

Cayton growled and looked to Whitby. "Speak sense to her."

"I haven't the time to try. I need to head to Yorkshire." As if he intended to walk there—though Kira knew from the map she'd consulted that it was nearly two hundred miles away—he headed down the driveway. "Can't trust this to a letter or telegram, you know. Ella?"

"Coming." Ella leaned up and planted a kiss on Cayton's cheek. "I'm going to adopt Brook's French ways. Just to watch you react like that."

The "that" was to pull away as if she'd shocked him . . . and turn his face to hide the pleasure in his eyes.

Kira bit back a smile.

Ella didn't bother biting back her laugh. "You're supposed to give me your other cheek."

"Go home, you little minx."

"I'll see you tomorrow. Practice your adoring face in the mirror." She stepped away, but she didn't follow Whitby yet. She paused before Kira. "It's a pleasure to see you again, Lareau."

*Belova—Kira Belova.* How long before someone used her real name again? She barely remembered to dip a curtsy. "*Da.* And you as well, my lady."

"Thank you for helping. Us and . . . and her. She needs friends."

Lady Pratt didn't deserve friends. But Kira swallowed those words down and inclined her head. "I will do what I can. For everyone."

"And we will do what we can for you. If you need our help, don't hesitate." Now the lady hurried after her chaperone, slipping her hand into the crook of his elbow.

Kira watched them for a long moment. "She is not nearly so cloying as Lady Pratt made her sound."

Cayton breathed a laugh. "A lesson in dealing with Kitty—the less she likes someone, the nicer they are." He paused, considered. "And the opposite too—the more she likes someone . . ."

Felicity being the exception, of course. Kira lifted her brows. "But she seems to like you well enough, my lord."

"My point exactly." Hands in his pockets and an odd smudge of white on the back of his neck, he wandered back toward the door.

# Nineteen

Ella scribbled another sentence onto her crowded page. Her handwriting had devolved since she began—first it was happy and full of her usual flourishes, with a few awful sketches in the margins to remind herself of what she was talking about.

That was twenty sheets and nine days ago. Now she dashed off whatever words she thought would get her point across to herself, with arrows often drawn across paragraphs, pointing elsewhere, or page numbers scrawled here and there.

Her eyes were ready to cross. She tossed her pen down and rubbed at them. "I think I may need spectacles before this is all over."

From the corner armchair, Cayton chuckled. "What about this one? Ayyappa? I see the word *tiger* in here."

"Ayyappa. Ayyappa." Ella flipped through her notes, looking for the double Y, the double P. "Ah. No. Ayyappa was just a godling who rode on a she-tiger."

"Blast." A thump sounded, the unmistakable sound of a book slapping the floor. "You do realize, of course, that there are probably scores of legends never written down and put into English."

"Really, James, if you have nothing helpful to say, I am quite happy with silence." She used his first name in a casual tone, but with tension inside—would he chide her for the liberty?

He grunted. "For about thirty seconds. Until you need to muse about the spelling of something or wonder what shade of yellow saffron is." Apparently the grunt wasn't over his given name.

She smiled, stretched, and let her gaze settle on the orange and white and black tiger that stared at her from the other side of the table where she'd propped the frame. "Dak says you should be nice."

"Dak?" The grunt this time had a laugh hiding inside it. "Who names a picture of a tiger?"

"*Moi.*" Her page was full. Again. She added a number to the bottom corner and shuffled it to the bottom of her stack of notes. Another blank page waited for her beneath it. "Did Lord Rushworth say anything yesterday?"

"No. Though he was in quite a good mood, for Rush, after tea. What did *you* say yesterday?"

Was it jealousy in his tone? She couldn't be sure. If it was, it sounded an awful lot like irritation. She rested her elbow on the table and her chin in her hand. "Well, he was telling me all about the countries in South America he has been longing to visit. I suspect that's where he intends to go if he can sell the Fire Eyes. But if he was in a good mood, it was probably because I said I longed for a dinner party and would try to convince Brook to host one after she begins to feel better. No doubt he had visions of me wearing the earrings so he can snatch them straight from my ears."

Cayton sat forward in his chair, all frowns. "He should try it, here, right under Stafford's nose. I daresay he'd get a fist in his."

"Well, Brook is still all but confined to her chaise, poor thing, so it was nothing but a carrot dangled before that would-be punched nose, at any rate." Her neck hurt from bending over the stacks of books so long, and her fingers were cramped. "Time for the next phase?"

"Might as well. I'll fetch Addie and tell Stafford where we'll be and meet you at the side door."

She nodded as he left . . . and plotted how to lead him off his set course while they were out walking. She appreciated, of course, that they were trying to determine who the spy was and so had to do what they could to see who could be watching them. But that meant taking very specific paths around the castle, and Stafford hovering inside trying to see which servants passed by windows from which they could spot them.

So very boring. And difficult, given that Rushworth didn't exactly say every day, *"So I hear you were in the lower garden this morning . . ."* He only occasionally made a comment to Cayton that he could decipher in such a way.

She also appreciated that the library was safe from prying eyes and ears, that people could only tell *that* they were there, not what they were doing. But it meant he stayed in his corner and she at her table. No hand tucked around elbow, no heads leaning together.

Yes, she was ready for the walking segment of their supposed courtship. It was far more fun.

She went ahead and turned to the next chapter in her current book, tidying her space so it was ready for her when she returned. The words *Dakshin Ray* jumped out at her from the new page. Sinking back into the chair, she read a bit. Just a paragraph. Or two. Or perhaps the page.

Her breath caught in her throat when she flipped to the next one. Coincidence? Coincidence or hope?

A knock sounded. "Ella, I thought you were meeting me at the door."

Not looking up, she waved Cayton over. "Here. This is . . . It could be it. Maybe. I don't know. Is it too abstract? A fluke of the translation?"

She heard the click of the door behind him, felt him as he drew near. Caught the scent of oil paints and turpentine and a not-quite-masking whiff of cologne.

He lowered Addie into her lap and leaned over her shoulder to better see the page where she tapped. "Flaming eyes. That does sound promising." He spoke more to the book than to her, turning back to the previous page. "This isn't a real tiger?"

"No. A statue."

"Statue." When he looked down and over into her eyes like that, she almost expected him to forget his fears and just sink another few inches to kiss her. "Did anyone ever mention a statue?"

Intercepting Addie's hand—which was reaching, as usual, for a curl—Ella shook her head. "Not in the story I overheard from Brice. But it would make sense, wouldn't it? Why else would there be diamonds called eyes, if they were not actually the *eyes* of something?"

"Excellent point. But what happened to the statue?"

"I didn't get that far."

"Hmm." He turned back to the book, shifting closer in his distraction, until he brushed up against her side. Though he moved away again, he didn't hurry about it, obviously lost in whatever he was reading. "Interesting. The idol, it seems, was stolen. And wherever it was seen, the tiger prowled, bringing death and destruction with it."

"That matches the story of the curse."

"Indeed." He straightened, his eyes cloudy with thought. "Walk?"

"Let's."

After helping her up, Cayton led her out of the library and then through the exterior door with a hand at the small of her back. Addie babbled something happy and full of *L*s and *B*s. Ella let herself imagine, for a moment, that they were a family. On their way from the Staffords' home to theirs.

Damp air greeted them, and the clouds rolling in promised rain before the morning was spent. She would probably have to give in to the offer of a car or carriage to go to tea today. A mile in the sun was one thing—a mile in the rain something else altogether.

Cayton led her to today's designated path and offered his arm. "So if they *were* part of a statue, what does it change?"

Addie was secure on Ella's opposite hip, so she accepted the offer. "I don't know that it changes anything, exactly. But it gives us more understanding of them. Of where they came from, their history. Did it say what became of the statue?"

"No. It didn't even say it had diamonds for eyes, just 'flaming' eyes."

"I'll contact a few of the museums in that region—perhaps one will know something. And in the meantime, I'll keep looking in other books on the area. Another may be more specific."

"Or lead us in more circles." He leaned close. "We all know how fond you are of going in circles."

She laughed as if he'd just told her she was the sun missing from the sky this day. "If you mean that to be an insult, you had better try again."

"Very well." He gave her a smile meant to look to any observers like he was trying to melt her heart. "Your hair's looking particularly red today, my dearest."

Too bad even that didn't keep the smile from working. "Better. Did Stafford mention whether he'd heard from Whitby?"

"A letter arrived while I was up there."

Ella lifted her brows. And then fluttered her lashes for the sake of the unseen observer. "I thought he said letters weren't to be trusted in this."

"Hence why it was so cryptic we had to spend half an hour deciphering it, I suppose. I believe the gist was that he had been unable to convince the constable to reopen the case, at first. He only just succeeded."

"How'd he manage it?"

"They found the body of the valet they'd assumed to be the culprit—on Delmore land."

"Oh." She buried her face in Addie's curls to keep her expression hidden. There was simply no way to look happy when getting that news, and it was all she could do to keep the churning of her stomach from demonstrating itself. "That's terrible. How did he die? Or do I not want to know?"

His other hand settled over hers. Perhaps part of the game, except that he moved his thumb over her knuckles in a way too subtle to be seen from a window. A way meant to give comfort. "Whitby's letter said 'like that soup you served.' We take that to mean 'like Stew.' Blow to the head, strangling."

She had to close her eyes, inhale through her nose, trust Cayton not to let her step in any ruts or puddles.

Addie's hands landed on her cheeks, caressed. "Lalala. La."

Ella pressed a kiss to the little one's downy head and forced her eyes open again. "Thank you, sweetling. You always know just what I need."

"I'm sorry, Ella." They reached the corner in the path, so Cayton led her around it. "I shouldn't have told you so bluntly."

"The truth is blunt. I wouldn't choose to be spared it though."

"Still, I could have been more delicate."

She gave the image a moment to fade, turning her face out toward the garden until it had. "How is the maid? Felicity?"

Cayton moved his head from side to side. "Good moments and bad. She had already mourned his disappearance, so perhaps that will help. I don't know. She's trying to put on a cheerful face, anyway. She and Mrs. Higgins are planning a birthday celebration for Lareau on Friday."

"So I've heard. It's kind of them to make her so welcome."

"Mm." He sent her a smiling glance. So of course, she knew to expect harsher words. "Don't get any ideas about showing up uninvited—you'd end up dancing with Rushworth."

"You know, I have my heart set on a novel Friday night, to distract me from Indian curses. Even the thought of bothering you can't overcome that." She could manage conversations with Rushworth without too much difficulty—but the two times he'd found occasion to take her hand or touch a hand to her back, she had nearly jumped away.

How much blood was on those hands?

"I thought bothering me was your life's work."

"Work? Hardly." She gave him her brightest grin. "It's far too easy to call it *that*."

He chuckled. And even his eyes were smiling. "I really don't like you, Lady Ella."

But he did, or he wouldn't be trying so hard not to. "I feel exactly the same way, Lord Cayton."

"Good." He faced forward again. "I think I'll avoid the celebration too."

"Catherine said she will be there. Something about playing the piano for them so she can see if Lareau can dance as well as she walks." Catherine had tried to sound snide when she said it, but it hadn't quite come out that way. Suspicious, perhaps. But not snide. "She is quite friendly with Felicity, isn't she? She mentioned her several times this week."

"Common ground, I suppose."

"Mm. Her brother disapproves. When she spoke of her, he smiled nearly as sweetly as you do when you're about to insult me."

He reached down to pluck two snapdragons, handing one to Addie and tucking the other into Ella's hair. "There we are. It clashes perfectly with that hair of yours." He lowered his hand again. "As for Rush—I find that a bit odd. I would have thought he would just be happy she was up and about, taking an interest in *something*."

Cayton looked out toward the pastures, that crease between his brows. "Personally, I wouldn't mind her taking a bit less of one with my household. When Tabby has Addie outside, Catherine usually ends up there too. I'm not sure what to think about that."

"She would never hurt Addie. Or any child." Of that Ella was absolutely certain. Catherine spoke of children with too much aching, too much longing. "I think Rushworth is right about one thing—what she needs is a husband and more children."

Cayton snorted. "Good luck to her. As much a shrew as Kitty is—"

"She is improving. But . . ." But she needed someone who understood what she'd suffered. Someone, perhaps, who already had children in need of a mother. Someone who knew how to keep her in check, who wouldn't let her slide back into the nasty woman she'd once been, who would urge her onward in her metamorphosis.

"What? Why are you looking at me like that?"

She blinked. And wished with all that was in her that she wasn't looking at probably the only man in England who fit that description. "Drat."

"What?" His lips twitched, either at the thought of her finding something to complain about or at whatever expression was on her face.

"You—that's what."

"Me? I wasn't aware that I had changed my name to Drat, but if you'd like me to answer to it, I suppose I can train myself."

She wanted to smile, but the sigh won out. "No. It's you who is perfect for her. You have a child, you understand her, you know her. You can make certain she doesn't slide back down into the woman she used to be."

"I beg your pardon?" He pulled her behind a large bush, flowering and leafy enough to block the view from the house. No amusement lurked behind his scowl now. "Now you're actually going to make me cross. Do you honestly think for even a moment that I would let that woman raise my child? Having a hand in all she has?"

Addie was reaching for a flower, the scene so picture-perfect that it wouldn't surprise Ella to find Cayton painted her just this way—except he'd have to leave Ella out. He wouldn't want her spoiling the image of his daughter. "I know what she was. I do. But can't you see how she's changing?"

"What I see is that she's an absolute wreck, and that though she may have put off some of her most objectionable pastimes, she is still no more what I would want in a wife than . . . than *Brook* is."

But she could see it. The symmetry of it—the newly changed man helping the woman to complete her change as well. It would be the perfect romance. If only it didn't involve the man she was pretty certain she loved and a woman she didn't quite like. "But she needs you." It sounded like a miserable statement, even to her own ears.

It must have sounded even worse to his. He straightened, sneered, and tugged his jacket back into place. "The only man she needs right now is the Lord—and thus far she won't listen to a word I say about Him."

"You've been talking to her of Jesus?" He really *was* perfect for her!

"Ella! You're missing the point. And *why* you're missing it is utterly befuddling. Are we not friends? Do you honestly want one of your friends wedding a criminal? Bringing the consequences sure to come down on Addie's head?"

*Friends.* That grounded her, brought her thoughts back into line. She shook her head and held Addie close. "Of course not. Sorry. Sometimes the ideas sweep me away, independent of the people they actually involve."

"Good." He smoothed a hand over Addie's hair, touched Ella's shoulder briefly, and then stepped from behind the bush. "If I ever hear you make such a suggestion again, I'm going to paint a picture of you with the most garish red hair ever seen in the world."

Ella laughed and followed him out, slipping her arm around his again. "Try it . . . and I'll kiss you in front of Brook."

He winced and led her on.

# *Twenty*

The music bounced and reeled. Kira had found an ancient tambourine in a little oddities shop in the village, and she shook it as she spun, as she twirled, as she laughed her way around the ballroom that Lord Cayton had granted them for the evening. A fiddle player had come from Ralin Castle, along with a few of the other servants. The room was full. Pulsing. Loud.

So beautifully loud that the music swelled her very veins, the clapping matched her pulse. The tune was Irish, they'd said, something the duchess's lady's maid had requested. She and her husband—the duke's valet—were leading the dance in the center of the floor, though others had joined in.

Kira didn't know half the faces, nor a quarter of the names. But she didn't care. She couldn't remember the last time she'd been in a room so full of life and noise and sweat and laughter and . . . and *joy*.

The music was Irish, but she could hear the familiar in it—the peasant dance. The one all rhythm and light rather than finesse and skill. She hadn't known she'd missed it so much.

Hands caught her about the waist, spun her around, and she laughed and spun with him, shaking her tambourine.

Her knee didn't hurt a bit.

The tune came to a jaunty cadence and then a quick halt. The fiddler let out a hoot and demanded a cup of water, waving a hand at the piano.

Lady Pratt slid onto the bench. Kira sucked in a breath and leaned against the wall. She hadn't realized her mistress was still here. When the fiddler had shown up, Catherine had deferred to him, had slid back. Kira had lost sight of her. Or perhaps had just wanted to think that she'd left, and so had granted herself permission to think so.

It was her birthday, after all. She was twenty-one years old. She hadn't seen Russia in three years, her family in five. She had taken the stage in St. Petersburg, in Paris, in Monte Carlo. She had collected admirers like they were stamps. She had won the wealthiest patron in all of Europe.

Lady Pratt struck up a less energetic song, though it wasn't somber by any means. Dorsey—it had been Dorsey to spin her around, of course—held out a hand. "Waltz with me, beautiful."

She smiled her reply, set down her tambourine, and let him pull her onto the dance floor, pull her in front of him, pull her too close. Why not? It was her birthday, and he was a handsome young man with that perfect wave of fair brown hair and dreams as big as her own had been.

The waltz came easily to her feet, her legs, her spine. The music filled her ears. She didn't have to think about it, to concentrate on stretching her leg out fully, landing on the exact beat, making sure her hand extended in time with the flourish. She could just dance and smile and enjoy the fact that the handsome man was smiling back.

"I believe this is the first I've seen you without a cap." Dorsey's gaze stroked her dark curls, warm and approving. "And in a dress with some color. You're even lovelier than I thought, Sophie—and that's saying something."

She laughed, letting her head fall back with it. She had missed styling her hair as she pleased. Missed having eyes turn her way when she entered a room. Missed wearing color. This dress was the least of the ones she'd owned, the only one she dared bring with her—but it was pretty. Blue, to match her eyes. "I am still not going to Africa with you, Dorsey."

"How about someplace closer, then? We could slip out to the carriage house. I could give you your birthday present."

More laughter bubbled up. He could have been any one of the village boys from back home, had he been speaking Russian instead of English. "Would that gift involve your lips on mine?"

His eyes twinkled. "Maybe."

She tilted her head. "Maybe." She shouldn't lead him on, she knew that. He wasn't Andrei, to chase her for a year. To know the game. But then . . . he wasn't Andrei, to look at her as though she were just another piece of art in his collection. Perhaps she *would* kiss him. Just once. For her birthday.

No, it wasn't worth the risk. She was still, for now, one of Andrei's possessions. She wouldn't betray him. Even in so small a way.

Dorsey grinned. "Does it require that much thought?"

"*Da*. Unfortunately. Nothing is ever simple."

"Don't know why not." He leaned closer, his chuckle rumbling up her arms, down her spine. "I'll be on my best behavior—I promise. Just a kiss. Happy returns and all that."

She laughed too. And considered it again, which she shouldn't have done. She knew that. But really, *she* was Andrei's spy here—he wouldn't have anyone else spying on *her*. And if by some chance he did learn of it, she could claim it was all in the name of prying information from Rushworth's valet, couldn't she?

He traced a little circle on her back as the song came to an end. "Meet me in ten minutes?"

"Maybe." She couldn't promise more than that. But given his smile, he had no problem seeing in her eyes that she intended to make excuses for herself until she ended up outside.

Just a kiss. It was no great thing.

The fiddler was back, but before Kira could take up her tambourine again, Felicity grabbed her hand and pulled her to the side of the room where chairs were set up. "I got you some lemonade. You must be parched."

"Oh." She was, though she hadn't paused to realize it. "*Spasibo*." She sat and accepted the cup.

Felicity grinned and rested a hand on her belly. "You're having a good time, I can tell. I'm so glad. And you look so beautiful!"

"*Spasibo*," she said again, smoothing a hand over the silk. Not high quality, but silk. Her skin had missed it.

Felicity touched a finger to the pale blue lace that edged the overlayer. "Wherever did you find such a lovely dress?"

"Paris. I had saved and saved until I could afford the material. A friend of mind did the stitching—I was never much with a needle."

"Well. Dorsey certainly seems to admire you in it." She grinned, eyes bright. "That's how Stew looked at me, when we met. Not that you'd know it now, but I was pretty." Her grin faded as she pressed a hand to her swollen cheeks.

Her eyes were still bright, but not joyfully bright, not healthily bright. Bright with a pain that pinched her face for a second before she cleared it again.

Kira grasped her hand, her delight with the evening seeping out. "You are pretty still, Felicity. I know Stew would think so too."

"Oh." She chuckled, waved off the comment. Swiped a hand over her forehead as if ridding it of a stray hair or bead of perspiration—but she pressed on her temple.

The lemonade refused to settle in Kira's stomach. "Have you a headache?" *Again*, she wanted to add.

"Just the heat, I think. The noise. I'll step outside in a minute and be right as rain, I'm sure."

"Do not push yourself too hard, *mon amie*. If you need to rest, then do. For the sake of the baby."

Felicity nodded and let the mask fade again for a moment. "I am rather taxed. And dinner did not settle well."

"I will walk you. I could use a breath of fresh air myself." She looked out at the crowd of near-strangers who had looked like neighbors just a few minutes ago. "They will not miss me for a few minutes."

They made their way through the crowd, into the hall—quieter and cooler by far—and toward their shared room. Felicity loosed a sigh. "Well, you do indeed dance every bit as well as I thought you would. Where did you learn? I could never move like that, even when I was a great deal lighter on my feet." Smiling, she cradled her extra weight.

Kira's smile hesitated. "I . . . I have always loved dancing. Much of it came naturally. I studied the rest."

"I can't imagine any famous ballerina having more grace."

A few came close. These days, some probably surpassed her. "I hear the duchess dances."

"Oh, beautifully! Nearly as well as you." Felicity bumped their arms together. "I've managed to peek in a time or two, at local balls. Did you know she trained for a while with that Russian company? In Monaco?"

"Lord Rushworth mentioned it. The Ballet Russe." Her tongue savored the syllables she hadn't said in far too long.

Felicity nodded. "That's the one. I should like to see a ballet someday. Perhaps I'll save up enough to catch a show in Gloucester."

"Let me know when—I will join you." A happy, completely unrealistic thought, given that Kira had no intention of staying in England. But she would dream. It was her birthday, and she would dream of being free enough to pick up and travel to another country just to catch a show with a friend. Perhaps that was the life that awaited her. Perhaps Andrei would be that generous with his parting gift.

Felicity rubbed at her ribs and swayed a bit.

Kira steadied her. "Are you all right?"

"Just tired. My eyes are blurry—time for bed, I suppose."

No. *Nyet, nyet, nyet.* Kira opened the door into their room and helped Felicity to her narrow bed. "Felicity . . . have you seen the midwife recently? Or a doctor?"

Felicity screwed up her face. "Not since you came. They'll only tell me that the babe will be here soon, which I know well enough. Another fortnight? Maybe three weeks?"

"I think . . ." Kira swallowed and leaned down to light the lamp. "I think you need to see the doctor."

"Oh, Sophie, I haven't the money for that. You know all they do anyway. You can do whatever needs done."

But she didn't. And she couldn't. She shook her head. "I left home when I was sixteen. My mother died two years before that. It has been seven years since I helped with anything, and I . . ." *I fear for you.* But who was she to say so, after admitting to being so long out of practice? When she couldn't even remember the name of the ailment she feared, just the symptoms?

Felicity settled on her bed. "How did your mother pass?"

"On her childbed. The bleeding would not stop, no matter what we did." She perched on the edge of her friend's mattress and pressed her hand to her forehead. No fever. "Have the midwife come by, at least. She will know better than me why you are having such headaches. Mention the blurry eyes. The pain in your ribs."

"Sophie. You're overreacting. I'm pregnant. It's uncomfortable business."

*Kira.* Today, of all days, she just wanted someone to call her Kira. She smoothed away Felicity's hair from her face. "You are my friend. I worry."

Felicity smiled and closed her eyes. "I'm glad you've come."

She couldn't bring herself to answer, didn't know what she could say. Was she glad to be here? No. She was glad to have met Felicity, but otherwise . . . no. Silently, she let herself out, eased the door shut behind her. Silently, she slipped up into the kitchen and out its door into the cool March evening. Silently, she made her way through the clear, damp night and to the looming shape of the carriage house.

Dorsey waited in the moonlight, leaning against the side of the building with his face turned toward the heavens. Wondering, perhaps, what the moon would look like from the African plains. Or how many more times it would wax and wane before he saw it there.

He turned when her heel crunched on the gravel of the drive, the pearly light catching on his even white teeth. "You came."

"I should not have. But yes." Because it was her birthday and no one knew her name and Felicity wasn't well and her knee didn't hurt but her dreams were still on the other side of an ocean, with some other woman's name on her posters.

She walked directly up to him, wrapped her arms around his neck, and pressed her lips to his.

He was taller than Andrei, by an inch or so. Leaner. He smelled of crisp English nights instead of heavy Parisian colognes. His arms came about her with every bit as much confidence—that borne of knowing he was handsome, knowing he was charming, rather than knowing he was rich enough to buy anything, any*one* he wanted.

And she wanted to weep and to find one of those boys from her village who would have been happy to make her his wife, one who had never had the boldness to steal a kiss and would have fumbled it if he had. One who spoke her language and shouted her name across fields ripe for harvest and waved to her when she walked by with her grandmother.

No. She just wanted her grandmother. Her father. Her brothers. To sit around the old, scarred kitchen table and anticipate the plate of honey-soaked chak-chak Babushka made for each birthday.

Dorsey pulled away and rested his forehead on hers. Distemper colored his tone, staining the evening still more. "Let me guess—you left someone behind in Paris."

*Worse.* She'd left them behind in Russia, and now too much of her life had passed without them. "It was over."

"But there was someone—of course there was someone. No one as beautiful as you goes through twenty-one years without a someone. Husband?"

She shook her head. Her eyes were going blurry, and she had no long-lettered ailment to blame it on.

"Well then." He kissed her again, quickly but determined. Like his tone still sounded to her ears. "I've a chance."

"As much as anyone. Perhaps more than most." She shouldn't encourage him. But it was her birthday, and his arms were pleasant, his lips confident. It was familiar.

Babushka's eyes would be blurry too, at how familiar it was when she had never had a husband.

Dorsey kissed her once more and then stepped away. "Happy birthday, Sophie."

Her eyes slid shut as he walked away. *Kira.*

# Twenty-One

Ella stepped out of the post office and into a bank of fog that hadn't been there ten minutes prior, when she'd made her stop in the telegraph office before coming here to post a letter home. The morning had dawned cool, so she'd slipped her favorite pea-green kimono jacket on, the matching toque over her hair. Just now she wished she'd worn something heavier. Or perhaps, as Stafford had advised from behind his newspaper at the breakfast table, she ought to have stayed in.

Brook had told her husband not to stifle Ella's adventurous spirit—then had moaned her way back to her "prison of a chaise," as she called it, calling out yet another suggestion that she carry a gun.

She shivered at the thought. Or perhaps at the fog. The library was sounding rather nice at the moment. She'd have a fire lit in the grate. Perhaps another cup of tea. And her chair was calling to her.

"Lady Ella!"

The chair was louder than she'd thought it could be, what with stuffing all down its throat. And sounded suspiciously like Lord Rushworth.

He emerged from the fog—making her wonder how he'd spotted her ten seconds earlier—with that smile he always wore. The one that promised all was well, the world was grand, and he was perfect, when she knew it was nothing but a lie.

She smiled right back. "Foggy morning to you, Lord Rushworth. You're out and about early today."

"I had a letter to post and a hat to pick up from the haberdasher." He was indeed holding a derby in his hands, which he put on now with more flair than she thought he had in him. "What think you?"

"Dashing." It did, in fact, suit him better than the fedora she'd seen him in before, but she didn't really want to say that. It might sound insulting. Or too complimentary. Or make him think, *"Oh, she's noting my hats—next stop, the altar."*

He adjusted its position and stepped nearer. "Are you headed home? Did you drive, or may I walk you?"

She ought to have accepted Stafford's offer of a chauffeur. Or Brook's insistence of a weapon. "I walked."

"Well then." He offered his elbow.

She had little choice but to set her hand on his arm, though she kept it light.

If he noticed, he gave no hint of it. "And what brings you into this foggy morn?"

"Oh, just posting a letter to my brother and his wife." She wouldn't mention the telegrams to the museums in India, not on her life. "I haven't got one from them in ages, and I require information regarding how Rowena is doing—she could have the babe any day now." The road out of the village had never seemed so long. Though that was likely because it vanished a few yards in front of them. For all her eyes told her, the world simply stopped there at the end of the sidewalk.

"Will you be leaving us when she does? Seeing how you are

with little Lady Adelaide, I think you must be eager for a niece or nephew."

"Most eager, yes. And I daresay I shall hurry home when the news arrives, though I am happy to give them some time to themselves for now."

"You are close? You and the duchess?"

She smiled into the cloud misting her face. "We are. We were friends as children. I never dreamed she would someday marry my brother, could scarcely believe it when it happened so quickly—and now can't imagine how Brice ever got on without her. They complement well. They're nothing alike, so you might not expect it—but there we have it. Foils to each other, I suppose."

"I have always thought that the best sort of marriage. One where a couple balances each other. The quiet with the exuberant. The steady with the bold." He, too, looked straight ahead, to where the road should be. Yet somehow made it clear his attention was completely on her.

Had it been Cayton, it would have been thrilling. With Rushworth, it sent a chill up her spine. "I suppose there's something to that, to be sure. I'm still not certain what would best balance me, but luckily I am in no hurry to discover it. I will patiently await my handsome prince." Hopefully he would read between those lines and deduce that it wasn't him.

His grin bordered on cynical. "Someone moody, perhaps? Surly? I ask because you seem rather fond of Lord Cayton."

She had been expecting the observation for ages—she didn't know how it could fit in his plan to pretend he was unaware of the court he'd forced Cayton to pay her. But still, it took her aback to hear him mention it now, and in the voice of a typical jealous suitor. Or what she imagined the voice of a typical jealous suitor would sound like. She'd never really had one, to know firsthand.

She tilted her head from side to side in what she hoped looked like indecision. "Well, he can be charming when he tries. Not that I forget how surly he is, as you put it, when he isn't charming. And I certainly can't forget how he behaved with Brook's cousin Melissa."

"Mm. He does have a bit of a history. We have long been friends, Cayton and I, but I cannot say as I approved of his . . . shall we say, previous exploits."

*Breathing calm. Fingers relaxed.* She mustn't show him his words bothered her. He was playing a game—that was all—trying to win her trust. "Nor do I, as I have made quite clear to him. Perhaps you noticed the mood he returned in the other day?"

"No, I can't say as I did." But he looked amused. More, he looked pleased. "Did you berate him for his indiscretions? I confess, I wish I had heard that."

She chuckled. "I daresay *he* wishes he hadn't. I wouldn't be surprised if he failed to call one of these days."

"Oh, I doubt that." Now he turned his head her way, that unnervingly steady gaze of his fixed upon her. "I doubt any man could really keep his distance from you if you welcomed him, Lady Ella. Certainly I can't fathom why he would *want* to do. You . . . you're perfection, clothed in beauty."

"Lord Rushworth." Just now, her fair complexion aided her well, letting her flush so easily. "You flatter me."

"It is hardly flattery."

"Well." She laughed, light and a bit hesitant. "You hardly know me."

"I am remedying that, am I not? I have so enjoyed the chance to converse with you each afternoon—and do appreciate that you've been kind enough to visit. She may never admit it, but it has been doing Kitty good." His face went solemn, caring.

"She is finally emerging a bit from her grief. I had feared she never would."

Truth, or just another part of his deception? She prayed it was truth, had been praying morning, noon, and night that it was truth. That the differences she noted each day in Catherine were God-given progress and not just a show, or a reverting back to her previous self. But Ella didn't really know her well enough to say. She had only faith that she was doing what she ought. "I have been praying for her."

It struck her only then—she hadn't been praying for *him*. Why, how had she overlooked that? She would remedy it the moment she got back to the castle.

His eyes softened. "You are so very good."

The soft gaze was as terrifying as the intent one. She looked back into the fog. "I believe that's your sister's greatest complaint about me. That, and that I'm generally happy."

"What does she know? They are your finest qualities. Lady Ella, I . . ." He paused and drew in a long breath, looking out into the fog again too. "I realize no one would approve. But I am earnest in my intentions toward you. Would you . . . ? May I court you? Without the excuse of my sister—just . . . me and you?"

The fog wrapped around her throat and squeezed. "My lord . . . I don't know how to answer. You should speak with my brother."

Rushworth sighed. "We both know what he'd say."

They did. Unless she warned him first, but . . . what would she say? She didn't want Rushworth to court her. But she didn't want him angry, either. "He is a fair man, my lord. And one well able to see beyond prejudice or past judgments. If he was wrong about you before, he will admit it."

He halted, just a step off the sidewalk, and looked down at

her. "Do you think he was? Wrong before? Do you think . . . What do you think of me?"

*Lord God, put your words in my mouth. Give me your judgment, for we all know mine isn't worth much.* She met his gaze. Held it. Didn't look away even when she wanted to. Within his eyes she saw everything and nothing, emptiness and fullness.

She drew in a deep breath and let it carefully back out. "I think . . . I think you have unlimited potential within you, Lord Rushworth. I think you have made yourself into a man who can be remarkable, or who can go without notice. I think that takes depth of character and determination and study beyond what most people would ever do—attention to yourself, your mind, your soul, and that boggles *my* mind. What I can't be sure of is what you've done with it. What is the truth and what is the mask."

He lowered his eyes to the hand she still rested on his arm. "What if the mask *is* the truth? What am I to do then? How can I reassure you?"

She lifted her hand and rested it on his cheek, gloves to flesh. He tensed, his breath catching, though it couldn't have surprised him any more than it did her. "A mask is never the truth, my lord. Or else it would not be a mask, simply a face."

"Then, perhaps I simply don't know which of my faces is most true." His lips tilted up, faded back down. "Tell me which you prefer. I'll make it my only one."

How many times had she wished she could just imagine her perfect prince into existence? How many times had she fashioned one in her daydreams, piece by piece? Wished she could just wish a man into her idea of perfection?

But to have one offer to remake himself to fit her desires . . . That left her shaking. No person ought to have that power over another. And even if she told him what never to do, what always to do, it wouldn't matter. It wouldn't be *real*. And he would likely do it only when she was watching. She withdrew her hand. "I want you to be who the *Lord* wants you to be, to fit yourself into His plan for your life. Not mine. It is the only way you'll ever be happy. The only way you'll ever know yourself. To first know Him."

He turned them toward the hidden road again, his stride slow and the tilt of his head contemplative. "I will think on that. And in the meantime . . . you will come for tea?"

"I will come for tea." Not sure if she'd dodged a bullet or taken one directly in the stomach, she waited for familiar spires and roof peaks to emerge from the fog.

⁂

"You want I should take her in, milord?"

Cayton took the pebble from Addie's fist before she could stick it in her mouth—everything was tasty these days, it seemed—and looked up to see why Tabby would say such a thing only five minutes after they'd settled in by the fish pool.

Catherine was meandering their way, Lareau trailing a step behind her. Neither looked particularly happy with the other, which made him wonder why they were out here together. At least until a few of their words drifted to him on the breeze. "Midwife" and "doctor" from the maid—"Felicity" and "fine" from Catherine.

Cayton looked to Tabby. "Is Felicity doing worse? No one has said anything to me."

"Nor to me, milord. Addie?"

"She's fine. No sense in rushing in." And he did agree with Ella that Catherine wouldn't hurt his daughter—as for the rest of Ella's ridiculous suggestion, his blood still simmered if he considered it too long. How could she suggest that he and Catherine . . .

It needled him even when he pushed it from his mind. He didn't want Ella to like him beyond friendship. Didn't want the faux courtship to be real. But apparently he also didn't want her suggesting he would be the perfect match for some other woman. Much like he gritted the enamel from his teeth every time he paused to consider that she was with Rushworth every afternoon in his drawing room. He kept nearly going down to join them and then stopping himself.

He'd probably just do something stupid to put the whole situation in jeopardy. It was what he was best at.

"Dadada." Addie, apparently deciding he wanted all the pebbles to be found, offered him another.

He smiled and took it. "Thank you, precious. This one is white. The other was grey. Do you see the difference? Can you point to the white one?"

For a moment he thought she might. She studied them, looking from one to the other where he held them in his palm. Then she simply reached for a third and plopped it down along with its friends. "Eedle um."

Cayton chuckled. "Never neglect the third option—how wise you are." And now he was talking to her as Ella did. When had he begun doing that?

"Leave it, Lareau." Catherine stepped onto the stone of the terrace. "If she needs a doctor, she will call one. I'm certain Mrs. Higgins would see to that, regardless of whether Felicity was being stubborn or not."

Addie scooted closer to Cayton's side. She no longer screamed when Catherine got close, but she certainly didn't ever go near her of her own volition. Cayton frowned. "Is everything all right?"

Catherine huffed and waved a hand. "Fine. May I join you?"

He nodded toward the bench under the lattice by way of

permission. He'd glanced out the window and seen her sitting here a few times. She had been all about his gardens, it seemed, with her maid or Ella or Felicity. She had color in her cheeks again. She'd lost that hollow look.

Which of them, he wondered, deserved the credit for that? Her maid or Ella or Felicity?

Catherine settled onto the stone bench. "Did you talk to Cris this morning? After his walk, before you left for Ralin?"

Cayton accepted another pebble from Addie and raised his brows. "I haven't seen him today, actually. Why?"

She shook her head. "He's been acting strangely. I think he must have bumped into Ella, though I haven't a clue what she said to him. Did she mention anything? Never mind. She wouldn't mention him to you—and for the record, I find it quite strange that you're both courting her, sharing a roof as you are right now."

"Well, we can agree on that." He shifted the rocks around his palm. Ella hadn't, as a matter of fact, said anything about bumping into Rushworth that morning. Perhaps Catherine was mistaken.

Or perhaps Ella hadn't wanted to share whatever it was she said to him.

It was concern burning a hole through his chest. Not jealousy. He knew well he had no reason to be jealous. Because Ella wasn't interested in Rush. And Cayton wasn't interested in Ella. And this was the most absurd situation. . . .

He shook it off and cleared his throat. "You're looking better, Kitty. More your old self."

"Am I?" She toyed with a ribbon that dangled from her dress, watching as Addie reached as far as she could for one particular little rock, nearly tumbling over rather than scooting closer to it.

Cayton steadied her. "Well, you are *looking* more like your old self—though I suppose you will never be quite the same person again. Such losses change us forever."

"They do. And they should, shouldn't they?"

"I—"

"Help! Somebody help me! Quick!"

Cayton was already on his feet, picking Addie up and passing her to Tabby. "Mrs. Higgins?"

"Hurry! It's Felicity!"

He heard Catherine's steps hurrying after his, and Lareau made it through the door ahead of him. He fumbled to a halt inside the kitchen, his eyes going wide. Felicity lay on the floor, her body convulsing.

Lareau had fallen to her knees beside her and held her head, muttering something in Russian before barking out, "Doctor! Now! She is having a seizure!"

He could do that. He could ring up the doctor. Though it seemed his feet wouldn't move fast enough, he skidded his way down the hall and into his study, where the candlestick phone stood waiting on his desk. He yanked the receiver off its holder. "Operator?"

"Good afternoon, Anlic Manor. How may I direct your call?"

He squeezed his eyes shut. "Dr. Fields. I need Dr. Fields."

It seemed to take an eternity for the lines to connect, for a voice to pick up. For the nurse to promise the doctor would be out right away.

How soon was "right away"? Soon enough? Could he even do anything for her?

Cayton sank onto the top of his desk. He'd promised her—he'd promised Adelaide he would always see that Felicity was taken care of. But what could he do? He hadn't been able to protect her husband from whatever evil had found him. And this?

"My lord?" The call echoed faintly down the hallway.

He slid off the desk and strode back to the kitchen. "The doctor is on his way."

Lareau nodded from her place on the floor. Felicity lay still now—it would have alarmed him more had the rise and fall of her chest not been visible. But there was blood matting her hair, staining Lareau's hands.

"Did she hit her head?" Not knowing where to stand, what to do, he hovered in the doorway.

Lareau nodded. "She must have. Mrs. Higgins is fetching the first-aid box."

Catherine, her face the empty one she had shown up here wearing weeks ago, stood at the side, staring down. "I don't understand. Does she have epilepsy?"

Lareau sent a scathing glare her mistress's way. "This is what I try to tell you." The Russian was heavier in her voice than usual. "Rib pain. Headache. Vision blurred. It is . . ." She squeezed her eyes shut, shaking her head. "I do not remember what it is called, but it is serious. More so now."

The fight went out of Catherine's stance, and she sank to the floor on the other side of Felicity. "Will she be all right?" Her voice sounded faint, faraway, young.

Lareau sighed. "I cannot say. My mother . . . if possible, she would recommend a doctor if this happened. The risks are high. They usually recommended taking the baby early. As soon as there was a seizure." Her voice was more measured again, the Russian retreating. But she probed at Felicity's stomach and shook her head. "She still has weeks yet. If it is a boy and they hurry along labor, he could have difficulties breathing. Boys always have a harder time than girls."

Felicity would never consent, not if it posed a greater risk to her child. He knew that without question. And didn't really want to know how doctors might hurry along labor in a woman still weeks away from it. It didn't sound pleasant.

But if they didn't? Would this happen again? Could seizures kill her or the child? He had no idea, but the thought turned him to a petrified statue.

The Lord wouldn't take both of them, would He? Adelaide and then her oldest friend? *Please, Lord, spare her. I beg you. Spare Felicity, spare her child.*

Mrs. Higgins bustled in with a box in her hands, and she and Lareau set about rinsing the blood from Felicity's head, examining the still-oozing wound. She made not a move, nor a sound.

The doctor came in while Mrs. Higgins was gently rubbing a salve into the cut. He listened as Lareau described the symptoms she'd observed, his lips pressing tighter with each added one until there was a white line around them. He examined the cut, nodded, approved the bandaging. Waved smelling salts under Felicity's nose until she groaned and rolled her head away, eyes blinking open. He rested a hand on her stomach and gently pressed.

It was Lareau's gaze he met. "I daresay you're right, my dear. It sounds like eclampsia. We need to take the baby as soon as possible. If we admit her to hospital, we can perform a surgery to—"

"No." Felicity, still blinking, squeezed Catherine's hand and reached for Lareau's. "It is too early. There is too much risk to the baby."

"And too much to you, the longer we wait." Dr. Fields patted her arm. "That is the one thing about preeclampsia and eclampsia—the symptoms vanish as soon as you are safely through the delivery. Once you have the child, you will be well."

Even from here, Cayton recognized the stubborn set to Felicity's jaw. "No," she said. "I will not put the baby at risk. I will be fine, I will stay abed, I will—"

"You cannot guarantee that. We cannot control the risks to you. We—"

"I said no. You'll not cut me open to take my child. We'll both be fine."

Cayton turned away. He wanted to believe she was right, prayed she was right. But too much in life was far from fine. And the Lord whispered no promises into his spirit.

# Twenty-Two

Kira's eyes stung, and her lungs were heavy and nearly useless in her chest. There just wasn't enough air. But she wouldn't gasp for it—she couldn't let the panic claw its way forward. That would only draw attention to her.

This wasn't about her. As the doctor left, she sealed her lips, determined to say no more unless someone asked her a direct question. She had said enough. She had warned, she had diagnosed, and she had been charged with keeping an eye on Felicity any time she wasn't tending Catherine.

The weight of it pressed her down. Maybe that was what sucked the oxygen from the room. So much responsibility, and for a life she so wanted to protect. *Two* lives she wanted to protect.

But she was just a ballerina. And a spy. A mistress. She wasn't a midwife. Certainly not a doctor. How was she to help, when it was a condition with no treatment?

Lord Cayton stood with Felicity in his arms, ready to carry her down to her and Kira's room. Mrs. Higgins fluttered around them, obviously set to follow. Lady Pratt still knelt beside the table, staring at where Felicity had been.

Blood pooled on the floor. Head wounds always bled so, and this one had been no exception—they just hadn't been able to fully see it through Felicity's curtain of hair.

Kira touched a hand to Catherine's shoulder. "Why do you not go and rest, my lady? I will clean this up and then check on you."

Perhaps the lady was too numb to consider arguing, because she actually stood and obeyed, moving woodenly out the door.

"What was all the commotion?"

Dorsey. The air felt even heavier. Kira stood and moved over to the drawer out of which she'd seen the cook get old rags. "Felicity had a seizure. She hit her head on the table when she fell. You can help, if you like."

She didn't look up to see if he would, just pulled out the rattiest-looking rags and turned back to the dark, sticky mess.

Dorsey was crouched down beside it, trailing a finger through the blood.

Her stomach turned. "What are you doing?"

"What?" He drew his hand away, a smile turning his lips. "Give me one of those. I'll help you."

For a long moment she just stood there and stared at him. The tip of his finger was still red, even as he held his hand out for a towel. Her lungs were useless, and her ribs squeezed like a vise. She handed him a rag.

By the time she knelt across from him, he had already wiped up most of it, all but a few streaks. She wasn't sure whether to be comforted by or wary of his efficiency. But she pasted on a wobbly smile and said, "Thank you."

He grinned. As if he weren't holding a bloody cloth in his hand, as if Felicity weren't being carried to her room, as if the air didn't weigh like lead. "I thought we could take a walk to the village later. It's your afternoon off, too, isn't it? They have ice creams at the shop there on the corner."

Maybe it was because he hadn't really seen Felicity. Certainly hadn't seen her convulsing on the floor. He had no reason to be in the clutches of terror. Maybe he simply didn't understand how much she meant to Kira, to Lady Pratt, to everyone else here. Maybe that's why he would propose something so ridiculous.

"I do not think I could stomach anything today, Dorsey. A walk might be nice, but . . ." She scrubbed at the streak, but it needed water. This bit had dried while they tended Felicity.

"Of course. Here, let me finish this. You can go and clean up. I'll wait for you outside, yeah? Maybe you can wear something pretty."

Something *pretty*? She pressed her lips together to keep from losing her temper—or her mind. Set the rag down and stood. "Thank you. It may be a while yet—Lady Pratt did not look well."

"Don't worry. I can wait."

Without another word, she stalked from the kitchen, feeling every bit as wooden as Lady Pratt had looked.

She went downstairs first and peeked in at her own room. Lord Cayton was hovering outside of the door while Mrs. Higgins settled Felicity. He chided her gently about her need to rest, and how she was to speak up immediately if she felt anything wrong—assured her he would take care of the doctor's fees, that he had promised Adelaide . . .

Kira headed back up the two staircases into the guest hall.

A sudden shrieking made her freeze a few feet from Lady Pratt's door. A crash made her lurch forward and grip the handle.

"Kitty, calm *down*! She is just a maid."

Another crash. Kira's hand shook in indecision. To intervene or not? It sounded as though it were the lady throwing things, and her brother trying to soothe her. Surely he would do a better job of it than Kira—Lady Pratt actually *liked* him.

"She is not *just a maid*! She is my *friend*. She is one of the only people in this godforsaken world who speaks to me as if I am a person and not a monster. She—" An enormous crash drowned her out, this one complete with the sound of breaking glass.

Kira squeezed her eyes shut. The mirror? A window? Lord Cayton would be furious.

He had nothing, however, on his guests.

"Kitty! If you don't calm down this instant—"

"What? You'll *what*? What can you possibly do to me that the curse hasn't done already?"

Curse? Kira's hand fell away.

"Don't be absurd. You have let the warnings of that ridiculous Highlander influence you too much. There is no curse, there is no—"

"My husband is dead! My baby is dead! Everyone I've loved, everything that matters—and now we come here, and what happens? My friend, the first friend I've ever made without lying through my teeth about who I am, is so ill she could die. It's the curse, it's the Fire Eyes, and I'll not have it! Do you understand me? I've had enough!"

"Stop it." There came the sound of someone striking someone, an *oomf*, springs squeaking.

Kira gripped the knob and turned it, stepped into the room.

Lord Rushworth's cheek was red, his eyes slitted and hard as he held his sister down on the bed while trying to stay out of reach of her clawing fingers. He looked up when Kira came in, his sneer nearly sending her running again. Until he barked, "Get over here and help me! She's going to hurt herself."

She already had, it seemed. Her feet were bare, bloody. Pieces of the mirror littered the floor between the bed and the wall, some of them red-streaked too.

Kira flew to the bed and held her down from the other side. Or tried. Who would have thought that the lady's gaunt frame could have so much power within it? She screamed and railed, though her words were either incoherent or the English was too much for Kira's mind just now.

Rushworth slapped his sister's cheek—not hard, not, it seemed, from anger. The kind of slap one delivered to rouse someone, to get their attention.

Catherine shrieked all the louder. *Curse* was the only word Kira could understand.

"Stop it! There is no curse, and even if there were, it would not be upon us. We have never even held the diamonds, Kitty—you know this. They were just rubies we had. They didn't kill Byron, they didn't kill Pratt, and they won't kill this stupid maid!"

She stopped struggling against them, though Kira wouldn't have called it calming down. The shrieking simply turned to sobbing, the flailing to an attempt to curl into a ball. She was shattered, pulling within instead of lashing out. As broken as the mirror, jagged and torn.

Rushworth muttered a word Kira didn't know and stood. "Hold her down. I'll be right back. Don't be fooled—she could turn violent again in a moment."

Kira could do nothing but nod. She kept pushing against the lady's shoulders, even though it felt useless to do so when she wasn't struggling against her. She held her down, and she smelled the metallic scent of blood, and she heard the words hammering against her skull.

*"It's the curse, it's the Fire Eyes. . . ."*

*"We have never even held the diamonds . . . They were just rubies we had. . . ."*

They didn't have them. Had never had them.

Andrei was going to be murderous.

Rushworth slammed back into the room, a vial in hand. "Are you holding her? You'll have to hold her—she hates this stuff."

Kira increased the pressure a second before Catherine tried to flail again. "No, no, no, *no*! Not the laudanum, Cris, please not the laudanum! I'll be good, I'll calm down, I'll—"

Lord Rushworth gripped her jaw. "Hold her forehead down." When Kira hesitated, he growled. "Must I get Dorsey in here to help me? Are you completely useless?"

Kira placed her forearm across Catherine's forehead, which meant all but lying atop her to hold her limbs down. Into her ear she whispered, in French, "Easy, calm down. It is for your good. You are overwrought."

Rushworth poured some of the liquid from the vial into his sister's mouth. "Swallow. Stop fighting me and swallow, Kitty. If you spit it on me again, I swear I'll bring Dorsey in here."

She swallowed. Stopped flailing. And her pleading, her shrieks, turned to sobs that seemed to start in her toes and heave their way up until they erupted from her lips.

Kira looked to Rushworth for permission to ease away. He nodded and recorked the vial, slid it into his jacket pocket. "It works quickly. She will sleep for a few hours."

She didn't know what to say. What to do. How to file away this information—that they didn't have the diamonds, had never had the diamonds. That this woman she couldn't like was broken in ways she hadn't imagined.

That this world she'd thought she wanted for her own might not be worth having. What was the point of it—of the riches, the sparkle, the gilding—if it couldn't protect one from the horrors? Death still stalked. Illness still pounced. Grief still ruled.

And she didn't have anyone beside her, anymore, to care if she suffered. No one to force medicine down her throat. To carry her when her knee gave out. No one to promise her all would be well.

Just a patron ready to write her a cheque and forget she existed, after she gave him what he wanted. Which she couldn't do.

She eased off the bed and turned to the door.

A hand slammed her to the wall, an arm pressed against her throat, pinning her there. Stealing the air.

As if she'd been able to breathe in the last twenty minutes anyway. Kira didn't gasp, didn't choke. She just looked straight into Rushworth's cold turquoise eyes.

He didn't sneer. He didn't rant. He just said, coolly and calmly, "Breathe a word of all this to anyone, and it will be the last word you speak."

She could see her reflection in his pupils. Not afraid, but not because she had any particular bravery. Because it didn't matter. She had nothing to lose. "The whole house would have heard the mirror."

He eased off only a bit. "I don't mean the blasted mirror. Mention the diamonds to anyone, and I will kill you in your sleep. Are we clear? You will be loyal, or you will no longer *be*."

Never in her life had anyone threatened to kill her. Shouldn't it have terrified her? Made her heart pound, her eyes weep, her limbs go weak? Yet all she could think was that dying in her sleep would be a far better option than whatever Andrei might do if she failed him. "If you are finished, I need to get the bandages and salve for her feet."

"I'm not just about threats. Be loyal, and there will be reward in it for you."

She saw no point in saying that there wasn't enough money in all the world to make her want to stay here, with them. "Thank you, my lord. Now if you please, your sister is bleeding all over the sheets."

He let her go.

She headed downstairs for the bandages, but then went down

still more. Lord Cayton was still in the servants' hall, just leaning against the wall outside her door, his eyes closed and his face a wreath of worry. Kira eased to a halt. "How is she? Resting?"

He nodded, not opening his eyes. "What did she break?"

It took her a moment to realize he meant Lady Pratt, not Felicity. "A mirror. Her brother sedated her."

"I went up—heard her shouts." He'd pitched his voice low now, quiet. "I thought I had better come back down here before Rush saw me. You heard her too. You know, now, what this is all about."

She had likely known it before he did, but she just nodded. Then said, "*Da*," when her tired mind noted that his eyes were still closed.

He opened them now, and they looked as weary as she felt. "Did he threaten you?"

"Of course."

He nodded and pushed off the wall. "If you want to leave, I can help you get passage away. Without him knowing, I mean."

And go where? Back to Andrei? She shook her head. Not yet. Not with only this to report. Not with Felicity as she was. "I am not leaving."

Lord Cayton rubbed at his neck. "Why are you women all so stubborn?"

"We have to be."

Her eyes went to her door, which was closed. She gave up on the whispering they'd both been doing. "I want to be here for her. I will not be able to do much, but it will give her comfort, knowing I am here. She has more faith in my skills than she should."

"You seem to know as much about it as the doctor does." He pointed himself toward the stairs she'd just come down. "Remember my offer."

She nodded and headed up the opposite way, toward the kitchen.

Dorsey still stood just inside, the bloody rags nowhere in sight and the floor spotless. His eyebrows were two slashes of suspicion. "Did I hear Lord Cayton say something about an offer?"

"To hire a nurse. For Felicity. I told him it wasn't necessary, I could handle it." The lie came easily, making the Babushka in her head cluck her tongue.

But Dorsey's eyebrows returned to their normal positions. "Was that Catherine throwing a fit—the crashing?"

*Catherine*? Yes, Kira had thought of her that way a few times. But she would never be so familiar in speech, not so long as she was her maid. There were rules. Everyone knew that. But then, he had been in their house so long—and she'd still been so young when he came. They must know each other well. "Yes. Lord Rushworth gave her laudanum."

The suspicion returned. Or no, it wasn't quite suspicion, it was . . . She didn't know what it was, but it darkened his eyes. "He didn't call for me."

"I helped him."

He didn't seem to hear her. "He always calls for me when he needs help sedating her. I hold her down. It's the only time he lets me touch her."

That sick feeling came back to her stomach. *Catherine*. "Why would you want to touch her?" Did she sound jealous—or concerned? "Do you . . . fancy her?"

Would that explain why he had served their house so long?

His eyes cleared, his smile flashed. "Nah. But she's pretty, aye? And she fancied *me* for a while, when she was younger. Not that I'd have anything to do with her, of course."

Hadn't she said she'd loved Pratt her whole life? Perhaps that didn't preclude a bit of an interest in another handsome man who lived under her nose, though. Kira couldn't really be sure. She'd had eyes only for ballet. Either way, she could see why Rushworth wouldn't like them near each other, if there were interest on either side. She nodded and reached for the bandages still sitting out on the table. "She cut her feet. I need to wrap them."

"Very good. Then that walk to the village?"

"All right." Maybe she'd just keep on walking. All the way to the end of England, across the Channel, over the Continent. All the way to Russia, where the snows would barely have begun to melt. Where her brothers could cajole her for staying away so long, for forgetting where she'd come from. Where Babushka would wrap her in her arms and say she had some chak-chak left, if she was in the mood for a sweet. Where Papka would tell her how much like her mother she looked.

Where life was simple and death was simple and faith was too deep to question.

She wanted to go home.

# Twenty-Three

E lla glanced at the clock on the mantel, trying to gauge how much time she had before Cayton was likely to join her in the library. It was eleven—a full hour after he usually came. Odd. She pushed to her feet, telling herself it was no reason for concern. He must just be talking longer than usual with Stafford—that was all. They were studying Romans—that could get interesting, and involving. Time probably slipped away from him.

Still, it was much later than usual. She had heard his car drive up before she made her way to the library, so there was no question that he was at Ralin. And her back was feeling tight, her neck getting sore from craning over her books. Her bottom had gone positively numb.

She needed her walk.

Well, he would find her if she started out on her own. She jotted him a quick note, left it on his chair, and hummed her way outside.

Sunshine had found their corner of the world again, and she welcomed it with a smile as she stepped out into the garden. Her ears strained for the sound of baby squeals, but all she heard were birds chorusing from the wood and horses whinnying in the pastures. Sounds of spring, of life.

*Life.* A letter had come from Midwynd yesterday. First a note from Rowena, saying all was well and that she missed her, that Annie—Rowena's stepsister who had been staying with them since last fall—wanted to know when she'd be home. That Sussex wasn't the same without her.

She'd smiled at that one. And then smiled even more when she'd read Brice's note, which told her that Rowena had been having contractions. False ones, but they indicated her time was likely to be soon.

Ella was going to be an aunt, and she couldn't wait. He'd promised to ring the castle the moment the baby arrived, and she was already anticipating the static-filled line, the familiar voice, the joyous news. *"Boy,"* he would say, *"and little Worthing is perfect."* Or, *"It's a girl, and she's as beautiful as her mother. Come meet her, Ella-bell."*

Maybe, when she was home visiting, she'd tell him about Cayton. About how Rushworth had told him to court her, about how he tried so hard to make it seem like he didn't want to.

About how she'd fallen in love.

Then she'd let him know oh-so-delicately that she knew very well where the Fire Eyes were, and she didn't much appreciate being kept in the dark about them when she'd been wearing them around as if they were nothing but priceless heirloom rubies.

Wait, that didn't sound quite right.

Then . . . then, while she was home, she'd have to go to the sanitarium where Stella lived now, locked away in a room where she couldn't hurt anyone. She'd have to listen to her oldest friend prattle about Brice and how happy they would be together someday. She'd have to look into troubled eyes and see the madness so clearly now and wonder for the millionth time how she had missed it before. How she'd been fooled for so long.

She stepped around a flowering lilac bush and came to an abrupt halt. Cayton stood in the middle of the path, staring up into the sky. Addie wasn't with him. Nor Stafford. No one was, but he had that look about him—as if he'd been standing there so long moss was likely to be growing on his shoes.

"Cayton?" He hadn't come to see her. It pierced, even as she told herself she shouldn't let it. Reminded herself it was just a fake courtship, so he was entitled to let it slide now and then.

But it wasn't. She had been so sure it wasn't.

He turned to face her, revealing a face etched with worry. "Sorry. I was going to . . . It's been a bad couple of days. Felicity had a seizure. Something called eclampsia."

"Oh, James. I'm so sorry. Is she all right?" She rushed to him, took his hand. Dared to touch a hand to his face.

Her mind flashed to a morning's fog, Rushworth's face. This one was so much better.

Cayton closed his eyes and gusted out a sigh. "I don't know. It could happen again, the doctor said. Is likely to, until she delivers. But she won't let them take the child, though he said it was less risky than the pregnancy continuing. She won't listen to anyone."

Of course not. Babies needed all the time they could get in their mothers' wombs. She'd read all about it when she learned Rowena was expecting. And a bit about eclampsia and its precursor too. That part had been terrifying, and she'd hidden the book to keep Rowena from picking it up.

There were some things people just didn't need to know about unless they needed to know about them. And since it wasn't as though there was anything they could do to prevent it, why invite worry?

She stroked her thumb over his cheekbone, feeling bold and yet *right*. "Why didn't you come and tell me about it? You needn't carry this on your own."

"Because . . . because I can't pretend today. I can't put on a smile for whoever's watching. I can't."

"No one would expect you to. And you don't have to pretend. We're friends, remember?" His cheek was warm under her fingers, his jaw just a bit rough. There was no paint on his neck today, and she found she missed it.

His eyes slid shut. "It's all coming to a head, I think. Maybe it's just my paranoia saying so, but . . . Kitty had a breakdown after Felicity's seizure. Rush was in a fit of his own because of it. Muttering all night about no more time, no more time. He's going to do something, Ella. Soon. Or make me do something. And I can't."

"You don't have to. If he tells you to, you come here, and . . ."

He shook his head, dislodging her fingers, and opened his eyes. An echo of anger painted shadows in their depths. "No one wants to listen—as if better answers will just appear. Whitby is still in Yorkshire. Who knows if he has gathered anything useful since he wrote that last cryptic letter. Stafford has been trying to locate more rubies to pass as the diamonds—but it wouldn't work a second time, which I have *tried* to tell him. But why should he listen to me?"

"Cayton."

"We may have found the legend about the Fire Eyes, but it doesn't really matter, does it?" He lifted a hand, rubbed at his neck. "He's threatened Lareau. He's threatened my daughter. I paid a call on the constable this morning to tell him, but he can't do anything either, not so long as it's just vague, idle-sounding threats with no evidence that he's anything but an arrogant lord who likes to sound powerful when he isn't."

Ella ran her thumb along the hand she still held.

He pulled it away. "And you, I notice, didn't bother telling anyone that you saw him in the village. But you did, didn't you."

"Yes." But she still didn't know what to make of it. How to tell anyone about it without it sounding unreal. *He offered to become whomever I wanted him to be.* "He didn't threaten me or anything. Just . . . just asked to court me. Officially."

"Just asked . . . Ella." He lifted both hands, framed her face. It sent a little thrill through her, until she saw that his eyes were far from soft and imploring. They were hard, determined. "He is dangerous. And he is unraveling. I don't think playing his game is going to work much longer. He's going to snap, to strike, to . . . I don't know what, but you can't be in his path when it happens, and he seems far too determined to keep you in his path right now. You have to go home. You *must*."

She could, perhaps. Say the letter from Brice had said the baby would come any day and that she'd decided to try to get there in time for it. Rushworth would believe her. "But how would that help? If I go, he would either assume I took the diamonds with me and come along—possibly waylaying me on the journey and stealing them—or if I left them here and we somehow told him, he would just strike the Staffords."

"I've a plan. You'll leave them here. I'll say you left in such a rush that you forgot them. I . . . I'll say I convinced Stafford to open the safe, to give them to me, that I'll take them to you."

His hands were cool against her face, but warming. And warming her. "So you'll keep all the danger focused on *you*? Cayton—"

"We can make it believable. We'll fight. Here, now. This is the one spot I'm absolutely sure someone is watching. Stafford has narrowed it down to just a few suspects. We fight, they report it, I go home and rant about it. Then you leave. He'll tell me to go after you, and I'll say I can use it as an excuse to get the diamonds. We have the constable and his men waiting. When he tries to get them, when I refuse, when he acts—they catch him."

Catch him with a gun raised, he meant. And what if he pulled the trigger before they could stop him? She shook her head. "Absolutely not. There has to be a safer way."

"Ella." His eyes went even harder. "This is the way we're doing it. Stafford approved it, more or less. You and I are going to argue. Loudly. Or better still, something visible. Slap me."

It was probably a bad time to be amused. But he honestly expected her to slap him? "I beg your pardon?"

"Slap me. Like you mean it."

Her lips tugged up. Just a little. "It would look ridiculous. I don't *want* to slap you. Why would I want to slap you?"

"Oh, use your imagination. Perhaps I insulted you."

With his hands framing her face like this? "You're always insulting me. But I'm just not the slapping type."

His eyes shifted, though she didn't know what words to use to describe the change. "Fine. I'll . . . I'll kiss you. You pull away and slap me for taking liberties."

"I—" His lips cut her off. They weren't gentle, probably by design. He did, after all, want her to pull away, to retreat, to get angry.

But his hands cradled her head and his mouth moved over hers, and her breath balled up in her chest and forgot whether it should be inhaling or exhaling. Her hands settled on his chest and then, of their own will, slid around him to hold him close.

"Ella," he breathed against her lips. "You're supposed to pull away."

"Was I? I forgot." She moved her face, just a slight tilt, to make her lips touch his again. Her blood hummed through her veins. Should it have felt so daring? So right? "Try again. I'll get it right this time."

He laughed. A rumbling in his chest, a pulling of his lips. "Liar."

"No, no, I'll remember. Kiss me. Make it count."

She felt his hum all through her, resonating. He pulled her closer, or perhaps she pulled him. Tilted his head. Kissed her again, but more.

He made it count. Parted her lips and made her head swim. Dug his fingers into her hair until it tumbled down around her shoulders. Held her so close the wind could scarcely breeze between them.

She forgot to pull away again. But apparently he forgot to remind her, so she saw no reason to speak up. Far better to savor the moment, to discover how he would move next, to learn how to respond.

Her first kiss—and she seriously doubted any other would ever surpass it.

She barely heard the gasp coming from the right, didn't quite register the sound of a book falling to the flagstone. But there was no missing the explosion of French that blistered the air. It ended with a heavily accented, "Get your hands off her!"

It looked as though Brook would provide their argument for them.

◈

A caged tigress, perhaps, might stalk around with approximately half as much fury and explosive energy as his cousin's wife. Maybe. Cayton could think of nothing else that would come close, unless one could bottle up a typhoon.

He slouched into his usual chair in the library, wishing he had thought to run for cover. He could have been home by now.

But that was the thing with Brook's tempers—they just swept all hapless bystanders along.

All right, he wasn't exactly hapless. But if she would stop ranting in three different languages long enough for an explanation . . . No, that would achieve nothing. What was he to say? Perhaps the idea had sprung from the right place—keeping Ella safe—but that had flown out the window the moment he'd touched his lips to hers, and they all knew it.

He was a cad. A reprobate. A selfish, untrustworthy rogue.

He risked a glance at Ella. She wasn't sulking in a chair like him—but then, she didn't seem to be swamped by guilt at her lapse in judgment. She stood before the towering window, arms folded, watching her friend pace. Not a hint of remorse on her face.

It was nearly as infuriating as the smirk upon Stafford's. Didn't she realize how terrible an idea it was to kiss him? She should have stopped him before he ever drew her closer. If she had so much as a stitch of sense, she would have.

Brook paused in her tirade—it had been in Italian now, he was fairly certain. Utterly incomprehensible. Ella lifted her brows. "Are you finished yet? Because I'd like to say something before you have to run from the room to lose your breakfast."

Brook narrowed her eyes, though it failed, somchow, to wither Ella. "I'm too angry to be sick." Anger sounded like French in her consonants and Monegasque in her vowels. "And all the angrier because this has obviously only been happening *because* I've been sick. What kind of friend goes behind my back with a man like *him*, knowing full well that if I weren't confined to my chaise, I would put a stop to it?"

Cayton had straightened a bit at that *him*. But she was right, so what in the world could he say? He glanced at his cousin.

Stafford, odd creature that he was, watched his wife with

nothing short of adoration as she fumed. "It isn't quite what you think, Brooklet. It's just a ruse to appease Rushworth."

Brook never had any compunction about whirling on the duke. Waving her arms about like a madwoman. Pointing accusatory fingers at one of her dearest friends. "That was *not* a ruse! And are you telling me you knew about this, Justin Wildon?"

"Now, *mon âme*." Having taught her last year how to box, Stafford was too smart to make any placating gestures. Or get within right-hook range. Cayton had glimpsed a few of the lessons, and he didn't mean to get any closer to the duchess. "We tried several times to tell you, but you were just so unwell."

Her fury was a thousand suns.

Cayton considered trying his hand at poetry to adequately capture it. Or perhaps paint her as an erupting volcano. He'd give it to Whitby for Christmas and earn himself a booming laugh.

"We'll discuss *that* later." She spun back to Ella. "I know playacting when I see it, and I know what it isn't. I'm shocked at you. Kissing him like that!"

Ella snorted a laugh. It didn't sound particularly friendly, which warmed his heart another few degrees. "Really, Brook, I knew you were many things, but I never dreamed you were such a hypocrite."

That managed to silence Brook, and drop her jaw too. For a moment. "*Pardonnez-moi?*"

Ella lowered her arms, looking ready to step into the boxing ring herself. "Will you try to tell me you never kissed Stafford 'like that'? What about before he ran off to India?"

Stafford grinned and tried to hide it behind a hand. Brook's cheeks went red. "That was entirely different."

Ella slashed a hand through the air. "It was *not*."

"It was! He was my best friend."

314

"Well, Cayton is *my* friend."

He shouldn't be. He should have found another way from the start, refused to go near her. He should have the good sense not to be glad to hear her declare him her friend.

Brook waved an arm at him, as if to say, *"How could he be? Just look at him."* And she had a point. "You barely know each other!"

Hopefully Ella wouldn't point out that they had gotten to know each other rather well over the last month. It would only remind Brook of all she didn't know.

Ella rolled her eyes. "We don't all have the good fortune of falling for our childhood friends, Brook."

*Good. No, no, bad. Very bad.* Cayton straightened, nearly brave enough to interject that "falling for" was not the appropriate phrase.

"*Falling for* him?" Brook went still, her eyes firing bullets. She spewed out something in French far too fast for him to keep up with.

Whatever it was, it must have been strong and pointed. The adoration shifted to anger on Stafford's face, and he stepped forward. "That's enough. You don't have to like him. You don't have to like the idea of them courting. But please don't speak that way of my cousin, not now. Not when he has worked so hard to become a better man."

Cayton hadn't realized he'd been amused by the situation. Not until it faded, hardened, turned achy. Until he wished he'd followed the rapid French. And then thought perhaps he should be grateful he hadn't. Whatever she'd said, it had probably been right. Certainly *used* to be right. And might be right again if he didn't manage to keep Ella—heart and body—safe.

He couldn't manage that if Ella were falling for him. Heaven only knew why she would, but—but he wasn't strong enough to hold out forever if she kept up those smiles and laughter and jesting and seeing right through his gruffness. If she kept looking at him as she'd been doing and finding excuses to touch his arm or hand. If she kissed him again like she'd done ten minutes ago.

He couldn't protect her from himself if she stayed so close to his side.

He pushed to his feet, met no one's gaze, though he kept his up in the same range as theirs. "You're right, Brook. I have no idea what you said, but I can guess. And you're right. I've proven myself to be a weak-willed and selfish man. Certainly not good enough for your friend, and just using her for my own means. In this case, to protect myself from Rushworth's threats. I kissed her for my own purposes, my own pleasure, with no intentions of following it up with any noble offers of marriage. With no intentions, even, of asking her brother for permission to court her. So . . . " He spread his arms, let them fall. "There we have it. Perhaps I haven't changed as much as I thought."

He had meant it to push Ella away. Not for it to sound so . . . *true.*

But it was. He was still everything he hated, everything he wished he'd never been. How, if the Lord removed his sin as far as the east was from the west, did he keep ramming into it every time he turned around?

Ella materialized before him, her face cut from stone. Her hair still down around her shoulders, where he'd put it. Her eyes blazing. She stepped close, too close, and lifted her hand. He expected . . . something deserved. That slap he'd asked for, a poke, a prod.

She settled her hand over his heart, fingers splayed. "Don't believe the lies, Cayton. Push me away if you must, but don't believe for a moment that you're still that man."

*Blast*. Why did she have to be so . . . Ella? His nose ached. And his eyes. "Go home, Ella. You're not needed here."

Her smile looked sad. "I would. But I can't. I can't leave you."

Brook made noises that were no doubt a protest. He couldn't really hear her over the rushing in his head. He couldn't look away from Ella's eyes. There were no eyes in the world like hers. No soul in the world like the one behind them. "Go home." *Don't beg. Stay strong.* "I don't want you here."

Her other hand touched his face, traced his jaw. "I know."

She did, too much. Too clearly. She knew the why behind the words, and she was just too stubborn to budge. He closed his eyes, though it did nothing to erase the image of hers. "Go home. I . . . I don't even like you."

Her lips touched his. Her voice, at his ear, said, "I love you too."

The world froze. He couldn't move, couldn't open his eyes, couldn't even breathe. If he did, it would all shatter, and the truth would drown him, and he'd have to face again the guilt of a broken heart laid at his feet. He just wasn't sure if it would be hers, this time, or his own.

There was more shouting. A flurry. Ella's hands fell away, and his lips went cool. Brook shouted something about Ella leaving. Ella shouted back her refusal. Then the massive library door crashed into the shelf.

Stafford was the first thing Cayton saw when he opened his eyes, and he looked as angry as his wife. *At* his wife. "Aren't you going to go after her?"

Brook threw herself into a chair, jaw set. Answer enough.

Stafford spun on him. "Cayton?"

His feet were part of the floor. He couldn't even convince his eyes to follow Stafford as he moved.

And move he did, with an exasperated huff and a Gallic toss

of his hands into the air. "Fine, *I'll* go after her. You two try not to kill each other for five blasted minutes, if that's not too much to ask."

The silence ticked. Then it tocked. Then it was ruined by Brook's loud exhalation. "Am I judging you too harshly?"

His heart, he was fairly certain, wasn't even beating. "No."

"He says I am. And my father says I need to forgive you. But you . . . Are you even capable of a good relationship? I don't mean it to be cruel, but . . ."

But she was Ella's friend. It was understandable. Cayton curled his fingers to his palm. "I . . . don't know."

She studied him too intently. And he had no idea what she saw. "Do you love her?"

He tried a swallow, though his throat felt tight and raw. "Does it matter? I thought I loved Melissa."

She rubbed a hand over her face and muttered a French phrase he'd never heard. "You do. So why are you pushing her away?"

She, of all people, ought to know the answer to that. Cayton straightened his fingers again. "Because if she stays, she'll get hurt. We have to get her away from here. Send her home."

Lifting her brows, Brook said, "She won't go. What am I to do, drag her out of the house?"

She *had* to go. It wasn't a choice. He sighed. "No. I think we need to be more extreme than that. I think we had better send for her brother."

Brook's eyes slid shut. "Who ever would have thought that we'd agree on something?"

It was probably a sign of the apocalypse.

## Twenty-Four

Kira slid the paper onto the counter at the telegraph office, praying she didn't look as nervous as she felt. Another letter from Andrei had arrived yesterday, filled again with sweet nothings that were only a decoy for that final line, in Russian: *Send me word, milaya. Or I send you a helper.*

Helper—one of his thugs, he meant, who would come less to help than to intimidate.

The man behind the counter greeted her with a vague smile. "Afternoon, miss."

"Good afternoon." She'd written her reply to him in French. *I am well, and working hard. You needn't worry for me, my friend. A little while longer and I shall return to Paris.*

She had no idea if the words about her return were truth or lie—but she wasn't about to send any more detail than that over the wire. She would have to write a letter detailing all Rushworth had said about them having had rubies, not the diamonds. Explaining that all her searching through Catherine's things had yielded nothing helpful, that she must rely now on what else she could overhear. She would write it in Russian, as he had instructed her before she left Paris. Using the code words they had agreed upon.

But that would take time, and he was getting impatient. It had seemed prudent to send something today.

The man looked over the page she'd provided, tapped a finger to the direction, and consulted a chart on his counter for the price. While she fished out enough coins to send the short message to Paris, noise outside drew the operator's gaze up. A smile touched his lips. "I'll get this right out, miss, just as soon as I see what the duchess needs—though yours will be in the queue ahead of hers, of course."

"Oh." *The duchess.* Her stomach dropped, twisted. "Of course. That is no problem." To prove it, she spun away, as if to study a map tacked to the wall.

But from the corner of her eye, she watched through the glass window as a servant opened the door of a car, as Brook climbed out and surveyed the street, offering a smile and wave to someone nearby.

Her mouth was tight, though, as she came in, and there was tension in her shoulders. She had always carried herself well, with a grace and poise taught to her by her actress mother and the royal tutors. But Kira could see unease behind the usual good posture.

She wanted to rush forward, to embrace her friend, kiss her cheeks. Instead, she turned her face away under the guise of studying the things on the walls, so that Brook wouldn't see so much as her profile. Then, once the duchess was fully inside and heading to the counter, where the man greeted her with familiarity, Kira eased toward the door.

Rain began to patter down, soft and cool, within seconds of her stepping outside. Kira sighed and opened the umbrella she'd brought along, given the gloomy grey clouds above.

"Sophie! Give you a lift?"

She looked up but was rendered immobile when she saw Dorsey behind the wheel of Lord Cayton's automobile. "Dorsey?"

"Come on, hen, it's raining—don't make me stand here with my head out the window."

Her fingers tightened on the handle of the umbrella. This couldn't be right. In the weeks they'd been here, she'd never once seen anyone but Lord Cayton himself drive the car. Not any of the staff, not even his own valet, with whom he seemed to be on especially good terms. Why would he allow some *other* man's servant to take it out?

She eased closer and checked over her shoulder to make sure Brook hadn't spotted the infraction—she'd have no compunction about storming out and dressing down any perceived wrong. But Brook's golden head was still bent over the counter, safely behind the glass of the telegraph office. Kira bent hers toward Dorsey. "What are you doing? Lord Cayton could not possibly have given you permission to take out his car."

Dorsey's eyes went flinty. His smile held fast, though it looked more chiseled in stone than warm. "How else would I have it, then? Are you walking back in the rain, Sophie, or getting in?"

The rain had gone from patter to steady drumming, and the hillside in the distance had almost vanished behind a curtain of heavy silver. Even with the umbrella, she was likely to be soaked within minutes if that downpour caught her before she reached the manor. Which it likely would.

"All right." She hurried around to the passenger's side and closed up her umbrella as Dorsey leaned over to open the door for her. Barely had she settled on the seat before he took off.

The look he angled her way was no warmer than the drumming rain. "What were you doing in the village alone? You said we'd get that ice cream the next time we came to the village."

Kira could only stare at him, but then said, "It hardly seemed a day for ice cream. It is cold and rainy."

Jaw ticking, he faced the road again. "You could have asked

me to come with you, at least. Unless . . . Who were you wiring just now? That man you left, that you said you're through with?"

Kira's fingers went tight around the wet umbrella. It wasn't the words. The words could have been nothing but pouty and jealous. It was the tone, and that flint in his eyes, that made her spine snap straight. "It is none of your business who I communicate with."

A mocking laugh whispered from Dorsey's lips. "Think you're too good for me, do you, hen? Is that it? Well, I always get my girl. *Always*."

Anlic was already at hand, but for a moment she feared he'd blow right past the turn. She gripped the edge of the seat. "That you may—but I am not your girl. Certainly not if this is how you behave when I dare to send a note home without asking your permission first."

He took the turn. Too hard, too fast, sending mud and gravel spraying out behind them. Lord Cayton would certainly not be pleased.

Dorsey grunted. "Home. To your mum, then?"

She drew in a breath. So little he knew her, if he thought her mother still alive. So little she had known *him*, if she had thought him charming. What was that verse Babushka always quoted? *"Charm is deceitful . . ."* It spoke of women, but it seemed to her it applied just as well to men. And she'd had her fill of charm that did nothing but hide the roiling darkness within a man.

The car jerked to a stop, and Kira let herself out without so much as a "good day." It wasn't one. And no others were likely to be as long as men's darkness ruled her life.

❦

The light was terrible. Lamps cast shadows, and he hadn't had the garret wired for electricity, and even if he had, the light from the bulbs wouldn't be at all right for painting. Cayton kept darting a glance at the canvas he'd barely put any color on, but he'd only ruin it if he tried to add more. He'd just have to be content with the blue sky and a few wisps of white cloud that he'd done yesterday evening, when trying to put the scene at Ralin behind him. Tomorrow would have to be soon enough to paint the autumn leaves floating down from unseen tree branches.

He wasn't content with sketching. He should have left his garret already. He should be on his way to Ralin, studying Romans with Stafford. Thinking about when he'd make his way down to the library, where Ella would be buried in a mountain of books. He'd toss her an insult; she'd bat it back with a laugh. He'd choose a book from her stack and start reading and pretend that he didn't glance up every minute just to see her bent over her own books.

But he couldn't go to Ralin today. Not after yesterday. And he couldn't paint. When he told her they wouldn't be heading to the castle, Tabby had taken Addie downstairs to distract the bedridden Felicity for an hour.

He spun to the window, watched yesterday's rain drip from the trees for a minute, and then gave up with a shake of his head. He would change into his riding clothes and head outside. Perhaps the damp air would wash away some of this nervous energy he couldn't shake. And if he happened to end up at Ralin . . . No, he wouldn't. Though if Ella happened to be as daft as he and was wandering around somewhere near his land again . . .

"You're an idiot, Cayton." Self-lecture delivered, he nevertheless stormed out the garret door, down the steep steps, and toward his bedroom. Evans would be taking the brush to yesterday's shoes this time of day, probably downstairs near his sister. He'd have to ring for him. He let himself into his room.

"Hello, Cayton."

He froze rather than jumping. His heart went still rather than racing. His eyes searched the shadows until he found Rushworth there, in the chair by the unlit fireplace. He slammed the door shut. "Really, Rush? My *room*?"

Rushworth didn't twitch. "I assumed, correctly apparently, that you would come here to change before you head to Ralin. Though you're rather later than usual."

And how often had he let himself in here to poke around? The question made Cayton feel prickly as a burr. "Get out."

"In a moment." Rushworth unfolded himself from his chair and stood. His motions weren't quite as smooth as usual. "We need to talk."

"About what? I'm doing as you asked, I'm—"

"I've changed my mind." Rushworth turned to the window, clasped his hands behind his back. But his fingers twitched. "Stop. Stop courting her."

"I beg your pardon?" He prayed he kept the panic out of his tone. The claws of fear that said, *Why? Why is he changing things now?*

"I said *stop*." His fingers curled, uncurled. The muscle in his jaw ticked. He drew in a slow breath. "You kissed her. I never told you to kiss her."

The spy had been watching then—or had just overheard the explosion to follow. He would ask Stafford which of their suspects had been working in the right area yesterday—the housemaid or the kitchen boy.

It probably didn't matter much at this point. Cayton let his face settle into the old one he used to wear on social occasions, when he wanted everyone to think him something other than what he was. "You told me to court her. To either win her trust or break her heart. How exactly did you expect me to do that if not by eventually kissing her and seeing how she responded?"

Rushworth's lips peeled away from his teeth. "Don't do it again. Are we clear? Do not *ever* touch her that way again."

*Ella, please be on your way home. Far, far away from him.* He effected a shrug. "I daresay it's irrelevant—the duchess isn't likely to let me in her house again. She was no happier to stumble upon us than you are to have heard about it. So . . . the ball is, as they say, in your court. Pick up the pieces, as you wanted to do."

*Be halfway to Sussex. Better still, halfway to the Continent. On a ship to America. Anywhere but here.*

Rushworth's nostrils flared. "If you've ruined this . . ."

*Lord, protect us. Protect Addie. Protect Ella.* He held his arms wide. "You *wanted* me to ruin it! To hurt her, to make her hate me. Didn't you? Isn't that what your plan was, so you could rush in and convince her to love *you*? *And* hand you the diamonds?"

"If you haven't sent her running back to Sussex, the diamonds in hand."

Cayton loosed a grunt that hopefully sounded just disgusted enough, just disinterested enough. He wrenched open the door of his wardrobe and pulled out his riding clothes, tossed them onto the bed. "What do you want me to do, Rush? Go back over there and try to see her again or let her think I got what I wanted and have lost interest? Just tell me."

Rushworth stood stock-still. Staring at him, hard and cold and calm, a million silent thoughts ticking away behind his eyes. An inhale, an exhale, a blink. Then a low, "It doesn't matter. Your time is up—you've lost your chance. She's too good for the likes of you."

"Indeed." And look at that—something on which Brook, Cayton, and Rushworth *all* agreed.

His door slammed behind his uninvited guest, all Cayton's feigned energy extinguishing with the draft. He closed his eyes and rested his forehead on the carved wood of his wardrobe. It bit. He didn't move. *Lord God . . . help us.*

Rushworth's angry footsteps faded away. Down the stairs. Down more stairs, toward the servants' quarters. Looking for his valet, perhaps, or checking on his sister, who wouldn't be budged from Felicity's side.

The room where Tabby was with Addie.

Cayton let out a breath. He had to get his daughter out of this house. He'd send her to his mother, but she and Aunt Caro could be heading home any time. He needed a different way. A way to keep *everyone* safe. And the only way to achieve that one way was to admit what he'd been denying.

Ella. He had to rely on Ella, trust Ella. *Love* Ella. Because if it worked, if everyone stayed safe, lived through this, she wouldn't let him off the hook when it was all said and done.

And . . . he didn't want her to. He had to protect her from himself, yes—but maybe he'd had it all wrong. Maybe the only way to make sure he didn't hurt her was to stay by her side. To guarantee that when she ached, he ached with her. To know that if her smiles faded, he could cajole them back.

What were those words he had read the other day at Ralin, with Stafford? From the fifth chapter of Romans—words that had brought Ella surging to his thoughts, to his heart. *"And hope maketh not ashamed; because the love of God is shed abroad in our hearts by the Holy Ghost which is given unto us."*

Hope. If it could take a physical form, it would have brilliant red hair and laughing cider eyes. And it would bid him believe that God loved him this much, enough to entrust him with the gift of her heart. That the Spirit could overcome his failings, could check him before he destroyed that fragile hope.

Or no, it wasn't fragile at all. It was linked to the very love of God. That made it the strongest thing in the world.

For the first time in his memory, light suffused his spirit, and he sank down onto his bed with the sure knowledge that this was *right*. That he could be what the Lord called him to be, with His help. That he could love, and accept love in return. He could be more than a good father. He could be a good husband.

He knew what he had to do.

## Twenty-Five

Foul moods didn't suit her, but Ella couldn't escape this one's fangs. She hadn't ventured out of her room since the argument in the library yesterday. She had wanted to—had wanted to go outside and let the rain wash it all away. She'd wanted to wander to the wood and pray. She'd wanted to get lost . . . and maybe to find her hope in the wilds.

But she kept hearing Brook in her head, chiding her for venturing out alone, unarmed. She kept seeing Cayton's irritated face when he'd found her on that first rainy walk.

She kept seeing Stella, madness in her eyes.

Ella pulled her knees up and leaned her head against the window, looking out at the weak sunshine trying to chase away the night's clouds. What if she was wrong? What if Cayton didn't love her, and she'd made a fool of herself yesterday? What if he really did intend to just let her walk away? What if his kiss had been nothing but pretense and a bit of physical attraction?

What if he wasn't the man God intended for her?

The thought made her heart twist and groan. So many things she'd been wrong about in her life, but it might just destroy her if this was one of them. If he didn't love her as she did him. . . .

328

She closed her eyes against the gaining sunlight and felt the cold of the glass pane against her forehead more than the meager touch of warmth on the rest of her face. Maybe she *should* just go home. Let this past month's memories fade into nothing. Let someone else deal with the diamond business, since no one wanted to include her anyway. Admit that she was always wrong about everything that counted.

*God?* She wanted to pray, but she couldn't find any words. Just a silent cry deep inside. A begging. A plea to know, to be sure, one way or another.

The sunlight shifted, painting colors through her eyelids. Transforming them into shapes. She saw autumn leaves in reds and golds and oranges. Falling, gliding through the sky like dancers upon an invisible stage. Rolling hills, the dusky green of cool weather, behind them. A man, smiling, dressed in his best. Dark hair, green eyes.

Her heart sighed.

A girl. Dark hair, blue eyes. Addie, but a bit older than Addie. Standing steadily. No, walking. Running. Chasing a butterfly, pure rapture on her face.

And a woman. She wore white, a perfect match to the lone cloud drifting through the sky. A veil in her auburn hair. A smile on her face.

Contentment.

A dream, that was all. The hope she'd clung to, put to pictures.

Ridiculous, unattainable pictures.

A light tap sounded, bidding her raise her head, even as the door opened with the silence of the staff. Ella looked over, saw a maid she didn't recognize, and failed to summon the energy for a smile.

The girl dipped a quick curtsy and kept her gaze on the floor.

"Excuse me, milady. The duchess sent me to inquire if you'd join her on a ride. She said she'd await you at the stables."

A ride? Ella glanced out at the muddy landscape, which would have deterred most people from such exercise. Not Brook, of course . . . but was she really feeling up to it? And didn't Stafford do his best to dissuade her from such things while she was with child? What if she just wanted to argue more? It didn't sit right.

But perhaps it was a peace offering. She pushed aside the disquiet and forced herself to her feet. "Very well. Tell her I'll be down as soon as I ring for my maid to assist me into my habit."

The girl flushed. "I could help you, milady. . . . That is, if you'd allow it. I'm only a housemaid at the moment, but I'd be happy to lend a hand."

Ella's lips tugged up a bit. The girl seemed nervous—at speaking so to her? Perhaps it was experience she could use for advancement, small as it would be. "All right. If you could just help me with my buttons."

It would have been quicker to ring for the borrowed lady's maid. The girl's fingers shook so badly it took a solid two minutes to manage all the buttons down Ella's back. But she gave her another smile and then slipped out of the day dress, into her riding habit.

She had no reason to feel such dread in the pit of her stomach as she considered walking down the stairs. No reason to narrow her eyes at the young maid's retreating back as they both stepped into the hall and the girl scurried away. No reason to want to slam back into her room and let Brook take her ride by herself.

A year ago she would have obeyed the feeling, reasonable or not. But what did such reactions ever get her but the chiding of her friends and family? *"Silly Ella,"* they'd all say, *"letting her emotions rule her like a child."*

Her fingers curled into her palm. Very well then—she'd trust reason above her own judgment. She'd face her stubborn friend. She'd listen to whatever words she wanted to say. She'd reasonably, logically decide which of those words to take to heart and which to dismiss.

Determination fueled her quick steps along the hall, down the stairs, toward the door. But then her feet came to a halt when voices reached her from the drawing room. Quite a few voices. All talking over each other. All familiar. But not all where they ought to be. Wondering if she'd somehow stepped through the looking glass, she walked in a daze to the drawing room door.

"Ella-bell!" Arms came around her and lifted her off her feet, her brother's laugh filling her ears. "Late riser today?"

"Brice." *Brice?* She shook her head, but the vision didn't change. It was still his brown eyes, his dimpled grin, his voice prattling on about train rides. She pulled away. "What are you doing here? I'd have thought Rowena—"

"Wouldna let him come on his own?" Her sister-in-law stepped away from Brook and Stafford, who'd been blocking the view of her, with open arms. "Ye ken me well."

Ella hugged her too, though she couldn't draw all that close, given the enormity of Rowena's stomach. She had most assuredly stumbled into Wonderland. "What are you . . . ? You're due any day! You've been having pains, he said. You shouldn't be traveling."

Brice grunted. "Thank you. Had she listened to that . . ."

Rowena sent her silver eyes heavenward. "Aye, and ye would have been so much happier had I stayed home, had the *bairn*, and ye missed it. We're together. As we should be."

"You . . ." Ella pressed a hand to her temple and thought to glance at Brook. Who, beneath the obvious concern for Rowena and the hint of green at it being morning, looked rather smug. Ella's spine snapped straight. "What are *either* of you doing here?"

Brice smiled and slung his hands in his pockets, as if she were silly enough to fall for his charm. "Can't a man come to see his sister and friends?"

"When his wife is due to have a baby any minute? *No.*" Ella spun on Brook. "You called him. You called my brother to force me home, when you *knew*—" Words failed her, so she settled for an exasperated growl and stomped closer to her interfering hostess. "I can't believe you!"

"What I can't believe"—Brice put a hand on her shoulder and pulled her back again—"is that my sister would make such a nuisance of herself that her hostess had to ask someone to remove her from her home. Really, Ella."

"Oh, shut up. You don't know what you're talking about. And you—" Brice's hand was too heavy, wouldn't let her move. She pointed at Brook instead. "How can you speak of independence as you do and then sic my *brother* on me?"

Brook crossed her arms over her chest. "Ella, I love you too much to see you hurt. You're going home. You're leaving the diamonds here. We'll take care of it."

"Diamonds." Brice hissed out a breath and let go her shoulder. "Ella . . . you brought the earrings with you?"

She folded her arms over her chest. "Well of *course* I brought the earrings with me. Though to be sure, I wouldn't have had anyone ever bothered to tell me what they really were!"

"And now the Rushworths are here. And they know she has them," Brook added.

Rowena drew in a sharp breath. Assuming it of shock or concern, Ella turned on her, fully prepared to assure her she had it in hand.

But Rowena was staring at nothing, a hand on her abdomen.

After a bare moment, though, she seemed to realize the conversation had ground to a halt and waved a hand. "It's nothing. Dinna mind me."

Brice was checking his watch. "Half an hour. It was forty minutes last time. They're closer."

"And it was twenty the time before that. It's nothing."

"I told you that you shouldn't have come." Brice brushed past Ella to put an arm around his wife. "You need to sit. Better yet, go and lie down for a while. They ease up when you do. You can rest while Ella packs, and then we'll be back on the train. Home again soon enough."

Ella pressed her fingers to her temples. "I am *not* going home!"

"Here." Brook hurried toward the sofa and arranged a few decorative pillows. "Rest here for now, Rowena. I can't believe you came. I couldn't be budged from the house when my time was near."

"They are false contractions, the doctor said. And if they become real . . . I willna have this *bairn* alone." She sank onto the couch, but it was more discomfort than pain on her face.

"Of course not. We're in this together, darling." Brice sat beside her, her hand in his. "Ella, go and pack. *Now.*"

"No." They weren't listening, of course. They never listened. If they had, she wouldn't be here with someone else's red diamonds, with criminals paying her court, with a sister-in-law who traveled all this way when she shouldn't have, so that she could stay by the side of a brother who oughtn't to have ever left home.

Ella didn't know whether to cry or shout.

Brook handed Rowena another pillow. "You might have to drag her out. Cayton's involved, and she thinks she's in love with him."

*Shout.* She definitely wanted to shout. Except that she'd no more than parted her lips before Brice spun on his seat, eyes wide. "*What?* Ella hasn't even *met* Cayton."

Perhaps she would try her hand at throwing things too. "Right. Because I'm all the time falling in love with people I've never met."

Her brother's eyes locked with hers. "You are, rather. Every single romantic story has you sighing over the hero, and——"

"Stop it, all of you!" She had a feeling it wasn't her volume that silenced them all so much as the sob that rose with it. She swallowed it down. "I know the difference between a romantic story and *love*, you idiot. I'm not going home. I'm sorry you came all this way, when . . . and she's . . . I'm sorry. But I'm not."

Brook stepped her way.

She backed up. "And *you* just stay out of it!" She spun on her heel and dashed from the house, ran all the way to the stables. A groom was just bringing out the horses—Star, the one she'd been riding since Whitby left with Tempesta, and another she didn't recognize. Perhaps Brook had actually listened to Stafford and wouldn't ride Oscuro while with child.

Well, she wasn't going to ride with Brook anyway. "The duchess isn't coming."

The groom opened his mouth, something that mixed alarm with confusion in his eyes, but it snapped away quickly, replaced by a smile. "Shall I accompany you, milady?"

*No.* She felt the word resonate inside. Her own stubborn desire for time alone, no doubt. Well, she wouldn't be foolish. She wouldn't, no matter how much she wanted to just gallop off into the wood and see where the horse led her. It would just give her family and friends more fuel, another reason to force her into their way. She bit back the refusals clamoring and nodded.

The groom helped her mount, mounted himself on the second

horse, and took off into the lead while Ella was still positioning her skirts. "This way, milady. I know just the spot to show you."

Her spirit strained for the wood, the trees, where the weak sunshine would be painting greens through the leaves and the branches would whisper solace to her.

He headed the opposite direction, toward the rolling hills that led to the road, the village. But perhaps there was some little oasis of peace that way she hadn't discovered yet.

They trotted for a few minutes parallel to the drive, and the ride did nothing to soothe her. She needed solitude. Trees. Perhaps the river. This was wrong, all wrong. Then he led her into a copse of trees. It was pretty enough, but not *enough*. She could hear a cart driving by on the main road, and even the rumble of an engine.

"This way." The groom sent her a tight smile and motioned to the right.

The engine sound grew louder. Ella reined her mount to a halt, resistance making her stomach tight. "I don't care to head toward the road. I would prefer—"

"We don't much care *what* you'd prefer."

Before she could do more than part her lips, rough hands grabbed her and jerked her down from the horse. Before she could draw in air to scream, fingers clamped over her mouth.

A *click*. A cold circle pressed to her temple. She turned her eyes just a bit and saw that, yes, it was a pistol pressed to her head. Images of Stella, gun in hand, flashed before her eyes.

She may be sick.

The groom turned his horse around, but he made no shout. His bearing held no panic. "My money?"

Dread sank in her stomach. Of course. Brook hadn't been dressed to ride—the second horse had never been for her. It had all been a ploy, a plot. Get Ella outside, tell her the duchess was too sick after all, offer to take her instead. They wouldn't have expected her to even run into anyone in the house. And the groom obviously had no intentions of telling anyone where she was. He'd say she took off on her own, and everyone would assume she was out on one of her larks. It would be hours—*hours* before they came looking for her.

Crunching leaves signaled a new arrival, and Rushworth soon appeared through the trees. "Did you cut the phone lines too?"

The groom nodded.

Rushworth tossed a little pouch at him. "There you are, then. Split it with your girl and leave the area, as we discussed."

His girl. The maid.

The man holding her chuckled. "Nice little spitfire you got there, by the way. I greatly enjoyed convincing her to help."

Fury blazed up in the groom's eyes, but he banked it, pocketed the pouch, grabbed Star's reins, and dug his heels into the horse's flank without another word.

*Father God . . . Lord above . . . God in heaven. Help me.*

The arms holding her relaxed, moved. But the gun didn't leave her temple, just traced a path to between her eyebrows as the man moved in front of her. A face appeared behind the gun, showcasing a wave of brown hair and a smile that would have been handsome had he not been baring so many teeth at her. "In the car with you now, love. Hurry up." He leaned closer, close enough that she could see something in his eyes that was more animal than human. "Or don't. Put up a fight. It won't please Rush, but it would sure please me."

Even in her madness, Stella had never looked like *that*. Ella couldn't stop the shiver, even though it made him laugh.

Rushworth took another step toward them. "Dorsey, do stop terrifying the poor girl. My apologies, Lady Ella. I hate having to unleash him on you, but he is . . . very effective."

*Unleash the monster.* Ella had assumed Catherine meant a

monster within her brother. It had never once occurred to her that he kept one as a pet. Knowing she was shaking and unable to stop it, she met Rushworth's gaze. "Why are you doing this?"

He looked sad. Full of regret. Yet he walked to the car—Cayton's car—idling on a little rutted road beyond the copse and opened the passenger-side door, motioning for her to get in. "I hope you'll forgive me. It isn't how I planned it, but we're out of time." He studied her so intently. His eyes were empty, dark, hollow, and she had a feeling he only kept one monster on a leash because he had another inside to keep it company. "Come, my lady. Get in."

The car looked so *black* inside. She dug in her heels. She needed to scream. No one from the castle was likely to hear her all the way out here, but there was always a chance someone was on the road and—

"Can I gag her yet?" Dorsey sounded far too eager. "Or I can knock her upside the head."

"Dorsey, *please*. Lady Ella is going to be on her best behavior. Aren't you, darling?"

The other man loosed a growl. "You said I'd get to have fun today."

She was definitely going to be sick.

"And there is a whole castle full of people with whom you can have fun if Ella doesn't cooperate. And her precious *Cayton* and his brat, for that matter—they should be finishing up their errands in town and heading to the castle any minute. You can start wherever you like, if she doesn't get quietly into the car."

She got quietly into the car. An unexpected peace settled on her as she did, coating over the fear and the sick and the surety that she was an idiot. An unexpected peace that whispered an unexpected realization.

She should have trusted her instincts.

# *Twenty-Six*

"D o you have absolutely everything you need?" Cayton stood in the doorway of Ralin's nursery, too unsettled to keep from showing it. He put his hands in his pockets, drew them out again. Paced a step forward, stopped.

Addie was already playing with her cousin and his blocks, those happy squeals bludgeoning him. He couldn't let her go. He *had* to let her go. It was ripping him to shreds.

Tabby smoothed her apron and nodded. "Enough to get us through a few days, and the duchess will supply what else we need before we go. I couldn't pack too much, milord—it would have looked strange."

"I know." He wanted to pick Addie up again. Hold her close. Breathe in talcum powder and lavender one last time before leaving. But he probably shouldn't disturb her. Sometimes she could be so sensitive, picking up on his mood. He'd likely set her to crying, and then they'd all be miserable.

But he'd never been away from her for more than an hour or two.

Unable to stop himself, he strode over, scooped her up, and

pretended to gobble her belly so he could hear her soul-deep laughter.

Addie held on tight once he righted her, grinning that perfect baby grin, and leaned forward to press her mouth to his cheek in a sloppy baby kiss.

He was undone. Ripped to shreds. "I love you, angel. Be good for Tabby. And for Ella. Make her smile for me, and laugh, and she'll do the same for you."

He had yet to talk to Ella, of course, didn't know for sure she'd agree to his plan. But he'd seen to everything in the village anyway. He'd bought the tickets to put her on the southbound train with his daughter. He'd sent a wire to Midwynd Park, in case her brother hadn't left yet. He'd sent another to his mother, telling her to head there too when she arrived back in England.

He knew this was the one plea that would convince Ella to leave. There was no possible way she could deny him when he asked her to keep his baby safe—when he put his precious Addie into her care until all this was over. She may have a few choice names to call him for manipulating her so, but she would agree. She would leave, taking Addie with her. And he would send them off with the promise that when it was all finished, he would come for them both. They'd have a proper courtship. He'd whisper the truth of his love in her ear and let her plan that September wedding.

Assuming he lived to keep his promise.

Tabby eased closer, a frown in place. "You'll be up again before we go, won't you? And you'll follow within a day. It's just a day."

"That's right. Just a day." Unless something went wrong. And recalling the roiling hatred in Rushworth's eyes, he couldn't shake the feeling that something was very likely to go wrong. He turned to Tabby. "If something were to happen—which it won't, of course, but if it *does*—the houses, everything will go to Addie. I've already arranged that. Stafford will be in charge of the trust until she comes of age, but I've long ago set aside enough for your family. You'll stay, won't you? She'll need you, especially at first."

Tabby's eyes had gone wide as twin moons. "Why are you talking this way, milord? Nothing will happen, you said. The authorities will be there, everyone will be safe."

"Of course we will be." Unless they weren't. He attempted a smile, though given how weak it felt, it probably did little to convince her. "I'll just feel better knowing Addie has everyone she loves around her if the unexpected happens."

Tabby's hands fisted in her apron. "You're the one she loves best, milord. She'll not be happy without you. Remember that today."

"I will." He pressed a kiss to Addie's forehead and then set her back on the floor. "Just promise me."

Tabby blustered out a sigh. "I promise. I'll see Addie's as happy as she can be. And my brother can see that *you* don't get in any trouble you shouldn't."

Evans was already at Ralin too, ready to help however they needed. Felicity's labor had begun as Cayton was calling for the carriage—Cayton had spent half an hour trying to track down Dr. Fields in the village, only to be forced to resort to the midwife. But Mrs. Higgins had banished all the menfolk from the house as Cayton left, saying they were none of them needed underfoot.

Just as well. All hands may be needed in this plot, so they were now belowstairs with Ralin's menservants. "He will. And I thank you." He set a hand briefly on her shoulder and then forced himself out the door. "I'll be back up before you go."

The train heading south left in three hours. Hopefully it

would give him time enough to convince Ella to be on it, even if her brother hadn't yet arrived to drag her home. Then he and Stafford could call the constable, and they could put this scheme into action.

He took the stairs down two at a time, feeling more unsettled with each footfall. He needed to see Ella. He'd take her in his arms again, without any pretense of a faux argument. He'd hold her tightly, kiss her softly, as she deserved to be kissed, and confess his heart. He'd beg her to take Addie and go.

His feet headed, therefore, to the library, rather than to his cousin's study. Yet as he drew near, he saw the library's thick door was open—unusual. And from within came not the sounds of Ella's muttering to herself or her pen scratching furiously over paper, but male murmurs. Stafford's, and another he couldn't place so readily. Whitby, perhaps, back from Yorkshire? Cayton stepped in, then nearly retreated again when he saw it was Nottingham with his cousin. They fell silent at his entrance.

He took a step back. "I didn't mean to interrupt. I was just looking for . . ." He trailed off at Nottingham's raised brows. Cleared his throat. "I'll just go and—"

"Oh, I don't think so." Nottingham didn't so much as budge, just stood there with his hands slung in his pockets and a benign smile upon his face. "Sit down. Now."

Cayton really wasn't all that fond of dukes who thought they ruled the world.

He sat down.

Nottingham didn't, just turned toward Cayton's chair and towered over him. "Good to see you again, Cayton."

"Likewise." If he could have avoided the duke until all this was over, he would have been thrilled beyond words. Then he'd have earned himself a bit of credit by putting the needs of Ella and Addie first and seeing that everything was finally resolved.

Now . . . now he probably looked exactly like the man he used to be, kissing a girl in one moment and declaring he didn't even like her in the next.

Though perhaps Ella hadn't told him about that. He could hope.

Nottingham smiled. "Hard to believe it's been nine months already. Last time I saw you, you were deprived of sleep and all but unconscious on Whitby's couch."

"And you hadn't been married a fortnight yet." He forced a smile, prayed it looked pleasant. "I hear congratulations are in order on a new generation coming any day."

"Thank you." Nottingham beamed. "And *I* hear you and my sister have come to know each other a bit this last month."

Nottingham might just kill him before Rushworth got the chance. Cayton dug his fingers into the arms of the chair and tried again to clear his throat. "A bit."

"Or maybe more than a bit, if I'm to believe Brook."

And he hadn't even gotten to kiss her again, to say good-bye. Would it be unmanly to beg for mercy? He rubbed at his neck. "We've become friends."

Nottingham arched a brow.

Cayton's throat refused to be cleared. "Good friends?"

Nottingham's other brow joined the first. "Good friends, yes. That's . . . closer to what Brook describes. Good friends who . . . close themselves off in the library for an hour each day. And then go for long walks together. Every day."

He knew Brook had never liked him, but he wouldn't have thought she'd sign his death warrant so blithely. "She's . . . good company."

Nottingham snorted a laugh and let his brows return to their usual positions. "I've never been much for playing cards, Cayton, so I'm just going to put them all on the table. She loves you—you know that, don't you? She loves you so much that she's quite determined to stay here, no matter the risk to herself."

Cayton surged to his feet. "You can't allow it, Duke. You can't. It's far too dangerous, and I didn't go behind her back to call you up here just so she could talk you into letting her stay!"

Nottingham's lips twitched up. He turned to Stafford, who sat grinning on the sofa. "You're right. He does love her just as much."

"Told you."

Cayton hissed out a breath and pivoted away, back again. "I don't much like either one of you. Do you know that?"

The dukes laughed, and Nottingham came over to clap a hand to Cayton's shoulder. "You're going to have to get over that, if we're to be brothers. You *do* intend to marry her, don't you?"

His hand wasn't exactly light and friendly. Cayton scowled. "If she'll have me once all this excitement has worn off. Though if she has a lick of sense, she probably won't."

"Oh, don't worry, Ella has never had a lick of sense. Right, Stafford?"

"I once thought she did, but she proved me wrong by falling for him." Stafford looked positively jovial as he stood, as if it weren't a day for fleeing and giving up one's daughter and quite possibly putting oneself in the path of a madman's bullet. "Relax, Cayton. He just had to be sure. She's his only sister."

"And I'd still like to see you together. I can't quite picture it yet. Do you know where she is?"

And now they were to be stuffed pheasants on display. Cayton rubbed at his neck again. "I couldn't say. I rather thought she'd be down here."

"No, we sent her out in a rage. To ride, given her attire. That was, what, an hour ago?" Nottingham looked to Stafford for verification, and they exchanged nods. "She ought to wander back soon, I should think."

Cayton snorted, warmth blooming beneath it. "If she hasn't lost herself, you mean."

"Her favorite thing to lose. Well, let's set out and see if we can find her." Brice patted his shoulder, using it to give him a push forward. He turned back to Stafford. "You're right—this *is* fun."

"I imagined it would be."

Cayton shoved his hands in his pockets, though he doubted it had quite the same effect as when Nottingham did it. "I really, really don't like either of you." He didn't know what he'd done to deserve such friends—a cousin who was always looking out for him, a woman who knew his past and his present and wanted to be part of his future, a brother-in-law who would always peer into his soul and speak the truth.

The Lord had no reason to bless him as He'd done. If he died today, he would die more fortunate than he had a right to be. He would die with hope gleaming in his soul.

Stafford led the way outside into the gaining sunshine, toward the stables. Over his shoulder he said, "We had a wire from Whitby this morning too. He'll be arriving on the afternoon train. I daresay he has much to tell us."

"Much as I would like to see him, let's hope we miss him and are on our way back home by then." Nottingham stepped into the shadows of the stables. "Though I may have to bind and gag my sister to achieve that goal." He shot a grin at Cayton.

Cayton idly noted his own horses in their usual stalls—the roads were too muddy to risk his Renault. To Nottingham's grin he had only a sigh to return. "I have a plan for that. I . . . I'm going to ask her to take Addie with her."

Stafford blinked at him. "You've never been apart from Addie for any amount of time."

"And I don't want to be now, but I can't have her here, in harm's way. Where Rushworth could . . ." Nostrils flaring, Cayton shook his head. "She needs to be away. And I trust no one more than Ella to see to her safety."

"Manipulative. I fully approve, in this case." Nottingham nodded, smiled again. "She'll never be able to turn that plea down."

Stafford was peeking into the row of stalls. And frowning. "Star is here—she's been Ella's mount since Whit left with Tempesta. They're all here that should be, other than the ones being exercised this time of day. She must have come back, slipped inside."

It should have relieved Cayton, if it meant she wasn't out wandering on her own, that he could see her the sooner. But it only made urgency redouble in his chest. And the two dukes were walking too blasted slowly as they turned back to the castle. Didn't they feel this electricity sizzling through him?

Maybe not. They hadn't seen that look in Rushworth's eyes barely an hour and a half ago. They didn't know how close he was to snapping. And that Ella was his focus.

He had to find her, now. And get her out of the area, Addie in her arms, as soon as humanly possible.

They ended up in the drawing room, where a pale Brook occupied a chair beside the couch—it took a moment for Cayton to realize there was another duchess reclining there, eyes closed and mouth tight as she rested a hand on her burgeoning stomach.

Her obvious condition reminded him to say a quick, silent prayer for Felicity. First babies could be so slow in arriving, he knew—none of the men would be welcome back at Anlic for hours yet.

Nottingham seemed to forget his sister in light of his wife. He kneeled at her side and inspired her eyes to open with a brush of fingertips across her cheek. "Have the pains got worse?"

The Duchess of Nottingham's face relaxed as she smiled. "No, they've stopped again, as they do. I told you, it willna be today."

Nottingham's hum sounded dubious. "Can I get you anything?"

"Lilias has gone to fetch me some tea."

"Lilias is back with the tea, actually. Excuse me, Yer Grace."

Stafford and Cayton took a step backward, making way for a middle-aged woman with a steaming cup. She slid it onto a table and settled beside Nottingham, fussing over her mistress with all the love of a mother.

Stafford repositioned himself to be close to his wife's side. "Have any of you seen Ella, by chance? Her horse is back in the stables and Cayton has a foolproof plan for getting her on that train in a few hours."

Brook's brow creased. "She hasn't come this way. Though if she's still upset with us, she wouldn't." She pushed herself up. "I'll check her room. Or perhaps the library."

"We were just in the library." Stafford quirked a brow at Cayton. "Where else is she likely to go?"

Nottingham's gaze on him felt as heavy as an obligation and as sharp as Brook's tongue.

Cayton rubbed a hand at the back of his neck. "I know of no other places inside. She is always eager to get out-of-doors. The gardens, but only as a means to get to the wood. She always wants to head to the wood."

Nottingham's mouth turned half up in a crooked smile. "You know her well. Perhaps we should divide and conquer. We can check the outside. I'll cover the gardens."

Stafford nodded. "I'll take the front acres, toward the road. She hasn't gone there so far as I know, but she may have tried something unusual today, just to avoid us."

Brook pushed herself to her feet. "We ladies shall check the house."

Nottingham pointed a finger at his wife. "This lady will not budge."

Her maid straightened. "I'll happily look for Lady Ella while Rowena rests, Yer Grace."

"Excellent. And Cayton can take the wood."

It was the most likely place to find her, and he knew well the dukes were granting him a favor by letting him cover that section of ground.

So why, then, did the tightness in his chest only get worse?

# Twenty-Seven

Kira's heart pounded, her nerves were frayed beyond repair. And it wasn't just the fault of the scream that tore from Felicity's throat or the way her whole body curled upward, around her stomach, with the pain.

That was normal. The stubborn tilt to the midwife's chin was assuredly *not*. "I said get *out*. I don't need the likes of you crowding my birth-room."

It wasn't *her* birth-room, though Kira bit back the words. It was their bedroom, and Felicity wanted her here. She'd said so before the pains were so great, before she stopped caring who or what surrounded her. "I will not interfere, madame. I will just help. Fetch what you need. You can think of me as an apprentice."

The tall, bony woman narrowed her beady eyes. "What help do you think you can be, you who can barely speak English? I said to get out, and I meant it. Now get *out*."

It was no wonder Felicity hadn't wanted to call this woman. Kira drew in a deep breath that didn't calm her and worked to keep the Russian from her words. "Felicity wants me to stay."

The midwife sneered. "She's a child. She doesn't know what she wants. Now get out before I call someone to *drag* you out."

There was no one here who would, with all the men banished, but Kira didn't point that out either. Even the other maids had scurried away for their half day off when Mrs. Higgins told them to go, once the midwife arrived. The housekeeper was the only staff still here, and she certainly wouldn't interfere on this shrew's behalf.

"Martha, stop." Felicity panted and fell back onto her pillows again. Sweat gleamed on her forehead in the lamplight, and her face was so very pale. "She is my friend. My husband is dead. At least grant me my friend."

Kira's fingers curled into her coarse skirt. If she closed her eyes, she saw Felicity seizing again, there on her bed. And then she heard again that first cry of pain as the convulsions sent her into labor.

Martha sniffed. "You never did know how to choose your friends, Felicity. First you let your mistress make a puppy of you, following her around, and now some foreigner?"

Felicity pinched her nose. Her head hurt, she'd said. Terribly.

It wasn't good. It was so very far from good, and the doctor was nowhere to be found, and the hospital too far away. Kira, ignoring the useless midwife, sank to her knees beside the bed and squeezed Felicity's hand. "Tell me what you need. A drink?"

"Don't be a fool—she can't have anything to drink while she's in labor." Martha pushed her aside. "Now. Tell me who the father is, Felicity. I'm bound by law to report it."

Felicity's eyes burned bright as fever. Her gaze met Kira's over Martha's sharp shoulder. "Get Lady Pratt."

Yes. If anyone could put this woman in her place, it was Lady

Pratt. Kira spun from the room and ran through the house. It felt empty with the servants gone, with no baby squeals from the nursery.

She shook it off and kept going. Lady Pratt had reverted to hollowness again, but this might just rouse her. Spark her anger on behalf of the maid she was so fond of, remind her of who she was. Kira didn't much *like* who she was, but she certainly knew how to talk down to people, and that was what they needed just now.

With a cursory rap on the door, she let herself in.

Lady Pratt sat in a chair by the window, her hands idle. She looked up when Kira came in, then back to the outside. "I heard screams. I trust it isn't Felicity in labor, or surely someone would have fetched me."

She was already angry, Kira could see that now in the way her hands gnarled around each other, in the rigid line of her back.

Felicity's first screams had been two hours ago. She hadn't come down, hadn't investigated—had she just sat here the whole time, too proud to come unless she was asked?

Kira sighed. "She had another seizure, my lady. I feared leaving her, and Mrs. Higgins had everyone trying to find the doctor or midwife, then sent them out of the house. This is the first I could get away. She wants you."

For a moment, Kira thought pride would keep on holding her there in her chair. But it wasn't Felicity she was angry with. She exhaled in a gust, stood, nodded. "Of course I'll come. I'll— Cris!"

The door crashed the rest of the way open behind Kira, making her jump out of the way.

Rushworth thundered in, but not alone. He had Lady Ella by the arm—her wrists were tied behind her back, a gag in her mouth, and her hem and shoes were caked in mud. Her face, however, looked perfectly calm.

Dorsey was the last to enter, closing the door behind him. He had a gun in his hand—and that same look in his eye as when he'd trailed his fingers through Felicity's blood.

Kira slid backward until the wall welcomed her.

Catherine's expression edged toward panic. "What are you doing? Cris, what have you *done*?"

Another cry echoed through the house.

Rushworth removed the gag from Lady Ella's mouth with surprising tenderness. "I'm sorry to have had to do that, darling. But it was for your own good. If you spoil his chance at a fortune, Dorsey probably wouldn't listen to a thing I say. No one would really notice if you scream now, though."

"Cris." Catherine's voice shook along with the hand hovering at her mouth. "Cris, you're not like him. You . . . you swore you'd never do this. Kidnapping? You're not like Pratt."

"I hadn't any choice, Kitty. He's moved up his deadline. We've only got a week to get the diamonds to Paris, or he'll kill you." Rushworth drew a folded piece of paper out of his pocket, held it out. No one took it. With a shrug, he dropped it onto the bed and then stroked Lady Ella's cheek. "You understand that, don't you? You would do anything to protect your family. You don't want anything to happen to Nottingham or his very pregnant wife."

Kira pressed her palms to the wallpaper behind her. Andrei. He had sent a threat, even though she was here. Didn't he care that he might be ruining everything? Putting her in danger? Putting so many innocent people in even worse danger?

No. He cared only that he got his diamonds.

Lady Ella somehow managed to smile. "Of course I understand, Rush. You can untie me. I won't fight you." She darted a glance at Dorsey and shuddered.

Dorsey grinned like a wolf.

"In a moment. Once Kitty promises she'll be on her best be-havior while I see to this nasty business. You can stay here with her, Ella, out of harm's way, since the house is all but empty."

Catherine still stared at him in horror. "You're going to get us all arrested or worse. Can't you see that? Can't you see that this crazed pursuit of the Fire Eyes will be your undoing? I don't want a part in it, I told you that! I'm *through*, I've already lost too much!"

Rushworth's face twitched. He took a step away. Lifted a hand. That was all, just lifted a hand and quirked a finger.

Dorsey started forward.

"No!" Catherine scrambled away, over the bed, obviously aim-ing for the door. "You promised. You *swore* he'd never touch me!"

"Calm down, Kitty. He's just going to tie you up."

Kira inched toward the door, praying they wouldn't even notice her against the wall. If she could get it open, make ready an escape for Catherine . . . That would still leave Ella in the room, but if the men pursued Catherine and Kira, she could get away.

Rushworth got to the door first and sent Kira a disappointed look. "You were supposed to make her accept the inevitable. I swear, it's so hard to find good help these days."

Catherine screamed, jerking Kira's attention back to the corner where she huddled, the bed and the wall providing too narrow a passage, Dorsey looming.

Ella had somehow scrambled over the bed too, despite her hands being tied, and jumped between them.

Dorsey growled. "Rush! Your woman's in my way."

Rushworth gave Kira a push away from the door. "This is getting rather annoying. Ella, darling, I'll be kind and godly and perfectly good in a few days, I promise you—but just now

I'm trying to save my sister's life. So if you would kindly step aside, I need to keep her from ruining it all and getting herself killed."

Ella didn't move, didn't look away from Dorsey. "Call off your dog, Rush. Catherine won't do anything stupid."

"History says otherwise." He gave Kira another shove. "Look, how about the three of you lovely ladies just sit on the bed for a moment, hmm? Before Dorsey loses his restraint."

Since it seemed the only good chance to keep everyone un-harmed, Kira moved to obey—and reached over to press Cath-erine into doing the same. Once they were both on the edge of the mattress, Ella slid to a seat beside them.

"Thank you. You may be useful yet, Lareau. Another reason we came here, actually . . ." He drew out another paper and handed it to her. "This arrived last night, and I hadn't the time to find another translator. If you would?"

Kira took the paper and skimmed through the Russian words. From an investigator, it seemed, trying to discover the identity of Rushworth's buyer. "He seems to think it is Prince Vitaly. His daughter has been heard speaking of red diamonds she will soon have." That stupid, stupid girl.

"Prince Vitaly." Rushworth seemed to be storing the name away, though apparently not making an immediate connection to the princess who had supposedly recommended her. Western-ers rarely understood their naming system. "Does he include any information on him? How dangerous he is?"

"Yes, but . . ." Kira sighed and put the paper aside. She couldn't let them die—and they would, if Rushworth thought he was facing only the prince. He would do something foolish, try to cross him, and they would all pay. "It is not the prince. Your man is wrong. Andrei Varennikov is the one who wants the diamonds."

The tic in Rushworth's jaw proved he knew the name. "Andrei Varennikov. The merchant who owns half of Russia."

Dorsey pressed the gun to Kira's head. "And you know this *how*, hen?"

She straightened her spine and kept her gaze on Rushworth rather than Dorsey. "Because I am not Sophie Lareau. I am not a lady's maid. I am Kira Belova, of the Ballet Russe. Andrei's mistress."

She expected Ella to recoil from her. Certainly not to turn *toward* her, eyes wide. "But you're Brook's friend, then! She has a poster with you on it. Her grandfather sent it. You're listed as the prima ballerina."

"Do not tell her, please—that I am here, that I . . . that I am his . . ." She squeezed her eyes shut.

The gun pressed harder to her forehead. "Well, well. Quite a 'somebody else,' love. What you want me to do with her, Rush? I can take her out into the wood. Won't take me but half an hour to take care of her. Bury her near where I did that stupid bloke who wouldn't cooperate. Think anyone will mourn you like his little wife did him, hmm?"

Stew? He'd killed *Stew*? She blinked back unexpected tears. But kept her eyes shut—to keep out some of the horror. He must have tried to buy him off, to feed Rushworth information—"*he'd never met a stranger,*" Felicity had said. He knew everyone, everyone loved him. He would have been a perfect spy, in that regard. But if he was anything like Felicity described, he wouldn't have had it.

And it cost him his life.

A prayer formed on her lips. She didn't want to die, didn't want to suffer whatever else Dorsey would do to her first. She wanted to get everyone out of this, to find a way home to Russia. To walk up to that little cottage she had once only wanted to escape and cry with her grandmother and fight with her brothers and breathe in the scent of her father and grandfather. She wanted to hear someone call her *Kiraka* and yell at her for all she'd done wrong and pull her close and tell her it was never too late to do what she should.

"Later. I need her to help with my sister for now. Keep her calm, La . . . *Belova*. Keep both of them calm. Tell them a few stories about how ruthless your man is, what would happen if we don't deliver these gems by the twelfth of April. Tell them of how he strikes for the heart, which is why he has promised to tear my sister limb from limb to get the diamonds from me." Footsteps sounded, even and unhurried, as Rushworth moved toward the door. "Dorsey—outside the door. Eyes peeled, ears attentive. You're only to come in if it sounds as though they're trying to escape, and if I find you entered when you shouldn't have, you'll regret it."

Kira opened her eyes just as Dorsey pulled the gun away. He smiled at her, and it looked exactly like the charming one she'd found so attractive just a few days ago. "Soon, hen. Soon."

She scooted a little closer to Ella.

Rushworth opened the door. "I'll be back with the diamonds. If Cayton happens to come home, or anyone else who would interfere, shoot him. And if the ladies make noise enough to bring the housekeeper or midwife up here, shoot Belova."

Dorsey's grin widened. "Yessir."

Ella leaned in until their shoulders touched. When the door closed behind the men, she murmured, "I'm not sure which of them is the bigger monster."

Catherine surged from the bed. "A useless question—they feed on each other, make each other worse. I am not even sure which of them came up with this plan." She spun to face them, her glare focused on Ella. "I *told* you. I warned you. And what do you do? You go and fall in love with Cayton and are stupid enough to kiss him where Cris's spies can see!"

Ella's shoulders finally sagged. "Did you honestly think I could fall for your brother? If he hadn't protected you all your life, would you even *like* him? When he would sic that monster on you?"

Catherine leaned against the wall at her back, face pained and eyes closed. "Will this Russian really kill me? So gruesomely?"

Another of Felicity's cries echoed through the walls. Kira's breath shuddered. They should be down there with her. Not trapped up here, a madman with a gun at the door.

"No."

Catherine opened her eyes, and Kira met her gaze head on. Her voice, she knew, hadn't sounded promising. "He has men like Dorsey to do it for him."

Catherine, shoulders sagging, sat on the bed again and went to work on the ropes binding Lady Ella's wrists. "So be it. If it will end all this madness, then . . . let them come. I'll turn myself over to them."

"No." Ella slipped one hand free when she could, rubbed it against her leg. "You're not going to die over the diamonds, Kitty. We'll find another way."

Kira expected a harsh reply. Instead, Catherine's head bent forward, and she sniffed. "Is that your infernal optimism speaking, or do you actually believe it?"

Her second hand free too, Ella reached for Catherine's. "I believe it."

Catherine looked up, and something odd and unexpected lit her eyes. It took Kira a long moment to realize it was hope. "All right, then. We're in this together—we'll solve it together. We'll stop them. No one gets hurt."

"No one gets hurt."

Kira drew in a long breath. They had far more faith than she had.

◦◦◦

Cayton whipped another branch out of his way, huffing a bit as he came up the last rise, to their rendezvous. Stafford and Nottingham were already there, every bit as muddy as he was, and looking every bit as dour.

"There were prints in the copse near the little road heading south." Stafford's nostril flared. "Two horses, then footprints. Looked like a scuffle, and they led to the road. Tire marks. A car."

The tight ball in his chest twisted and churned. "He's taken her."

Nottingham ran a hand through his once-immaculate hair. "Was Rushworth at your house this morning?"

"Yes. Yes, he . . . he threatened me. I left soon after, in the carriage. He could have taken my car." How could this be happening? He should have disabled the thing. But it hadn't occurred to him. The car always got stuck in the mud, and his only thought was to leave as quickly as possible. To get Addie out of the house, and to convince Ella to take her to Midwynd.

But all that time he'd spent in the village, arranging things . . . all that time Ella could have been missing. Rushworth could—likely *did*—have her even now. He could have knocked her out. Tied her up. Trapped her in some dank, foul hole that would contain her sunshine.

Nottingham started back for the castle, his step not so slow now. "Someone has to have seen something. Servants?"

Cayton shook his head. "Mine were all sent out—a maid is in labor." Then his eyes went wide, and he dragged in a breath. "His valet is likely helping him—but Kitty's maid stayed there, with Felicity. She could have seen something—she would tell us if she did."

Stafford nodded. "We'll send someone to ask her."

Nottingham's pace increased still more. "He has to be somewhere nearby. Stafford, where would he take her?"

His cousin shook his head. "We've searched all the places I know to check. Cayton likely knows them better than I do—he grew up here. If there is a dark hole or abandoned building somewhere, I daresay he explored it as a child. Or we can ask Brook, she has explored incessantly too, and she always seems to know where to direct us when we're looking for Ella."

Nottingham looked to Cayton. "Can you make us a list of the places you know? How to find them?"

"Of course." Assuming he could convince his hand to uncurl from its fist.

They hurried in silence for a nerve-racking five minutes until the castle finally came within view again. Then Nottingham drew in a shaky breath. "What will he do to her? I don't know him that well. I don't know what to pray against."

Stafford shook his head.

Cayton sighed. "He . . . he loves her, as much as he knows how. I don't think he'd harm her, but he may . . . He obviously plans to run once he gets the diamonds. He may try to force her to go with him."

Nottingham's lips thinned.

Their pace increased until they were running, and every footfall became a prayer. *Please, Lord, protect her. Lead us to her. Help us find her.*

Stafford led the way into the castle, bellowing for his butler. Mr. Norton appeared straightaway with a bow. "Your Grace?"

"My wife. Do you know where she is?"

Mr. Norton's brows lifted. "She and the Duchess of Nottingham went out, Your Grace. And Your Grace. And my lord."

The dukes stared at each other. "Went out?" Nottingham echoed. "With my wife in the state she is?"

"I beg your pardon, Your Grace. I tried to dissuade them, and the duchess's—of Nottingham, I mean—lady's maid was beside herself to find her mistress not resting when she returned from looking for Lady Ella. But the duchess—of Stafford, that is—was quite insistent. As she often is. She said they must compose a reply to the note."

Cayton's blood ran cold. "What note?"

"I certainly don't know, my lord. It came addressed to the duke, but she snapped it up. As she often does." Mr. Norton inclined his head, apology clear in his eyes.

Stafford growled. "I'm going to throttle her. Then I'm going to kiss her. Then I'm going to lock her in her room for the next ten years."

"She'd only climb out the window," Nottingham pointed out.

"Or cut a hole through the wall with a butter knife and a serving spoon," Cayton added.

Mr. Norton cleared his throat. "She did, however, ask me to give you this." He held out a folded piece of paper.

Stafford flipped it open and barked out something sharp and biting in Monegasque. "She says to call the constable and have him post men at all the possible routes away from Anlic, but for him to be discreet about it."

Anlic. Cayton strode toward the corridor that led to Stafford's telephone, the dukes a step behind. His heart felt so tight and heavy it was a wonder he didn't sink through the floor. Anlic—all the servants had been sent away. The house would be virtually empty. But still, it seemed a risky place for him to hold Ella. Unless he weren't really *in* the house, just watching it.

Stafford drew even with him. "Do you really think he's at your house? With Ella?"

"He could be hiding nearby, watching for someone to arrive with the diamonds." The claws of fear dug deep. "Gregory can lead the constable and his men in without being seen, and show them where to wait. We should ask him to meet us here first. And check the safe. If Brook took him the diamonds . . ."

Or, perhaps worse, if she hadn't.

# Twenty-Eight

Ella had already examined all the windows but wasn't entirely certain that the three-story drop would leave her able to run away and get help. Plus they squeaked when she raised them, which had brought Dorsey back in, looking far too ready to hurt someone. She had mumbled some excuse about needing air, but she hadn't argued when he slammed the pane back down to the sill.

She'd just been glad he left again.

Catherine had sat in a chair by the one window, wincing a little more each time one of Felicity's cries reached them. Kira paced the room, mumbling in Russian.

She hadn't told them any stories about Andrei Varennikov. Ella was rather glad of that too.

Where was Cayton? Addie? Her brother and Rowena, the Staffords? What was Rushworth doing? How did he mean to get the diamonds? Had there been time to fetch the authorities after they got whatever message he had probably sent?

"What was that?" Kira paused in her pacing, face blank. "Is that a motor? A car?"

Ella turned back to the window, her eyes going wide. "It is

Stafford's Rolls-Royce! It's Brook and—" She cut herself off with a hand to her lips when Rushworth emerged into view, a pistol extended. It nearly turned to a whimper when she realized Rowena was in the car with Brook. "No, no, no. What are they doing here? Why would they . . . ?"

"If there is danger to be had, you know well Brook will find it." Kira peered out the window too, shoulder to shoulder with Ella. "She will have a plan—she must. Will he bring them up here, do you think?"

Footsteps on the stairs a minute later answered that question. Even Catherine got up, all of them rushing to the door to listen. They backed away just in time to avoid it hitting them as it swung open.

Ella shook her head at the sight of her sister-in-law and friend, Rushworth's gun pointed at their backs. And Brook hadn't even the sense to look worried. "What in the world possessed you to do this?"

"A lovely question, my sweet." Rushworth tossed them into the room, his careful mask cracked and rage visible through it. "I ought to have known my darling cousin would ruin everything. *Sit!*"

Brook just crossed her arms. "You might as well give up, Rushworth. You'll never make it out, especially given that you're stupid enough to hole up *here*."

Rowena, hands supporting her stomach, shrank into a corner made by the armoire.

Rushworth snarled. "Dorsey! One. To the head."

"No!" Ella flew for him—not Dorsey, he'd just toss her aside—knowing she'd never make it to him before a bullet could be fired, knowing he wouldn't have time to call off his beast, but needing to try *something*.

She landed on Rushworth, meaning to beat on his chest. But

he pulled her too close, her fists could barely strike him. And he looked down at her with a terrible smile.

Dorsey didn't raise his gun. He raised his hand and sent it into Brook's skull with enough force to knock her to the floor.

*Lord, the baby! Protect the baby!*

Rushworth's hand moved over Ella's back. "Quite right, my love. My thought exactly. You and I shall slip away from all this commotion and wait for the duke to bring me my Fire Eyes."

Brook was pushing herself up to sitting, dabbing at the red-stained corner of her mouth. Fury burned in her eyes. "A bit hard for him to do, considering I have your note here with me, *cousin*, and he never saw it."

Rushworth's arms turned to a visc around her. "You try me, Brook. You so try me. You better have brought them then."

Ella's gaze found her sister-in-law, still in the corner. Rowena's eyes were squeezed shut, her face pale.

Brook smirked. "Why in the *world* would I have done that? Then you'd win. And you are *not* going to win. No, cousin, what I did was leave instruction for the constable to cover all escapes from Anlic."

His arms were crushing her, but Ella didn't dare make a sound.

"After I *explicitly* instructed you—" His grip loosened abruptly, and he dragged in a quick breath. "At least the phone lines are down—we have some time. Our second plan, then, Dorsey. You scouted the rendezvous?"

Dorsey studied Brook as if waiting for an excuse to hit her again. "Aye, my lord. The old church we found is definitely abandoned and far from any homes. A good view from the bell tower."

"Perfect. We must be quick, before they can set up checks along the roads. I'll make sure the constable is drawn away from here. You keep an eye on these women, especially my idiot cousin. I'll send another note to Ralin directing Stafford to bring the diamonds to the church or he will be responsible for the consequences. Give me two hours, then secure them all—don't hurt my sister—and meet me there." He pulled Ella into the doorway. Then stopped. "Or . . . Kitty, you can come with us. If you don't come now, I don't know when I'll see you again. I can't return."

Her eyes were tear-filled, her limbs quaking. She shook her head. "I can't have any more part in this, Crispin. I told you that. I meant it."

His larynx bobbed at Ella's eye level. "I'll try to find a way to see you have what you need. It may take some time to set things up so the money can't be traced back to me."

"Don't. I don't want it." Catherine wrapped her arms around her middle. "I'll get on just fine."

"No you won't. They'll seize everything. You'll be a pauper."

Her expression didn't change. "Better a pauper than to live under that curse."

He shook his head, tightened his arms around Ella again, and pulled her from the room. "Foolish girl. After all we've been through, all we've done to get here . . ."

Ella just had time to glance at Rowena and note that her face had eased. Just enough time to meet Brook's eyes once more before Dorsey slammed the door between them. Her friend was smiling. *Smiling.* She definitely had something up her sleeve, Kira was right about that. All Ella had to do was keep Rushworth calm until she could manage it.

He didn't pull her straight for the stairs as she had expected, but rather into the next room over. Her throat closed off when she realized it was his bedroom, but he only stepped to the wardrobe and opened a cabinet, a drawer. He pulled out a sealed piece of folded paper.

And the gun he had apparently tucked into his belt once he'd forced Brook and Rowena into the room.

Ella forced a swallow. "You don't need that. I won't fight you."

His smile would have looked tender, loving, had he not just pulled out a *gun*. "It isn't to use on you, dearest. But the duke will be in a rage, and *he* doesn't need to know that I won't hurt you." He cradled her head—with the hand holding the gun—and kissed her forehead. Lingering there until she feared he'd sense her fear, her revulsion.

He rested his forehead on hers. "I'm sorry. I have to use you as a hostage—just for his sake. I won't hurt you. Know that—no matter what. I won't hurt you. You don't need to be afraid."

She drew in a breath but couldn't force any words back out.

"It'll be over in an hour or two. We'll have the diamonds. We'll be on our way to France. We can marry there, and you can decide where we'll go." He dipped his head, caught her gaze. "I'll buy you a villa, a mountain, anything. The world will be ours for the taking."

She could only nod. He must have been satisfied with that, or else feeling too pressed for time to waste any more on reassuring her. He pulled her out of his room, down the stairs, into the weak sunshine.

They headed for Cayton's car once more, his fingers tight around her arm and that gun far too present in his other hand.

But Brook had a plan. And the men would come soon—surely Brook really had left them a note or some instruction to fetch the constable. That couldn't be just a bluff. It would be well. She'd be fine.

She just had to keep him calm.

⊰✥⊱

Kira rushed forward the moment Dorsey slammed the door. "Brook! Brook, *est-ce que tu vas bien?*"

She fell to her knees beside her old friend, noting the crack to her lip—and the healthy-looking anger in her eyes. Praying there were no unseen injuries, that the child she carried was well.

Brook met her gaze. She was as beautiful as she'd been as a princess—and every bit as friendly as she'd been as an opera-singer's daughter, laughing when recognition struck, throwing her arms around Kira and nearly pulling her over with it. "Kira! What are you doing here?" Her question, like Kira's, was in French.

She prayed Dorsey didn't speak French.

Kira hugged her back. "Nothing good. You know Andrei Varennikov?"

Brook pulled away and made a distasteful face. "I know *of* him."

Dorsey stepped forward. "What are you saying? English, both of you."

Kira ignored him. "I know him considerably better than that." She paused for a moment for that to sink in.

But Brook didn't pull away. Condemnation didn't shadow her eyes. She just sighed and reached for Kira's hand and said, "You wanted to avoid that."

Dorsey grabbed Kira by her collar and yanked her up. "I said *English*."

Kira pasted on a smile. "I am sorry, Dorsey. I forget myself."

"*Ne t'inquiète pas,*" Brook said. *Don't worry.* She didn't try to stand, just pulled her knees up and sat there on the floor, her arms around her legs as if she were perfectly comfortable. "Varennikov?"

"He is the one who wants the diamonds." Brook was smart—

she would be able to piece together the rest. And Brook had no doubt heard all the stories about the Russian mogul during her years in Europe. She would know what that meant, the price he could pay. The price he would exact if they failed.

Brook, indeed, sucked in a long breath and looked to Catherine. "No wonder your brother is worried for you, Kitty."

Kira shook her shoulders, and Dorsey actually let her go. Though probably only so he could ease to a position where he could better keep them all in the sights of his pistol. He moved it between them, even taking in the other woman, large with child, who clutched at her stomach and squeezed shut her eyes.

Brook looked her way too. "Rowena? Are you all right?"

The woman drew in a long breath. "Dinna worry for me. It will fade again. I'm sure." *It.* Pains? Kira edged a bit closer to her. Rowena let the breath back out. "Catherine . . . is it ye this Russian is threatening? Is that why yer brother is going to such lengths?"

Catherine sniffed and leaned in to the window. "Don't give him so much credit, he had no idea who the buyer was until Lareau—or Kira, or whatever her name is—told him. And we thought *she* was just a lady's maid, the daughter of a midwife."

"Oh, you were the one . . ." Brook laughed . . . and her hand inched toward the back of her leg. "No wonder I've been dreaming of the ballet!"

Kira glanced at Rowena again. She was watching Dorsey warily, but her face still showed pain and had a gleam of perspiration on it.

Catherine pressed a hand to the glass. "There they go, Cris and Ella. I certainly hope you have a plan, Brook."

"*Ne t'inquiète pas,*" she said again. She whipped her skirt up a few inches, pulled out a revolver she'd had strapped to her calf, and leveled it at Dorsey's knee. A *bang*, and he fell, screaming, his gun clattering to the floor. Brook was quick as a flash, picking it up and cocking it and pressing it to his chest. "I have a plan. Be still, you rat."

Kira knew there was a reason she'd always liked this girl. Even Catherine looked impressed. Rowena, however, seemed more horrified.

Dorsey whimpered and clutched at his knee. "Don't. Don't, I-I'll help you."

"Oh, you ridiculous man—I don't *need* your help."

Kira winced at the *crack* when Brook struck him in the head with the butt of the gun, but she had no sympathy for him at all. Only relief when he slumped, his bleeding knee sliding back down. Brook looked up at Catherine. "There, see? A plan—I knew they'd bring us to you, being helpless women as we are. Have you something to tie him up with in here, or do we need to go farther in our search?"

Mute, Catherine spun for her wardrobe and tore through it, eventually coming up with the belt for her dressing gown. "It is silk. Is that a problem?"

"Stronger than hemp, actually, if we wet it. Someone help me roll him over."

Kira hurried over, shoving him onto his stomach and wrestling his arms together at the small of his back. Brook dipped the belt in the basin of water Catherine handed her and made quick work of tying his wrists, her knots tight and precise.

Catherine hovered behind them. "You're so very strange, cousin. But just now, I'm rather glad of it."

Brook nodded to Kira and stood, turned to face Catherine. "You declined helping him—does that mean you'll help me, or do I have to tie you up too?"

Catherine turned her face away, staring at Dorsey. "I told him, I was through. I tried to talk him out of it."

"He won't listen. You surely know that."

"Yes, but . . ." She backed up a step. "Just promise me he won't get hurt."

"My only goal is to get Ella away from him and see he meets justice."

It meant Catherine would meet it too. She surely saw that. Her shoulders sagged, but she nodded. "I'll come with you."

Not exactly a promise to help, not a promise that she was on Brook's side. Kira opened her mouth, ready to insist on explicit words—not that Catherine wasn't capable of lying—but her attention swung back to Rowena when she gasped. Her hands clutched her rounded stomach, and a pool of fluid soaked the rug beneath her feet. Her eyes were wide and horrified. "Oh. Brook. It wasna to happen today. It wasna—ah!" She doubled over.

Kira rushed forward to support her. "All right. You are all right. Come, sit through it. Come." She got her to a chair that was closer than the bed, letting her grip her hand through the pain. "Good. Good. Keep breathing." She looked to Brook. "Was she having pains before?"

Brook came and took the woman's other hand. "They had stopped when she rested. I'm so sorry, Rowena, I shouldn't have dragged you along on this!"

Rowena shook her head. "She is my sister. I had . . ." She squeezed her eyes shut, words giving way to a grimace. "Go! Get her!"

"But . . ."

"Go." Kira patted Rowena's knee as the contraction ebbed, but she looked to Brook. "I can care for her. You go. Find Lady Ella."

Catherine pulled Brook up. "We have to hurry." Her gaze

found Kira's. "Tell Felicity I will be back as soon as I can. I will be here. Will you tell her that?"

Kira nodded.

Catherine kicked Dorsey once, in the stomach, then stepped over his prone form. "They no doubt cut the phone lines here too, but I'll find someone, somewhere to drag his sorry hide to jail. Do you think you can figure out where Cris means to have the men meet him, Brook?"

"Give me a bit of credit, Kitty." A gun in each hand, she strode for the door. "He might as well have drawn me a map."

"I always knew I liked her," Kira said as their footsteps echoed down the hall. The room seemed a good deal emptier without Brook and Catherine in it—and a good deal fuller than she wanted it, with Dorsey's prostrate figure taking up so much of the floor. She prayed a silent prayer that Catherine would cause Brook no trouble while they were out. Or that, if she tried anything, Brook could handle her as easily as she had Dorsey.

Rowena loosed a breath of a laugh. "I didna, at first. She's terrifying."

"*Da*. That too. Would you like to move to the bed?"

Rowena nodded, and Kira helped her up, helped her walk with slow steps around Dorsey, to the mattress. By the time she got her settled, heavier steps were pounding up the stairs, and Gregory came in, huffing, another groom behind him.

"His lordship sent us to sneak in," he said between wheezes. "In case Rushworth was here. We missed him, didn't we? I saw tire tracks, and they looked fresh."

"*Da*. And he has taken Ella. But you're still in time to be useful." She nodded toward Dorsey. "He needs to be taken to the constable."

"Happily." He bent down, hooked his hands under Dorsey's

bound arms. Then glanced up again. "Have you checked on Felicity, Lareau?"

"It is Kira. My name is Kira. And that is my next stop." She looked to Rowena. "If you are all right for a moment."

Rowena nodded and closed her eyes. "As long as he's gone, I'll be fine."

She prayed the same could be said for Felicity.

## Twenty-Nine

Ella watched out the window, trying to take note of where Rushworth was driving. There were trees and hills and honeyed-stone cottages with thatched roofs . . . and then there were just trees and hills and birds flapping overhead, and the road gave way to a track whose mud sucked at the tires, and then the mud was too deep and the tires just spun.

"End of the line." Rushworth didn't sound put out by it. "Now you see why I arranged for horses for the trip back out?"

She hadn't dared to voice a question about that when he idled to a halt in the last village they'd gone through and passed a few pound notes to a stable boy. He was just a lad, no older than the one he'd hailed at the village near Anlic, to run a note up to the castle, *if you would be so kind.* No older than the one he'd paid to deliver a verbal message to the constable—that they'd headed the opposite direction.

Each time they stopped, she'd been tempted to shout for help or try for the door. But he had her pressed to his side, an arm around her. And the gun in the hand at her side. Silence had seemed the wisest course—and this time she would obey her instincts, no matter how illogical they seemed.

372

He scooted out the door now and held out his free hand toward her.

Brook had a plan. The men too. The constable would surely see through the boy. They'd find her, and all would be well.

And he had a gun, dreadful and cold and loaded.

She put her fingers in his palm and let him help her from the carriage. Her shoes sank into mud up to their laces.

Rushworth sighed. "I do detest the mud. And the rain, and the cold. We should pick a warm, dry place to settle. What do you think?"

She hadn't said a word since he pushed her into the car. If she spoke, her true feelings might come slipping out in her tone, and that wouldn't be a good thing.

But he was waiting for an answer, even as he led her through the muck, her hand held tightly in his.

Ella cleared her throat. "I am bad at geography. I daresay you have studied it out, haven't you?"

"Well, yes, hence my thought of South America. There are wet parts, to be sure. But it's warm. And we could buy ourselves half a country with the money the Russian will give us."

"I don't need half a country." At his sharp glance, she attempted a smile. "I just want a family, Rush. I don't much care where I live, or how well. So long as there is love and laughter."

"That's what I adore about you." He halted, pulled her close, cradled her head with his gun hand again. Lowered his head.

She closed her eyes and saw autumn leaves drifting down. Cayton smiling. Addie laughing. Herself in white. A sigh slipped out. Perhaps it wasn't just a fleeting hope. Perhaps it was a reminder, sent by God. A reminder that hope wasn't in vain—not if it was rooted in Him.

She fluttered her eyelids open again, and Rushworth was pulling away.

His eyes gleamed, his lips tilted up. "You understand what matters in life. You would do anything to protect your family. You wouldn't turn a blind eye if someone hurt them. Certainly would never *be* the one to hurt them."

"Of course not." She moved along with him when he turned toward the track again, glad the gun was not at her head anymore. "Kitty told me about your father."

He went stiff at the mention of him, but his fingers were gentle around hers. "Did she mention our mother? How she would just let it happen? Pretend she didn't see the bruises? She would tell me that if I were just a good boy . . . But none of us could be good enough to please Father."

Ella shook her head. "No. She didn't mention her."

"I was glad when she died." He paused, glanced at her, continued in his even stride through the mud. "I'm sorry if that sounds terrible. But it's the truth. She never thought of anyone but herself."

"I'm sorry." She didn't know what else to say. And she *was* sorry. Had his mother intervened, had his father not been so cruel—Rushworth would be a different man. Perhaps a good man. Perhaps even a man she could like. "I'm so sorry you had to go through that."

"But then that left us with *him*. I was afraid to go to school, afraid to leave Kitty there, alone with him." His fingers tightened around hers.

She squeezed them back. "You have always been a good brother. I know you found ways to protect her."

"He had a bad heart." This he delivered in a flat tone, utterly devoid of emotion. "The doctors knew it. So they didn't think to question it when it stopped."

"Didn't think to . . ." She stumbled, would have gone down into the mud had he not caught her. She would have preferred the mud to looking up into his eyes. "Rushworth . . . what are you saying? You couldn't have killed your own father."

He righted her, pulled her onward. "I used to dream of it, of someone bludgeoning him as he did me. That was why I went hunting for Dorsey. . . . Well, I went hunting for the man who killed Pratt's father. I thought perhaps he could do the same to mine. I couldn't find him. I found Dorsey instead, wanted for the murder of his aunt. We were of an age. Understood each other. Struck a bargain."

She squeezed her eyes closed and walked blindly. "But he's so . . ."

"Violent, yes. I decided, after all, that it wouldn't do. Not if I wanted to avoid questions. So I gave Father some laudanum. He used it habitually, so it was easy enough to increase the dosage in his vial. Then some drops of belladonna in his eyes to hide the contraction of his pupils, and no one was the wiser. They all thought he'd died in his sleep. Heart failure."

She shuddered, couldn't help it. A murderer was holding her hand. "Rush."

"Well, it was him or my sister. What would *you* have chosen?"

"Another way. I would have chosen another way."

He sighed and halted again. Gave her that strange, tender look. "Yes, you would have. Because you're so very good. And I'm sorry that I'm not, not yet. But I *will* be. For you. And I want no secrets between us, which is why I'm telling you all this. That yes, I killed my father when I was eighteen, to protect my little sister and myself. I pray you can forgive me for it, given the reasons."

She forced a swallow. Opened her mouth to assure him she understood, even if she didn't agree with it—which she did, somewhat. But instead of that, she said, "What about your nephew? Did you use the laudanum on him too?"

His eyes flashed dark—then bright. His lips curved up. "Look at you, you clever thing." He tugged her onward. A clearing was just ahead, and in it a tumbling-down church. "It was a miscalculation, and I have repented of that, I assure you. I never thought it would hurt her so badly."

*Oh, Lord God, what am I to say?* "Hurt *her*? What about the boy?" Probably not the best choice.

"The boy." He released her hand and took her elbow instead. He spoke of his nephew as if he were saying *"the dog"* or *"the horse."* "He never should have existed. If Kitty hadn't behaved so with Pratt, forcing a wedding—but she was always stupid when it came to Pratt. When I realized what they'd done, I nearly let Dorsey have at him, as he suggested. But Pratt said he was close to the diamonds." He shook his head. "Had it been a girl, it would have been nothing but a minor inconvenience. But a boy—that tied us forever to Delmore. That wasn't part of the plan."

He stopped abruptly, spun on her, took her head between his hands again.

A sound escaped. She knew it was a whimper, but hoped to him it would just sound like surprise. And hopefully he wouldn't notice the tears blurring her eyes.

"Ella, I'm sorry. I-I didn't mean it—I was making it up. Dorsey always does that, exaggerating his exploits. I suppose the habit has rubbed off. But it's a lie. I didn't kill him. Of course I didn't. It was the crib death."

He must think her an idiot. And she must let him. Though she couldn't even nod with her head trapped between his hands. She could only bite her lip to keep from saying something stupid and try to keep the gasps from turning to sobs.

"Shh." He wrapped his arms around her, rubbed a hand up and down her back. "I'm sorry. I shouldn't have said such things.

I didn't mean to make you frightened of me. I won't hurt you, Ella, and I will never, never hurt our children. You must believe me, after all I did to protect my sister. We can have a family, as many children as you want, and I'll adore them all."

Brook's plan had better be appearing soon. Ella couldn't keep the shaking from her limbs much longer.

The sound of an engine rumbled through the stillness.

Rushworth pulled away. "Ah, good. They got my message. Come, my love. We'll take the high ground." He pulled her toward the crumbling church on the little rise.

She saw autumn leaves falling, heard imagined laughter echo. And said a prayer that she lived to see it, and Cayton with her.

⟳⟳⟳

Cayton slammed the door of the car, tempted to kick the wheel of his own as he stomped past. Couldn't the thing have seized up for Rushworth? Stalled out? "Hurry up—the engine's still ticking, they can't be far ahead of us!"

But they'd lost so much time already. That interminable walk to the telephone, only to discover it dead. They'd had to drive to the constable, afraid to approach Anlic themselves lest Rushworth was watching and would react in panic. But then the boy had rushed in and said he'd spotted a man and a woman with a gun, headed south.

Stafford had wanted to head straight out. It would have been the logical thing, but something in Cayton had fought the instinct. Had insisted they first head back to Ralin to see if any other messages had arrived for them.

He'd never in his life been so glad he'd heeded that quiet advice, and that the dukes had listened to him. He still had Rushworth's second note in his pocket, with instruction on where to rendezvous. With the diamonds.

Stafford hurried, checking his pistol again as he did so. "We'll catch him. We'll get the women. It will all be fine. He won't hurt them so long as we have the diamonds." He craned his head around. "Nottingham?"

Nottingham lifted the black velvet bag, his face as hard as stone. He had refused the offer of a weapon. "I don't like this. Who knows when the constable's men will make it out here—it's just us against him."

"I like those odds." Stafford lowered the pistol to his side but didn't holster it.

A good idea. Cayton pulled his out too. "Those are the real Fire Eyes, right? He'll know if they're not."

"They're real." Nottingham didn't sound pleased about it. "You two both promise you won't shoot to kill—we're out for justice, not vengeance."

Cayton didn't dignify that with a response. Neither, he noted, did Stafford. They trudged a few steps up the track. He held out an arm to block the others, his eyes on the ground. "Two sets of footprints. A man and a woman, as the boy said."

"Catherine." Stafford bent down to get a closer look. "They're no deeper than his, to indicate a struggle. It must be Catherine."

The odds were still in their favor, but the likelihood of something going wrong felt greater.

It couldn't—that was all. At least not until Rushworth told them where he had the women. They had to assume he had the duchesses too. And Ella. *Ella.*

She would tell him it would be all right, if she were beside him. He knew she would. She would smile that bright smile of hers and tell him not to fall back into the fear, into the recriminations. She would tell him it wasn't his fault.

Except it *was.* If he hadn't told Brook to call for Nottingham, then Ella wouldn't have stormed out and been caught. If he hadn't kissed her yesterday, they never would have had the argument with Brook to begin with. If he hadn't fallen in love with her, then he wouldn't have thought kissing her a good idea.

The recriminations pounded for a few steps, louder than any drum. Calling up those old wells of hatred, loathing, all aimed at himself.

Then he saw Ella's smile in his mind's eye, and the drumbeat stilled. She would say it was worth it. She would say that no matter how they planned their ways, it was the Lord who set their path. She would assure him that He would take care of them. That it wasn't his fault.

He pushed ahead. It had been years since he'd been out here, but he remembered the ruins of the old church in the clearing, from a time so long past that the stones were marked with Latin and anything once wood had rotted to nothing. It was the kind of place he'd liked to have taken Ella, someday. Let her think she was wandering aimlessly through the wood but then lead her out into the clearing. He could imagine her delight at discovering it.

They stepped out into the meadow, his eyes moving to the church—and his blood freezing in his veins. "No."

Stafford gripped his arm just before he surged forward. "Easy. Think it through, James."

How was he to think it through? Rushworth had Ella on the church steps, a gun to her head and an arm clamped around her waist. Her red hair blew in the wind, begging him to hurry. He had her—he had her right there, and Cayton couldn't do a thing. *Dear Lord . . . I thought it was for me—for me to protect her, to redeem myself.*

"Easy." Still gripping his arm, Stafford urged him forward. "Rushworth!" he called out as they neared. "Let her go. We have what you want."

They were close enough now to see how pale she looked, how still she stood. Afraid, surely, but brave. Faithful. Trusting the Lord. Because that was his Ella, so very Ella.

"You had better," Rushworth called back. "Stop there. That's close enough. Where are the Fire Eyes?"

Nottingham lifted the bag in trembling hands.

"Take them out. Let me see them."

He untied the bag and jiggled the earrings out into his palm. His jaw was clenched so tightly it had to hurt.

Rushworth nodded. "Good. Toss them this way."

"No." Nottingham's voice was thick, heavy. "Not until you let my sister go."

"Aw." Rushworth pursed his lips and held her closer. "I do understand the need to protect one's sister, Nottingham. I do. But Ella is quite safe right now, so long as you do as I say. Toss the diamonds as far as you can in this direction, and she and I will go together to retrieve them while you heroic men stay right where you are. Isn't that right, darling?" He trailed his nose down the side of her cheek.

Her nostrils flared.

Cayton sprang forward. He didn't mean to, and he didn't get but a step before Stafford dragged him back. But Rushworth saw, of course.

And he laughed. "How perfect! You love her. That makes this all the sweeter. Tell him to stay away, Ella."

She swallowed and pulled out a smile. A strange, fragile one he'd never seen on her before and prayed he never saw again. "Stay back, Drat. I don't need you rushing to my rescue." She closed her eyes when the gun shifted against her head. "I don't even like you."

*I love you too*, he wanted to say.

"The diamonds, Nottingham!"

Nottingham closed his fist around them. "Ella? Tell me what to do, Ella-bell."

"Wait! I'll help you, Cris!"

Two blondes emerged at a run from the back of the church, Catherine pulling Brook by the arm.

Rushworth shifted with Ella. "Kitty?"

Ella sighed. "Do what Catherine says." Perhaps she was talking to Rushworth. But Cayton didn't think so—she was answering her brother.

They had a plan, those crazy women. And it would be all right. His hands still shook, his heart still trembled, but they would be all right.

Cayton and the two dukes shifted as Catherine pushed Brook closer to Rushworth. Stafford muttered, "What are you doing, Brook?" and looked more puzzled than worried. Well, no. But *as* puzzled as worried.

Catherine wheeled Brook to a halt beside Rushworth. "I'm sorry I'm late. But I'll help."

Her brother frowned. "Why did you bring her?"

"How else was I to find my way? Besides, I don't know how to drive that car of hers. Stay right there, cousin, or my brother will put an end to your insipid little friend. I'll fetch the diamonds, Cris."

There was no possible way Brook would have led her here to help. Not unless she had a reason to want to. It *was* part of whatever plan they'd hatched—and Ella wanted, needed them to trust her.

"All right. Go." Rushworth shifted a step away from Brook, pressed the gun harder against Ella's temple. "Don't try anything, Brook."

Brook held her hands away from her side.

Catherine sped across the grass between them, her face more

harried than he'd expected, and more sorrowful. She stopped in front of Nottingham and grabbed not the earrings but his hand. "It'll be all right. I promise. Just . . . trust me. I know you can't, but trust me." She scooped up the gems and spun back.

They could have seized her and mirrored Rushworth, pointing a gun to the head of the one who mattered most to him. But it wouldn't have been right. His hands still ached to move, to grab, to force, but he held himself in check. He would trust. Her, and the Lord. "Let it play out," he murmured, as much for his own benefit as the dukes'.

Stafford nodded. "He's right. Brook wouldn't have brought her here unless . . ."

But unless *what*? Could they really trust Catherine? Ella apparently thought so. Still, Cayton gripped his gun, knowing he couldn't use it, not with one pointed at Ella, but taking comfort in its warm metal. It would be all right. It would.

No it wouldn't. It would all go wrong, Rushworth would get away with the diamonds, and he just *knew* . . .

Nothing. He knew nothing.

Catherine stopped halfway back to her brother and squared her shoulders. "Let Ella go, Cris."

Rushworth's brows drew down. "What are you doing, Kitty? I have this worked out. You don't need to interfere."

Catherine didn't budge. "But you don't mean to let her go. I know you don't."

"Kitty."

"I appreciate that you want to save me—and that you want a life with her. But you can't see clearly through the curse, Cris." She shook her head, and her voice sounded clouded with tears. "You'll never have what you want, not like this. You'll never be happy. You'll never run far enough or fast enough, and it will always haunt you. All the greed, all the death—it'll take it all.

Strip you bare. You'll lose her, if this is how you get her. You'll lose your children, as I lost mine."

Rushworth stared at his sister for a long moment, his thoughts impossible to comprehend behind the careful mask he lowered into place. But then he moved the gun. It was still at the ready, but it wasn't pressed to Ella's head. And he loosed the arm around her waist, though he then gripped her arm. "I'll let her go. Bring the diamonds here, and I'll let her go."

He wouldn't. And Catherine had to know that. But she eased forward. Blast her, she was easing forward.

"You don't really love her. That's what you always told me about Pratt—remember? That I didn't really love him—I loved the idea of him. What he used to be. That's what this is too—you love the idea of her. The thought of someone who will always smile at you, always be kind. But do you really think she will, that she will be, when you force her away from her family?"

Cayton edged away from Stafford. Just a shuffle to the side, so he could see Ella more clearly, so Catherine didn't block his view of her. And of Brook, as it happened. She had edged just a bit behind them and was reaching for something. Knowing Brook, a weapon.

Rushworth's jaw ticked. "And you never listened to me about Pratt—you told me to stay out of your love life, and I did. Now, kindly return the favor and *bring me the diamonds*. Or I'll make a quick stop on my way out of here and put a bullet through that little maid's skull."

Catherine jerked.

Ella sucked in a breath. "No, you won't. That isn't your way, Rush. Is it? You prefer quieter deaths. You'd have to slip laudanum to her. Then belladonna in her eyes to cover the signs of it. Like your father. Like your nephew."

Cayton watched Catherine as the words sank in, as they

became more than mere words. As they became the most hor-rifying truth a mother, a sister could ever comprehend. Then she leapt into the air, flying across the space, keening—a sound too raw and throbbing to be called a cry. Cayton charged after her even as Brook tugged Ella away. Which of them would Catherine attack? Brook, for bringing her here? Ella, for say-ing such things?

Rushworth. She landed on him like a cat, all claws and rage. He'd been distracted by Brook stealing his hostage, looking at Ella, reaching for her. But then it was all flailing arms and screams. And Ella, red hair flying out behind her, was charging Cayton's way.

He was there to catch her, and if he crushed her too hard to his chest, she made no complaint.

The gun's report tore through the meadow, bringing silence in its wake. Brook? But no, she had edged back into the stone arch of the church's doorway, and she had no gun in her hand. Ella winced and buried her face in his chest.

Cayton forced himself to look to see who had been hit—because if no one had, there would still be struggling, not this sudden, eerie quiet.

Catherine staggered back, blood covering her torso, horror in her eyes. "No. No. *Cris.*"

Rushworth crumpled to the ground, red staining his abdo-men. The pistol was already lying there. His sister fumbled to her knees beside him and cradled his head. "Cris . . . how could you? How could you do this to me? *How*? He was your nephew!"

He lifted a hand an inch, let it fall. "Diamonds. Paris. You . . . must."

She balled her hands in his jacket. "I don't want the dia-monds, I don't want the money. I don't care if he kills me—I just wanted my *son*."

Ella moved in Cayton's arms, turned her face to look at them. Rushworth lifted his head a bit, grunted, searched with his gaze . . . then saw them. His eyes flashed with anger.

No, with pain. Then nothing. His head fell back, his limbs went slack, and his sister's keening filled the meadow.

Brook slid to her knees by Catherine's side and put an arm around her. She held out a hand. And Catherine slid the diamonds into it.

Cayton closed his eyes and held Ella close, the words tumbling from his lips. "I love you."

She held him back, tight and then tighter. And her voice sounded like perfect hope, like perfect faith, as she murmured, "I know."

# Thirty

Night had fallen, and Kira couldn't remember ever being so tired. She sat on the hard, bare chair in her hard, bare room and could only stare at the hard, bare wall across from her. A baby cried, in the corner of the room. A baby laughed, in the kitchen. A baby slept, upstairs in a duchess's arms.

But Felicity didn't move. Wouldn't move. And the night was dark and colorless because of it.

Dr. Fields rested his hand on Kira's shoulder. They had been red with blood ten minutes ago, from where he'd had to perform an emergency surgery to save the child. Felicity had already been gone. Another seizure. And bleeding, so much bleeding. They could have lost them both, but the doctor had been quick. Just quick enough to pull a blue little boy from his mother.

Kira had done what her hands had done before, when it was Mamochka's voice giving quick instructions. *"Rub the chest. Slap the back. Clear the nose. Rub the chest, slap the back again."* He had squalled, flushing pink.

Her hands felt useless now though. Her knee didn't ache. But her heart . . . her heart would never feel quite whole again.

In the corner, Catherine sat on Kira's bed and held the baby close. Tears still streamed unchecked down her face. She had been crying when she entered the room, crying for her brother. Kira wasn't sure if she had never stopped, or if she had started again.

"You would be a welcome addition to these parts, if you stay here," the doctor said. "Felicity isn't the only one who didn't want to call Martha."

Kira shook her head. If she could somehow avoid Andrei, there was only one place she would go—home.

Mrs. Higgins sniffed from the door. "She can't be gone. My sweet Felicity. What will I do?"

Kira lifted a hand, and the older woman gripped it. "You will live. You will remember her. You will tell her boy how she loved him, how his father would have loved him."

"That wasn't what she wanted though." The housekeeper sniffed again and gripped her hands together. "She knew I was too old to raise a child. We all heard her—we all know what she wanted. We will honor her wishes."

Kira settled her gaze on Catherine again. She held the babe as she would have her own—probably as she *had* her own. She couldn't nurse him, of course, but Tabby would help with that, for now. Until another wet nurse could be found. "She wanted you to take him, Catherine."

The lady looked up, tearstained and grieving. "Pardon?"

"After the last seizure. She knew she was fading. She said to give the child to you, if you would take him." Kira slid her hand free of the housekeeper's. "She said her babe would need a mother, and that you needed a child."

Mrs. Higgins sidled into the room, over to Catherine. "You can give him a better life than I could. So long as you let me be a part of it, my lady."

Catherine turned her face into the woman's apron and wept.

She would take him—Kira was certain. She would love him, she would tell him of his mother. She would let what family the babe had left come whenever they pleased, stay however long they liked. Or perhaps she would stay here, near them. Assuming she avoided prison.

Kira pushed to her feet, nodded to the doctor, and slipped from the room. She hadn't heard what all had happened after Brook and Catherine left. Just that Rushworth was dead. That everyone else was unharmed. That Brook's father had returned sometime during the aftermath.

She headed up the stairs and nearly turned toward the next set of them and all the people crammed into Catherine's bedroom in the guest hall to check on Rowena and her child. But she went to the kitchen first. No one here would understand—she knew that. But Felicity had been a friend. In some ways a sister. And Kira would honor her as she knew how.

Addie and Tabby had been in the kitchen a few minutes ago, but now it was quiet. Kira pinched off a crust of bread from the loaf on the counter and slipped a piece behind the stove. Pinched another off and tucked it behind the spices on the windowsill. Went to the door and threw the rest into the wind. "For your soul, my friend," she said in Russian, softly. "On its way to heaven."

When she stepped back inside, Brook was there, hand outstretched. "Will you come up, Kira? We need to speak with you."

She had never been so tired. She had just lost a friend. But her knee didn't ache, and Felicity's boy was healthy, and Rowena's daughter too. And Brook looked at her and didn't judge. Just held out a hand.

She slipped hers into it and went with her up the stairs.

They should have all given Rowena some privacy. Kira probably ought to have insisted, or Dr. Fields. But other things had

ROSEANNA M. WHITE

stolen their attention, and Rowena didn't seem to mind the teeming life filling the chamber. She was nestled beneath the covers of Catherine's bed, pillows propping her up and her daughter sleeping in her arms. Her husband sat beside her, gazing down at the newborn with reverent awe. Cayton and Ella stood by the window, hands linked together, and Whitby leaned on the wall near to them. Stafford greeted his wife—and Kira—with a smile.

He held his hand out to her. "Brook has told me about you over the years—I never dreamed I'd make your acquaintance quite this way."

She let him take her hand, as plenty of dukes had before, and kiss it. But he wasn't like any of the other dukes, and she wasn't the same girl who had smiled at them and ducked her head and judged just how much to flirt and when to retreat. She offered what smile she could and curtsied as was polite. "I have heard much about you as well, Your Grace. Back when you were Lord Harlow and Brook was *not*, she insisted, in love with you."

Brook laughed and shooed her husband out of the way. "I have no recollection of such a time."

Stafford chuckled and positioned a chair in front of her. "You look exhausted, Kira. Please, have a seat. We have much for which to thank you. And a few questions besides."

Nodding, she sat, glad when Brook took the chair beside her. "I do not need your thanks. But I am happy to answer your questions."

"Start with Varennikov, if you would." Brook positioned herself sideways in the chair so she could see her. Though she still looked like the princess. The duchess. "He is the buyer Pratt struck a deal with two years ago?"

Kira nodded and filled them in as best she could—she told them of the statue for sale in the museum basement, Andrei's impatience, the deadline he had apparently set for Lord Rushworth and then moved up in that recent letter.

Lady Ella stepped forward when she had finished, her lovely brows pinched. "We know the threat to Catherine if the diamonds are not delivered—but what will he do to *you*, Kira?"

*Kira.* She drew in a breath and shook her head. "I cannot say. Perhaps he will deem it beyond my influence and not punish me for it. Perhaps he will be in a bad mood and . . ." She shrugged.

Ella looked at her brother, at Brook. Quickly at Cayton. "They didn't win—that's what we wanted to avoid, isn't it? They didn't profit from their crimes. Rushworth is dead, Dorsey in jail and likely to hang for the murders of his aunt, Hannah, the valet at Delmore . . . and Stew—and they were the ones who had done all this. Catherine knew about the crimes, but she never took part in them. I don't see the point in punishing her more. Do any of you?"

Brook shook her head. "She has enough grief to deal with, especially after today. I know it was an accident, I saw it all, but still—it will not seem that way to her. Her brother's death will haunt her. And I don't exactly want to sic Varennikov on her."

Stafford sighed. "What do we do then? Go to Paris with the diamonds? Sell them to him as he wanted? It would keep Kira safe."

It would do more than keep her safe. It would get her that flat she didn't want anymore. Baguettes and café au lait and all the jewels she once coveted. A view of the Eiffel Tower stretching to heaven, and shopkeepers who put aside their ancient brooms to kiss her cheeks whenever she passed by.

"No." She leaned her head back. "No, what I should do is tell him I found exactly what he wanted me to find—information. And that information is the simple truth: they never had the jewels. They had rubies."

Frowning, Brook reached for her hand again. "But if he's in a bad mood. If he would hurt you—"

"I do not think he will." Not if she handled it right. He would just refuse to reward her. And she was happy with that.

"What then, with the diamonds themselves? I don't want them in my safe anymore." Brook reached over to a side table and picked up two dangling earrings. Rubies and gold and . . . probably not rubies, given the conversation. She held them up to the light, and a scarlet rainbow shot onto the wall.

Kira sucked in a breath. They were lovely, and that rainbow . . . but they were just two little gems. What had made Andrei willing to kill for them?

Stafford leaned into the side of the wardrobe. "I vote we toss them in the sea—as we should have done two years ago."

"No, donate them. Loudly, publicly—and with a lot of private security." Nottingham took his daughter from his wife's arm, as carefully as if she were made of glass.

Kira smiled. There was nothing like seeing a doting father hold his new babe.

"No." Ella grinned, wrapped her arm around Cayton's, and leaned into him. "No, we have a much better idea than that. Don't we, Drat?"

Cayton angled a crooked smile down at her. "I dare not guess what you're thinking, love. But I'm with you, whatever it is."

# *Thirty-one*

PARIS, FRANCE
APRIL 12, 1913

Cayton stood back, well out of the way while the Duke and Duchess of Stafford performed the glad-handing they were such experts at. Brook had been to the Musée National des art asiatiques Guimet before, as it happened. She had met the director, who had first greeted her today as *princesse*—and then launched into a very long congratulatory speech when he learned she was now a duchess. He beamed when he heard she had the most brilliant little boy now—who, no, wasn't with them *here*, at the museum, but was indeed in Paris. His first trip abroad.

Cayton leaned against the wall. This could take a while. His eyes traveled over the pieces on display, half his mind wondering if Tabby had gotten Addie down for her nap, or if she and Abingdon were keeping each other awake. Or if Mother and Aunt Caro were doing the keeping-awake, as the case may be—they'd been in raptures at the early reunion with their favorite little ones.

Ella returned from her "prowl" around the first room in the

museum and tucked her hand into its spot against his forearm. "Stop it," she whispered. "You look suspicious. Stand up like an earl instead of slouching like an art thief."

He chuckled and slouched a bit more. "I am an earl. I'll slouch if I want to do."

Her eyes twinkled up at him, her dimple winking. "You have the worst posture I've ever seen, Drat. I can't believe your mother let you get away with it."

"Neither can she. You two can bemoan my spinal failures when we're done here." Not surprisingly, his mother had adored Ella on sight. She probably would have begun planning the wedding whether he'd given her leave to do so or not.

Which, of course, he had done. His only whispered request was that she wait until he'd had a chance for a proper proposal, after all this was behind them.

Ella tugged him upright. Though apparently it was because Brook had progressed the conversation and was motioning them forward. She made introductions to the still-beaming director of the museum, and then said, "Do you remember, *monsieur*, when you let the prince and me into the basement? Do you think . . . ?"

The director, somehow, beamed even brighter. "Of course, of course! And if anything catches your eye, know that it is all for sale—for you, that is. Right this way."

"That was far too easy," Ella whispered. "No doubt there are booby traps. Hidden doors. Monsters waiting to spring from the walls. Tread carefully, dearest."

She would be telling stories about this for decades to come. Their great escapade—the grand adventure—the fitting finale to the tale of the Fire Eyes.

She would probably conveniently leave out the complete lack of excitement about it all.

He would let her.

They followed the director down the stairs. He chattered on about something or another from Nepal, and Brook replied as if she knew exactly of what he spoke. Who knew? Perhaps she really did. Stafford piped in here or there, but mostly his job in this grand adventure was to subtly prod the director toward the north end of his large basement, while Ella and Cayton headed for the south.

Monsieur Director didn't say anything when they slipped away. And if he *did* notice at some point, Brook would chime in with some offhanded statement about how they were exploring. He would think nothing of it, she had assured them as they hatched the plan. This was Paris, after all. They rather expected two young people in love to sneak off for a kiss now and again.

Not a bad idea, once they took care of business.

"Oh!" Ella batted at something, shook her head wildly.

Cayton chuckled and caught the strand of spider's silk that she had walked through. He could just barely see it in the light of the bulb overhead. "Careful. You walked straight into a monster's trap."

"Luckily you were there to untangle me, my valiant knight."

"Lucky indeed." He took her hand and led her to the end of a row of shelves, around a corner.

Ella tugged him to a halt. "It's not that way—I studied the diagram."

"Ella . . ." He shook his head and pulled her forward. "You'd have us back at the stairs in no time. This is my part. You get the diamond bit. Remember?"

She blustered out a sigh. "Very well, then. But only so that you feel useful."

They followed the directions Kira had drawn out for them until they ended up before what appeared to be just another shelf filled with boxes of all shapes and sizes. He set his gaze on the middle one and scooted the boxes this way and that until the dark form came into view. Ella reached in and pulled it forward. The light struck the clay tiger's crude face and illumined its empty eyes.

He rested his hand on her shoulder. "Ready?"

"Ready. Check to make sure we haven't set off any silent alarms. Called in any thugs. No assassin-acrobats dropping down from the ceiling—"

"Ella." He laughed, because he couldn't help it, and leaned over to kiss her cheek. Because he wanted to. Into her ear he whispered, "Do your part, love. Send them home."

"Right." Ella reached into her handbag and extracted the black velvet bag. "Though it feels a bit anticlimactic. No one threatening me or confessing their secrets or anything."

"I can confess my secrets, if it will make you feel better." He helped her with the drawstring when it caught and shook the gems into her palm. They were loose again, the Nottingham earrings holding only rubies now.

Ella grinned at him over her shoulder. "Would you? Make them good."

"All right. Well . . ." He waited for her to reach forward and work the first of the diamonds into the eye socket. She turned it this way, that, and for a moment he thought they were wrong, all of them wrong, that this wasn't the statue of Dakshin Ray they had come from, it had all just been a mistake.

Then it slid into place and held steady.

Cayton breathed again, though he hadn't realized he'd stopped. "My first confession—I have at least three Shakespearian plays memorized. Top to bottom and inside out."

She sent him a quick, wide-eyed stare. "Impressive—and yet you've never quoted them to me! Which ones? *Hamlet*?"

"Not in full—*King Lear. MacBeth*. And . . . *A Midsummer Night's Dream*."

"Ah, perhaps I shall call you Puck instead of Drat." She reached toward the second eye with the second diamond. "What about *Much Ado About Nothing*? I always fancied that one."

"That doesn't surprise me in the slightest—everyone ends up married."

She drew her hand away, smiling. It faded into something not quite happy and not quite sad. "There."

"There." He slid his arm around her again and studied the statue for a moment. It looked . . . *right*. Like more than it had been—a frame without a painting. Yet not what someone had probably thought it was once—a god. It was clay, molded by man's hands. Clay made to frame diamonds likely mined in blood. Jewels worth more than any two rocks had a right to be, nestled in dried mud.

Shakespeare would have loved such ironic poetry.

Ella elbowed him. "Whistle."

"Right." He chose a tune she'd been humming to Addie that morning as they all strolled down the Champs-Élysées and pushed the statue back to be in profile, into the shadows.

A few minutes later the Staffords meandered their way, still chattering at the director.

Ella put on her brightest smile and hurried over to Brook with that bounce that only Ella could make look so natural. "Brook! It's here, it *is*. I thought it must be. The whole collection from the Madhya Pradesh. The tiger, the boat, even the—"

"Ella, calm down." Brook laughed and settled a hand on Ella's arm. She turned to the director. "Forgive her. She has become overly fascinated with all things from India."

The director smiled, but his brows pulled down. "From

Madhya Pradesh? *Non, non, mademoiselle.* These are all from Jaipur—I found them myself, from an antiquities dealer there."

Ella straightened, lifted her chin, and shook her head. "That may be where *you* purchased them, *monsieur*, but I assure you— they are from Madhya. I have been researching it extensively, and—"

"Here we go." Cayton stepped forward and took her arm. "Ella, he doesn't want to hear about your endless research."

She spun on him, mouth agape. "Well of *course* he does. It's his job!"

"*Oui*," the director agreed, stepping forward from between the Staffords. "I am much intrigued. How can you be sure of their origins, *mademoiselle*?"

She turned back around, giving him the full force of her smile. "Oh, it's very simple. You see, I stumbled across a book. . . ."

Cayton only listened with half an ear as she spun the tale she had indeed pieced together from her notes. Of artifacts raided and stolen and cursed, of the British tromping in and seizing them, of East India Company men trading and selling and buying until they landed in Jaipur some two hundred years later. Statue and diamonds separated, though Ella didn't mention that part.

The director listened with rapt attention. "*Incroyable.* You must have done nothing but read for months, *mademoiselle*, to find all that."

"I have absolutely ruined my eyes." She clapped her hands together. "And there they are. So remarkable, *monsieur*. I have dreamed of finding them, of shipping them all back to the museum in Madhya, where they rightfully belong, righting a wrong wrought by my English forebears—they are for sale, you say? My brother—the Duke of Nottingham—has granted me fifty pounds to spend on this enterprise, though he deems it nonsense. Will that be enough? I already have the director of the museum in India waiting, eager to welcome them home."

The director was back to beaming. "Of course! And for a friend of the *princesse*, I will even offer to ship them back to India for you."

Ella bounced again. There was something enchanting about it, the way her curls sprang up and down. The light in her eyes. "Oh *monsieur*, how generous you are. I have the direction right here!" She pulled a slip of paper from her handbag and waved it in the air. "Cayton can help you box them all up. Can't you, darling?"

Cayton sighed. "I'm sure Monsieur Director has men to handle this properly, my dear. He won't want to worry with it *now*."

Monsieur Director waved at him. "*Non, non,* now is good. Here, I have a crate. We shall right a wrong. Beautiful. *Très, très belle.*"

And so a crate was brought out and Cayton cajoled into loading the tiger—its face turned from the director—into it, along with a boat and a something he couldn't quite identify but which looked a bit like a very small building. They added straw, Ella gushed, Brook chattered, and Stafford nodded in an approving, ducal way.

The director himself nailed the lid onto the crate, looking as though he were returning the Holy Grail to King Arthur. "*Voilà!* I will see it is shipped at the first possible moment, *mademoiselle.*"

Ella leaned over and smacked a loud kiss to the man's cheek. "You're an absolute doll, *monsieur*. Shall we handle paperwork once we are upstairs?"

Monsieur Director's cheeks went pink. "*Oui.* And I do hope you mention our humble establishment to your brother."

"Of course I shall." With a sigh of satisfaction, she tucked her hand back into the crook of Cayton's elbow. "I'll write him straightaway."

Cayton let her pull him a few feet before he cleared his throat. "Ella."

"Hmm?"

"You're going the wrong way."

"Right." She did an about-face and had the good sense to let him lead her out.

Once his back was to the director, he let himself grin. It was a rather grand adventure after all.

Kira stood alone in the vast foyer of Andrei's vast Parisian home and waited. She wore a pretty dress in pale blue, to match her eyes. But not one that he'd bought her—one she'd purchased before, when she was just Kira Belova, ballerina, and not Kira Belova, Andrei Varennikov's mistress. She'd done her dark curls up in a simple chignon, set a fashionable but modest hat upon her head.

She'd seen Sergei that morning. Her friends at the ballet. They had all kissed her cheeks and asked how she'd been, and she'd done a pirouette just to prove to them that she could—that *they* could, if ever they suffered an injury. Sergei had watched her closely through the impromptu scene from *The Rite of Spring* that she'd joined them in, and he had offered her a place in the corp again.

It had felt good. To prove the doctors wrong. To know she still had the skill, the strength.

But somewhere in England's rains, the desire had faded. She'd smiled at him, thanked him, and said she needed to go home. She hadn't seen her family in too long.

He was Russian—he understood.

Andrei was Russian too, but she doubted he would understand. He had worked too hard to escape his roots, and he would not respect her desire to return to hers.

He didn't have to respect it. He just had to promise not to hunt her down and take out his anger on her family.

*"Ma chérie."* He emerged from his office, a smile on his face, and paused a few feet away to look at her. Just to look at her, as if she were another painting on his walls, another statue for his conservatory. "I missed you."

"Did you?" She had her doubts, but they weren't to the point. She folded her arms over her chest. "That letter you sent with this deadline nearly got me killed. He went mad—Rushworth. Absolutely mad."

Andrei chuckled and waved it away. Nothing but a fly, a nuisance. "He needed inspiration. And here you are, back in Paris—I trust they are here too? With my diamonds?"

She sighed and dropped her arms again. "Andrei, there *are* no diamonds—or at least, not with them. They never had them. They had only rubies."

He froze, muscle by muscle. *"Pardonnez-moi?"*

"Rubies. They had only rubies, and now Rushworth is dead too. I did what I could. I brought the proof of it all." She reached into her handbag—blue to match her dress—and pulled out the folded sheets of paper, crafted by Stafford's jeweler. Letters of authenticity for two rubies, two carats each, valued at but a few hundred pounds British sterling.

She handed him the paper. And then the stones. Two rubies, two carats each—provided by Catherine, who had fished them out of her brother's things. The rubies that the Nottinghams had planted for them to find last autumn, to mistake for the diamonds.

Andrei cursed and tossed the rubies to the floor. "Unacceptable!"

She didn't flinch. She certainly didn't dare tremble. She raised her chin. "Indeed. And I am sorry I could not return with better news. But I can give you only the truth. Perhaps the Fire Eyes are out there somewhere, but they are not in England."

Andrei turned away, cursing again. In French, in Russian. Then he took a deep breath and faced her once more. His hands were in fists, but he held them against his legs. "You did your best, *ma belle. Merci.*"

"You are welcome. But before you go on, allow me to say . . . I appreciate all you have given me. But you will marry soon, and my career is done, and I miss my family. I plan to go home. To Russia. I will not need the flat or the clothes or the jewels." She motioned to the boxes that she had paid to be carried in along with her stacked just inside the front door. The silks, the furs. The diamonds and sapphires and emeralds.

His fist relaxed. His face moved from careful civility to bemusement. "What will you do? Without the ballet, without your flat?"

She spread her arms and had a feeling her smile was one he'd never seen on her before. "I'll live, Andrei. I'll go to Optina on pilgrimage, to Kitezh on the solstice. I'll listen for the church bells and to the chanting of the monks."

He shook his head, but it wasn't a denial. Just more confusion. "You can give all this up? Paris, this life?"

"It was never really mine. It was yours."

"Ah, Kira." He closed the distance then, but there was no threat in the line of his shoulders. He just came close, set his hands on her shoulders, and kissed her forehead. "Take the jewels, at least. The ones I bought for you. Your family may need them someday."

She could only shake her head. "No. I will not be in your debt, Andrei, I will not—"

"What need have I of a few baubles? Take them, *milaya*. Sell them before you leave Paris if you prefer, but do not return home empty-handed."

Her eyes slid shut. He could be so cruel. And he could be so kind. "For my family, in case we come on hard times."

He rubbed her shoulders and then slid his hands down her arms to grasp hers. "It was a good year. I will remember it fondly."

It hadn't been a good year. She'd try to forget him. But it had led her where she needed to be. She slipped away from his hands, from his house, and ran back to the taxi waiting for her outside—his servants hot on her heels, loading the jewelry cases back in. She would sell them today, she would go home, she would dance with a tambourine in hand, and her knee wouldn't hurt.

She would live.

# EPILOGUE

E lla stroked Addie's hair down one more time, smiling at the way it curled around her ear. At how her mouth pursed in her sleep, trying to suck on the thumb that had fallen out. She was the sweetest thing. So very beautiful. Ella couldn't wait to start teaching her to say "Mama," but that seemed like something that should wait until the little one's father actually proposed.

Susan, Lady Cayton, smiled and eased down into the rocking chair Tabby had just vacated. "It's good to be home. It'll be better when we get to Azerly Hall—you'll join us in Yorkshire, won't you? Your brother and his wife can come with you, or your mother."

"Mama would probably agree, though I daresay Rowena just wants to get back to Midwynd." They would be on their way in the next few days, now that Augusta was two weeks old. They hadn't wanted to travel too soon.

"Oh good." Susan leaned back and set herself to rocking. "I

403

can't tell you how glad I am, Ella. I just can't tell you how glad. I wasn't sure he'd ever give himself another chance at love."

Ella laughed. "He didn't. I just didn't give him a choice."

"Good. He's in his garret now, I daresay, if you want to find him. I think I'll just sit here for a while and watch my beautiful little girl sleep."

Ella bounced. "Perfect—how do I find this garret?"

"Up the stairs at the end of this hallway. You can't miss it."

She doubted that but tried it anyway. And given that there was only one set of stairs and only one door on the hall at the top of them, she might indeed get to claim a victory in following directions. An occasion surely worthy of a celebratory kiss. Moving silently, she stepped through the door.

The room was awash in colors. On paper, on canvas, a few random splashes on the walls that made her grin. She feasted on it for a long moment before turning to look for him.

He stood near the window, his back to her, an easel before him. Intent upon his task, he didn't seem to hear her, so she slipped farther into the room and looked around a bit more.

She paused before the winged unicorn, nearly ruining her stealth with a gasp of appreciation. It was exactly as she'd pictured it that night in the garden. The cloud-castle in an evening sky, sunset colors painting its foundation. The creature magnificent in the foreground, soaring through the sky. And Addie, a bit more grown up, running up the stairs. Addie and *her*.

She blinked back tears and pressed a hand to her lips. It was the best gift anyone could ever give her, and it wasn't even for her. She couldn't wait to see it hanging upon the walls in the nursery, where Addie could wonder at the beauty. And then someday wonder at how her father could have captured it so perfectly.

Needing him, Ella gave up on silence and spun, giving him

time only to lower his brush before launching herself at him. "You magnificent man."

He *oomfed* at the impact. And laughed. "Far better than Drat."

"You put me in the cloud-castle with her." She cupped his face, let herself get lost in the summer-green of his eyes. "I could kiss you."

"I won't stop you." Mischief in his eyes, he set his brush onto the palette and slid both onto a table. "But if you liked that one . . ." He nodded toward the painting he'd been working on.

The white of the canvas was still visible in a few places, but the color in the rest took her breath away. Crimson on one leaf, floating down from an invisible branch. Orange and saffron behind it. An azure sky with a few white clouds.

Cayton, smiling. Addie, laughing as she chased a butterfly. And *her*. In bridal white. The very image the Lord had given her.

The tears wouldn't be blinked back this time. She gripped his hand, certain she was dreaming. *How else . . . ? How . . . ?* "Cayton, I . . . What is this?"

"A question." He slipped behind her, arms around her waist, his head right beside hers so he could look at the painting with her. "I haven't got a ring yet—all the family jewelry is in Yorkshire. So I thought I'd give you a painting for now. Do you like it?"

Her laugh was half a cry. She turned, wrapped her arms around his neck, and pressed her lips to his.

When he pulled away a long minute later, his eyes were bright, his smile sunny. "Is that your answer?"

"Maybe." She made a show of looking at the painting, tapped a finger to her lips. "Though I do have one complaint. You made my hair *red*."

He cleared his throat and tugged on a curl. She wasn't sure

what his purpose was until he'd maneuvered her head next to the canvas and held the real curl beside her painted ones.

"Drat." She pulled the lock free of his fingers. "Perfect match."

Cayton chuckled and slid his arms around her again. "Yes," he said against her mouth. "Oddly enough . . . we are."

# AUTHOR'S NOTE

Thank you so much for traveling with me through the tales of the Fire Eyes and the group of friends who found themselves in possession of them! I had fun in this final installment wrapping up the mystery of the red diamonds and expounding a bit on their history. When I decided they should have come from a statue, I had a wonderful moment in discovering that there really was a museum dealing in Asian antiquities in Paris at the time—utterly perfect for my plot!

We get to see a bit more about the Ballet Russe in this one, as well. I, like Europe at the time, am a bit enthralled with all things Russian, and dove headlong into study of the culture so I could create Kira to be authentic. I hope you enjoyed the glimpses of Russian life, and if you want to know more, I can't recommend enough the book *Natasha's Dance: A Cultural History of Russia* by Orlando Figes. My ballerina would have been born into a free generation, but her grandparents would have been serfs—and the life they would have known was at once intriguing and often horrifying. We, as readers, know that even this Russian culture was marching toward change in the

Bolshevik Revolution of 1917. But at the time of this story, it was still at its height.

I'd also been waiting not-so-patiently to take my stories into the Cotswolds, where I'd situated Ralin Castle among the picturesque countryside full of cottages of honeyed stone with thatched roofs. I hope you enjoyed the glimpse of this beautiful landscape. The descriptions of Anlic Manor are based on an actual manor house in the region, Temple Guiting Manor—which is now a vacation property available for rental. And yet no one volunteered to send me there to write this book! Shocking, I know. As always, you can see photos of the locations and characters on my Pinterest boards at www.Pinterest.com/ RoseannaMWhite.

Finally, a word about my characters. While I realize that few gentlemen were involved with their children at this stage in history, I loved the idea of making Cayton an exception to that, proving himself so very different from the character who made brief appearances in the first two books. And I could think of no better foil to his personality than the optimistic Ella—who *may* (ahem) be more like me than any other character I've ever written. Not that I get lost *quite* so often (only about half as much . . .), but it's well known in my house that putting something into my care will likely result in it disappearing into a vortex and never being seen again.

This time around, both of my characters had to struggle with trust: trusting that God had something good in store, and trusting their own ability to recognize it—and receive it. I hope and pray that you, too, will see that whatever path you're on in life, God means it to enrich your heart and soul. And that no matter how many mistakes we make, in our actions or our judgment, we can always trust His voice to lead us . . . so long as we know how to hear Him.

**Roseanna M. White** pens her novels beneath her Betsy Ross flag, with her Jane Austen action figure watching over her. When not writing fiction, she's homeschooling her two small children, editing and designing, and pretending her house will clean itself. Roseanna is the author of over a dozen historical novels and novellas, ranging from biblical fiction to American-set romances to her new British series. She makes her home in the breathtaking mountains of West Virginia. You can learn more about her and her stories at www.RoseannaMWhite.com.

# Sign up for Roseanna's newsletter!

Keep up to date with news on Roseanna's upcoming book releases and events by signing up for her email list at
http://bit.ly/RoseannaWhiteNewsletter

# More From Roseanna M. White

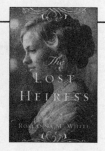

When Brook Eden's friend Justin, a future duke, discovers she may be an English heiress, she travels to meet her alleged father. Once she arrives in Yorkshire, Brook undergoes a trial of the heart—and faces the same danger that led to her mother's mysterious death.

*The Lost Heiress* by Roseanna M. White
LADIES OF THE MANOR

BETHANYHOUSE

# You May Also Like . . .

Lady Georgina Hawthorne has kept a secret her entire life. She must marry during her debut season or she could lose everything—and Colin McCrae is not her idea of eligible. But as their paths cross, their ongoing clash of wits has both Georgina and Colin questioning their priorities.

*An Elegant Façade* by Kristi Ann Hunter
HAWTHORNE HOUSE
kristiannhunter.com

When disaster ruins Charlotte Ward's attempt to restart a London acting career, her estranged daughter, Rosalind, moves her to a quiet village where she can recover. There, Rosalind gets a second chance at romance, and mother and daughter reconnect—until Charlotte's troubles catch up to her.

*A Haven on Orchard Lane* by Lawana Blackwell

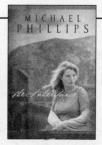

In Scotland's Shetland Islands, a clan patriarch has died, and a dispute over the inheritance has frozen an entire community's assets. When a letter from the estate's solicitor finds American Loni Ford, she sets out on a journey to discover her roots—but is this dream too good to be true?

*The Inheritance* by Michael Phillips
SECRETS OF THE SHETLANDS #1

# ◊ BETHANYHOUSE

Stay up to date on your favorite books and authors with our free e-newsletters. Sign up today at bethanyhouse.com.

**f**  Find us on Facebook. facebook.com/bethanyhousepublishers

Free exclusive resources for your book group! bethanyhouse.com/anopenbook

anopenbook